After suffering a humiliating divorce, infuriated Catholic Jude Matawapit bolts to his family's Ojibway community to begin a new job—but finds himself thrown into a battle for chief as his brother-in-law's campaign manager. The radical Kabatay clan, with their extreme ideas about traditional Ojibway life, will stop at nothing to claim the leadership position and rid the reserve of Western culture and its religion once and for all, which threatens not only the non-traditional people of the community, but Jude's chance at a brand-new life he's creating for his children.

Recovering addict Raven Kabatay will do anything to win the respect and trust of her older siblings and mother after falling deep into drug addiction that brought shame and anger to her family. Not only does she have the opportunity to redeem herself by becoming her brother's campaign manager for chief—if he wins, she'll have the reserve's backing to purchase the gold-mine diner where she works, finally making something of herself. But falling in love with the family's sworn enemy—the deacon's eldest son, Jude—will not just betray the Kabatay clan. It could destroy everything Raven believes in and has worked so hard for.

Sanctified
Copyright © 2019 Maggie Blackbird
ISBN: 978-1-4874-2704-7
Cover art by Martine Jardin

Published by eXtasy Books Inc or
Devine Destinies, an imprint of eXtasy Books Inc

Look for us online at:
www.eXtasybooks.com or www.devinedestinies.com

Sanctified
Matawapit Family Book 3

By

Maggie Blackbird

DEDICATION

For my brother and sisters: Curtis, Connie, Christine, and Allison

Thank you to my husband and the Mals for your never-ending support and love.

A big thank you to my editor Emmy, my proofer Bri, my cover artist Martine, EIC Jay, and Art Director Angela.

CHAPTER ONE: BREAKDOWN IN PARADISE

Jude signed away the last of his marriage, signed away the last of the life he'd built since his first year at university. Finished by a simple signature on a piece of paper.

He tossed aside the pen. It rolled across the polished surface of the boardroom table and bumped into another one, the same as his ex-wife had *bumped* into another man. A man who was supposed to be Jude's friend and colleague, the very man Jude had introduced to Charlene and their two children, a man who'd eaten dinner at his house.

Stephen Baker wasn't even here to witness the destruction he'd caused. He was living his brand-spanking-new life in Kenora with Charlene.

The secretary poked her head in the room. "Mr. Matawapit, would you like another cup of coffee?"

"This past year, I've consumed enough to cause a bean shortage in Brazil." Jude shoved back the chair in the same way he'd shoved away the anger, bitterness, and disgust when Charlene had broken down and admitted to the affair.

"Save the cup for the next guy who has to come in here and sign away his life." He handed the secretary the mug she'd given him earlier, after leading him to the boardroom to address his divorce papers in private. She'd led many a man or woman to this room of wood wainscoting, leather chairs, polished hardwood floors, and coffered ceiling.

The lawyers should be able to afford fancy furnishings, at

the rate they'd charged Jude for an uncontested divorce. A great pity to the poor suckers who couldn't mediate their split and had to march into court to fight over the kids, money, possessions, and the house.

When Jude stepped outside, big fat snowflakes fell from the overcast sky. He stuffed his hands into his coat pockets.

There she stood in the parking lot, beside her fancy sports truck—little sister Bridget in a knitted cabled toque to match her fluffy high-collared black swing coat with the big buttons. Even five months pregnant she was classy as always, just like Charlene had dressed.

"You're not at work." Jude strolled over.

"I got you a *Coffee Coffee.*" Bridget held out the paper travel cup.

"*Coffee Coffee?* Seriously?" Even though he'd become officially divorced moments ago, Jude couldn't help the smirk tugging at his lips. "C'mon, you're not supposed to show the enemy any pity. Get me your famous tar you're loyal to."

He took the cup, which immediately warmed his cold hand, since he'd yet to don his leather gloves.

"I thought the enemy deserved what he truly wants instead of Reggie's Donuts after what he's been through." She looped her arm through his. "How you doing?"

"Considering I signed away my marriage a few minutes ago, not too shabby." Jude sipped the bitter caffeine he used to savor that was as pungent as the sour pit in his stomach.

Bridget halted. She wrenched her arm free. Her boot heels squeaked along the snow. She faced him. "Will you please stop it?"

"Stop what?" Jude sipped more battery acid.

"The big brother mode. Say it for once. Please." Her pitch-black eyes flashed.

"What would you like me to say?"

Bridget might be a year younger, but no older brother cried

on his little sister's shoulder. Big brothers remained strong for the family, never showing a hint of weakness, like Dad always did.

"Something. Anything."

"Maybe this is the best way to start a new year. Newly divorced."

The sound of a radar going off came from Bridget's purse. "Oh geez. Now what?" She withdrew her cell phone.

This was a perfect opportunity to escape. "Look, I'll talk to you later. Work beckons after a two-week Christmas break."

"Never mind work." Bridget read her text message. "The center is functioning fine without me. The school won't fall down if you're not there." She slapped her hand over her mouth. "Oh my God."

"What?" Adrenaline pumping, Jude leaned in. Something bad better not have happened back home.

"Chief Willie died last night." Bridget gasped. "And . . . the principal quit at the high school."

"Died? Quit?" Mom, Dad, and Emery must be birthing sixteen dogs after getting slammed not once, but twice, back at the reserve. And why hadn't Dad texted? The parents always contacted Jude first.

"Mom says Dad's going to fill in until a new principal's hired. As for Willie . . ." Bridget's eyes sagged at the corners.

Jude yanked his cell phone from his jacket pocket. He furiously typed in . . .

Dad, what happened to Willie? And what's this about the principal quitting? Call me at once.

He sent the message. Something resembling a disgusted frown forced his lips into a scowl. He didn't need *not* to be bothered—if Dad thought to spare Jude's so-called full plate after signing his divorce papers. Everyone knew he put others first and himself second.

The text popped up.

I planned on calling you tonight. You signed your divorce papers this morning. I didn't wish to bother you right now . . .

Jude clenched his teeth or the growl threatening to climb up his throat would escape.

Bridget slid her arm back through his. "C'mon. Let's get a coffee."

"I already have a coffee." He held out the paper travel cup.

"We'll get one where we can sit and talk." Bridget trudged to her truck. "No excuses."

He gripped the phone. "I'm fine."

"No, you're not. For once, let someone inside your head. You're worse than Dad." She threw open the truck door. "The *Coffee Coffee* on Waterloo."

"Do you think he'll have a traditional or a Catholic funeral? He practiced both faiths." Raven poured a refill into her brother's mug.

Clayton grabbed the sugar packets from the small bowl on the counter. "We'll talk later."

"Order up." Cookie banged the bell.

"Okay." Raven set the coffee pot on the back counter's burner.

In respect to Willie, the diner's tables and the main counter were full. Whoever couldn't get a seat stood, holding their coffee-filled mugs. Everything stopped after a community member died, except for *Kiss the Cook*, where the people of the reserve liked to gather if the home of the grieving family was too packed.

The diner door swung open.

Raven turned to Darryl Keejik and his husband, Emery Matawapit, entering. With the next election coming up in

April, and Willie going unchallenged for fourteen years, Darryl was probably campaigning to fill the spot as the new leader of Ottertail Lake—especially after becoming a full-on Matawapit by marrying two summers ago into a traitorous Catholic family who shunned their own culture.

Balancing four plates, Raven wove her way through the crowd to the back table where four old women sat. She set down their breakfasts. "Here you go. Do you need more coffee?"

"Yah. *Meegwetch.*" The one woman patted Raven's arm. "Very sad about Willie, huh?"

"Very sad." Raven wiped her hands on the apron wrapping her waist. "I should get—"

"But it's how the circle goes," the old woman rambled on in her smoker's voice. "Creator has plans."

"Yes, Creator does." Raven inched away. Impolite, but she had other people to serve.

She turned and banged into Darryl, who steadied Raven's wobbling balance. Emery stood behind him.

"The tables are full. Help yourself to some coffee." Raven used a nice voice. To give them the usual stink-eye after the chief's death was disrespectful. Even enemies set aside their feuds burning hot on the campfire.

"You need help?" Emery asked in his perennial soft-spoken tone. "I can go around refilling everyone's mugs."

Leave it to Mr. Outstanding Catholic to volunteer assistance, since he volunteered everywhere else. His wavy black hair, flashing white teeth, green eyes brighter than summer grass, and pale skin a shining rosy hue from being out in the cold coughed up a gag in Raven's throat. How could someone be so perfect, even perfect-looking? But she wasn't dumb enough to pass up an offer for an extra arm in this mob.

"Sure. Thanks a bunchies." She flashed Emery her pearly whites. On the fake side, but she'd give herself an A for effort, since she was getting mostly A's at her adult education classes at the school.

She grabbed three more orders to take to another table while Cookie kept manning the full grill of frying food.

"Over here," another regular called out.

"This isn't for you." Raven sidled around his chair and cooed into his ear, "It's for over there. Wait your turn, handsome."

"Handsome, that I am," he replied, although he sure wasn't, at seventy-eight years old with a big pot belly.

Raven giggled and dashed to the table the food belonged to. "Okay, here we go. Four Hunter's Breakfasts. Eat up."

"What you think's gonna happen?" the one man asked. "Bi-election? Can't see it. Not with elections happening in April."

"Don't know." Raven set down the other plates. "Ask my brother. He's on band council."

"Where's ol' Clayton, anyway?" The man looked around.

"At the counter." Raven stepped back. "Emery has the coffee pot. If you need a refill, give him a shout."

"Gotcha." The other man dug into his breakfast of eggs, steak, pan fries, and pancakes.

Raven snaked her way through the crowd.

Laughter erupted at another table. She spared a glance at the three women a couple of years older than her huddled together. Her heart tugged at their kinship. It'd been a long time since she'd last experienced womanly friendship from females who weren't her relations.

The women glanced up, shooting Raven dirty looks. She shot one straight back.

"Slut." The hushed insult was loud enough to reach Raven.

An angry knot of tension erupted across Raven's shoulders. Under any other circumstance she would have stormed over and called out the bitches, but now wasn't the time. Not during the chief's mourning period. If those ugly witches wanted to behave in a disrespectful manner, they could go on right ahead. It wasn't Raven's fault men liked her.

She huffed into the kitchen.

Cookie stood at the other counter, while Raven's step-nephew had taken over the grill. Only fourteen, and in grade nine, Tyrell was present because there'd be no school in respect to Chief Willie.

"Hey, hey, hey, I'll need someone to take this over to the chief's place." Cookie set the last of the muffins into a cardboard box.

"I'll ask Darryl. He's hanging around while Emery's serving coffee." If Raven sent Darryl off on his way, he wouldn't have time to start promoting what a great leader he'd make.

"Perfect, perfect, perfect." Cookie patted the box. He squinted at Raven. "Too bad about Willie. What'cha think's gonna happen?"

"Ask Darryl when he comes back here to get the food. I'll get him." This was a perfect opportunity for Raven to unearth what the traitor was up to.

She darted back into the main area of the diner. After worming her way through the pile of customers, she found Darryl standing at the back window, surrounded by a few people from the Traditionalists Society.

Just as Raven had suspected. Darryl was promoting himself to those fierce in protecting their culture.

"I hate to interrupt, but Cookie needs help."

"Oh? What does he need?" Darryl held a mug of coffee.

"Someone to take the care package over to Willie's place." Raven motioned at Darryl to follow.

She wound her way back to the kitchen while being asked by a few customers about their orders. They could wait. They wouldn't die of starvation if they had to sit another five minutes.

"Here he is." Raven scooted into the kitchen.

"Good, good, good." Cookie smacked his hands together. "I need someone to take this food over to the chief's house."

"No problem. Lemme get my jacket. Emery can gimme a hand." Darryl started for the boxes.

"I'll go." Tyrell whipped around from the grill.

"Stay put." Raven used her lips to point at Darryl. "He's going. We need you on the grill. So . . ." She folded her arms, sending Cookie a stomach-poking look.

"Oh yah. Yah." Cookie popped four slices of bread into the toaster. "What's gonna happen now? Bi-election?"

Darryl's small, dark eyes widened. He hefted up a package. "Uh, I'm not sure. We probably won't consider meeting until a couple of weeks. Joe's deputy chief."

"Yah, I know, but deputies only fill in when Willie's away." Cookie reached for the butter.

"We'll have to wait and see." Holding the cardboard box, Darryl edged toward the swinging doors. "Until then, everyone knows Joe acts in Willie's place."

"But he's a band councilor." Cookie scooped up a knife.

"Yeah, he is. That's why we appointed him deputy chief. For emergencies like this. We'll wait until the funeral's done. The coroner still has to fly up. Then Lucy has to plan his funeral." Darryl vanished from the kitchen.

"He never gives me a second to talk to him." Cookie threw up his hands. "Tyrell, take the orders out. I need to speak to Raven."

Raven retrieved the plates sitting on the warming tray and handed them to Tyrell, who took the orders and dashed out to the eating area.

"Soo . . . y'know how old I'm getting."

"Seventy-two is hardly old." Raven washed her hands at the sink just as the toast popped from the toaster. "I'll get those. You watch the grill."

"See what I mean, eh?" Cookie flipped a couple of eggs over easy. "You always tell me what to do."

"I'm only trying to help." Raven buttered the toast.

"You run this kitchen like I do. That's what I'm looking for. Someone who's gonna care about this place as much as me."

The sizzling grill, constant chatter, and even roars of laughter from the dining area filled the kitchen. Raven checked the order lading. These were individual side dishes. She set the two plates of toast on the higher counter facing the main area and rang the bell for Tyrell.

"Of course I care. I love working for you." She set two more orders of toast into the toaster. "You . . ." He'd given her a chance when nobody else had. "I'm always here whenever you need me."

"Yah, that's it." Cookie eased the eggs onto three plates. He added the bacon and ham. Then he dished up the pan fries. "You're always helping out. Always willing to come in whenever someone's sick or something. Keep this place clean without me having to tell you to. Always busy doing this or that."

"I enjoy it." The sight of dirt, after living in it for so long, made Raven's stomach queasy. Filth, even a smidgen of something not put in its proper place, produced an itch on her skin.

"If I was forty years older, I'd marry you, sweetie. Keep your apartment at the senior center super-clean. Make sure you're fed each night . . ." She shook her hips.

"Ho, ho, ho." Cookie threw back his head, laughing. "Always make me smile. But I'll take you as a daughter."

Raven giggled. She pecked his cheek, then reached into the deep freezer to retrieve the chicken strips someone wanted to eat at nine in the morning.

"And that's why I wanna . . ." Cookie placed his chubby finger over his skinny lips. "It stays between us."

"Gotcha." Raven twisted a pretend key at her mouth to seal

the imaginary lock. She set the chicken strips into the deep fryer.

" . . . sell you *Kiss the Cook*."

It was a good thing she'd performed her task first, or she would've dumped the order into the fryer, splashing hot grease over herself.

Kiss the Cook? The gold mine of Ottertail Lake? The place where everyone had been gathering for over thirty years after Cookie had sobered up? But for Raven to secure a place like this, she'd for sure need her brother to become chief during April's election, and that meant making sure Darryl Keejik didn't win—no matter what.

Chapter Two: Something Better

The pile of books came crashing down from the shelf in the study. Jude bolted out of the way. He growled. Even though he had thirty days to vacate his sanctuary, packing came slowly. Now he had another mess to clean.

He plopped in the chair and faced the French doors leading to the empty deck and snow-covered pool. There also went his children's sanctuary, a once-favorite family spot, since their should-have-been forever home had sold after finally putting it on the market three months earlier.

Downsizing. He'd looked at houses in Bridget's neighborhood. At least something good had come out of his divorce. Last year, his sister and brother-in-law had bought a great three-bedroom bungalow over on Dalhousie Drive. Noah and Rebekah could walk to school and chill with Kyle, Bridget's adopted and her husband's biological son. There was also a great park for the kids to play at.

Walking to work was great exercise, since the school was right there on Redwood Avenue.

Jude's gut blackened. At least the pitiful glances had stopped from his staff, the people at church, members of the Catholic Men's Association, and acquaintances from the golf course and curling rink. He didn't need anyone's pity.

His landline rang. Dad. Without looking at the call display, Jude picked up the cordless. "Hey."

"How're you?" Dad cleared his throat.

"S'okay. How about you? You're the one filling in when you're retired."

"I don't mind. I'm more concerned about Willie's family."

"Yeah, that's too bad. Heart attack, hey?" Jude turned the chair.

"Yes." Dad heaved a big breath.

"What is it?" Jude stuck the end of the pen into his mouth and planted his feet on the desk. He crossed his legs at the ankles.

"You know, sometimes the Lord is speaking to us, but we don't hear Him, because we're too busy looking and listening elsewhere."

"I'm still going to church. I'm still a member of the Catholic Men's Association. I'm still on the pastoral council. Charlene's the one who's initiating the annulment, not me. I assume she'll start the proceedings now."

"This isn't about attending Mass or supporting honorable causes. This is about daily reflections with our Lord."

"I'm praying every morning, Dad." A lie, but Jude made sure to add a dash of conviction to his words. He crumpled a ball of paper and fired it at the empty pen mug, since he'd already packed away his putter and pro-putter machine. The paper was a ringer. *He shoots, he scores.*

"Prayer sometimes isn't enough." Dad's tone altered from authoritative to gentle, but a hint of commanding remained. "We must contemplate what He exactly wants and discern the right direction He wishes for us to take. I faced complete distress after He called me home when you and Bridget were almost finished high school. The heartbreak your mother and I faced having to leave you in Thunder Bay with Aunt Patti and Uncle Robert."

"Dad, the Lord called. You went. Bridget and I were fine." Jude aimed his fountain pen at the mug. The pen rolled across the mahogany desk—his pride and joy—and hit the hardwood floor.

"We are without a principal. This is why we had the

education institute provide the teachers program up here. Because teachers not from the community kept leaving. Only those from here will stay."

Jude sat up. His feet hit the throw rug surrounding the desk. This was perfect. Why hadn't he thought of this sooner? The principal's job was his chance to leave Thunder Bay. Leave this house. Leave a job that served the Lord who'd turned his life into a disgraced mess. "I see . . ."

"You were thinking about it?"

"Err . . . yes . . . I was."

"Really? I didn't think you were. You should have told me."

"I only recently found out. Perhaps the Lord wants me home." Jude tried not to snort aloud at His Holiness's name. "I have thirty days to vacate the house. It's enough time to provide notice at the school." A school geared toward a God that didn't deserve any notice.

Dad again cleared his throat. "I'm sorry. So sorry for what happened. You're a good man. I'm thankful you have the children. If you need to talk —"

"They'll be okay." Again, Jude's gut blackened. He had to speak to Bridget.

Jude waited for his sister in his study. He ran his fingers along the mahogany desk, another *something* he'd sell, because there'd be no room in Ottertail Lake to accommodate anything in his study. The kids would lose their haven, too — the family room. But they'd have a lake to swim in, new places to play, a rec center to go to.

The front door opened and closed, followed by the walk-in closet door opening and closing. Footsteps scampered to the family room. Kyle was no doubt searching out Noah and Rebekah. Heels clicked against the hardwood floor.

His sister appeared in the double-door entrance, frowning.

"What's going on?"

Jude used his chin to point at the side table. "Coffee? I picked up a packet of Reggie's decaf last night for you and the little one. It's freshly brewed."

Bridget stamped to the table. "Reggie's? Seriously? I'm not going to like this, am I?"

Again, this was Charlene's fault. If she hadn't humiliated him and stolen his faith, he wouldn't be leaving. Fingers seemed to curl around Jude's heart, squeezing.

"This isn't easy for me." How could he leave his other half behind? Bridget was more than his sister. She was a part of him, as if they'd grown in Mom's womb together and divided the egg to share for the rest of their lives.

Bridget fixed her coffee. Hand trembling, she sat on the edge of the chair facing the desk. "What's going on?"

Jude sucked in a deep breath and folded his hands on the desk. "I'm moving."

"Oh? That's why you scared me half to death? Your text frightened me into next week." Bridget's tone was scolding but also impish. She plopped in the chair.

"Fort William or Port Arthur?" she asked, referring to the city's two major neighborhoods, once separate municipalities.

"Neither." Jude had to force the word from his mouth.

Bridget clicked her long nails on the small table beside the armchair. "I see. I see." For a moment, thunder clouds gathered in her dark eyes, then the corners wilted. She stared beyond the desk to the French doors.

"You're taking the principal's job, aren't you?" Her voice was small, which was rare, because nothing sent his sister scuttling to a corner.

Jude's abs contracted, as if someone had punched his gut. He licked his lips. "I'm sorry."

"No. No. Don't be sorry." Bridget kept speaking in a small voice, head bowed. "I get it. I do. What she did . . ." Her

brown skin with red undertones whitened. "Fucking bitch —
"

"Whoa. Easy." Jude hadn't heard her use this kind of language.

Bridget looked up through hate-filled eyes. "Well, she sure didn't think of anyone but herself. She didn't think about the kids. She didn't think about you. She didn't think about the life you two built together. Ever since she left, I've been playing surrogate mother to Becky and Noah."

"I know. It's tough. Y'see, leaving's for the best. Mom and Dad are there. Mom'll watch them after school. It's what they need right now. There're too many memories here for them. Too many memories for me."

Bridget brushed at a lock of her long, black hair. "I wish I could spend more time here, but my schedule's so — "

"Don't." Jude raised his finger. "The kids are my responsibility. You have a family of your own. And it's growing." He motioned at her belly, where her unborn daughter was growing.

"I understand. I do." She set aside the mug. "Did you already give notice?"

"No. But I'm working on my letter." He pointed at the laptop. "I'm emailing it to Sam tomorrow."

"Oh geez." Bridget sagged in the chair. "Sam's retiring in two years. You wanted to be the next Superintendent of Education."

More than the Superintendent of Education. In time, Jude had planned on working one more step up to the ultimate position — Director of Education.

"I can't . . ." As tempting as both jobs were, what man wanted to stick around when everyone knew his Catholic wife had cheated on him and then had left him for a colleague?

Jude picked up his coffee mug. "I already talked to Dad. I

wanted you to know right away."

"She's not even here anymore." Bridget thrust her free hand outward, palm up. "She's in Kenora. Tons of women at the university have been asking me—"

"Nope. Don't go there." Jude raised his own hand. "I just got divorced. I don't want any blind dates—"

"I wasn't going to set you up on a blind date." Bridget made a face. "And it's been over a year since you two separated, more than enough time to—"

"Not interested." He sipped his coffee. "Anyway, there's stuff I won't be able to take with me." Shit, a lot of stuff. "The house they have for the principal is about twelve-hundred square feet, or smaller. I'll have to sell some furnishings, but what I don't sell, I want you to have, or Adam can have, or Kyle can have . . ."

Cookie flipped over the closed sign and locked the door.

Raven couldn't help cupping and un-cupping her coffee mug.

"Well, well, well . . . finally a break." He drew out the chair and sat. "So, what'd you think of my offer?"

"I'd love to, but how am I gonna get the cash?" No bank loaned band members money for a business based on the reserve. "I guess I could check around and see what kind of funding's available. How'd you go about getting the diner set up?"

"It's not available anymore, but the feds were offering a program to support Indigenous businesses. An interest-free loan."

"I s'pose I could ask Clayton if there are any kind of programs like that now." Then there was the economic development officer, who might have some leads.

"Why the sagging shoulders? It'll happen." Cookie slurped

his tea.

Because sleeping with men was the only way Raven had gotten anything she'd wanted, and now she had to rely on her brains. She crumbled the napkin in her hand. "I hope so."

"Hey, lookit the chance the funders took on me. I had to get the band to write me a letter of recommendation. You can, too."

"I'll let you know."

"Sure. Think it over. I think this place'll be perfect for you."

"I'm going to recommend Joe remain deputy chief." Clayton stood outside the chief's house, puffing on a cigarette.

Raven stamped her feet. Even with long underwear and mukluks, and the pine trees offering protection from the January north wind, the cold still seeped through her parka and jeans. She should have worn snow pants. "Why?"

"The election's in April. I need to campaign. Devote my time to winning. The first thing I'm gonna do as chief is take back the Traditionalists Society. It's ours. It belongs to the Kabatays."

Her brother should. As a founding member, he'd worked hard to develop a group intent on following their culture in every aspect of their lives. Darryl Keejik had no right serving as chairperson. And she'd championed Clayton for walking away from what he'd formed after Darryl had manipulated The Traditionalists Society into accepting the church in the community.

"What were you meeting with Cookie about? He gonna finally put a stop to the rumors about his retirement?"

There was her opening. "He's retiring."

"He is?" Clayton puffed on the smoke again, his beady eyes studying her. "Who's he selling the place to? It's a gold mine."

"If I can come up with the money — me." Raven rubbed her

17

shivering arms. "Nobody's gonna loan me money. It's not like the bank can come on the reserve and seize the diner. And I sure don't have any kind of credit rating . . ."

Clayton's slim lips spread into a wide grin, the first true grin Raven had seen in a long time after the Matawapits and their church had screwed up his plans for the reserve. "I need a campaign manager."

He set his palm on Raven's shoulder. "You do this for me, I'll more than guarantee you the diner if you make sure I get in as chief."

Raven's stomach somersaulted. This was the reason for her adult education classes and why she studied so hard.

"Oh my gosh, I don't know what to say." She sputtered.

"Say yes." Clayton's grin always resembled a coyote on the prowl, ready to attack.

"Yes. I'll do it."

"Remember, I need to win." Clayton thrust his finger.

Raven drew back. Pointing was a grave offense, highly rude. "I won't fail. I'll make sure you have the best campaign possible."

"I mean *whatever* it takes. Are you ready to go that far?"

"Yes." She'd stop at nothing for her brother to become chief and the chairperson for the Traditionalists Society again.

They'd both get what they wanted. He'd rule the reserve as a chief should—dedicating his efforts to making Ottertail Lake a true *Anishinaabe* community, and only *Anishinaabe*. And she'd finally gain some respect, instead of sneers from Mom, her sisters, and the community.

Jude set out the plates on the table. He'd made sure to order the kids' favorite treat—*Romeo's Pizza*, the best in Thunder Bay, homemade crust and Romeo's secret family sauce. There was cheesecake for dessert he'd picked up at *The Bistro* after work. Pop, another treat, was chilled and ready for drinking. Rebekah loved orange, and Noah adored root beer.

He'd spent the week contemplating, but no matter how many times he assessed the pros and cons, the school needed a principal—one who wouldn't leave. The children needed a principal—one dedicated to his job, not present to gain work experience for a résumé like all outsiders did, putting in their obligatory year and then splitting.

If Dad could pack up and leave, so could Jude. Emery had done just fine in his new environment at age eight. So would Rebekah and Noah, who'd turn eight and nine this coming spring and summer.

"Noah. Becky. Dinner. It's a surprise."

The kids scampered from the family room and into the dining room.

Jude sat. After they ate, he'd tell them they were moving to Ottertail Lake.

CHAPTER THREE: SINGING THE BLUES

Jude threw up his arms as he surveyed his new house. Talk about downsizing. He'd gone from a castle to a wigwam.

At least while he'd been in Thunder Bay transporting his belongings to the reserve with the help of Darryl, Emery, and Dad, Mom hadn't had much to scrub from top to bottom in the twelve-hundred square foot, three-bedroom, pre-packaged home.

Leaving his job early had been a must in order to use the winter road, because he'd refused to fly in their belongings. Too expensive. Praise Father Arnold for his letter to the Catholic School Board, urging them to accept an early resignation from Jude so he could leave to answer the Lord's call. A lie. But it'd worked in his favor.

The first week of February. And he was in Ottertail Lake. Noah and Rebekah remained in the city at Bridget's place. When Emery and Jude returned the U-Hauls, they'd retrieve his truck and send the kids in on the plane.

"I made the right decision," he said to the white walls needing a new coat of paint.

"If you think you did, then you did."

Jude whipped on his heel at Emery lounging in the back doorway. "I thought everyone left."

"Mom and Dad did. I told Darryl to come and get me." Emery pointed at the year-old dining set Jude had carted from the house because Charlene had taken the original one after they'd separated, an antique set belonging to her great-grandmother.

Jude had also brought the bedroom, kitchen, and family room furniture. All the essentials for a home. Even a shitload of groceries, and the deep freezer he kept on the supposed back deck because there was no room inside.

"Want some black tea?" Emery sidled up to the chipped and stained kitchen counter. Even the one measly row of four cabinets required a refurbishing.

There were no more marble countertops, four-place eating bar, hardwood floors, industrial-sized fridge and freezer, walk-in pantry, six-burner gas range top, two wall ovens, and a breakfast area built into the bay window that overlooked the deck and pool to enjoy coffee and the newspaper. Jude sagged against the table.

"It'll be okay." Emery removed the digital kettle from a box. "Once we get everything unpacked, it'll be as cozy as—"

"I don't need a pep talk." Jude dug inside another box for mugs.

"I know, but you lived in a beautiful house." Emery filled the kettle. "You had a six-figure job."

"And I'll rebuild." Jude set the cups on the dining room table that had no business being in the kitchen. "I'm not sure how, but I'll figure out something."

If only the general public knew the difficulties band members faced. A building loan? Not happening even with a five-star credit rating, because banks and other financial institutions couldn't enter the reserve to foreclose, so a person had to have enough equity or collateral to match the loan, located off the reserve the bank could access.

Then there was the ministerial guarantee, which meant the involvement of band council. Dad had gone this route to build his house. Jude would, too, depending on who sat at the leadership table after April's election. If Clayton Kabatay became the big pooh-bah, crumbling ground zero might become

Jude's forever home, or until the next election.

Another option was putting his name on the housing list, but he'd have no say in the design or size. The reserve purchased construction packages, which was why every damned house on an Indian Reserve looked the same, starting with this junk pile of wood and nails.

"Your vein . . ." Emery grinned. "The one on your forehead . . ."

"Is sticking out?" Jude switched on the water taps. "I'll give these a cleaning." He set the mugs in the sink.

"Don't wash too much. Mom said she'd be here bright and early to get the house settled. She knows you want to go to the school right away." Emery dug around in another box. "Where are the tea bags?"

"Forget it." Jude switched off the taps because the bottle of Sunshine Soap was hidden in one of the bazillion boxes.

Emery moved to the sink. "Sit. I got this."

Jude plopped in the chair. "Y'know, I'd let the kids stay in the city to finish the school year, instead of coming up to this disorganized mess, but the last year has been difficult enough for them."

"Disorganized? True. But Mom'll settle you in. She kept a fire burning ever since we left for Thunder Bay."

A woodstove. Jude stifled the spittle itching to escape his mouth and hit the smooth wood finish of the table. He'd have to figure out how to keep the place warm, but not too warm. At least the house was located a road away from the school in the district everyone referred to as *downtown*, so he could sneak over on his lunch hour and reload the woodstove.

"I learned how to make a fire when I was eight. I had to know. The kids'll grow up fast here," Emery said, as if reading Jude's mind.

Jude glanced away from the woodstove in the corner of the living room. "They're seven and eight. I don't want my kids near a fire."

"They're going to be eight and nine in the summer. They have to learn." Emery withdrew the dish soap from a box. "I was chopping wood at their age. It's different up here for kids. They're a part of the community and expected to participate, not like in the cities or towns where they can be sheltered. We don't have that luxury up here."

"It was a different time when you were growing up."

Emery threw on the taps. Water shot from the faucet. "I turned twenty-nine in November. I'm not that old."

"Okay, you can teach Noah how to build a fire, but you have to supervise him at all times." Jude lifted his finger.

"I'll watch him," Emery replied in a reassuring tone. "And don't be pointing. You're as bad as Dad. You know it's considered rude."

"He only does so to get his point across."

"I know. He did it to me all the time." Emery's cell phone dinged. "It's Darryl. He's on his way. I'll wash a mug for him."

"How goes your schooling?"

"Good. It keeps me too busy. A lot of papers, research, and studying. Sometimes I wonder if I should have been content with my BSW." Emery kept digging around in the boxes and setting the items on the counter.

"Is that why you didn't apply for the mental health counselor job? I thought for sure you would've. You were a shoo-in."

"Darryl kept telling me we didn't need the money and he wants me to concentrate on finishing my master's."

"Speaking of finishing schooling . . ." Jude folded his arms. "I need to get on the adult education files, pronto. I'm meeting with Dad tomorrow morning at the school."

"He'll be glad to hand that stack over to you. The one student isn't very cooperative." Emery filled the digital kettle and plugged it in.

"Oh? Who?"

"Raven Kabatay. I guess she was doing terrific. Straight A's, except for math. Now, she's arguing with Dad about everything."

"Great. One of Clayton's sisters, right?"

"Yes." Emery set three teabags into the teapot.

"Anything I should know about her?" Scratching his brow, Jude stifled a sigh.

"She works at Cookie's. A waitress. She's big in the recovery program, too."

"Recovery?" He sat up in the chair.

"She's a recovering addict." The kettle beeped. Emery lifted it off the stand and filled the teapot. "Darryl said she moved back about two and a half years ago after she got out of treatment."

Shit happened. Bridget's husband was a recovering alcoholic. "Good on her. If she wants to better her life, why's she — Never mind." Raven was a Kabatay, and the Kabatay family were determined to keep the so-called family feud burning.

Headlights appeared in the kitchen window. Jude's brother-in-law had arrived. A truck door slammed. Barking ensued.

"He brought your fur kids?"

"Of course." Emery placed the mugs on the table. He dug around in another box and produced the honey.

The back door opened, then slammed shut. "*Aniin. Aaniish naa ezhiyaayin?*"

"Quit showing off and speak English," Jude muttered. "As for how I'm doing, I'm here, aren't I?"

Darryl swaggered into the kitchen, having doffed his parka on the hooks next to the door. "You're still not enjoying yourself?" Amusement glimmered in his small, dark eyes.

"What do you think?" Jude couldn't help the dryness in his

tone.

"Easy. Now that we got you cornered, I need to talk to you about something."

"You make fun of me, and now got the nerve to ask me for a favor?" Jude shook his head, a smirk forcing his lips to move upward. "What is it?" He took the cup Emery held out.

Darryl accepted the other teacup Emery offered. "I'm running for chief."

This wasn't a big shocker. Darryl already served on band council, and he'd gotten in on his first try at the leadership table. Considering he held a master's in Indigenous Governance, his education and personality made him a winner in the political ring.

"And . . ."

Darryl's vest had embroidery of his clan stitched in a circle on the left breast. He reached inside the inner pocket and produced a fist-sized leather pouch.

Jude held his breath.

Darryl pinched the tobacco between his thumbnail and index finger. He placed the contents in front of Jude.

"What am I—" Jude took the tobacco.

"I'm asking if you'll be my campaign manager." The slant of Darryl's eyes confirmed how serious he was.

"Campaign manager?" Jude couldn't say no. To be asked was an honor. Especially since most candidates didn't campaign on reserves, not like in Western culture. Communities were small and very tight-knit. Roughly over two thousand people lived in Ottertail Lake. Everyone knew everyone.

He cleared his throat. "I was under the impression you were running for council."

"That was the plan." Darryl added a dollop of honey to the tea. "But Roy asked me if I'd run for chief."

Roy Morrison was Dad's BFF, and he also sat on band council. "Why?"

"Politics. What else?" Darryl set his elbow on the table and rested his round chin in his palm. "Roy figures with Willie gone, Clayton'll go for chief and try his best this time to have a quorum in his favor."

"He hasn't in the past, has he?" Of course not, otherwise Dad would have been ousted as principal.

Darryl sipped his tea. "There's the self-governance model that I developed."

The project was the reason for Darryl's return to the reserve. He'd been hired on to manage the self-governance initiative, which was now complete.

"Do you think he'll readjust the model you developed?"

"More so." Darryl lips firmed. "What Clayton wants is everyone with white blood off this reserve."

Jude glanced at his brother. Irish and German descent ran through their veins from Mom.

"And you know he'll go after the church again," Darryl added.

"Naturally." Jude sat back and massaged his temples. "What about the school? We have two non-native teachers."

"He'll oust them. He'll oust you, too."

"Nope. I didn't give up six figures, a great pension, and my dream house for nothing. And he's not screwing around with my kids' education."

"That's why I need you as my campaign manager. You're a natural leader." Darryl kept gazing at Jude, his eyes crinkling at the corners.

Jude glanced at Emery, who sat in silence across the table, nursing his tea.

"We talked about it," Emery began. "I agree. I think you'd be an excellent campaign manager. Politics . . . you know it's not my field."

"It's not my field either." Jude picked a pen off the table and stuck the end in his mouth.

"Sure it is. You've served on the pastoral council at your church in T. Bay. You served as president for the Catholic Men's Association. You sat on the board for your golf course. You became a principal before you were thirty-five. Not too many people your age achieve what you've accomplished. Leadership's part of you." Darryl tapped where his heart lay beneath his vest.

"Becoming a principal was a lot of work." Jude set aside the pen. "A lot of night school."

"Isn't that why you and . . . ah, well, your ex-wife held off on kids? You both wanted to concentrate on your careers first."

True. Well, Jude was starting over here. Starting over at thirty-eight. This was his new home, and his kids' new home. Becoming involved in the community was imperative. He wasn't going to sit on his ass while others did the work to make Ottertail Lake the best place to live.

"Okay. I'm your campaign manager."

"I knew you'd say yes." Darryl's palm came out. "With you as my wingman, I know we can go up against the Kabatays."

Jude clasped Darryl's hand. "They're a huge family, aren't they? We got our work cut out for us."

"We sure do." Darryl grimaced.

"They won't fight fair." This came from Emery.

"Yeah, they'll try dig up dirt on you. If there are skeletons, you'd better let me know. Pronto." Jude winked.

"None that I can think of." Darryl shrugged.

"What about when you lived in Winnipeg?" Jude's brother-in-law had been a single man and hurting big-time after being dumped by Emery.

Red crept onto Darryl's face. He glanced away. "I was in my twenties. I went out bar-hopping and whatnot."

Emery's normally fair skin pinkened. "Maybe we should focus on our strategy."

Jude's gaze darted to a still-staring-at-nothing Darryl and then to a still-pink-faced Emery. Was there something they weren't telling him — something possibly dirty enough to cost Darryl the election?

CHAPTER FOUR: THERE'S SOMETHING I LIKE ABOUT THAT

Frost nipped at Raven's exposed skin, the kind of frost that burned. At least there wasn't a wind chill, or minus thirty-seven would become minus forty-seven. She scurried from her sister's truck she'd parked, dashed up the shoveled walkway, and into the school.

All was quiet, classes for the kids having finished for the day. The scent of pine cleaner permeated the squeaky-clean hallway. She hurried to the adult education classroom. Since her vehicle was the lone truck in the lot, she might be the only one here. Even the new principal wasn't present, unless he'd foolishly walked over.

She entered the classroom to Jude Matawapit sitting at the teacher's desk, hunched over, writing on some paper.

"I was beginning to wonder if any of my students would arrive." His strong fingers gripped a pen. His jet-black hair with blue undertones was slicked off his face and tapered to a short-trimmed back. Dark irises richer than a moonless night, so dark his lashes gave the illusion of a generous coating of mascara and liner-rimmed eyes, stared at her.

Not gawked, not ogled, not leered like every other guy did. He simply stared. His plump lips didn't form into a flirty smile, either.

Jude stood. A white dress shirt hugged his pumped biceps and shoulders that formed into the size of baseballs. A black belt wrapped his ultra-slim waist. And a gold clip kept his line-striped burgundy tie secure. "Have a seat. It looks to be you and me tonight."

Raven inched up the aisle. Her boldness remained at the door, where she'd probably dropped her tongue. She clutched her books and sat at the desk directly in front of him.

"I've been reviewing your file." He closed the folder, and just like Deacon Matawapit, crossed his strong arms. They even shared the same rich baritone — direct and full of authority. "You were an A-plus student, but as of late you haven't been handing in assignments. Once you get behind, it's difficult to catch up. I've seen this happen too many times during my years educating others. When a student falls behind, most give up."

A flame of annoyance flickered in Raven's stomach. Never mind Jude Matawapit's handsome white teeth, flawless red-toned brown skin, or run-her-nails-along-his-muscles build. Who was he to talk down to her like a kid? He was worse than her siblings and Mom.

Raven stared up at the white stucco ceiling. "I've been extremely busy. Not all of us make big money and do what we please. I've been pulling extra shifts at the diner."

"Did you review your last three assignments, then?" Jude stuck the end of the pen into his mouth.

There was something about the way his red lips and white teeth nibbled on the cap. And she hadn't witnessed a man in his late thirties gnawing on one like a hungry beaver.

Jude popped the pen cap between his rich lips, as if sucking on a lollipop, and released it. When he rounded the desk, his thick fingers glided across the top. He stopped in the middle, the fingers of his left hand still lingering on the desk's surface. He rested his buttocks against the edge while crossing his sturdy thighs.

His stance, a get-down-to-business sort of manner, should have intimidated Raven but failed. His brows-bunched-together stare and drawn-in cheeks seemed to coax her to lean in closer and rest her elbow on top of her own desk. She set her chin on her knuckles. "I'm completing them here tonight."

"Do you have any questions?"

She shook her head, still holding his stare. "I guess I should get comfy, huh?"

"Comfy?"

"Removed my toque and coat." She sat back, hands brushing the edge of her desk and arms spread wide.

Jude shouldn't care if Raven was about to undress. He'd seen many students remove their outerwear in class. But the down parka on Raven didn't swallow her ballerina-lithe body like a garbage bag. The coat was the fashionable snug style, silhouetting her supple form. Long strands of black hair lay against her sharper-than-razors cheekbones.

Her perfectly applied winged eyeliner gave her slanted black eyes a mysterious cat-shape appeal. Rich burgundy lipstick, matching the shade of his tie, plumped her lips to a sensual pout, or maybe her mouth naturally retained a pucker. As she stood to drape the parka over the chair, she gave him a nice view of the skinny jeans painted on her slender thighs and gently rounded butt.

She whipped her head around, peeking at him through the fringe of her super-long lashes.

Heat climbed onto Jude's face. He shoved the pen back into his mouth and chewed on the cap. Adult or not, she was a student—his student. Maintaining a professional distance was a must.

Raven's moist-looking mouth tugged at the corners. A hint of triumph flashed in her eyes. Well, well, she'd stolen a look purposely, expecting him to check her out. A hot coal flared in Jude's chest. He rounded his desk, making sure to move slowly, heels clicking one after the other on the floor. She'd get the hint he meant business.

"Why don't you catch up on your lessons? There's no point in reviewing the next one until you're finished those." He used his pen to point in her direction. Traditionalist or not, she could suck up his supposed rudeness. In his world, pointing told another a man wasn't screwing around or willing to play games.

Raven sat. She flipped open her textbook and binder.

"Which lesson are you working on?"

"History. A pity. We are the First People, but it's all about . . . those who sailed over here." Her husky voice, deeper than most women's, with a light scratch to the tone, was sensual nails grazing Jude's skin.

He gripped and re-gripped the pen. "At my former school, we were building the curriculum into the current courses."

"Did you teach high school or elementary? You taught for the Catholic Board of Education, didn't you?"

"Elementary."

"I see." Raven lowered her head. Her black hair veiled her face. Not narrow, like Clayton's hawkish looks. The hollowed cheeks, delicate long nose, and tapering chin complemented Raven's smoky eyes and wide mouth. A traditional diamond-shaped face, like the Indigenous people of the old days.

No wonder she'd stolen a glimpse at Jude when she'd removed her parka. Raven was probably used to men gawking at her wherever she went. If the fashion designers ever took a chance on hiring Indigenous women to model, they'd be scrambling to photograph Raven.

Why was he still thinking about her anyway? This was ridiculous.

Jude plopped in the chair. If she didn't require assistance on her lessons, she should've finished her assignments at home. All Raven had done was make him stay late.

Nine o'clock. Class over. Two hours of reading through files and catching up on work while Raven had done her assignments. Jude slid the files into his briefcase.

Raven looked up at the clock.

Jude stood and closed his briefcase. "How'd you do?"

"Great." Raven shut her notebook and textbook. "I finished my lesson. Only five more to go."

"Well, you showed dedication by coming here tonight. The other four didn't even call to explain their absence."

"Get used to it. You're on an Indian Reserve. Nobody calls or confirms anything. Or shows up on time."

"You showed up on time." Jude motioned at the clock. "Five to seven."

Raven's husky chuckle matched her voice. She slunk into her parka like Marilyn Monroe shimmying into a fur coat. "I'd better text my sister. Hopefully bingo's done."

"That where she is?"

"Yeah. They all went, except for Clayton."

Jude slid on his own parka. It'd be a cold walk home, even if his place was only a road over. The weather could force a polar bear to pack up and head for the Bahamas.

"I have to get Fawn." Raven checked her phone. "I'm using her truck. They're finishing the blackout. They should be done in about another twenty minutes."

Jude headed for the classroom door. The bottoms of Raven's mukluks brushed against the floor. He turned off the lights.

They meandered down the hallway. He wasn't in a rush, and she didn't seem to be either, maybe because of the bingo thing.

Percy, the evening custodian, had probably called it a night. Once someone went outside, there'd be no going back in, because the doors automatically locked behind them,

33

except Jude could reenter, since he had a key.

"You don't have a vehicle yet?" Again, her husky voice scratched at Jude's flesh, kitten claws playfully nicking him.

"No. I'm getting it this weekend when I get my kids."

"How many do you have?"

"Two."

"Oh yeah, that's right. How old are they now?"

"Seven and eight. My daughter, Rebekah, we call her Becky, is in grade two. My son, Noah, is in grade three." This was weird. Raven didn't seem like the enemy. Polite. Asking perfunctory questions anyone else might ask to fill the gap as they walked to the main doors. The only shot she'd got in was the history curriculum not including enough about the Indigenous people.

"What about you? Any children?"

"No. There's still lots of time. I'm only thirty-one."

"You were two grades ahead of Emery?"

"Yep. But you know how it goes. You stick to people your own age in school."

"True."

They reached the end of the hallway.

Jude pushed on the door.

Whenever emotion didn't fill Raven's words, her sandpaper voice became a caress, warm against Jude's ear, even when she stood a foot away from him.

"Ladies first."

Raven edged outside, glancing around. She'd already pulled up the hood to her parka. A scarf hid her slim chin.

The chill bit at Jude's exposed face. Funny how people assumed extreme cold temperatures made a person freeze. Not true. The icy air hurt. Even burned.

"C'mon, I'll give you a lift." Raven's truck already hummed, her having hit the starter from the classroom window.

"Sure." A warm vehicle was too good of an opportunity to pass up.

They scurried to the truck, where white fumes rushed from the exhaust pipe, offering Jude a sniff of smelly gasoline.

He hopped into the passenger seat and quickly shut the door to a blast of hot air from the vents. He rubbed his gloved hands.

"I guess we got another week of this." Raven also rubbed her mitten-covered hands together.

"Did you make those?" What she wore was stunning — perhaps crafted from moose hide. Fringed. Trimmed with red trade cloth and beadwork stitched into a floral pattern. Rabbit fur was sewn to the top and bottom of the cloth.

"Yeah." She shifted gears. "My kokum made sure we all knew how. She taught my kokum, who taught my mom." She backed out of the parking spot.

Many referred to their grandmother as kokum on the reserve. Jude never had. He'd never known his paternal grandparents. "Your grandma taught your grandma?"

"By your definition, great-grandmother. To me they were simply kokum. Both. She died when I was twelve."

"That's a long time for her to live."

"She was like any other *Anishinaabe-kwe,* married when she left the residential school at sixteen. Had a family right away. But her kokum taught her how to dress a moose hide, how to hunt, set fish nets, harvest wild rice. All that stuff. My great-grandma was born on the trapline. She was *Biidaaban.* Then *they* forced her parents to give her an English name."

"What does it mean?"

"Dawn is approaching. It's when she was born, the approach of dawn, or so Mom told me." Raven finally engaged the gear to drive.

They left the parking lot.

Jude's chest sank. It'd been an interesting conversation. A

pity they might not speak like this again.

Raven wasn't going to do all the talking. Jude had a mouth. She guided the truck onto the main road. "What about you? Why come live up here? You lived in the city your whole life."

"The school needed a principal. Somebody who'd stay." Gone was the understanding tone from seconds ago. Jude's vocal cords had morphed to direct and full of authority. Too bad. There was a nice guy hiding beneath his Deacon Matawapit impersonation.

She shouldn't have offered him a ride, but not to do so was rude. Nobody deserved to walk in the extreme cold, not even her supposed enemy. But how could Jude be classed as an enemy? True, he was a Matawapit, but he didn't belong to Ottertail Lake, unlike Emery who'd arrived as a kid and made the community his home. Jude was more outsider than band member.

"I see. That was generous of you. I know teachers and principals in Ontario make excellent money. They probably have a good pension plan, too. I bet you made six figures." Raven steered the truck onto the other road. Up ahead was the principal's house.

"Sometimes it's not about money." The way Jude answered, he sounded like he was trying to convince himself he'd made the right choice.

"No regrets then?" Raven pulled up at the box-shaped house.

"None." Jude lifted his briefcase off the floor. "Thank you for the ride."

When he made no move to open the door, the saliva in Raven's mouth vanished. The silhouette of his square jawline, aquiline nose, and sensual lips sent jitters down her spine.

In the old days, he'd be marked as a handsome and skillful

hunter, capable of generously providing for his family. Not a hint of his white heritage lurked in Jude's features or coloring. He appeared one hundred percent *Anishinaabe.*

"You take after your dad." As much as Raven loathed to admit it, the deacon had aged well. Jude, upon reaching his sixties, would maintain his youthful handsomeness, too. Like most *Anishinaabe* men, he'd enjoy a lack of gray peppering his super-thick hair until his late seventies, maybe even his eighties. Kokum hadn't grayed until her eighties.

"Is that a compliment?" His voice rose an octave, impish.

Raven hadn't meant to flatter the guy, and her mouth remained dry. "I guess it is."

"Thank you. The . . ." He cleared his throat. "The women of your family are also . . . nice."

"Uh . . ." Nobody had ever called Raven *nice.* "You mean nice-looking?"

"I'm your adult education teacher. I'm attempting to, well, err . . . I don't need to get slapped with a sexual harassment suit."

"Oh yes, the suing thing." Raven couldn't help the laugh. "I can't afford a lawyer. Go ahead." She sat taller, waiting for the flirty words like all men lavished on her.

"Go ahead?"

"Say what you wanted to say. I won't be offended or go running to the board."

"Ookay." Jude's chuckle was as sexy as his handsome face and deep, smooth voice. "The women in your family are beautiful. You come from a line of attractive women."

"That's a neat way to put it. You're really sharp at twisting it up, hey?"

"Twisting?"

"Instead of saying I'm super-hot, you said the women of my family are."

Jude again chuckled. He fingered his thick, black brow,

shaking his head. If it wasn't so dark, Raven would probably catch a grin and some dimples.

"What?" She shook back her hair.

"I never had a woman demand that I tell her she's pretty. You're upfront, aren't you?" Teasing lurked in his words.

"Always. Why not? Are you used to demure women?"

His chuckle vanished.

"I'm not demure." Raven couldn't help the slyness creeping into her tone. "If I want something, I ask. If I like someone, I tell them."

"Bold, then?" If the interior lights were on, she'd probably catch a grin from him.

"Not bold. Honest."

"Honesty's a good trait. Blunt, too?" He sounded like he'd quirked his brow.

"I've been told. Some say I can be mean."

"Mean?"

"Yep. If someone pisses me off, I can get mean. Maybe I'm the B word."

"Look, we've never formally met until tonight. How about you let me draw my own conclusions?" His reply wasn't an order, since warmth filled his words.

"Okay. I'll let you draw them." A ding sounded. "That's probably Fawn." Raven reached inside her pocket and withdrew the cell phone. She checked the message. Bingo was over. Mom and the others hadn't won tonight, either. "Big sister awaits. I gotta bounce."

"Enjoy the rest of your evening. I'll see you on Thursday. Be sure to try to get caught up on all your assignments." He shifted in the seat, completely facing her.

She faced him. "Will do. If I'm caught up at work and the diner's quiet, Cookie lets me study. He knows how bad I want my high school diploma."

"I'd like you to also graduate, Raven," he said sincerely.

"I . . . I will." Raven shivered, and it wasn't from the cold.

"Then I'll see you on Thursday."

"Thursday. It's a date."

CHAPTER FIVE: I'VE GOT YOU FIXED

Raven parked at the community center, located in the Sandy Point district. People scampered from the building, dashing to their running vehicles. Fawn bounded to the truck, her breath a fog of white in the air.

"Frick, it's freezing." Fawn slammed the truck door shut. She stuck her face in front of the vent. "I was crazy to go out tonight."

"Did you at least win at the pull tabs?" Raven guided the truck through the parking lot, following a trail of vehicles.

"Nope. Nada. Nothing." Fawn turned her parka pockets inside out. "All I got in here is lint."

"That's about all I've got, too." Raven folded her lips.

"How'd your class go?"

"S'okay." Tingles still coated Raven's skin.

"Don't be that way. Your lips are folded. You always do that when you're hiding something."

Older sisters. Raven hit the gas. "I'm not hiding anything."

"Are, too"

"Am not." Any other time, Raven would blab to her sisters about the latest stud who'd snared her eye, but this was different. Jude was a Matawapit.

It'd been ages since she'd last gotten under the sheets. For the first two years at the reserve, she'd concentrated on recovery. But this last year, her clit was leading the way, wanting some action. But there'd been no guy who'd claimed her attention . . . until Jude Matawapit.

Jude sank in the recliner. He glanced at his mug, made a face, and sipped what should be a glass of scotch instead of the lemon tea he was forced to drink because of a dry reserve.

The fire in the woodstove crackled. Flames flickered behind the glass door. He set aside the mug and removed his sweater. The too-much-warmth vanished now that his arms were exposed. Hot. All because of Raven Kabatay.

She seemed a little on the sassy side, could probably morph into bitch-mode, too. He chuckled and tilted the mug. His buddies on the golf course always said those kinds of women could get wild in bed.

The picture of his children in a silver frame sat on the coffee table because he'd yet to find a place for it in the too-small living room, since the photo had once sat on his mahogany desk in his former study. He reached over, cradled the frame in his hand, and traced his thumb along their bright smiles. Trusting smiles. Smiles that had faded over a year ago after their mother had moved out.

He set aside the frame and stroked his mouth. The woodstove kept throwing heat at him. A smidgen of sweat broke out down his back. He shouldn't have tossed in a helping of ash after he'd gotten home. Pine would have sufficed. He stood, carried the mug to the sink, and dumped the tea down the drain.

He circled the wood table and skimmed his fingers along the cushioned chairs. There wasn't a chance he could engage in a fling, even though his dumb dick urged him to get selfish for a week or two. He pressed his crotch. Yep, half-hard. Some hand action while watching a video on his laptop of Dita Von Teese performing seductive burlesque should help.

He ground his fist on the table. If he dared to let temptation lead him in the wrong direction, for sure he'd get another slap across the face. And using a woman wasn't right, even if she was offering.

His dick now pushed out against the sweatpants he'd changed into after arriving home. Yep, his cock thought different. The ol' sausage wanted to go to the diner and hunt out Raven and her more than beautiful buns.

Raven finished stacking the clean coffee cups on the tray. At ten-thirty in the morning, only a few people mingled in the diner. The cold had probably kept everyone else away. A flash of black caught her eye. She held tight to the dish rag. Her heart did a *ba-bump ba-bump*. Jude was here. She wasn't supposed to see him until Thursday.

Her damned clit could remain hidden behind its protective hood. He might simply want a coffee break elsewhere from the school. Oh heck, never mind modesty. Men liked her. And so did Jude.

Just as the diner door swung open, Raven spared her reflection a glance in the window of the pop cooler. Everything was perfect — makeup, false eyelashes, hair neatly secured in place with a nice beaded barrette she'd crafted.

Raven swiveled on her comfy shoe sole designed for being on her feet all day. Too bad she couldn't wear her favorite *fuck-me* heels. Rosy cold red flecked Jude's dark skin. Even frost dusted his black eye lashes.

"I'm guessing you want something hot." Uh, she hadn't meant to toss out a double meaning, as she was prone to do, because she'd sincerely meant a cup of coffee or tea.

"Hot?" Jude's slanted thick black brow quirked.

Raven had guessed correctly about dimples when they appeared on his strong face. "Yes, hot. Can you think of anything . . . hot . . . on the menu?" Okay, that'd been intentional.

Jude's dimples deepened.

"Well?" She held up the coffee pot.

"Hmm, besides coffee?" He continued to smile as he removed his parka and set the heavy coat over the back of the stool at the counter.

"Oh?" Raven used her sassiest voice. "And what are you thinking exactly?"

Turning over the mug, Jude winked. "You're the student. It's up to you to provide the answer, not me."

"You know all the answers to the questions? And what other kinds of questions do you have for me?" Once Raven poured the coffee, she stared directly at Jude and stood straight in front of him. She set her free hand on the counter and clattered her nails.

His gaze roamed to her hand and then traveled upward, lingering on her apron and tucked-in blouse to highlight her super-slim waist. When his admiring peep settled on her breasts, she went hot and cold. Just as fast, his dark eyes drew back to hers. That was not a perverted gawk but a very appreciative gentleman admiration.

"You're a master at your craft." She almost had to draw out a fan in minus thirty-seven-degree weather.

"My craft?" He retrieved two creamers from the small bowl.

"I didn't think you'd be so . . . smooth." Raven giggled.

Jude chuckled. Red slid onto his cheekbones. He set his forearm on the counter. "Not smooth. I'm simply not the kind of man who . . ." The sound of his tongue clucking the top of his mouth echoed.

Warmth coated Raven's skin.

"I guess it's a good thing you're a Catholic boy. Something tells me you're capable of a lot of trouble." Raven snatched a menu from between the sugar container and salt and pepper shakers.

"Nah. I did your usual high school and university mischief-making—"

"I never heard it called mischief-making." She again giggled. He had a way of making her stomach tingle with laughter.

"I'm a principal. I make sure to use proper language. Remember, I was responsible for elementary-aged children."

"Okay, I'll let it pass. What would you like?" She pushed the menu in front of him and withdrew an order pad from her apron.

Jude's pupils deepened, smothering his irises, and his eyes crinkled at the corners. He set the tip of his finger against his mouth.

The breath caught in Raven's throat. The word seemed to dangle in the air—*you*. His potent look was twisting her into a pile of goo, ready to melt all over the floor.

He leaned in over the counter slightly. "What do you recommend? You've been at this longer than I have." His lips tugged upward.

If Raven's heart pounded any faster, she'd have to jump into the snowbank to cool off. She flipped over the menu. "The bagels are fresh. Cookie came in early and made them."

Bad Raven! Why'd she skitter under the bed to hide? No, she wasn't afraid. No man scared her. She scared men.

"Fresh? Anything else fresh?" Jude kept smiling. Not a friendly smile. Coy. Frisky. Daring.

Raven's throat dried. Screw the snowbank. Water. Where was a pitcher of water?

"Hey, hey, hey. Order up." Cookie banged the bell.

Cheesy, yes. But the bell had saved Raven. With all the courage she could muster, and in her smokiest voice, she choked out, "Take a good look around. You'll see for yourself what's fresh."

She set the coffee pot on the burner, scooped the order off the stainless-steel counter Cookie used to set orders on from the kitchen window, and dashed off to deliver two Hunter's

Specials to Mick and Moe—like a pathetic coward, instead of a flirty seductress.

The grin reverberated in Jude's chest. He couldn't resist and turned in his seat as Raven headed off with the two plates, her hips tilting side to side, giving him a great view of her heart-shaped ass.

What a wiggle. She'd had to have rehearsed that kind of move to make her sassy walk become a natural part of her. Subtle lift of the shoulders. Suggestive elongation of her back. Hadn't Marilyn Monroe intentionally va-va-voomed men into submission using coy body language?

Maybe this was why he preferred old-school movies and the women of the past—Liz Taylor, Sophia Loren, Marilyn. They used their body to talk to men. No need to run around half naked. Sex was in their voices, in the seductive tilt of their heads, in the way they smacked their lips at a man, in their husky or sweet girlie voices, in the way they traced their finger along a rim of a glass.

He fixed his coffee and stirred it. Raven returned to the counter. Her false eyelashes weren't over the top, either, like the creepy spider look Hollywood starlets mirrored. Just the right amount of length and fullness to enhance the natural tilt to her eyes. Or maybe her sharp cheekbones were responsible? The slant of her brows and sleek nose drew her angular features upward.

"How long's your break?"

"Fifteen minutes." Jude sipped the coffee, a fresh-tasting brew that warmed his chilled insides, although Raven was also partly responsible for the additional heat.

The diner door banged open, ushering in a helping of cold air. Jude shivered. The dance in Raven's dark eyes became two left feet trying to find a rhythm to the beat.

"What's the special, sis?" Clayton hefted up to the counter, chest puffed and chin up.

"Steak and eggs with shore lunch pan fries."

"Shore lunch?" Clayton produced his usual sly grin. "Mushrooms and green onions?"

"Yep." Raven's natural husky voice fell flatter than a bad music note.

"I never had the chance to welcome you, Matawapit. How you enjoying the rez so far?" Not a hint of sincerity lurked in Clayton's greeting.

"I'm enjoying it." Jude wasn't about to force a smile, or force anything, not after what Clayton had done to Mom, Dad, Emery, and the parish laity two summers ago, or the protest Clayton had held outside the Healing the Spirit workshop the following fall.

"Guess we'll see if you like it enough to stay, hey?" Clayton plopped on the other stool.

"I'm here, aren't I?" Jude continued to gaze at Raven, whose usual warm lips had caved downward.

"That you are. My portfolio on band council is recreation. Maybe after the election, I'll take on education?" Clayton motioned at his mug. "The special and a cup of coffee. We need to talk."

"Lemme put in your order." Raven's strained smile never met her eyes.

"Go on ahead." Clayton made a shooing gesture at the swinging kitchen doors.

Raven vanished behind them.

"Darryl running for chief?" Clayton rudely reached in front of Jude for the creamers and sugar packets.

"Why don't you ask him?"

"'Cause I'm asking you."

"I'm the school's principal, not the reserve's newspaper reporter." If Clayton wanted to be rude, Jude could dish out a serving, too.

Clayton snickered. "Easy. Just asking. Don't get bent out of shape."

"Do I look like I'm bent out of shape?" Jude glanced down at his straight torso. "Everything seems fine to me. No zigzags going on here."

"Good. You're good." Another snicker erupted from Clayton's thin mouth. "How're you enjoying the job? I'm asking as a band councilor."

"A band councilor? You said your portfolio's recreation. And I'm accountable to the education board. Now if you want to ask as a band member of Ottertail Lake, I'm spending my time going through the files and familiarizing myself with the policies and procedures."

"Heard so. Evie mentioned you called a staff meeting."

Evie was the *Anishinaabemowin* teacher. "Yes, I did." If Clayton wanted to ask more questions, he could make an appointment. Jude shoved away his coffee. "Break's over. Gotta jet."

"That was quick."

"I'm on a fifteen-minute break."

"You'd better set your clock to Indian time. Nobody expects you back on the dot. Acclimatize yourself to the reserve."

"I am." Jude stood. He withdrew five dollars from his wallet and slid the bill beneath his mug. Clayton had better not steal the leftover change that was Raven's tip. "See ya."

Jude threw on his parka and left, anger simmering in his gut, something he hadn't experienced since he'd left Thunder Bay behind.

Now that Jude was gone, Raven forced herself to step from the kitchen. This wasn't good. She loved when her brother visited the diner before heading for the band office. But the way Clayton had slid beneath Jude's nails like splinters off an old board had knotted her stomach.

She shouldn't care Clayton had tried to get a rise out of Jude—a man who practiced the Catholic way and had bought into Western indoctrination. If only her pinched chest would listen. And her overworked libido.

She pushed on the swinging doors. "I'm going to make a fresh pot. Did you want more?"

"Let me finish this first." Clayton sipped on his coffee.

"Okay. I'm going to make some new stuff for Mick and Moe. I think Shirley and Adrianne want more, too."

"They probably do. It's colder than a moose's ass out there."

Raven added a packet of coffee to the filter.

"We have to meet about the campaign. Nominations open in two weeks."

Dread creeped up Raven's spine. She couldn't let her clit do the thinking. Establishing herself as more than the fuck-up little sister who needed saving eight times a day was done. The community had begun to show respect. She wasn't a man-crazy, drug-chasing, using bitch anymore. Even the young girls whom she'd helped when she'd been a part of the Traditionalists Society had started to look up to her.

"When did you want to meet?" She added water to the coffee machine.

"Right away. I know Darryl's running."

"Did Jude say so?" Raven pivoted on her shoe. From what she'd overheard, Jude had told Clayton to man up and ask Darryl himself.

"Nope. But he is. He's not saying anything yet. And I know who'll nominate him."

"Who?"

"It won't be any ol' body. He'll get Jude."

"Jude?" But he'd only just moved here. Why would he involve himself in reserve politics? He was all about education and the church.

"I can't see it. I can see Roy. Roy's a die-hard Catholic." Raven couldn't believe Roy had once been devoted to his culture and a huge champion of the Traditionalists Society, but well over five years ago, he'd turned traitor and joined Team Matawapit.

"Roy won't, because he's running for band council again." Clayton sipped more coffee.

"Did he say so?"

"Nope. But he will. He's been a shoo-in for the last twenty years."

"What about Emery?"

Clayton almost spit out his coffee. His body shook. "Him? Emery doesn't have the balls for politics. I know saints who're eviler than that guy. And he's Darryl's ol' man. Better for it to be someone else, and it's gonna be the brother-in-law."

Raven's pulse points ceased to operate for a moment.

"What's wrong?" Clayton peered.

"N-nothing."

"You sure? You folded your lips."

She swiped up a dishcloth. "I'm thinking about a lesson that's due, and it's kicking my butt. I hate math."

"One thing I need you to do." Clayton hunched over the counter.

Raven leaned in, placing her forearms on the smooth surface she'd cleaned a half an hour ago. "What?"

"Find out what you can about Darryl."

"Darryl?" Raven whispered. "What about him?"

"There's gotta be some dirt on him." Clayton fingered the handle on the mug. "He was away for ten years. Schooling and work."

Darryl had resided in Winnipeg for a decade, but they'd

traveled in different circles. He sure hadn't been skidding in the North End, like she'd been.

Before she'd gone full steam with recovery, fighting dirty had been her mantra. The twelve-step program had taught her to play fair and accept life on life's terms. But she needed her family's trust. Their respect. Their admiration. Most of all she needed the diner.

Chapter Six: Crazy Talk

A gain, the cold spell had kept the other students away, who'd never bothered to inform Jude they wouldn't be present at class tonight. He glanced at the clock. Two minutes to seven.

From inside the classroom, the echo of a door opening and closing carried to where Jude sat behind the desk. His heart ramped up a couple of clicks per hour.

He snatched his pen and tossed open a student folder.

Footsteps carried into the classroom.

Jude glanced up to Raven sashaying to her desk.

"How'd you do on your lessons?" Perfect. His voice didn't hint at the apple caught in his throat from the sight of her lithe body poured into the snug parka.

"I finished them all except for math. Math's always kicked my ass." Raven swept the parka over her chair as if she was laying a blanket on the ground for a picnic. "Once this requirement is out of the way, I'm never looking at math again."

"That's why I'm here." Jude stood. His chest puffed. *Down, boy.* He was her teacher and sincerely wanted to help, not ride to the rescue on his horse. Well, being Ojibway, it'd be paddle to her rescue in his canoe. "Let's have a look."

"Are you always gonna teach adult ed.?" She flipped open her textbook and notebook.

"We don't have the funds to hire an extra teacher." Jude pulled over one of the student desks closer to Raven's. The scent of her soap tingled under his nose. No perfume, even though she dug makeup and styling her hair. He should've noticed her lack of a strong scent.

"You completed quadratic equations. Why're you finding analytic geometry difficult?"

"Why do you even care?" Raven sank in the chair and folded her arms.

Jude hadn't expected frustration. "You really hate math?"

"Yes." She stared at him, her lower lip protruding. "I hate it. But I have to . . . I have to learn it."

"Is this why you left high school? I reviewed your file. When you left at sixteen, you were still trying to acquire grade nine math. According to Mr. Dewey's notes, he coached you last year and you received your credit."

Jude leaned in closer, since Raven was glaring straight ahead. He rested his hand on her notebook. "All you need is this one credit to finish grade ten. You're already on to grade eleven subjects in the other courses. You're not going to let this hold you back, are you?"

"You don't get it." Raven blew a puff of breath from the side of her mouth. "I'm not good at math. It goes over my head, no matter how it's explained to me."

"It's not as bad as you think. You passed grade nine."

"I think Mr. Dewey gave up and passed me so he wouldn't have to stay late after each class. I managed a D."

"A D is better than an F, isn't it?" She was smart—smart enough to kick drugs, smart enough to find a way to get out of gangbanging and the streets.

"Why do I need to know analytic geometry anyway?" She shrugged.

"It's the curriculum and what the government requires."

"Yeah . . . the government, again telling us what we can and can't do." She turned in his direction, their knees almost skimming.

Their faces were inches apart. Her light breaths for air were a heartbeat against Jude's ears. Close enough to see how flawless her makeup application was. Close enough to almost touch the rich black lashes she'd pasted to her eyelids. Close enough to smell her frustration.

"Why your grade twelve?" He did his best to soften his voice.

"It's something I need to do."

"Many try for their general equivalency diploma."

"I don't want the *good enough* diploma." Annoyance crept into her eyes. "I *need* my grade twelve. I . . . I have to know this stuff. That's all."

"I see . . . You do know GED is acceptable."

"I said I don't want the *good enough* diploma."

"And I asked why grade ten math is important to you."

Her throat bobbed. A long, sleek neck made for tender kisses and gentle nibbles. "It just is."

"It'd help if you told me why. I'm trained to offer guidance to students." Again, he did his best to keep his voice soft. Too bad he didn't have Emery's coaxing tone that would've cajoled Hitler into curling up like a kitten.

But maybe Jude didn't need his little brother's fingers-skimming-a-person's-hair voice, because the annoyance in Raven's eyes vanished.

She folded her lips, still staring. "I—I w-want to prove I can finish my diploma."

"Prove to whom?"

Her legs slithered back beneath the desk. "You have my file. I split for the 'Peg. I . . . I didn't think I . . . uh, I needed my culture." Her eyes moved back and forth. She blinked a few times. "It, y'know, seemed dumb to me at the time. I didn't want to be an Indian. I wanted to be me."

"What's wrong with being Ojibway?" Jude hadn't thought about his race up until two years ago. He'd been so immersed in Catholicism, his life spent amongst other educators, golfing with buddies from church, his culture had been miles away.

Perhaps he should ask himself the same question.

"Nothing." She faced him, shrugging. Her eyes ceased moving back and forth. And the blinking had stopped. "My cousin lived in Winnipeg, so I got a job waitressing and moved in with her. She was . . . quite the party girl. She showed me the bar scene."

"Hey, everyone in Manitoba who turns the big one-eight thinks about the bar. You don't think I wanted to check out the bar when I turned nineteen?" Jude made sure to add a sweet amount of teasing to his words. He winked. "How'd you think I celebrated the big one-nine?"

"But you had boundaries, didn't you?" Raven rested her elbow on the desk and snuggled her temple against her knuckles.

Jude set his elbows on his knees and clasped his hands together. "Yeah, I did."

"I bet you had a nice girlfriend to keep you in line."

Warmth rose to Jude's cheekbones.

"I bet she was the blue-eyed blonde girl-next-door all guys dream about marrying." A tinge of disgust lingered on Raven's wistful words.

A thundercloud of anger smothered Jude's gut.

"Did I hit a sore spot? That's quite a scowl. I even see a vein sticking out on your forehead."

If she was being honest, so would Jude. "Maybe . . . but we're talking about you."

"Not until you tell me why your vein is sticking out."

Ah, stubborn, too. Jude should have guessed as much. "You're right. I married the blue-eyed blonde girl next door."

"You divorced her, from what the moccasin telegraph said. Why? I heard . . . rumors."

"We hit a rough patch. Something I ignored. She didn't ignore it. She . . ." Grit sanded Jude's tongue. "She found someone else."

"I see. Gave up. I thought as much. You don't seem like the type who gives up when the going gets tough."

"I don't. But sticking your head in the sand doesn't help, either." At least he could admit that much about what he'd done wrong.

"You didn't stick your head in the sand. You acted like a typical man who needed his butt kicked back into the game. Why didn't she kick your butt?"

"Maybe she tried to, and I didn't notice." No, Jude couldn't recall a kick to his ass, or a smack. They'd both simply . . . gone their own ways. Perfunctory morning talk over coffee. Perfunctory chit-chat at the dining table. Perfunctory sex.

But Raven, she was the kind of woman who refused to be ignored. She would've caused a scene at church, of all places, to get her point across.

"What?"

Jude peered. "What do you mean?"

"You're staring at me." The scowl that had plastered Raven's face since she'd arrived at the classroom vanished.

"Just thinking."

"About what?" She moved in closer, and their knees brushed.

The warmth coming from beneath her painted-on skinny jeans tingled along Jude's arms and swirled around his stomach. "What kind of woman you are."

"Oh? You've already sized me up. What's the conclusion?"

"You'd have yelled at me. Banged a pot over my head. Kicked me in the butt." Laughter crawled up Jude's throat, and he chuckled.

"For what?"

"Ignoring you. Us. Everything. You don't strike me as a woman who accepts being ignored."

"No, I don't. And you strike me as a man who'd never cheat, even when she's not putting out." Raven's lips formed into a coy grin, the same brash sneer as her brother.

"Putting out? Nice way to say . . ." He couldn't say *sex*.

"Sex?" The way Raven had said the taboo word, she might as well have blown in his ear like Brigitte Bardot.

More heat warmed Jude's face. "I think we'd better change the subject."

"Why?" Raven almost seemed to snort. "Y'know, everyone seems to tuck it in a corner like a flashing purple elephant. If not for sex, this world would be empty, wouldn't it? Even the birds and bees do it."

"It's not a proper conversation one has with their student." If Raven said the *sex* word one more time, Jude's dick might join the discussion.

"I don't buy into Western civilization's view of sex. I'm *Anishinaabe-kwe*. We were never chaste, but encouraged to explore our desires. The only thing frowned upon was if we married too many times, so we ensured to choose our husbands wisely. Your church is responsible for trying to make us into pure virgins, when we were never virginal to begin with."

Jude couldn't will away the constant heat on his face. All during Raven's rant she'd held his stare, unashamed of her God-given sexual desire. Finally he responded, "One shouldn't use another to fulfill their wants. I was taught to give than receive."

"Who said anything about using? When two consenting adults hook up, they give pleasure and also receive pleasure."

"Hooking up?" He stifled his scoff. "Yeah, that's it exactly. You're using each other to get your rocks off."

"Nope. We're using what Creator gave us. And we choose who we'll pleasure and allow that person to pleasure us."

All this talk about pleasure, sex, arousal . . . Jude stood. If he didn't, the sticky heat coating his arms and legs would travel to his crotch, which had already begun to warm. "We should start your lesson."

"I'm not finished."

Jude set his hands on his own desk. He faced the white-board. "I don't think—"

"I'm traditional. I believe I can spend the night with a man if I choose to."

"I see." He chewed on his inner cheek.

"I get it. You'll be sinning if you hook up."

"It's not hooking up to me." He kept facing the whiteboard. And he didn't care about pleasing God or the church any-more.

"Neither is it to me."

"You told me seconds ago *when two consenting adults hook up*—"

"I spoke in general terms. Did I once say, *when I hook up?*"

"No." Jude ground his knuckles into the top of the desk. "Why are we discussing this anyway? We should be talking about analytic geometry."

"I can't remember how we got on the subject." Raven gig-gled.

Her sassy chuckle grazed the back of Jude's ear. Every muscle wound tight. Because... dammit, his hot crotch wished she'd come up behind him and slide her arms around his waist and giggle in his ear, even nibble on his lobe. He'd turn, take Raven's slim face in his hands, brush his mouth against her red-painted lips and find out how bold of a woman she was.

"Well?"

The word bumped on his spine. He swiveled. "Uh... what?"

"Didn't you hear me?" Raven's elbow rested on the desk. Her fingers twisted around the strands of black hair cascading across one breast.

"No. I was thinking how to steer this conversation back to

analytic geometry."

"I asked if you wanted to stop our discussion." Raven's husky reply was sandpaper brushing Jude's skin.

Nope, he didn't wish to end their discussion, but as her educator and a gentleman, he must. "Do you?" The answer tumbled from his mouth with the same heat swathing his skin.

The color drained from Raven's face. "Your voice. It gets deeper. It's not as serious when . . ." She glanced away.

Jude gave himself an illusory pat on the back. Up until now, she'd gotten beneath his skin, scratching him like a playful baby lynx. Yes, a lynx, because Raven was as dangerous as a full-grown female. She'd been in kitten mode earlier, but this woman was as feral as a big cat on the prowl for a mate to snarl at, scratch, and bite.

"When what?" With confidence swelling his chest, he swaggered to her desk. He set his hands on top and leaned in.

Raven flipped open her notebook and textbook. "Analytic geometry."

Jude snickered. She wasn't a man-eater. "Analytic geometry. Okay. Let's begin your lesson."

After a half hour of their lesson had passed, Raven was finally able to accept the warmth coming from Jude's firm body, the breaths from his mouth when he spoke, and the scent of the rainfall-scented bar of soap he'd undoubtedly slathered over his skin.

He'd tenderly taken her through analytic geometry. He'd gently explained lectures one and two. He'd kindly used examples she could understand. And she did. She could complete her next two lessons because of Jude. Not once had he'd used big words, over-the-top illustrations, or shaken his head in frustration. He clearly wanted her to learn.

She closed the textbook. "Thank you."

"You're quite welcome." His black eyes reflected his satisfaction.

"You're good at your job. Why become a principal?"

"Because I want to make sure my teachers provide the same care that I do when I teach. My main job is managing the administrative tasks of the school and supervising the students and teachers. I don't want a school to succeed for my ego. I want my school to produce students who learn and teachers who enjoy helping students learn."

"I think you're gonna do a great job here." But if Clayton became chief, he'd send Jude packing, because Clayton didn't want some *goddamn Catholic apple*—red on the outside, white on the inside—*turning our children, our children's children into goddamn Catholics.*

"Everything okay?"

Raven swallowed. "Yeah."

"You don't seem so. You just scowled." Jude bared his dimples. He could look rather sweet because of those indents beneath his cheekbones. Less serious. Maybe the deacon appeared the same way when he smiled. "C'mon, we talked about me. What about you?"

His teasing words seemed to walk along Raven's spine in a playful manner. "It's hard for you to understand. You're . . ." *Perfect.*

"I'm what?"

"I bet you never had a bad day in your life."

Jude laughed lightly, shaking his head. "I've had my bad days. Bad moments. Bad weeks. Even bad months."

"Riiight. Tell me another one. You're the kind of man who joins his buddies somewhere on the weekend for a couple of drinks and then goes home."

"What's wrong with that?"

"That's what I mean. You wouldn't understand."

"Try me." His smile vanished. His dark eyes searched hers.

"For starters, I'm the youngest. Fawn's forty-three.

Clayton's forty-two. Lark's forty-one. Wren's forty. Then I came along. I'm thirty-one."

"You're like Emery. He was a surprise baby, too."

"And I bet you watched over him."

Jude's strong jaw tensed.

Raven had guessed correctly. He'd played big brother to the hilt, the way Clayton did, since under tradition as the eldest and only male, his job was to take care of the family.

"They all turned out fine, y'know." Raven gripped her pencil. "My sisters are married. Have kids. Made Mom a grandma. Clayton lives with his girlfriend. They foster his girlfriend's nephew, Tyrell."

"And you?"

"What'd you think?" Raven half chuckled and half snorted. "Gonna be three years for me this coming summer."

"My brother-in-law, Adam, proved people can change." Jude's tone remained deep, even when he tempered his voice.

"I knew Adam well."

"That's right. I recall Bridget mentioning you dated one of Adam's old buddies."

"I was . . ." Raven wet her lips. "I was always known as the fuck-up." There, she'd admitted it.

"And?"

"You don't get it, do you? I bet if your life was still super-perfect, you'd look at me differently."

"My life was never super-perfect." Jude's voice remained supple. "My divorce more than proves that."

"Before your divorce . . ."

"It wasn't perfect either. Otherwise my marriage wouldn't have sunk."

"Don't blame yourself. She let a great catch get away." And Raven wasn't tossing out flirty words to stroke his ego like she'd done in the past.

"Yeah?" He quirked his brow.

This was dangerous territory. They were knee to knee. Breath to breath. Only her jeans and his dress pants kept their skin from touching. She shuddered, because her clit was throbbing.

She more than wanted Jude, and not for a one-night stand either. But a Matawapit? She wasn't his type—Miss Perfect Catholic who only believed in sleeping with someone she loved.

She was the bad girl mothers warned their sons to stay away from.

CHAPTER SEVEN: DON'T SHOOT ME DOWN

Raven was the type of girl Mom and Aunt Patti would've disapproved of when Jude was in high school. But he wasn't in high school. He was an adult, and he and Raven sported thick bruises from life's many kicks.

"Do I get a ride home again?" Flirting was new. He hadn't flirted in years. Unless his ex-wife counted.

"Sure. It's cold outside. Y'know, I could've gotten you." Raven's hands trembled.

She was nervous. So was he. Heart pattering a little too fast. Saliva gone sticky in his mouth. A smidgen of sweat at the back of his neck. He'd only gotten divorced last month, after a year of separation required by the province of Ontario. Raven was a recovering addict sorting out her life. But she'd been sober for two and a half years.

"We should . . ." She licked her lips. "I guess we're done, hey?" She reached for her parka.

Jude's stomach drooped a smidgen. He stood. "You're right. We should get going. I have to finish packing."

"Going back for the weekend?" Raven zippered the coat.

"Bright and early. Emery and I are returning the U-Hauls. And I need to get my kids and the truck." Jude forced himself to the teacher's desk. He donned his coat and slid the files into his briefcase.

Part of him anticipated seeing Noah and Rebekah, but the man who'd spent since the age of nineteen enjoying a healthy sex life needed a companion for the night. He was more than a father, teacher, so-called Eucharistic minister, so-called lector, and so-called member of the Catholic Men's Association. He was a flesh-and-blood man. And his flesh burned hot for a real woman, not one on his laptop undressing ala burlesque style.

"Ready?"

Jude swiveled, clutching the briefcase. Raven stood at the doorway, hugging the books against her chest.

"Yep." Jude strode across the floor.

They meandered down the hallway as if neither wanted to reach the main door. Jude wasn't in a hurry. He was returning to an empty house that wasn't a home yet. Once the kids arrived, maybe they'd add something to the cold place devoid of warmth only a family produced.

"You working tomorrow?"

"Yeah. I get Sundays and Mondays off."

"Those the quiet days at the diner?"

"Sunday is, but Mondays are nuts."

Their footsteps were the only sound present. A *click click* from his boot heels, and a *smoosh smoosh* from her mukluks, reaffirming they'd reached the dreaded uncomfortable silence.

Jude couldn't ask for a date. His parents would freak. His brother and sister would freak. Okay, maybe not Emery. But Bridget . . . oh boy.

Raven pushed on the door. A blast of cold and the familiar scent of winter swept into the building.

"How's your, err, brother doing?"

"He's fine." Even with the icy air nipping at their skin, Raven didn't dash for her truck. She kept dragging her feet along the walkway.

Jude ambled beside her. He stole a peek at her face hidden by the faux fur lining of her upturned hood. Screw it. He'd been alone for too long.

"How about a coffee?"

Raven stopped. Her mittened hands drew the books even tighter against her parka. Tight enough to show off her flat stomach hidden beneath the barrier of clothing.

"We . . . um . . . yes, sure, but can we go somewhere besides the diner? I . . . um . . . I work there all day. It's, uh, the last place I wanna be."

Jude swallowed. "Sure. Where do you wanna go?"

"Uh . . . what about the staff room? We're already here."

"True." Downtown and Old Main were the hub of the reserve. And they both lived in the busiest areas of the community. "I'd like to say yes, but I can't use the school for . . . err . . . personal business. And having a cup of coffee off the clock would be . . . personal."

"What about the church?"

"The church?" Shock gripped Jude's spine. Miss Antichurch and religion was willing to go to a place she hated, just so people wouldn't see them together, but was desperate enough to be with him that she'd step inside a place she considered the annihilation of their once prosperous race?

Dad had given Jude a key, first thing he'd received upon moving here. Funny how he'd been annoyed at receiving it, thinking he might be able to put in his obligatory Sunday for the sake of his kids and family. Now it came in handy.

"Okay. To the church." There was a nice seating area at the back where the chair lift staircase was located.

Talk about desperate. Raven had to be out of her mind to suggest the church. If her family found out, they'd lose the smidgen of respect they had for her. But where else could they meet without anyone seeing them? Nobody ventured down Church Road but the people who went to church. And at nine-fifteen at night, the only person around was Father Bennie, since he resided at the rectory across from the church, but at his age, he'd probably gone to bed.

Most of all, she was risking her chance at the diner.

Raven kept her foot on the gas pedal as she headed for the Grassy District or Catholic City known by her family. Normally, she drove straight to take the road to the nursing station or the baseball field. She turned right onto Church Road.

Neither had spoken during the drive. Her heart kept an even thump because they'd talk at their intended destination.

She couldn't fathom Jude making out in a church, not her good little Catholic boy. Uh, wait. *Her* good little Catholic boy? He didn't belong to her. And she didn't belong to him. They shared a mutual attraction. Way more than an attraction. She itched to see him take off his clothes, and he no doubt felt the same way.

The lights were out at the rectory. Raven pulled into the church's parking lot.

"Keep driving to the other door."

"How many doors does this place have?"

"Three. One beneath the car port." Jude pointed. "And one that faces the lake. The other is the main door up the stairs to get into the church. We're using the basement. There's a seating area where Father Bennie or Dad meet with parishioners who need spiritual guidance."

Raven stopped at the main staircase. The steps led to a landing and then up to the church entrance. She switched off the truck.

Jude dug inside his parka and produced his keys.

"That's a lot of keys."

"I always have this many. It's no different here." He chuckled.

"Keys to where?"

"Everywhere." Jude got out.

Raven followed him to the door beside the main set of stairs. She stamped her feet and spanked her mittens together. Exciting? Positively, absolutely yes! She was about to go on an unofficial date with a guy who'd never have spared her a glance in high school if she'd lived in Thunder Bay.

"What is it?" He opened the door and flicked on one light from the set lining the wall.

"You woulda looked away from me if I'd gone to your school." Raven shut the door and shrugged off her parka.

"Maybe your assumption's wrong." Jude also shrugged off his coat. He motioned at her to follow.

He turned on one row of lights and led them to the front of the basement. Or the back. Or whatever church people referred to both entrances as. There were two doors with signs indicating the men's and women's washrooms.

He opened another door and led them into a room. With a flick of the light switch, a spotless kitchen appeared.

"Lemme put on a pot." Jude sauntered to one of the many cupboards and withdrew the coffee supplies.

"You come here lots, don't you?" Raven glanced around at the off-white cabinets, main sink, another big sink, fridge, and oven. Two shutters above the counter closed off the kitchen to the main area. This was probably where the women served food.

"Oh uh . . . yeah. Before the move, the kids and I attended Mass here if we were visiting. We'd also drop in if something was going on." Jude readied the coffee.

"What else happens, besides church, and . . . Healing the Spirit." Raven squirmed, thinking of her own family's protest when the workshop had taken place two falls ago. She'd eagerly held one of the signs stating the Catholic Church should never receive forgiveness for what it'd done to Canada's Indigenous People.

She'd also gladly participated in the protest two summers

ago Clayton had led against the church—when they'd demanded chief and council stop paying the parish's hydro bill, rescind their decision to fund Healing the Spirit, and stop giving money to the church.

"Here we go." Jude held out a paper cup.

Raven eyed the industrial-style coffee machine, the same kind Cookie had at the diner. Very expensive. Who'd paid for it, if the church forever complained how broke they were?

"What is it?" Jude turned to the coffee machine.

"Nothing." Raven shrugged. "When did this get remodeled?"

"Six years ago."

"Six?" Her blood heated a notch. Again, band council had forked out cash to the church when Clayton had said there was no such funds.

"I take it you don't approve." Jude leaned against the counter.

"Why do you say that?"

"You're frowning." The inquisitive look vanished. "I was hoping to . . . ah . . . generate something other than a frown."

The heat left Raven's blood, and warmth caressed her tummy. "What were you hoping to generate?"

He used his elbow to shove off the counter. His lips spread into a sly grin as he swaggered over to her, strong thighs gliding one in front of the other, and his chin angled slightly downward while gazing at her through a thick fringe of lashes. "A smile . . . perhaps."

Raven used her tongue to trace the rim of her mouth. Something maddening and exciting fluttered between her legs. "A smile. That's it?" She stood on her toes, leaning a smidgen forward. "I thought you'd ask for a little bit more."

"Well, we're in a church. A smile'll suffice." He kept grinning.

For once, she, Ms. Expert at Flirting, couldn't find a

comeback, even after searching her blank mind. No, not blank. The word *sex* kept blinking on and off in her brain like a cheap neon sign outside a Motel Six.

Hand trembling, Raven lifted the paper cup and sipped the coffee. "This is . . . um . . . very good. Rich. Where'd you get it?"

Jude snickered. "C'mon." He motioned at the door. And he didn't saunter ahead. Instead, he waited for Raven to vacate the kitchen and walked by her side.

They headed for the indoor staircase where the lift chair was available for disabled parishioners. She sat in one of the comfy armchairs. There was a small, circular wooden table where she could set her coffee cup.

"Where'd you get it?" Raven held out her cup.

"*Coffee Coffee.*"

Coffee Coffee? That was Canada's biggest chain, known for its fine roasted brew.

"This stays between you and me. I donated the coffee." Jude sipped from his cup.

"You did? You do?"

"Yes."

"Why?"

"My father's a deacon here. I made a more than generous salary at the time. There're people here who're like family. I give to, uh . . . many charities on a regular basis."

This was something new. Sure, there were food drives and stuff happening on the reserve, and everyone pitched in to help if someone lost a loved one.

"Which charities?"

"A few." Jude glanced away and picked at some imaginary lint on his pants that had a strong crease down the middle. "Catholic Northern Missions. The Open Door. It's a shelter for the homeless in Thunder Bay. My weekly donation to Saint Patrick's Parish. I'll switch it over to here now. Cancer Care for Kids. The Diabetes Association."

"I bet you donated to Healing the Spirit."

"Yep. It's not something I talk about. I keep my monetary donations to myself."

"What else do you donate?" Raven's previous boyfriends hadn't bothered to give to anyone or do anything for others.

"My time. You volunteer. Darryl told me, even though you have a busy schedule, you helped the young girls who belong to the Traditionalists Society by teaching them about their culture."

"I . . . did." Something tight seemed to wrap around Raven's ribcage, and she forced out the words. "I help out where I can. I keep the recovery meetings open."

"You chair them?"

Raven nodded. "We have three a week. Mondays, Wednesdays, and Fridays. There's talk about a Saturday meeting. Weekends are hard for people in recovery."

"I bet they are." Jude pursed his lips. "My brother-in-law's a recovering alcoholic."

"Adam. We go way back."

"So you've said. Bridget mentioned he attends meetings here when they're visiting, if a meeting's available."

Raven worked off her mukluks. She drew her legs up against her chest. All she needed was one of the blankets she'd crocheted. "I put in my name for a place. I'm hoping I can get something."

"Where do you live now?"

"My mom's." Raven's skin went cold. "You know about the housing shortage on reserves."

"I sure do."

"I doubt I'll get my own pad. Housing always goes to families first." And she'd be stuck at Mom's, the very place she'd run from at sixteen.

"It's understandable. Parents need a place for their

children. Is that whose truck you have? Your mom's?"

"Yeah. She doesn't lend it to me very often. She thinks I'm going to fall off the wagon and wreck her vehicle."

"You live in Old Main then. That's where the Kabatays live, right?"

"Yep." She tilted her head. "The more I talk to you, the more I had you pegged wrong. I thought you were very serious, much like your dad. One of those strict Catholics who thinks everyone's sinning. But you're friendly and you like to tease."

"I'm the eldest child. Teasing and tormenting my younger siblings is part of the big brother job description I take very seriously." Dimples crept onto his face. "As for being a super-strict Catholic, I'm divorced, aren't I?"

"Through no fault of your own. Can you still go to church? Isn't divorce a sin?"

A smidgen of red tinged his cheeks. "My ex started the annulment proceedings."

"Annulment?"

"If approved, the church will deem the marriage null and void. If it's approved . . ."

"I see." She fingered the cup's rim. "Are you happy about that?"

"I really don't mind."

Raven's mouth dried. If they engaged in sex, Jude would be sinning until this annulment thing was approved. Yet, he'd asked her for a date after class. He did really like her.

Chapter Eight: Let It All Begin

Jude hadn't noticed before, but there was sadness within Raven, a loneliness he'd never seen until tonight. Although he'd taken courses on drug and alcoholism addiction as part of his professional development, Emery might know more. He did have his BSW and was starting his second year for his master's. Since little brother was traveling with Jude to Thunder Bay, maybe they could talk on their way home.

"What're you doing this weekend?"

"Working. Homework. I want to get caught up on my math lessons since I now understand analytic geometry a little better, thanks to a fabulous teacher." She fluttered her lashes.

She sure knew how to plump a man's ego. Jude couldn't help his grin. "If you run into problems, text me. I might be out of service sometimes, though."

"Sure."

"Well?" Jude withdrew his phone. "Here's mine." He flashed the numbers on the screen.

Raven withdrew her phone. Her cherry-painted lips formed into a smirk. "Here's mine." She held up the phone.

"What's so funny?" He typed on his keypad.

Using her long nails, she also typed away. "You. Was the *text me if you have problems* your sly way of getting my number?"

"Honestly, no. But it worked in my favor, didn't it?" Jude chuckled. "I do sincerely want to help if you need me."

"Then if I need you, I'll text. When're you driving back?"

"Sunday morning after the . . . uh . . ." How he'd give

71

anything to skip church, but if he did, he'd get raised eyebrows from Emery and Bridget. " . . . nine o'clock church service. We're staying at Bridget's. It's a three-bedroom home. Emery and I get to fight over who gets the pull-out bed in the living room and who gets the air mattress."

"The kids have the spare room? I know Adam has a son."

"Their son. Bridget adopted Kyle."

"Cool. What about you? Will this stepdad have a say in your kids' life?"

A flash of red heat invaded Jude's chest. "No. I'm the parent. Charlene's the parent. He makes no decisions whatsoever." It was a good thing he didn't point his customary finger. A high five was well-deserved.

"I just wondered, that's all. Clayton has a say in raising Tyrell, even though he's only the step-uncle."

"But they're fostering Tyrell, aren't they?" Which was far different from Jude's situation.

"Yep. His mom's in Vancouver somewhere. Drugs. Drinking. I hope she gets clean, but Tyrell's been with Clayton and Tanya since he was eight. He's in high school now. Grade nine."

"I'll most likely meet him. I'm having a special assembly when I return. I'd like a chance to meet everyone, and for everyone to meet me during a sociable time. Basil Skunk and Darryl are going to have a special ceremony to welcome me to the school."

"Really?" Raven's reddish-brown smooth skin brightened. "You're okay with it?"

"Why wouldn't I be?"

"You're Catholic."

No, I'm not Catholic. I'm not . . . anything. "Just because I'm Catholic doesn't mean I don't recognize my culture. When the Indigenous Women's Alliance held their protest walk in the city for the children in foster care, I was more than glad to participate."

"Yeah. Saw you there."

"Saw you there, too."

Raven's mouth widened into a deep smile. She sat straighter, shaking back her long hair. "And?"

"I was married at the time."

She waggled her sleek brows. "I must say I rather like your answer. Even though your marriage was in the dumps, you were still loyal to your wife." She squinted. "I don't get it."

"Get what?"

"Why your wife let you get away." Raven sipped more coffee.

"I guess I have a lot of faults, or so someone told me." His voice was dryer than the desert, pretty much how the end of his marriage had left him feeling.

"Your ex-wife?"

Jude nodded. Funny, he'd revealed more to Raven than to his own brother and sister — heck, his whole family.

"I prefer to find out for myself." Raven shrugged.

"Find out what?"

"All those horrible things your ex must have said to you."

Jude half snickered and half snorted. "I'm a stubborn, domineering, tight-lipped man who doesn't speak enough about his feelings but expects everyone to divulge theirs to me."

"I heard lots, and we only officially met on Tuesday."

"I heard lots, too. Like why'd you stop? What shook you back into reality?"

Raven's slim jaw stiffened. "I was sick of it." She shuddered and cupped her shoulders, as if transported to the awful place she thought about. "I woke up dope sick. Really dope sick. Unless you've been dope sick, you'll never understand. Sully . . . he wouldn't give me any more. He said I was cutting into too much of the profits. I . . . I started doing stuff I shouldn't have." She glanced away.

"Stuff like what?"

"You don't wanna know." Her voice was smaller than her rounded shoulders.

"Try me."

Her eyes narrowed. "If I told you, you'd be running out the church door. Shit. What I say might burn down the church."

"A lot of people sit in these chairs to speak about their feelings." Jude patted his armchair. "I'm sure what you have to say won't be any worse than what they needed to talk about."

"Religious people don't sin." Her scowl was part sneer and part disgust. "They're almost perfect—"

"Don't sin?" Clayton must've given Raven this false information. "Do you know why people attend church?"

"Because they're perfect little Catholics." She flicked her hand.

"Wrong." Jude couldn't help the natural authority jumping into his voice, as if he was standing in front of a class. "Why do you attend twelve-step meetings? Are you a perfectly sober person?"

"Perfect?" Raven's eyes bulged. "I attend because I couldn't manage my own life. I messed up bad. I've always been a screwup."

"And what do these meetings give you?"

Raven's chest sank. She kept her knees drawn against her breasts while rubbing her foot along the cushion she sat on. "Peace."

"That's why we attend church." *Well, why I used to. And why am I defending the damned church?* "It's not very different, is it? We both worship a higher power. I'm not sure what you call yours. I call mine God." Well, he used to.

"I call mine *Gitche Manidoo*. Or Creator."

"You never answered my question." Jude shouldn't prod, but he needed to know the truth.

"You mean about what I did? All the evil skeletons—Wait,

they're not skeletons. Everyone knows what I did. Ask around." Raven stared at her coffee cup, hair falling around her face.

"I won't judge you like the others did." But would he? Was he ready to hear her answer? Yes. Like the adulteress woman the scribes and Pharisees had condemned for her sinful ways, so had the people of Ottertail Lake judged Raven. Jesus had told the woman to *go and sin no more.* In her own way, through twelve-step meetings and her culture, Raven was doing her best to go and sin no more.

Shit, now he was thinking about the Bible. Damn the Catholicism Mom and Dad had poured into his blood.

"I used men for drugs, for money. Whatever they could get me." Raven's voice didn't shake. Her hands never trembled. She stared straight ahead, chin lifted.

"Used?"

"I fucked them." Her voice didn't rise in anger. Never lowered in shame. Her tone remained even. "Sorry. I'm in a spiritual place. I shouldn't swear. I'd never swear in a sweat lodge, so I'd better keep my language G-rated."

"The sanctuary's upstairs." Jude pointed upward. "We're in the basement."

"It's still a spiritual place." She turned her head, gaze cold and smooth like a frozen lake. "And if you ask me how many men I slept with, I can't tell you, because I never bothered counting. They were a free pass to what I wanted at the time."

Jude nodded.

"Now you know the truth." The only hint at her nervousness was the twitch of Raven's foot. "What about you? I expect you didn't sleep around."

"I was nineteen when I met Charlene. You do the math." Jude grinned. He wasn't ashamed the only woman who'd seen him undressed was his ex-wife.

"That's not going to take analytic geometry to figure out."

Raven's coy smile appeared. "I'm honored." Her voice was rich in respect.

"Honored?"

"That a man like you, who's very . . . um, choosy, asked me for a date tonight." She raised the cup. "You make a mean pot of joe."

"Brewing the coffee in the morning was always my job. It still is."

"So . . ." She wet her lips. Someone was moving into vixen mode. It was rather nice to see Raven being Raven again. "You'd brew me a cup of coffee?"

"If you spent the night?" Jude's throat dried. He squirmed. The itch in his pants resurfaced. "I'd even cook you breakfast. I make a mean steak and eggs."

"Steak and eggs sounds awesome." She slid her long nails into a few black strands of hair.

Something tugged at Jude's insides. Something tugged at his mouth. Want. Need. His palm ached to caress Raven's shiny black hair. His lips yearned to taste the tongue that had licked at a droplet of coffee sitting on the rim of the paper cup Raven held.

What about the kids, though? He gripped the cup. They'd be devastated. They needed more time. Maybe he also needed time. When he'd moved up here, a relationship was the last thing on his mind. And he sure hadn't counted on Raven Kabatay to sashay into his life.

They were hiding in the church basement for a reason—to avoid gossip. Her family hated his family. He couldn't even tell her about being Darryl's campaign manager for the election, because her brother was running for chief.

"What is it, Jude?" she whispered.

Her supple words caressed the shivers along his back, caressed the ache in his pants threatening to bulge, caressed his hands holding the cup.

Enough of torturing himself. He set the cup on the table and leaned in, clasping his fingers.

Her black eyes studied him, a hint of curiosity lurking in their dark depths.

"I'm going to kiss you, Raven, if I may." The pounding of Jude's heart battered his chest. Was he downstairs in the basement at Jennifer Mayman's birthday party, ready to kiss her because she'd boldly dared him to as a gift? With the way his stomach lurched, his intestines twisted, and his blood raced, he was again a silly twelve-year-old ready to experience his first kiss.

"I . . . I . . ." Raven's slanted eyes widened. "I never had a guy outright ask me."

"I'm asking." Jude heaved out a racing breath.

Raven set aside her coffee. Her slim socked feet glided against the floor. She also leaned in, wetting her lips. "Yes." The word was a delicate hiss.

Jude shifted to his knees and snuggled between Raven's spread legs. He set his hand on her thigh that quivered beneath his palm. The heat from her crotch warmed his stomach. He glided his other hand behind her neck. Raven's ultralong false eyelashes fluttered. He gazed at perfectly applied makeup. A light dash of shadow on her lids. A darker and heavier application in the crease. And a glittering golden-white shade beneath her black brows. Gorgeous. Damn, she was sexy with the tipped liner running across the bottom of her lids.

He slid his mouth along Raven's puckered lips. A sweet sensation dribbled down his back. The lushness of her flesh and the moistness of her skin seemed to skim his spine. The heat of her breath dusted the dip below his nose, even caressed the small indent.

She moved her lips in rhythm with his slow strokes.

The door burst open, and a shot of icy wind followed.

Jude jumped to his feet. Raven yanked her knees to her chest.

Emery gaped at them.

"What're you doing here?" Jude sputtered. A church, of all places, his little brother thought to interrupt.

"I . . . I . . ." Emery stamped his boots on the mat. "I wasn't sure who was here. I came to . . . I came to think . . . upstairs."

"Think?" Jude kept the growl from popping out of his throat. "It's . . ." He scrambled for his phone on the table. "It's nine-forty at night."

Raven scooted into her mukluks and yanked on her parka. "I should go." She squared her shoulders. "Good seeing you, Emery. Bye, Jude." She tilted her gaze his way, raising her sleek brows.

Awesome. She wasn't offended at being caught by dumb ol' Emery, which was expected since she was a bold woman, unashamed or unfazed by anyone or anything.

"I'll . . . text me if you need help with your lesson. I mean it."

"I will." Raven marched to the door, head still held high, and vanished.

Jude snatched the coffee cups from the table. "Well, go upstairs if you need to pray bad enough to come here at this hour."

Fine, he was complaining and behaving like an ass, but dammit, his crotch continued to throb. Raven's kiss, the velvet taste of her lips, and the warmth of her mouth kept taunting his heated skin, heated blood, and heated dick.

"I'll . . . I'll go upstairs." Pain reflected in Emery's green eyes. His pale skin was paler than usual.

"No. Wait. Gimme a second to tidy up." As the eldest, Jude must put his younger brother first.

"I'm fine. Go on ahead." Emery lifted a shaky hand at the door Raven had used to leave, taking her yielding mouth, yielding body, and yielding boldness with her.

"My ride split." Jude headed for the kitchen.

No footsteps followed, but the light sound of Emery ascending the carpeted stairs where the lift chair was located carried to where Jude emptied the cups into the sink.

Something terrible must have happened. After accepting his sexual orientation and marrying Darryl, the confusion and bleak stare that had once kept Emery from Mass for two weeks had resurfaced tonight.

Jude tidied the kitchen in under five minutes and darted up the stairs. Emery sat in the front pew. Head bowed. Hands clasped in prayer. Only the emergency lights saved the church from being engulfed in blackness. The red hues cast the odd silhouette here and there.

"Hey . . ." Jude plopped in the pew. "What's up?"

"I need time to pray." Emery lifted his head. Pain still lingered in his eyes.

"What's going on? Did you and Darryl have a fight?" Boy, could Jude relate. Fights were a normal part of marriage.

"Uh . . ." If light was present, Emery's face would come up red. "I don't want to talk about it right now."

"Ignoring problems gets you nowhere. I speak from experience. I spent over a year ignoring problems in my marriage. Lookit where it got me."

"I'm still trying to digest everything." Emery fingered his lower lip.

"What happened?"

"We were talking about the election and if anything . . . Remember what you said about skeletons?"

Jude braced himself. "Darryl has skeletons?"

Emery's jawline hardened. "I'm not ready to talk about it." He held up his hand, clearly stating there'd be no more discussion.

They had the drive home from Thunder Bay to talk. If

Darryl had done something to hurt Emery, there'd be hell to pay.

"Where were you? It's ten o'clock. I phoned your sisters and your brother. None of them saw you. How's my truck?" Mom sat on the sofa, still threading the needle through the deerskin.

Raven removed her parka. She should've taken a drive, because Jude's kiss still lingered on her lips. He was the kind of man who took charge and was probably the same in bed — yanking her against him, smothering her mouth with his, but gentleman enough to let her come up for air. Most likely he fucked the same way, with nibbles on the neck, low groans by her ear, coaxing her to open to his cock, even whispering for her to lock her legs around his hips while he teased her with sassy pumps that became plunging, fast thrusts.

He probably ate pussy the same way. Licks and pecks to her thighs. Sweet kisses on her cunt lips. Tongue moving slow and easy around her clit, even suckling it. Maddening. Did he like to slide a finger up a woman's coochie and asshole while feasting? Raven shivered. If she kept this up, she'd have to rub one out before going to sleep.

And damned Emery. Maybe the interruption was a treasure in disguise. Coyote loved to thwart or confound situations for a good reason. But kissing in the seating area at the church was far from a situation. More like a make-out session. She hadn't made out in years. Kissing led to sex. But this time she'd been cock-blocked by a little brother.

"You never answered me." Mom kept sewing.

"I went for a drive."

"I loaned you my truck to go to school. We're in Old Main. It's a ten-minute walk, so I expect you to drive it to the school and back."

If Mom was giving Raven this much grief about taking the

truck out late, the family would disown her if they found out she'd gone on a *date*.

What could she do? She had nowhere to live. She depended on her siblings for rides or the use of vehicles. Clayton had gotten Raven the job at *Kiss the Cook*, asking Cookie to give her a chance.

After completing step nine, making amends to those Raven had hurt during her addiction, she'd hoped Mom, Clayton, Fawn, Lark, and Wren would've forgiven her, but they still didn't trust her. She might as well be newly clean for all it mattered.

The program said actions spoke louder than words. So Raven's actions had to convince her family she'd changed. And there was only one way to convince them.

Chapter Nine—Heavy

Emery drove, having taken over the wheel upon meeting the ice road at Manidoo Lake. Jude covered his mouth to stifle the big yawn leaving his throat. What a long day. They hadn't left Thunder Bay until after breakfast, when they'd seen Noah and Rebekah off at the airport. Thank God they'd gained an hour, since they were in Central Standard Time now.

When they'd left the city, they'd traveled the Trans Canada until they'd hit Ignace, where they'd turned off on Highway Five-Ninety-Nine, which ended at Frog Lake First Nation. From there, it was a snow-covered bush road up until the junction.

First thing that morning, Bridget had asked Jude about Emery. He'd reassured her he'd talk to their little brother on the drive home.

News squawked from the radio, the only sound in the truck, except for tires rolling over snow.

Jude reached for the thermos in the backseat to pour them another refill. "You finally gonna talk to me?" He'd made sure to keep his voice gentle, which wasn't an easy feat. Damn his natural direct, authoritative tone.

Emery drummed his fingers on the steering wheel. The high beams caught the endless sea of spruce trees and snowbanks, since they were cruising over land to get to the next lake. "Darryl . . ." He took a big breath. "Darryl has an enormous skeleton in his closet."

"What skeleton?" Jude refilled Emery's travel mug and then refilled his own with a good helping of *Reggie's Donuts* special brew he'd bought, all to please his little brother.

"I don't know if anyone will find out. And if they do, I don't know if they'll use it against him during the election."

"Did you want to tell me?"

"Don't go all Dad on me." Emery's quick-snapping answer was a dog's jaws clamping onto Jude's hand.

"Whoa. Easy. I was only asking a question." For Emery to lose his temper, the skeleton had to be the size of the Sleeping Giant, a massive rock formation of a man resting on his back out on the bay of Lake Superior, one of Thunder Bay's main attractions. "I'm trying to help, if you'd let me."

"Sure, like you let me help you through your divorce." Emery flicked his hand resting on the steering wheel.

"Whatever it is, I'm sure it can't be that bad."

"Easy for you to . . ." Emery leaned his head against the headrest. "Sorry. I shouldn't have . . . Lookit what you went through. My problem seems minor compared to what's happened to your family."

"Never mind. What's going on?"

"Darryl . . ." Emery moved his head off the headrest and re-gripped the steering wheel. "Darryl hired a . . . he hired a . . . he hired a prost-prosti . . . he hired a pr-pr-prostitute."

Jude jostled to balance his travel mug before it fell in his lap. "Wh-wh-what?" He slammed the mug into the cup holder. "That son of a bitch—"

"No. Put your rifle away. It's not what you think. It happened a long time ago." The words raced from Emery's mouth. "His buddy was getting married. Darryl served as best man. This was during his university days. When he was finishing his master's."

Jude's rising temper returned to its proper spot. "What happened exactly?"

Emery made a *pfft* sound full of revulsion. "I guess they were drunk. Riding around in a limo. Someone dared someone to stop where the prostitutes hang out. They called one over. And they paid this guy . . . he serviced Darryl and one of the groomsmen . . . as a joke. Some joke."

Typical of a bachelor party? Yes. But still not good. It was time to slide into big brother mode. There wouldn't be another Matawapit getting a divorce—not after Emery and Darryl had only clocked in a year and a half of marriage.

"He didn't even tell me. He never planned on telling me, otherwise he wouldn't have kept this from me until Thursday night. The only reason he said anything . . . he was scared someone might find out and use it against him." Disgust spat from Emery's mouth.

"I know it's a shocker. I'd be pretty upset, too." Jude must make sure and take Emery's feelings into consideration. Darryl had been hurting big-time after the nasty breakup when they'd been teenagers, which had kept the two estranged for ten years. "But try to remember how he was feeling then, and why he felt that way."

"It doesn't excuse what he did," Emery muttered.

"No. It doesn't. But he went on a splurge because he couldn't have you. Do you think he would've behaved like a man-whore if you two had stuck to your original plan and gone to university together?"

Emery frowned. He raised his hand. "I don't want to hear it."

Nope, little brother wasn't ready for reasoning. He needed time to lick his wounds. "Pride can be—"

"Yes, my pride. One of the seven deadly sins. But I'm a man, not a saint. I can fall victim to my pride, just like everyone else. And my pride is hurting big-time. Not only did he hide this from me, what am I supposed to do or say if anyone finds out? He not only embarrassed himself, he embarrassed me. I'm married to a pervert who cruises the red-light district for—"

"I know you're hurting. I know you're angry. I went through the same thing with Charlene. She kicked my pride into the ground when I confronted her."

Emery stroked his mouth. "Is that why you divorced her?"

Jude gazed out the passenger window. "Darryl never cheated on you."

The radio continued to squawk, and the squashing noise of the tires rolling over the snow-covered road kept carrying into the vehicle.

"No, he didn't." Resignation filled Emery's reply.

"How was he when you left him?" Jude turned to face his brother.

"I don't know. I crashed in the spare room."

"The spare room?" Jude's words formed into an exclamation. "I can't see Darryl letting you get out of the house without talking."

"Oh, he tried — when I returned from the church on Thursday night. I told him to get the fuck in the bedroom and leave me alone or I was going to your place to sleep. He listened."

Oh man, little brother was taking up his lance and tomahawk. "You cussed him out?"

"Yes." Emery's answer was a fast snap.

"What about the dogs? The cats?" Dumb question, but for once Jude had no idea what to say.

"They slept with me. They're my dogs and cats. Not his."

The dogs and cats belonged to the two of them, but if Jude pointed out the obvious, he might get a punch in the face. He'd better save the *it happened a long time ago, and has nothing to do with your marriage because you two were estranged,* since Emery, the most logical of the family, wasn't ready for logic.

"Enough about me. What about you?"

"What about me?" Jude lifted his travel mug from the holder.

"Thursday night. The church. Raven."

"There's nothing to speak about."

"Do you see what I mean?" Frustration crept into Emery's tone. "You're always ready to dole out advice, butt your nose into my business, but you don't let me near your problems."

Jude sucked in his cheeks. He wasn't about to hear a lecture from a brother who was nine years younger. "Like I said, there's nothing to discuss."

"Then I don't have anything to discuss either."

"You're not the kind of man who huffs off to pout."

"Pout? I don't pout. I deal with problems. You hide from them."

Indignation erupted in Jude's chest. "I don't hide from anything."

"Did you ever think . . ." Emery clucked his tongue. "Charlene sent me a lengthy email."

"She did what? When?" Jude almost dropped his coffee again.

"After the divorce was finalized. She asked if I'd, well, uh, consider being a witness for the annulment."

"A witness?" Blood-red hate boiled in Jude's gut.

"I told her I couldn't."

"Thank you." The balls on that woman.

"But she had a lot to say in the email."

"I can well imagine." Jude sneered.

"You do know it takes two, right?" Emery's voice relaxed to its natural gentle tone.

"Okay, if it takes two, I'll talk if you talk."

"Talk about what?"

"Maybe you're overreacting? What Darryl did is in the past. I don't think he owes you an explanation about his sexual extracurricular activities while you two were estranged."

A very rare scowl, ferocious enough to punch someone, formed on Emery's face.

"Admit you're jealous."

"I'm. Not. Jealous."

"Look, you pretty much lived like a monk. I think you might have regrets. Hey, we all do. Maybe you wanted a chance to fuck around."

"Fucking around, as you so nicely put it, goes against my beliefs," Emery coolly replied.

"It goes against mine, too, but we're men, not saints, as you like to put it. There were times I was tempted. Can you say the same?"

The radio kept squawking to fill the silence of doom that confirmed Jude had hit a nerve.

"If I throw on the light, will I see a red face? Am I right?" Jude inched his hand to the light between them on the roof.

"Fine. There were times I was tempted." *I give up* filled Emery's answer.

"It's not easy following one's beliefs." Jude rested his hand on the console while still facing Emery.

"Speaking of beliefs . . ." A very un-Emery-like sly grin wiped away his look of resignation. "What about Raven then?"

Jude flopped back in the seat. "Let's say I'm pretty damn tempted."

"You're looking for an . . . extracurricular activity?"

"That's a very tactful way to put it."

"You used it first, not me." Emery turned his head, smiling.

Jude sank in the seat. He could admit the black gut of doom had lifted after finally speaking about what he kept hidden to his little brother. Maybe there were times he needed an ear instead of always being the ear.

But would he have unzipped his mouth if he was still married? His stomach re-blackened. Probably not. It took a divorce to make him understand there might be changes he needed to make. Like Raven. She'd been easy to talk to. Something he'd never done with Charlene.

"Okay. Lay it on me. What'd she say?"

"Who?"

"My ex-wife. I can take it."

"She explained her side. Why she had the affair. Why she felt you weren't right for her anymore. Why you two weren't right for each other anymore."

"Did she admit to pursuing Stephen? The jerk was *very* interested in Bridget before Charlene picked up her chess pieces and got in the game."

"She told me she simply wanted a man who would take her out for dinner and truly listen, instead of always feeding her directions, trying to solve her problems, always giving his opinion on everything."

Jude winced. Maybe he wasn't ready for the truth. He wasn't some ogre like Charlene was painting him out to be.

"And she admitted she was jealous of Bridget."

"What? Bridget?" Jude hadn't seen that coming.

"Think about it. You married while you were finishing your teaching degree. Charlene had started working at the hospital. That's awfully young to be tied down."

"I see . . ." Jude ground his teeth. "She had regrets, hey? Didn't get to screw around. One dick wasn't enough for her." *My dick wasn't enough for her.*

"It wasn't about dicks. She admired Bridget because, well, she stayed single for a long time. Bridget got to do everything Charlene didn't. Vacations. A Caribbean cruise. Skiing in Banff. A road trip out to BC. Dating. Her own circle of friends."

"Friends? Bridget's about as close to her friends as I am to mine." Jude couldn't help getting on the defensive. He'd given Charlene everything. "And we went on a cruise."

"Uh . . ." Emery cleared his throat. "You took her on the *Magical Castle* cruise."

"What's wrong with the *Magical Castle?*" Jude threw out his hands. "The kids loved it. Water slides. Theme shows.

Theme state rooms. Tons of *Magical Castle* animals running around."

"Did Char?"

"Yes." Or had she?

"They were all family vacations," Emery said quietly.

Jude fisted his hands. Yes, he'd shelled out big bucks to take his family on great vacations, but he'd been so busy pleasing his kids, maybe he'd forgotten that his ex-wife had needed a good dose of romance. Date night didn't cut it. Every man took his wife out to a favorite restaurant and then a movie on Friday nights. At least he'd assumed as much. Unexpected flowers. He'd done that, too. Jewelry. Chocolate. What more had Charlene wanted?

Of course they'd used the money from their wedding for a down payment on a starter home, because a house was more practical than wasting free cash on a honeymoon.

Stephen was probably going to take Charlene on a romantic vacation.

"Fine. Yeah. They were family vacations," he huffed out.

"I'm not blaming you. Okay? I'm saying she has a side and you have a side. I know you did your best."

"Guess it wasn't enough." Jude stared out at the blackness of the passenger window.

"What about Raven?"

"What about her?"

"Err . . . are you two . . . dating?"

Jude puffed out a good helping of air. "I don't know."

"You don't know?"

"I'm Darryl's campaign manager. Her brother's running for chief. How do you think this'll play out?"

Emery grimaced.

"Yeah. That's what I thought, too." The first time he'd taken an interest in a woman, and she stood behind enemy lines.

They sat, as they always did, for Sunday dinner at Mom's before everyone went to bingo. Kids ran around. Raven's sisters, their husbands, and children took up every inch in the tiny house. Mom's only great-grandchild occupied the highchair. Fawn's son, Bryan, and his girlfriend, Yolanda, were in the living room, enjoying a break from their baby, who Fawn cooed over as a proud kokum.

"We owe it to Annie. She started the Traditionalists Society." Mom offered a spoonful of mashed potatoes to little Brittany, passing on eating, as she'd done ever since Christmas, always complaining about a sore stomach, acid reflux, and indigestion whenever she ate. But she needed to eat. Mom had lost ten pounds on her already slim frame. "She's probably turning in her grave over what Darryl's done."

Mom shook her head and shoveled another helping of mashed potatoes into Brittany's waiting mouth. "Marrying a Matawapit." The wrinkling of her nose matched the deep wrinkles around her eyes and lips. "He'll probably start going to church again."

"I'm taking care of it." Clayton cut into his roast, a delicious smoked side of moose he'd hunted this fall. "I'll win this election."

"Have you heard if Darryl's running?" Mom looked at her own food, made a face, and shoved away the untouched plate.

"I don't need to ask," Clayton said. "I know he'll run."

Fawn turned to Raven. "This is your chance to finally help your family." Her hard stare said *don't screw it up*. "She's going to inherit what we leave behind after we're gone." Fawn used her chin to motion at her ten-month-old granddaughter.

The food sat funny in Raven's stomach. She had to find a way to resist Jude. She wouldn't screw up her campaign. The next time he came to the diner, she'd treat him as a customer, and only a customer. At school, she'd treat him as her teacher, and only her teacher.

Chapter Ten: Makin' Time

For two weeks, Jude never had a moment alone with Raven. She was working hard on her lessons each time she appeared at class, offering him a mere perfunctory smile and hello. He'd been busy acclimatizing himself to the reserve and school. Work and kids were his life. Mom had offered to help, but Jude had said no. The children were his responsibility. He had relented and allowed Mom to watch Noah and Rebekah after school.

Seeing Raven Tuesday and Thursday evenings, knowing they couldn't speak intimately, left an uncomfortable ache in Jude's gut. Today, he'd find out if she felt the same way, since he was finally taking a well-deserved coffee break away from the school.

They needed to talk. Nominations opened Monday night at the community center, and once Jude started campaigning for Darryl, his schedule would double.

His ears seemed to smile at the *crunch, crunch* of snow beneath his boots. One of his favorite sounds. Even the smell of winter was a taste of heaven. Sure, he came from a city known as a big town deep in the Shield, surrounded by thick forests, swollen hills comparable to small mountains, and Lake Superior right there, but being isolated from the main world of traffic, stop lights, constant people, endless distractions was a welcome break. Maybe that was why he'd always spent a good two to three weeks of summer at the folks' house.

At least the cold spell had broken. Minus twenty today. Freezing to most people, but in the northwest of Ontario, the temperature nipping at his exposed face was the average.

Someone drove by and tooted. Jude waved. The truck looked like Old Joseph's from church.

Jude headed up the shoveled walkway and pushed on the glass door. All was quiet inside the diner. He'd timed his break perfect at eleven o'clock. The breakfast crowd was gone, and it was too early for the lunch crew. Only Hank Snowball occupied a table near the back next to the window.

Jude strode up to the counter. Raven appeared from behind the swinging doors, having probably heard the bell tinkling overhead when he'd first arrived.

"Hey." He removed his parka, slung the coat over the back of the stool, and sat. "I guess those lessons are going well, hmm? I haven't heard from you." He set his cell phone on the counter.

"I haven't heard from you, either." She flipped over his mug and poured the coffee.

He'd itched to call, but the kids' reaction had kept floating through his mind. Yes, they seemed fine, but he'd had to make sure they had his attention before he tried sneaking around again.

"Honestly, my paperwork's this high." He raised his hand off the counter to indicate a stack of work. "And I had to settle in my kids."

"How're they doing?" Raven's dark eyes brightened with curiosity.

"Fitting in. They like school. They know a lot of kids from their visits here. Same thing at church."

She set her hand on the counter. Another good sign. She hadn't made an excuse of being busy.

"Becky has a sleepover at a friend's tonight, and Noah wants to stay at his grandparents'. It's a sibling rivalry thing. When one's at a sleepover, the other has to sleep somewhere else, too. It's not any different up here."

Raven's skin glowed. "Cute. My nieces and nephews are the same way." She pushed the menu in front of him. "What can I get you?"

You. Yep, he'd missed her. Missed their talks. Missed the flirting. Missed the company of a woman as stunning as Raven. "A bagel. And . . ." He leaned in. "Seeing how I have the night off . . ."

She squared her shoulders, and her gaze darted about. Jude's shoulders also tensed. *Second thoughts? God, no. Please.* Hopefully she hadn't changed her mind.

"I . . . Gosh, there's so much going on. Nominations are on Monday night . . ." She clicked her painted nails on the counter.

"I'm a dad. I don't get nights off too often. Say yes. Please." He kept his voice low. And he meant *please.*

Her deep gaze pierced his, searching. Deep enough that he held his breath while the seconds passed, seconds seeming to drag on long enough to punch his contracted abs. Finally, she nodded.

"Okay," Raven whispered, leaning in slightly. "We . . . can. Where're we going? I—"

"I'll get you. Take a walk down Turtle Road."

She folded her arms across her flat stomach and again nodded. "What time?"

"Seven. I'll have the kids dropped off by then. You can show me the camp. Do they still keep the road plowed?"

A ride out to Geoff's Camp was the perfect spot. The small resort closed for the winter, but people still used the road. At least Jude hoped so.

"Yeah. They do."

"Then that's what we'll do. I'll bring along some hot chocolate."

The bell over the door tinkled. Jude swiveled in his seat as two old women came in. When Raven dashed off, he couldn't resist checking out her long legs and perfect ass. The minutes would drag until he saw her again.

Raven should have held firm to the promise she'd made and told Jude no. She quickened her pace on Turtle Road. Jude should arrive any moment. Was he looking to get laid? In the past, she wouldn't have cared, because sex was sex. Now? Apprehension tingled along her spine.

The twelve steps sat in her head, reminding Raven she must focus on what she could give, instead of what she could get. Did this mean her intentions to campaign for Clayton were wrong? But she needed some respect back, and that would happen through the diner. The members surrounding the big table at the recovery center would insist she put this in her higher power's hands.

From behind her, headlights appeared on the road. Her limbs tingled.

The humming engine and tires rolling over snow carried to where she'd stopped. A midnight-blue crew-cab short-box truck pulled up beside her. Nice ride. Sexy ride. The big handsome truck suited Jude. Not a rebel bad-to-the-bone truck, but classy and striking, just like him.

The window lowered. "Hey, good-looking, need a lift?" Humor sparkled in Jude's teasing question.

Raven giggled and opened the door. She sat on a welcoming warm leather seat. Such a gentleman, having turned on the heater button for her. "Sure could use one. Is this what you do? Ride around the rez rescuing damsels in distress?"

"Riiight . . ." Jude chuckled. "Only one in particular." He winked.

She dug his wink. It produced a boyish glitter in his black eyes, a devilish smile to his red lips, and his devastating dimples made an appearance. "I guess it's a good thing I decided to take a walk tonight, then, huh?"

"A very good thing." He steered the truck off Turtle Road and onto Racoon Drive. "You ever go up to the camp?"

"When I was little. Mom worked there as a housekeeper. Sometimes she'd let me tag along. I played in the cabins while she cleaned. But most of the time Kokum watched me."

"You and Emery have something in common, being much younger than your siblings."

That was all they had in common. In high school, Emery had been a nice guy, quiet, and stuck to Darryl. As amazingly gorgeous as Emery was, magazine-cover-model stunning, she'd never desired to date him. Neither had her friends. Probably because Emery's congenial disposition landed him in the category of guys girls dug as friends only. A great ear to blab to or a shoulder to cry on.

Now Jude, he might not have Emery's devastating beauty, but big brother ranked higher because his handsomeness was stylish, classic—rugged, even, when he dressed down, passing on his usual business attire.

Tonight, he smoldered of ruggedness, from the teal sweater hugging his solid build to the black jeans clinging to his strong thighs. No parka, which he must have shucked in the backseat.

Raven removed her coat and mittens. She tossed them in the back, where there was a ton of room. Being the rez, she'd never made out in the backseat of a vehicle. Growing up, none of the boys could afford cars or trucks.

"When'd you get your license?"

"Sixteen, like any other teenager." Jude guided them down Camp Road.

Oh boy, here they went. Alone and away from everyone. Raven's heart rate matched the dribbling of a basketball. "I still don't have mine."

"What?" Jude sputtered. "But you drive."

"It's the rez. Our rules are different up here."

"I know. I gotta get my brother and brother-in-law to start wearing helmets when they're burning around on their four-wheeler. They only reason they wear helmets snowmobiling is so they don't get cold."

"Emery's as rez as everyone else. Your kids will be, too. They're the same age as him when he moved up here."

"Rez . . ." Jude snickered. "And what is rez?"

"You should know. We ignore the rest of planet Earth and live by our own rules."

"Very true."

They were enclosed in bare brush resembling skeletons against the flash of the high beams. The road, mirroring a roller coaster, was only wide enough to accommodate one vehicle. They were climbing a hill on a turn.

"You should get your license, though. It's good to have one."

"I don't have a vehicle to use."

"What about one of your family's?"

"They always fly into the 'Peg or T. Bay."

"I don't blame them. It's a long haul from the city to here."

"And a lot of gas. Did you fill up in the city?"

"Yep. Then we refueled in Sturgeon Creek."

"Big price jump, hey?"

"Was it ever." Jude shook his head. "Why do you think I walk to work?"

"You'll get used to it. In time, you'll be driving everywhere like everyone else." They were climbing another hill, this one straight up and no turn.

After a few more turns and hills, they pulled up at the main area. All was quiet, except for the light wind rustling through the spruce trees. Jude reached into the back seat and set a thermos between them.

"I thought you'd like some tea."

"Awesome. Honey, too?"

"Already added." He removed two small travel mugs from a cloth bag and set them on the console.

Once he poured, Raven took her cup and sipped. Chamomile. Perfect.

Jude switched off the high beams to the daytime lights.

"I hope you don't waste too much gas."

"I gotta run the truck or we'll freeze." He snickered. "As you said—I'll get used to the prices up here."

"You will. Each time you head for the city, you'll feel like a big sale's happening."

"I won't be going back for a bit. Too much to catch up on at the school."

Raven worked off her mukluks.

"Did you make those, too?"

"Kokum did." She sipped more tea. No stars. No moon. They were wrapped in the pitch-black night.

"Are you the kind of girl who knows how to hunt?"

"Of course." Silly man. "I used to help Kokum check the trap lines. She taught me how to skin them. And cook them. When I was ten, she made me a rabbit coat. I loved it. Too bad everyone's against fur now."

"I don't think the anti-fur movement pertains to Indigenous people." Jude tilted the mug. "I'm assuming most of society knows a lot still rely on trapping for an income. Trappers bring their furs in for trade to make the trip into the city to buy Christmas presents. Food for dinner."

"That's what my dad did, I guess. Guided during the summer, hunted in the fall, and trapped in the winter, Mom said." Too bad the bottle had sucked the life out of him. Maybe that was why Mom remained angry. The Indian Residential School had cost her a husband, forcing her to raise four kids on her own while pregnant with a fifth.

Would Jude understand? Probably not. He'd say his dad

had gone to the residential school and had overcome his demons.

"I hope they do. This fall, I went out hunting a couple of times with Clayton and my cousins," she said.

"Get anything?"

"A deer. Those mittens you saw came from that deer. Kokum taught me how to skin one when I was twelve."

"You know so much. Why leave?"

Raven sipped more tea. The chamomile and honey warmed her limbs and chest. A man from a perfect family wouldn't understand. It was best to lie. "I told you, I wanted to be like other girls. Makeup. Hair. Hip-hop. Dating. I loved Winnipeg. It was different from the rez, but in some ways not that different. Maybe it was the nabe? My cousin lived in Lord Selkirk Park. Y'see a lot of *'Nish* from the northern reserves there."

Jude grinned. "*'Nish.* My brother-in-law uses that a lot. Adam. Even Darryl the odd time. Is it a Winnipeg thing?"

"I thought everyone used it." Raven chuckled, since *'Nish* was slang for *Anishinaabe.*

The tea deserved a vape. Her taste buds craved a taste of *Totally Wicked,* her favorite e-cigarette flavor. "Gimme one sec."

Smoking was frowned upon nowadays. Was Jude one of those offended anti-smokers? Once she donned her mukluks and parka, she cracked open the truck door and got out. Maybe around minus sixteen. A welcome respite from minus thirty-seven. She withdrew her vape.

The other door cracked open just as she inhaled the delicious vapor.

"I didn't know you vaped." Jude's boots crunched against the snow as he strode over. "My brother-in-law quit for the new year. Bridget bought Adam a vape."

"I quit six months ago." Raven held up her hot pink e-cigarette. "If not for this, I'd still be smoking."

"Nicotine?"

"You betcha." She took another puff.

"How do you get your e-liquid?"

"The mail. I order from a place in Winnipeg." Raven puffed again. She sipped from the mug. The combination of chamomile and tobacco-tasting vapor was delicious.

"It's healthier than smoking."

"Please don't give me the *smokers are a drain on the healthcare system, they're selfish for risking their lives and lungs, they have families to think about* speech. Or I'll talk about how nobody eats for fuel anymore, but emotional comfort, and what a drain it is on the healthcare system."

Jude threw back his head and laughed.

Low. But not scary. Handsome, like him.

"I won't say anything. My dad smokes."

"Yeah, I see the deacon sneaking a ciggie on his daily walks."

"I will say I'm glad you quit. I didn't even know you smoked."

"I was a heavy smoker. Quitting wasn't easy. I still get cravings."

"Did it go hand in hand with your addiction? I know Adam liked smoking and drinking. I was surprised when he quit."

"It does. I started when I was twelve."

"Twelve?" Jude's eyes popped.

"Drinking. Smoking weed. Smoking. I was bad, I told you."

"When'd you start using drugs?" He folded his arms.

Raven puffed on the vape. "It went from weed to booze. When I moved to Winnipeg, the stuff was around at parties. I liked the feeling." She shuddered. "I loved chasing the dragon."

"Chasing the what?"

"Smoking heroin. Some smoke crack. I found I got too

hyped on crack. The first time I smoked heroin, it was completely . . ." How to describe the feeling? Impossible. "You get this really awesome rush. They say it's better than sex. At the time, it was. No orgasm can compare to the feeling. Then you go into this dream-state. You float to the clouds. You don't wanna come back down."

"I see." Jude tilted his head. "Was it easy . . . quitting?"

Raven's stomach seemed to follow her lowered head. "It was really hard. I had to detox first. Then I went into treatment. Clayton took care of me. I owe him my life. If not for him . . ."

She'd be selling herself on the street. Pain scratched at her skin. The same curled-up pain she'd experienced balled up in the corner, rocking from dope sickness. Puking. Crying. Wanting to die and get off the planet, even jump out of her own skin.

"I stayed in treatment for three months. It was an aboriginal healing program. They used our culture and the twelve steps to help us. Clayton came and got me after I finished. He hauled me on the plane and brought me back here. They're only three meetings a week. I was going to meetings twice a day before that. We had meetings in the morning and meetings in the evening.

"He . . . he sat with me each night, reading from the twelve-step book, even though he's not an addict or alcoholic. Everyone else had given up on me, but not Clayton. He's a true big brother."

Her throat swelled. "I know everyone calls him a shit-disturber, a troublemaker. But they don't understand what he did for the family. After Dad's death, he looked after us. He sacrificed his own life for ours. He fished, hunted, and trapped to feed us. He dropped out of high school to guide at Geoff's Camp so Mom had another income."

"C'mere." Jude crooked his finger, wiggling it for her to

step closer.

She did.

He draped his arms around her waist, and she snuggled against the safety of his strong chest.

Chapter Eleven: Don't It Make You Feel Good?

Jude's beating heart warmed Raven's ear. Warmed her chilled body. Warmed her quaking insides. His palm caressed the small of her back.

"Do you understand why he wants to see the end of the church now? It robbed him of a family."

"You said he's only forty-two. He's still young enough to have a family of his own," Jude murmured.

Raven's stomach tightened. He didn't understand or didn't want to understand. "He's raising Tyrell. See? The residential school again."

"Tyrell's mother attended?"

"No. Her parents did." She lifted her head.

He gazed down, sifting his fingers through her hair.

Yes, they'd come out here for a reason. To hide from those who might tattle to their families. But even knowing what she'd lose, the ache throbbing inside her panties screamed for Jude. Screamed for his touch. His lips. His hands. His cock.

His mouth came down on hers. Raven's limbs melted from his scent swathing her, a combination of honey and chamomile tea. Each soft pucker Jude lavished on her lips awakened flutters in her belly. The urge to squirm surfaced. Wiggle against him. The heat in her panties cajoled Raven to fondle Jude's groin with her crotch. She met thickening dick beneath his jeans.

He moaned. His tongue slipped between her lips. She

matched his sensual licks with teasing strokes. Damn, he was a good kisser. Gentle, but a hint of want in the potent exploration of her mouth.

She locked her arms around his broad shoulders. Gosh, she could ski off these babies since they were the size of baseballs. His cock bloomed to a full erection pressing on her belly. She almost squealed inside his mouth.

Still kissing, he steered Raven to the truck. She peeked at his half-open eyes. He peeked back and broke the kiss.

She leaned against the rear passenger door. "I never made it in the backseat of a truck. Is it as big as it looks?"

"Is what bigger than it looks?" Teasing invaded Jude's question. His dark eyes glimmered.

"Silly man." She poked his flat stomach. "You know what I'm talking about. Considering you stayed at your uncle and aunt's as a teenager, I'm betting you got some experience back there." She used her chin to motion at the truck.

"Sure do." He opened the door, still grinning. "But not what you think. Remember, I was raised a good Catholic boy."

"Never took advantage of a girl, hmm?" Yes, marriage had granted Jude sexual experience, but his lack of partners was a turn-on. She'd be the second woman to jerk his prick, suck his balls, and lick the head of his cock. "What're we waiting for?"

"Lemme flip up the seats."

"Oooh, they flip up?" Excitement curled around Raven's clit, hot enough to wet the skimpy panties she'd made sure to shimmy on earlier. Hopefully Jude loved itty-bitty pink lace. She draped her arms around his waist while he pushed a button and folded the seats.

"C'mere." He climbed in.

She snaked in beside him. As roomy as the back was, they were snuggled tight together.

He used his boot to close the door. "I should take these off, hey?"

"Let me." She leaned forward and removed his snow boots. Then she made sure to worm out of her mukluks. "There."

He'd plumped up their parkas to use as pillows.

She settled beside him. He was probably about five-eleven. Not too tall for the back. The deacon needed a thank you for gifting his son with a height beneath six feet.

Jude's arm wound around Raven's shoulder, and he drew her against his solid chest. They both had to keep their knees bent to fit. This was the time Raven cursed her own height. To be five feet and able to fit anywhere.

Her mouth met his lips. He lavished a steam-coated kiss on her. Each pucker and nibble curled her tummy with sweet tickles. This was nice. Kissing. She'd never simply kissed since she'd been a teenager and first experimenting with boys. Leave it to Jude to take his time. She wasn't in a rush either. The caresses he lavished on her hair, the delicate licks and strokes of his tongue exploring her mouth wrapped Raven in sultry warmth.

She brushed at his hair — thick and coarse. He'd never lose these babies, not when his father still had a full jet-black mane. She glided her nails along the smooth skin of Jude's face while he continued to taste her tongue, and then she traced the strong bones of his cheek and jawline.

Just their breaths and the humming engine filled the truck. She could have stayed out here forever, exploring his face, massaging his hair, sampling his tongue. The *mmm* noises he made were deep and full of satisfaction, enough to elicit a shiver from her.

His fingers wandered along her spine, his erection rubbing her thigh.

Raven wormed her hand downward. A bold move, but it'd been too long since she'd last jerked cock. Jude's breathing heaved, his tongue plunging and searching. She curled her fingers around the button of his jeans. Her clit throbbed with anticipation. Just as she was about to unfasten the button, his hand seized her wrist.

Raven froze.

Jude broke the kiss, hand still locking her wrist. He gaped at her, Adam's apple bobbing.

"Wh-what is it?" she stammered. She'd never gotten this kind of reaction. If alone with a guy, the horny hunk couldn't keep his pants on.

"I . . . I . . ." He released her wrist and settled his palm on her cheek. "I . . . I can't think when I'm around you."

Jude buried his face into Raven's hair.

She skimmed his back with her nails. A good Catholic boy. According to his church, he was married until his annulment.

"I understand . . ." Something smothered Raven's chest, maybe the disappointment invading her queasy stomach.

"No . . . don't." Jude's deep voice was hushed. "This isn't about you at all. It's about me." He pecked the top of her head.

"It's your marriage, isn't it?" Raven kept her face buried in his chest.

"No. It's . . . my kids."

"It's okay." She fingered a strand of his hair.

His dark eyes brightened. "It is?"

Raven nodded. "Can we at least kiss?"

Jude traced Raven's cheekbone, the print of his finger leaving a delicious silken echo in its wake. "These are lethal. Beautiful."

Flattery warmed her belly. "Thank you."

"They are. You could cut diamonds with your cheekbones. A true Indian face. All your features are so defined. So . . ." His tone kept softening until his lips skimmed hers.

Raven accepted the melodious kiss. She'd never met a man who wasn't ruled by his dick. Or a man who struggled with putting his own needs aside for those he loved. She was special to Jude. His actions more than said so. *He wants more than sex from me.*

She shuddered and molded herself against his strong body. His erection met her stomach. He was dying to have her but making no move to sneak his hand up her sweater or grab her ass.

In the past, violent poison had filled her mind whenever she saw a Matawapit or Darryl. Now, the venom was fading.

"Hmm . . . what is it? Are you okay?" Jude's sleepy eyes peered at her.

Shit, she'd been too busy thinking that she'd forgotten to return his kiss. "I'm fine. Keep at it."

"You sure?" His eyes questioned her.

"More than sure." They were alone after two weeks apart. She deserved a night of wherever this led, whether taking a cold shower upon returning home or lying in bed savoring the moment of having a man deep inside her again.

She covered his mouth and feasted on his wet tongue that eagerly explored hers. Everything about him was clean and handsome. Mouth. Straight teeth. Outdoorsy breath. Shiny hair. Smooth, flawless skin.

Raven couldn't resist and slid her hand inside his sweater to meet Jude's firm back muscles. Gooseflesh pimpled his skin. She traced her fingers over the tiny bumps. He gasped in her mouth. She kept tracing the excited raised marks that said he enjoyed kissing and touching her, because his hand sat on her hip, rubbing.

His erection pressing along her stomach kept goading Raven. What did he feel like? Look like? She edged her fingers from his back and wormed her way to his jeans. His breathing hitched. He slid his hand from her hip to her ass and massaged her cheek. His palm seemed to burn through her back pocket.

A groan snuck from her throat. Jude broke the kiss and

pecked her jawline. A path of pecks. A kiss to her lobe. A nibble behind her ear. A light lick on her neck. The steam and fever kept mounting. They should have turned down the truck temperature before getting in the back. Sweat crept between Raven's legs, along with her wet excitement. Her panties would end up soaked if this kept up.

"You feel so good. Smell so nice." Jude's voice was as hot and wet as Raven's pussy. He kept kneading her ass. His lips suckled her throat.

She gulped for breath. Her hand remained on his button. She unsnapped it.

He stiffened but kept planting kisses on her neck.

She edged down the zipper. Beneath her palm, his cock flickered. Her heartbeat jumped. She edged her hand inside the nest of warmth. Hair as coarse as his black mane brushed her fingers. Heat from his flesh scorched her hand. Thick pre-cum seeped along her fingers. Her clit kept throbbing. Tingles kissed her skin and slithered up her inner thighs, massaging the spot that always coaxed her to spread her legs and raise her hips.

She needed a taste of cock. Her cunt screamed for him.

When Raven gripped Jude's thick erection, she cupped his wide girth and long, straight length. His cock thrust between her fisted hand. Moans deep from his throat moistened the skin of her throat. If she didn't get her clothes off, she'd come in her jeans. The tingles were everywhere — on her spine, teasing the wet skin between her pussy lips, coiling around her clit, slithering down her thighs.

"Jude . . ." So hard to talk. Just panting.

"Oh God." He gasped. His lips left her neck. They stared at each other. "C'mon."

He struggled a bit but sat up. When he removed his sweater, Raven groaned at the dips and contours of his flexing muscles and dark skin. Her mouth filled with wet anticipation, aching to suck on his bare flesh.

She unfastened her jeans and wiggled from the tight denim. If she was smart, she would've worn leggings.

"Nice . . ." Jude's gaze pierced her pink panties. "Very nice. I didn't think you were the kind of woman who preferred practical white cotton."

Raven squirmed beneath Jude's hot stare and the lack of room to remove her clothing. Poor Jude managed to free himself from part of his jeans, but he'd never get them fully off.

As for her sweater and bra, she'd have to keep them on. Her ache was too great, and so was his, to try to remove the rest of their clothing.

"C'mere." He patted the carpeted floor.

She rested on her back. Her breaths kept coming fast. He moved half on top of her. His hand slid between her legs. God, she swore her clit jumped from its hiding spot to reach for his fingers. The shivers wouldn't stop. Everything pulsated — thighs, skin, pussy.

His fingers eased between her cunt lips, and Raven sucked in air but gasped as he massaged her slippery flesh. The scent of her excitement filled the truck.

"Oh, you're so ready for me." He almost seemed to coo since his look was tender yet raw.

"Please . . ." Begging wasn't something she'd ever done. She attempted to spread her legs.

Jude's finger traced the rim of her clit, tormenting the sensitive area that quivered. She tried to raise her hips but couldn't. He was half on her, his weight keeping her pinned to the floor. He circled and stroked, petting her pussy. Each swirl, each caress spurred her juddering clit to surrender.

The waves of crackling heat struck her hard and fast. She gasped as the explosion of pleasure gripped her cunt and flickered along her skin and thighs. Fevered. She thrashed beneath him, gasping and groaning.

"Oh yeah, that's it. Look how beautiful you are," he said, voice thick with excitement.

The sizzling fever dissipated. Raven panted. Gosh, how she wished to hang tight to the quivering sensations that had rocketed her from earth seconds ago. But Jude's lush voice and the arousal in his eyes wrapped her in a puffy white cloud she found ten times better than an orgasm. Nobody had ever called her beautiful after she'd gotten her rocks off.

"Jude . . ."

"I need you, Raven." His low voice remained thick.

"Please . . ."

He moved on top. Raven cursed her sweater. But there'd be other times when she'd experience their skin as one. She locked her legs around his hips. His cock was brushing the opening to her pussy. When he eased inside her, the same fever erupted and heated her clit. His cock was a welcome invasion, pure pleasure as he spread her flesh to accommodate his length and thickness.

"Oh my God!"

Jude stiffened. His eyes flew open. "What? Are you okay? I'm not hurting you, am I?"

"Condoms. I used to be religious about condoms. I don't have any. I haven't bought any in—" How stupid! Cock-blocked by her own senselessness.

"It's okay. Trust me. There isn't a chance anything'll happen."

What did he mean? But from what she'd learned of Jude so far, he was an honest man and no liar. If he said they were safe, they were safe. Whew. They wouldn't have to stop fucking.

"Then what're you waiting for?" She brushed his face. "Fuck me."

"Oh, I'll fuck you, all right." His mouth claimed hers.

She tangled her fingers through his locks, *oohing* and *aahing* with each delightful pump that taunted her pussy. Slow and easy. Meant to be savored. She licked at his tongue while he continued to gently thrust.

His mouth traveled from her lips to her neck again. "You feel so good." He panted. "Oh, you feel so good."

Hmm, a talker. Her favorite kind. "You do, too. Fuck me harder." Her cunt demanded a good pounding.

He didn't need to be told twice. She was as eager as him to get her rocks off. His thick prick moved hard and fast, forcing her to accept his length and girth. The hot tingles resurfaced, crackling along her limbs and swirling around her clit.

His moans and gasps called to her. She was the woman he'd chosen to give himself to, after a year alone. He'd chosen her. Raven Kabatay. A recovering addict and nobody from the rez.

Chapter Twelve: Things Keep Changing

While Raven puffed on her e-cigarette, Jude poured more tea for them to enjoy. What a night. If possible, they'd get between the sheets again. He still couldn't get over her boldness. Even her understanding when he'd had second thoughts. The girl was special.

He carried the cups from the truck to where Raven stood in the headlights. Swathed in her parka, long hair spilling down her back, she was as lovely dressed as she had been undressed.

"Here." He held out the cup and nuzzled against her backside he'd caressed earlier.

Raven craned her neck, grinning. Her beautiful white teeth flashed at him. "Thank you. Such a gentleman. Is this also a part of your good Catholic upbringing?"

"It has nothing to do with Catholicism. It's thoughtfulness." He pecked her cheek.

She gripped the cup he held out. The scent of her pussy lingered on his fingers. She had a charming, strong aroma. He couldn't help taking a deep breath to allow her lingering fragrance of musk to invade his nostrils.

"What're you doing?" She giggled.

"Enjoying a sniff." He couldn't resist teasing her. "What man doesn't enjoy smelling his fingers after they've been inside a woman?"

"You guys are all the same." She playfully smacked his

112

hand.

"Easy . . . you'll lose your tea."

"Hmm, tea and a vape after sex. My fave." She swiveled on her heel. Her stare twinkled like the stars above them.

He kissed her forehead. So much warmth standing out in the cold.

"Are we gonna run outta gas?"

"Yep, if we don't get going soon . . ." His chest sagged.

"You're busy the rest of the weekend?" Her question mirrored his caved-in chest.

"I gotta get the kids tomorrow morning. They want to go tobogganing. Then it's home for dinner and a movie." He couldn't keep the regret from his voice. The children came first, though.

"It's okay." Raven's eyes matched the wilt in her voice. "I understand."

"I know you do, but it doesn't mean we both can't feel . . . a bit bummed about it." He leaned his forehead against hers. "I guess I'll see you . . ." Monday night was nominations. "Monday."

"I have to nominate Clayton. What about you?"

"I'll be there."

"Are you nominating anyone?"

If he told her the truth, she might become angry. Not how Jude wanted to end their perfect night. "Maybe we should leave politics out of our conversations?"

"I get it." She shrugged and stepped back.

Great. So much for their perfect night.

Raven stared ahead at the straight road. She'd vacate the truck pretty quick and start her walk home.

Jude reached over and laced his fingers around hers and squeezed.

The warmth of his palm produced a lightness in Raven's chest. She had a mad-on for him. A mad-on for everything about him. He was like everyone else on the reserve—wanting what was best for the community. Why else would he give up so much and move here?

She squeezed back.

He turned the truck onto Turtle Road. When he pulled over, he made sure he cut the lights and switched off the vehicle. Darkness engulfed them, since they were far from the four houses up ahead. "You gonna be okay walking alone by yourself?"

His concern touched her. How many times had she stumbled off home after doing her walk of shame from some guy's crib in the city? A guy who'd been passed out, not giving a shit what happened to her after they'd used one another?

"Thank you." She slid her nail along his finger. "I should jokingly say *it's the rez.* But y'know, I'm glad you asked."

"I wish I could take you home. I don't feel right dropping you off."

"I'm fine. Really." She peeked at him sideways, grinning. "Don't go feeling like you got your piece and now you're done with it."

"Don't say that. What we did wasn't *a piece* for me."

"It wasn't for me, either." She started to slip her hand from his, but he didn't let go of her fingers. "What is it?"

"Make sure and text me this time."

"I will."

"I'll text you, too."

"I'm all for it." She was. Excitement fluttered in her belly. "G'night, Jude."

"G'night." He leaned over.

This was risky, but they were in the dark, lights and truck off. She leaned in.

His mouth glided over hers. The heat of breaths from his

nose caressed the dip above her upper lip. Not a kiss meant to lead into sex, but a lingering kiss saying how much he cared by his gentle puckers.

Using her nail, she traced his strong cheekbone. Bold. Powerful.

He pecked her mouth one more time. "I'll text you tomorrow when I get a chance."

"Okay." She rubbed his nose with hers.

They both chuckled.

"What kind of kiss is this?" His eyes crinkled.

"A northern one. It's meant to keep us warm in the winter."

"I must say I rather like it."

Raven did, too. There was something sweet about the tips of their noses touching. "G'night."

"Goodnight."

Raven forced herself from the truck. She shut the door and scurried ahead so nobody would see her when Jude started the vehicle. After a few more quick sprints, the headlights hit her backside and lit the road. She kept walking. The truck rolled by, but she continued to stare at the snowbank, since she was upon the first house. People had to believe she was out taking a stroll because the night wasn't the bone-chilling Jack Frost coat of ice they'd endured for over a week, and everyone poked their heads out when the temperature lifted to the minus twenties.

Two kids who should be in bed were playing with their plastic toboggans at the big ditch. They laughed and giggled while sliding downward. She used to do the same, too. It was a weekend. They probably lived at their grandparents'.

Her cell phone beeped. She removed her mitten and reached inside her parka. When she gazed at the message, her heart thumped.

Sweet dreams.

Yes, she'd have sweet dreams of Jude. She texted back.

You, too. And they'd better be about me.

She couldn't help the giggle. A couple of seconds later, the message popped up.

Bossy lady. I bet you're bossy somewhere else, too, hey?

Raven slapped her hand over her mouth. She texted back.

Stick around and find out.

Her heart held its breath as she waited for his answer.

Oh, I'll definitely be sticking around. Can't wait until next time. G'night.

She texted back a goodnight. It was a good night. But her pattering heart deflated over Monday night just around the corner. She stuffed the phone into her pocket. There must be an answer to balance her commitment to her beliefs and her feelings for Jude.

"I guess it's a good thing I tagged along, since you're not answering my texts." Emery stood, hands in pockets, watching Rebekah and Noah slide down the big hill.

Jude gazed out at the endless sea of spruce on the other side of the lake. Various ice roads led to different islands where people fished or camped out. "Didn't you two ever get cold when'd you'd stay out here in the winter?"

"No." Emery stepped in front of Jude. "How're you doing?"

"How're *you* doing? Still sleeping in the spare room? It's

been over two weeks."

"This isn't about me."

"Look, this isn't like you to stick your nose where it doesn't belong. What gives?" Jude folded his arms.

Emery motioned up and down. "Most people would call this a closed-off, defensive stance, but technically it isn't. It's called a self-soothing stance when a person is attempting to draw comfort during an uncomfortable situation."

Letting out an exasperated breath of air, Jude dropped his arms. "Are you taking lessons from Bridget?"

"Bridget?"

"Yes. She should become a private detective instead of the director at the Indigenous Students Center."

"I'm not being nosy. I'm being . . . y'know, it's okay for you and Bridget to butt into my life, but whenever I try and speak to either of you, the walls come up." A hint of frustration lurked in Emery's voice.

Jude wrapped his arm around his little brother's shoulder and steered them away from the edge of the steep hill leading to the frozen water covered in snow. "Feeling left out?"

"Uh . . . no. You're living up here now. I think we can start being brothers instead of teacher and student."

"I don't treat you like a student." Jude stopped. "I'll answer you if you answer me. What's going on with you and Darryl? If I'm his campaign manager and have to push to get him elected, I need his full cooperation, not a moping guy who's upset because his spouse won't share his bed."

Emery's face reddened. "If you must know, we're in the same bed."

Jude grinned. What man could deny himself sex? Not even Emery could say *no* to a roll in the hay. "That's progress, but you still got him on ice, don't you?"

Emery's face remained red. He ducked his head. "I guess we're trying to jump the first hurdle all married couples have to either jump or walk away from."

"You don't strike me as the kind of man who gives up."

"No, I won't give up. I made a commitment. When I said *till death do us part*, I meant it. Although the church doesn't recognize our marriage, in my eyes it's a sacrament. I'm . . . simply disappointed in him. He kept the truth from me. What he did might cost him the election if anyone finds out."

"Nobody's going to turn on him 'cause he solicited the services of a prostitute."

Emery scowled. "See? Every time I hear that, I—"

"Get mad? Burn?"

"Yes."

"Give it time. If you'd been a man on the loose—" As if Emery would get drunk and holler at a prostitute to come on over and suck his dick. "Remember, evolution made us all—"

"Evolution? Don't you mean God?" Emery studied Jude, curiosity glittering in his green eyes.

"Yes, God. He made us different for a reason. Think about how the world would be if six billion Emerys were running about."

"It'd be pretty boring, hey?" Emery grimaced.

"Not boring. A little intense, but not boring. If you were boring, Darryl would've found someone else. You two balance each other. Darryl gets carried away with causes he believes in. Carried away with everything. He's ruled by his emotions. You pull him back and make him contemplate his decisions.

"As for you, Darryl loosens you up. He makes you act on instinct. Sometimes the gut feeling works. Spontaneity can be fun."

"Balance. True. Darryl's a big believer in balance. For him, it's the Ojibway world. And the Ojibway world follows nature's law of stable equilibrium."

"No good and evil, hey?" Jude had to agree with Darryl. His brother-in-law's philosophy was a heck of a lot better than reenacting the Bible's story of Job.

"Okay, we talked about me. What about you?"

Jude wasn't about to confess he'd had sex. That was between him and Raven.

"Well?"

"I guess I'm gonna have to wait and see." Jude shoved his hands inside his parka pockets. "I worry how it'll affect them." He used his chin to point at Rebekah and Noah running back up the hill, laughing and rosy-cheeked from the fresh cold.

"And don't tell me to put it in the Lord's hands." There, he'd shut down his little brother before Emery could give his usual answer.

"Why not? If He can create all of this . . ." Emery used his hand to make a sweeping motion. "Why can't he resolve your problem?"

"Are you using Him to resolve yours?" Jude winked.

"It's taking time, but I'm learning."

"What've you learned?"

"To let go of the past and past regrets. I kept blaming myself for Darryl's, uh, bold behavior while we were estranged. But I'm not to blame. Darryl chose to do what he did as a single man. I chose something else."

"Such as the priesthood?"

"Yes." Emery heaved his shoulders up and down. "I made the right decision for me at the time. And I guess he did what he had to do. I can accept what he chose, but it doesn't mean I have to agree with him, or what he did. Am I disappointed? Very disappointed. That man isn't the Darryl I knew growing up. And he isn't the Darryl I know now."

"Who was he then?"

"An angry man. He did the *I'll show you and hurt me.*"

Emery cast Jude a weak smile. "Isn't that what we do when we believe we're getting even? We do things to spite others and hurt ourselves in the process?"

"Yeah, we do." Jude used his boot to brush at the snow. "I'm trying not to hold any resentments against Charlene. I'll be honest. Her emailing you really pissed me off. I can't believe she wanted you to witness at the annulment."

"Are you going to contest it?"

"No." Jude shook his head. "Why would I? The annulment will allow us to move on. She can marry the jerk." Not the snarling feeling again.

"Are you ready to . . . date?"

"Yeah." He honestly was. For a year he'd sat in gloom and doom. "But I don't know if *they're* ready for me to date." He lifted his hand at the kids. "Then there's the election. We try not to talk about it. There're some big differences we have that're gonna crop up the longer we see each other."

"When did you last see her?"

"Last night. We went for a drive to Geoff's Camp."

"Geoff opened the dining hall? I didn't think he was back from Mexico yet."

"He's not." Jude shot Emery a *don't ask* look.

"Never mind." Emery bit down on his lip. The smile appeared anyway. "Darryl and I preferred the Treaty Grounds. Adam and Bridget? They thought the trail at the church was a great place."

"Oh man . . ." Jude groaned. "Let's not go there. I don't even wanna think about my sister . . . Ugh. Get me some brain bleach. Geez."

Emery burst out laughing.

The most Jude could do was take the dating one day at a time. But the odds stacked against them . . . not good.

CHAPTER THIRTEEN: TOO MANY ENEMIES

Picking up Dad to ride together to the community center had been a great idea. Jude drove. They were leaving the Grassy District and heading for Sandy Point, where nominations were being held. Emery and Darryl had opted to stay home.

As for Mom, she was watching the kids. Although she'd gained status as a band member before Bill C-Thirty-One came into effect back in nineteen eighty-five—when the Federal Government had stopped allowing non-status women to become Status Indians under the Indian Act through marriage to Status Indian men—Mom never felt comfortable becoming involved in elections, but she did vote.

Jude never dared bring up the subject to Bridget or he'd get six hours of nonstop complaining. She loathed the Federal Government's patriarchal interference in determining who could or couldn't be classed as a Status Indian, since native women had lost their rights if they'd married non-status men.

This could one day impact Jude's children, because they claimed their Indian status through him. However, his grandchildren, if the government kept interfering, might not qualify, all depending on whom his grandchildren married.

At least women no longer lost their status—after the passing of Bill C-Thirty-One—if they married non-status men. And women who'd previously lost their status had had it reinstated.

For the sake of the future, maybe being dragged into politics was a good idea. As a deacon, Dad had to stay neutral.

"Roy'll be there to second the nomination. We have plenty from the church attending."

"That's great." Jude turned onto the main road to Sandy Point.

The big brown building was where bingo, suppers, and any other major-sized events took place. When he turned onto Lynx Road, the parking lot was already full. He glanced at the dashboard clock. They were twenty minutes early.

"This is serious business if they're on time. Hell, if they're early."

Dad chuckled. "They take their elections seriously."

Jude parked the truck. The spot near the ditch meant a jaunt to the building. At least the warmer weather was holding up at minus eighteen.

They entered the main lobby to people mingling about, holding coffees, and talking. As they wove their way through the crowd, they stopped to say hi and chit-chat for a few moments. Then they joined the table where the band members from the church sat.

"Norman. C'mon over here." Roy patted a seat beside him.

"Sit here." Jenny, Mom's BFF, motioned at Jude.

He slid in the chair beside her. She talked, but Jude only nodded. He couldn't resist searching out Raven, who Marilyn-Monroe-ed her way through the crowd, holding a tray of coffees. As Raven sashayed to the table, she laughed if one of the many men waylaid her, while the women shot her dirty looks.

She kept flipping her hair, wiggling and giggling at her fan club, who continued teasing her. It was hard to believe no male had piqued Raven's interest during the time she'd returned to the reserve. She was so busy putting on a show, she didn't seem to be searching out Jude.

Raven reached the table where the Kabatays sat. She bent over to set down the tray, which earned her spectacular ass many gawks from the men.

Jude whipped out his phone and typed out a message.

Evening. How'd your weekend go?

While Jenny continued to talk, Jude snuck peeks at Raven. A serious woman had replaced the vamp who'd strutted her stuff through the hall. Dark brows narrowed and red lips set in a straight line, Raven was leaning in, seeming to listen to what Fawn was saying.

The electoral officer stepped up to the small stage. In a few moments, nominations would be underway. The band office secretary and the administrative assistant were on hand to help. After a check of the equipment, the electoral officer stood at the microphone. She eyed the timer set up on a table.

"Good evening, ladies and gentlemen. Tonight is the . . ."

Jude again glanced at his phone. Nothing. He stole another peek at Raven. She was sipping her coffee, head down, but through the enormous crowd, he couldn't see what held her attention.

His phone dinged. A few people looked at him, and he switched his setting to silence.

Went okay. Finished my lessons for tomorrow night. How about you?

A bright glow filled his chest.

Took the kids tobogganing. Phoned my sister Saturday night. We video chatted for a good hour. Went to church on Sunday. Then had dinner at the folks. Maybe we could enjoy another coffee after school tomorrow night?

He hit send and sat back.

"As you can see, these are the nominations from the mail-in ballots from the off-reserve membership." The electoral officer pointed to the whiteboard where the band secretary frantically wrote. "Nominations for the on-reserve membership at this meeting are now open."

Raven stood. So did her other sister, Wren. They strode to the small stage.

Murmurs echoed through the big hall.

The electoral officer held out the mic to Raven.

"I nominate Ernest Clayton Kabatay for chief," she said into the microphone.

Wren leaned in. "I second the nomination."

"I also nominate Ernest Clayton Kabatay for band council," Raven added.

Again, Wren leaned in. "I second the nomination."

The girls moved to the table to fill out the form with the administrative assistant.

Jude nodded at Roy. They stood.

"They're making sure if Clayton doesn't get in as chief, he has a chance at band council again. We gotta do the same," Roy told Jude.

"Sounds good."

For some strange reason, Jude's heart rattled. He'd never participated in an election, unless his mail-in vote counted. Whenever band elections came around, he'd received the packet by post, which he'd filled out and had Bridget witness, and he'd done the same for her. Then they'd mailed their packages in the special envelopes.

He stood in front of the microphone the electoral officer held. "I nominate Darryl Samuel Keejik for chief."

"I second the motion," Roy said in his gruff voice.

They also nominated and seconded Darryl for band council.

The electoral officer motioned for Jude to see the administrative assistant. He withdrew his wallet and removed his Status Card, proof he was a band member of Ottertail Lake and held Indian Status recognized by the Canadian government.

Darryl was right. This election system had to change. Everything had to do with the approval of the federal government. Even the electoral officer, a woman from the Tribal Area Advisory Council, had to be approved by Indigenous and Northern Affairs Canada.

The rules had never previously bothered Jude, probably because he'd never lived on reserve and had a life separate from the Ojibway communities and people.

Once he'd filled out the form and signed and dated it, he headed for the canteen to refill his coffee.

"I'll tell you something, this is gonna get a little dramatic." Roy set his paper cup on the table. "Clayton's got the biggest bone to pick with Darryl."

"Yeah. I get it. Clayton feels Darryl betrayed him when they went after the church two summers ago."

"Yup." Roy scratched his chin. "Glad Darryl saw the light. Clayton? He'll keep rabble-rousing. Men like him never change. Not surprised he got his sisters to nominate and second him. Not surprised either that Raven's his campaign manager."

"She is?" Jude turned the spout on the big coffee urn. Why hadn't she said something to him? *Because I told her we shouldn't talk politics while we're together.*

"Clayton was bragging about it at the diner during supper."

Jude held out the cup he'd refilled for Roy. He snuck a glimpse at Raven's family. Her mother sat front and center, a woman who'd have possessed great beauty if not for the hostility hardening her face. A deep wrinkle was embedded between her black brows from constantly knitting them in disapproval. Wrinkles around her lips. Frown lines. And a helping of crow's feet from her perennial pinched expression.

"Let's go." Jude headed back to his table.

From what he'd heard, Arlene Kabatay, Raven's mother, had six other sisters and four brothers. A very big family, which was the norm for the older days. Dad's family was big, too, but not close. The Indian Residential Schools had done their job by destroying the kinship Dad had once shared with his siblings. His brothers and sisters lived all over Canada. Seven already dead. If not for Mom's side, Jude wouldn't have known family in an extended way.

At the table, Dad had a pad of paper out, writing down each person who was nominated for chief or band council.

Jude plopped in the chair beside Jenny, who'd also be nominated, since she already sat on band council.

"There'll be changes," Roy muttered. "I'll tell you something, after what's happened over the last couple of years, people are reassessing who they want as leaders." He slurped his coffee. "It's gotta be a strong campaign. And it'll be between Darryl and Clayton."

"Have you thought up any strategies yet?" Jenny asked.

"I'm going to meet with Darryl tomorrow." Jude snuck another peek at Raven, who was speaking to Fawn.

Sadie, Jenny's grandmother, shuffled to the stage. A traditional woman, she'd proven to be an ally for the church after taking Darryl's side during the first protest two years ago. She used a cane to walk now.

The electoral officer held out the microphone.

"I nominate Emeric Augustine Matawapit for band council." Even at her elderly age, Sadie's voice was firm and strong.

Jude almost fell out of his chair. Emery? Yes, the parishioners from the church had their strategy for nominations, and the Kabatays had theirs, but it was apparent the Traditionalists Society had gotten together to decide who they wanted at the leadership table, which was strange. because Darryl chaired the Traditionalists Society and should have known.

Since Emery was a former Grassy District resident, if he won, his seat would be from his original district, since each geographic area on the reserve had one representative at the leadership table.

"We need a seconder." The electoral officer's amplified voice carried through the hall.

Basil Skunk, a well-respected elder for the Traditionalists Society, rose. He hobbled up to the stage.

This wasn't a strategy. For some reason, Sadie had decided to nominate Emery without consulting him or anyone else. Jude withdrew his phone and quickly texted Emery.

You've been nominated for band council by Sadie Wasaya and Basil Skunk.

Dad frowned. Roy's beady eyes scrunched in confusion. It looked like they'd be meeting at Mom and Dad's tomorrow now that Emery was a candidate—if he accepted the nomination, since he could decline.

Sadie and Basil's nomination earned them stink-eyes from the Kabatays, Raven included.

Raven clicked her nails against the table. She sipped more coffee.

"Y'see why we have to take back the Traditionalists Society?" Fawn murmured. "I can't believe Sadie and Basil nominated Emery. It's bad enough the biggest traitor to his culture and people, Darryl, is now a part of them and running for chief. If they get in, the reserve's finished. The community will become a bunch of apples—white on the inside and red on the outside."

The diner would be in full swing tomorrow with everyone

arriving for coffee to gossip about tonight's nominations.

"Maybe he won't accept?" Raven tilted her cup to take another sip. She kept peeking at Jude over the rim. He was huddled with Roy, Jenny, his dad, and other people from the church.

"This means they have four from the church running for band council." Fawn held up four fingers. "Roy from Airplane, Jenny from Old Main, Emery's Grassy, and Darryl's Long River."

"Well, Grassy is full of Catholics. If the deacon could run, I bet he would. They had no choice but to nominate Emery." Mom sniffed.

Raven's family had nominated those they wanted from the different areas at the leadership table. She checked her sheet Clayton had provided. She had to make sure people voted for the seven councilors they'd chosen.

"She's no elder." Mom almost spit out her words while narrowing her eyes at Sadie. "She's just old. No true elder would do what she did—nominate a man who studied to become a priest, and who's loyal to a church that did its best to try and wipe us out."

Queasiness invaded Raven's stomach. But Jude had proven to her his family wasn't the enemy.

"Basil. Bah." Mom waved her hand. "He's no elder either. Not if he seconded the nomination. He had it in him to be a wise man. Now . . . he's nothing but senile."

If the venom kept dripping from Mom's mouth, she'd turn into a snake.

Raven checked her phone. She still had to answer Jude's text. This might get her into trouble, but Friday night kept pounding through her head.

Coffee sounds good. Geoff's Camp?

The message popped up.

Geoff's sounds good. I'll let Mom know I'm working late. See you tomorrow night.

No bantering. No teasing. From either of them. Already the politics Jude had insisted they steer clear of was beginning to interfere. He probably felt the pinch, too, since Raven's entire family seemed to pinch her backside.

Jude pulled up at Mom and Dad's house. He'd been able to get away from the school after letting the staff know he had a political meeting to attend. Emery and Darryl were present. Roy's old beater was also parked. The same for Jenny and a few others from the church.

Jude scooted up the porch steps and dashed inside the main hallway to a full living room.

Darryl strolled over, coffee in hand. "Thanks for the nomination and your support."

"And my brother? How's he feeling?" Jude shrugged off his parka.

"Shell-shocked." Darryl snickered. "He sure wasn't expecting that."

"Is he going to accept the nomination?" Jude hung his coat on the overflowing tree rack in the hallway. He followed Darryl through the archway into the living room.

"At first he said no way. But I reminded him two respected elders nominated him — for a good reason. If he declined, he'd insult them. So Em's keeping his name in the hat. He just didn't see it coming, that's all. He's only heard from those two what a great spiritual leader he'll be one day. They never mentioned him becoming a politician."

"In order to understand the community and their needs, sitting at the leadership table, if Emery wins a seat, will give him a clear view of what the people need." Jude could see

Basil and Sadie's reasoning. "A spiritual leader? They really said that? They do know he's not going to become a priest, right?"

"Yeah. But they still insist he'll lead us spiritually one day." Darryl steered them through the living room—after saying hello to the people seated on the couch, armchair, and love seat—and into the dining room to an already full table.

A red-faced Emery stood by the sliding doors in front of the screened-in deck.

"Congratulations." Jude smacked Emery's shoulder.

"Quit with the jokes, please." Emery almost seemed to groan. "I'm still digesting everything."

"You'll make a fine councilor if you get in." Jude headed for the kitchen opposite the dining room. "C'mon."

Emery followed.

"Am I going to be your campaign manager, too?" Jude filled his coffee mug.

"I'm not sure what I'm supposed to campaign about. I don't know anything about politics. Much less reserve politics."

True. Emery's field was social services and Catholic theology. "You've got Darryl to coach you." Jude fixed his coffee.

"They should've nominated you instead." Emery leaned against the counter.

"But they didn't. Hey, I just started living here. The community needs time to get to know me."

"They know who you are." Emery made a face.

"True. But they don't know me well enough."

"How do you feel about . . . *someone* being a campaign manager? You two are going up against each other," Emery murmured.

CHAPTER FOURTEEN: WE DON'T HAVE TO FALL IN LOVE

"I guess I'm gonna have to wait and see." Jude leaned against the kitchen counter. He had to deal with his pride. Taking advice from his nine-years-younger brother wasn't an affront to his capability of managing his own life. People a lot older had been more than willing to accept Emery as a priest by providing spiritual guidance to the laity and directing a parish.

"Be careful. The Kabatays are . . ." Emery kneaded the handle of his mug.

"Go ahead. Speak ill of them. God won't strike you down." Teasing lurked in Jude's reply.

"Clayton's going to use any means he can to win. Raven wants him to win. She's his campaign manager. Do you think . . ." Emery's lips formed into a straight line of concern.

The spittle in Jude's mouth morphed into a desert. Was his brother insinuating Raven was using him to gather information, or weaken his resolve so he'd lose sight of the election? "No. Can't see it." He shook his head vehemently.

But Raven had used men in the past for devious purposes. If Adam was here, who knew her too well, what would he say? But digging information from Adam was wrong, or was it?

"Text him . . ." Emery shrugged.

A ball formed in Jude's stomach. "Text who?"

"Who you're thinking about."

"And who am I thinking about?"

"Adam."

"He's busy. He's managing the kitchen now at Benny's. They have him there day and night."

"He's a manager, which means he can take a break to talk to you."

Emery and his damned logic. Jude chugged down a good gulp of coffee. What man called another man to ask about relationship advice? Hell, this wasn't even a relationship. They'd only started dating.

"It wouldn't hurt."

"Yep, I know." Jude swigged more coffee. "The thing is, we've only been on one date. And I don't want too many people knowing—"

"Can you seriously see Adam gossiping about who's dating whom?"

Nope, Adam couldn't care less about anyone's love life. He also wouldn't say boo to Bridget, since he was a man who stuck to the code of the streets and had learned to keep his mouth shut in jail and in prison. The clincher was Adam's participation in the twelve-step recovery program, which meant more zipped lips.

"No."

"Then ask him about her."

"You don't trust her?"

"I don't trust Clayton." Emery's brows wilted. "Which is disappointing, but Clayton is Clayton."

Jude shivered. No, he couldn't see Raven using him to win an election. As for consulting Adam . . . Jude squirmed. Maybe he should.

Raven might as well have brought a blank-paged textbook for all she'd accomplished during her lesson. The other four students yawned and stretched. One glanced at the clock, since it was nearing the end of the class. They'd gotten the low-down on more analytic geometry tonight.

She was *this close* to obtaining her grade eleven credits, with grade ten math still kicking her butt. But she'd nail the credit by the end of spring. One more year to go. Then she could proudly say she was a high school graduate. Considering the number of students who dropped out upon reaching sixteen years, it was too bad more adults didn't try to obtain their diploma. Most, instead, went for their GED.

If Raven graduated, she'd be the first of her family to finish high school.

Jude had his Master of Education, and he'd also acquired his principal's certification. The Master of Theology was a little strange. But he'd explained in one of his texts he'd needed it to teach religious education in the Catholic school. His ex-wife was a nurse practitioner, which meant a master's degree, plus a shitload of other education the job demanded.

What the heck did he see in a high-school dropout? A recovering addict. A woman who'd fucked almost every guy in Winnipeg. She was nothing like his ex-wife.

The other people rose from their desks, but Raven sat glued to her seat.

Everyone headed out of the classroom. Jude remained behind his desk, typing on his laptop, maybe preparing their next lesson.

Raven closed her textbook and binder.

Jude glanced up. "Ready?"

"Yeah." She stood and grabbed her parka from behind the seat.

"Lemme shut this down." He kept typing.

"Sure. No hurry." Raven donned her jacket. She sidled up to the desk and glided her nails across the smooth top. She stood beside Jude's chair. Leaning in, she inhaled his clean scent and the warmth coming from his ear. Something about campaign strategy was written on the spreadsheet.

Jude slammed the lid shut. He swiveled in the chair.

"I wasn't supposed to see that?" Raven moistened her lips. She sat on the edge of the desk, one mukluk off the floor, which she swung slightly.

A big grin spread across Jude's face as his gaze traveled up and down. "At times I wonder if you turn it off."

"Turn off what?" She walked her nails along the desk's top until they settled near Jude's hand that held a pen.

"The vamp." He slyly grinned.

"Oh? I'm a vamp now?" Flattering, but how had he perceived his ex-wife? Maybe Raven should ask. "Question." She rose off the desk.

"Fire away." Jude packed up his briefcase and laptop. He put on his parka.

"Why'd you get married really young?" The question was what anyone would ask, so he might not suspect she was digging for information.

He gripped the briefcase and laptop case. "Because I believed it was right for us at the time." He motioned at Raven to follow.

She switched off the lights.

They left the classroom.

"That's a really boring answer. I can admit why I saw Sully."

"Ah, Sully. The ex-gangbanger, or is he still gangbanging?" Jude fell in step beside her.

"Still gangbanging." He kept her pace—something Raven hadn't noticed until now. And he'd let her initiate the pace for sex, their talks, and even walking down a hall.

"Is he in or out of prison?"

"In . . . I think. Not sure. But I think he's in again."

"And?" Jude held open the door.

"And what?" Raven stepped outside to a slight chill. She peeked around at the empty parking lot. They were safe.

"You were telling me why you agreed to date him."

"Date." Raven guffawed. "We called it hooking up, getting together, shacking up."

"Okay. Why shack up?" Jude gazed at her.

"He had money and drugs." Raven hugged the books to her chest. "What did . . ." Here went nothing. "What did she have?"

Jude's eyes narrowed. "Nothing. I thought she was . . . someone different, but she proved me wrong."

"I'm sorry." Raven was.

"Don't be." Jude hit the switch on his keys, and his truck started. "Live and learn."

"Are you over it?"

"Do you mean am I still in love with her?" Jude stopped at the truck and opened the passenger door.

Raven got in. "Yes."

"I learned feelings change colors."

Colors? A person either loved someone or they didn't. Her heart pinched.

Jude set his briefcase and laptop in the back. He got in the driver's side. "She's the mother of my children. Therefore, I respect her. I don't wish ill health on her or anything."

"You don't?"

"It took me a long time to feel that way. I hated her at first, but I wasn't going to use the kids against her. That's not fair to Noah and Becky."

"The accepting she'll always be a part of your life kind of thing?"

"Yep. We aren't friends. But we're not enemies. We're co-parenting two kids we created who mean the world to us."

They rolled away from their spot.

His answer warmed Raven's skin. "I never saw boo of her.

I mean, I was away from here since I was sixteen."

"There's nothing to see." He shrugged.

"Did she visit a lot?"

"On holidays. She preferred to have the family at our house." Jude guided them to the familiar road leading to Geoff's Camp.

"She didn't like the rez?"

"I wouldn't say she didn't like it. She simply didn't know what to make of it. When she was here, we stuck to the house and church."

"You were the same way." When Raven had returned, she'd never seen Jude around. Except the one time he'd showed up at the diner with Emery and Darryl.

"Like I said, I never grew up here. Thunder Bay was my home. Don't get me wrong. I like Ottertail Lake. I think of it as my second home, but more so 'cause my parents live here."

"If they didn't . . ."

A sheepish smile spread across Jude's face. "I probably wouldn't have visited. Yeah, I'm a band member, but there're lots of band members who've never visited their home reserves, like Adam."

"He's from a rez in Manitoba."

Jude nodded. "I can't see him moving there."

"Neither can I."

They rode the crazy winding road with bare brush almost closing in on the truck.

"Is your mom watching the kids?"

"Yep." Jude's hand snaked across the seat, and he entwined their fingers. "I missed you."

Gah, he had a way of making her knees turn to mush. Even squeal like an excited little girl on Christmas morning. No guy had ever admitted to missing her, even Sully, and they'd shacked up for three years.

"I . . ." She'd never told a guy this—ever. "I missed you,

too."

"I like the way you flutter those lashes." Jude's deep voice caressed Raven's quivering knees.

"I fluttered my lashes?"

"You sure did. Were you being coy or a bit on the bashful side?"

Bashful? Her? But she had been. "You got me. You're the first guy to make me blush. Consider it an honor."

"I'm honored." He squeezed her fingers again.

The truck rolled up to the spot where they'd . . . had sex? Wrong. They'd had more than sex. They'd gently but urgently given themselves to each other.

Raven squirmed. "Did you bring tea?"

"No tea." Jude opened the door. "C'mon, now that I know you vape, you probably need to, right?"

"Smart man." Raven got out of the truck. "So no tea, huh?"

"Not tonight. It would have gotten cold. I brought pop instead. You want a cola?"

"Sounds good. Get it for me, pretty please? It's perfect for vaping."

"Gotcha." Jude swiveled and headed to the truck.

Raven dug inside her pocket and withdrew her e-cigarette. She puffed.

Jude returned, carrying the colas. "One for you." He held out the can.

"Thank you, gorgeous." Raven took the offered drink.

The boyish dimples appeared on Jude's face. "You like to tease, hmm?" He slipped his free arm around her waist.

Raven was drawn against his chest, still holding her vape and pop. His dark eyes sparkled.

"I know what this look means now," she murmured.

"What look?" His words twinkled just like his eyes.

"That you're being playful. That you like being teased." She pecked his lips.

"Teased by you? Definitely." His words didn't twinkle this time. They sparkled.

She was wrapped in the sparkles he rained down on her, as if he had a wand like in those kiddie cartoons she used to watch, a princess being gifted with all her dreams.

His lips covered hers. She melted her mouth with Jude's and sampled the fresh scent of cola. Each light pucker he offered wound her into a warm blanket that he hugged around her shoulders. Gentlemanly. Although the cold nipped at Raven's exposed skin, kissing under the stars was the most romantic place to be with him. Alone. Surrounded by the sea of spruce trees.

He broke the kiss. Through sleepy eyes, he gazed at her. "Care to join me in the back seat?"

"I thought you'd never ask." Raven tucked away the e-cigarette.

He took her hand, lacing their fingers as he guided them to the truck. Peaceful. Only their breaths appearing as white puffs on the air and the crunch of his boots along the snow.

Jude opened the back door.

Raven climbed in. She shrugged off her parka and set the heavy coat in the front seat. Jude did the same. His teal-blue sweater brought out the dark color of his skin. Black dress pants hugged his firm thighs.

"I rather like how you dress up." She cuddled up against him. "You're metro."

"You mean metrosexual?"

"Mmm-hmm. A metrosexual *'Nish.*" His arm wrapped her shoulder, and she rested her hand on his flat stomach, rubbing. His strong abs contracted beneath her palm. For once, she wanted to give something back, because this sexy man was deserving of a gift. And every man loved a blow job.

She walked her fingers along the button of his pants. His lips moved into a light smile. He bent and kissed her. While he smothered her lips with his, she caressed his hard-on through the plush material of his pants. His low moan filled her mouth. When she worked open the zipper and button, his waiting cock edged out from beneath his underwear.

Raven broke the kiss. "Let me. I've been wanting to check out your goodies ever since you first stood front and center in the classroom."

"Oh? You did?" He more than grinned, eyes crinkling.

"Sure did." She lightly skimmed his length with her nails. "The lighting sucks, but maybe I can see well enough."

If his grin got any wider, it'd stretch to his ears.

She scooted along the seat. His prick was before her. Straight, long, and thick. His scent was as ripe as him after being tucked away all day inside his underwear. She kissed the head, and he gasped. Maybe she did feel a bit vampy. In the past, she'd always brought a man to his knees. But screw showing off. This was about making Jude feel good. His pleasure was her pleasure.

His erection feathered her mouth, and she slid the tip between her lips. Warm. Hard. He pumped, his length moving in and out, filling her as she clamped tight and sucked in rhythm with his thrusts. The gasps and groans coming from him elicited sweet throbs in her panties.

Even his tempo was the same teasing strokes he'd used when they'd last come together, meant to coax her into submitting. Moistness invaded her panties. So much heat between her legs.

The only sound was Jude's gasps while he stroked her hair. She licked the tip of his cock. Delicious. As handsome as him. She sucked on his length, moving up and down. His fingers danced along her backside, tracing the bumps of her spine. For a moment she almost lost her rhythm because his exploratory touch was a mixture of sweet and sensual.

"Oh geez." He moaned again. "Raven . . ."

"Mmm." She wasn't answering. Sucking him off felt way too good. He was deep in her mouth, wet with her saliva, rutting smoothly between her lips. The suction produced by the friction they were generating was a light smacking sound toying with her cunt. Her thighs begged to open, spread out to take all of him.

"I need you. I wanna come inside you," Jude murmured, his voice pure silk that seemed to skim her clit.

"I need you, too." She popped up. "I wanted to give you—" *Never mind.*

She did her best to worm out of the painted-on jeans, which wasn't an easy feat. While she wiggled free, he kept touching her. Fingers tugging at her panties. Palms cupping her ass. Hands caressing her thighs. His dark eyes on fire. Licking his lips. Gaze full of awe.

Finally, she worked off the jeans and mukluks. Bare ass, bare cunt, and ready to get on him. She slithered onto his lap and silently cursed her height, because she was grazing the ceiling.

"Easy. I'll do the work so you don't hit your head." He drew her against him.

"We need a bed," she whispered.

"Maybe I can arrange that." His cock eased inside Raven.

"How?" His wide girth stretched her skin. Her favorite part—being opened by him.

"I'll tell you later."

She said nothing and let him fuck her.

CHAPTER FIFTEEN: RUN WITH ME

"I meant to ask you something." Raven nestled against Jude's shoulder. She'd already planted her feet on the headrest of the front seat.

"What's that?" Jude's mouth grazed the top of her head.

"When we were last together, you told me not to worry about protection. You, um, guaranteed me we were safe. We didn't use protection again."

The sound of Jude wetting and smacking his lips carried through the hum of the truck. His chest heaved slightly.

Raven stiffened. He couldn't have something like a low sperm count. He had two children.

"I had a vasectomy." His answer was quieter than the stillness of the night.

Disbelief surged through Raven's veins. Weren't Catholics not allowed to use birth control? She straightened and stared at him. "Uh . . . I thought you couldn't—"

A deep breath came from Jude's mouth. "I told my brother once, if I didn't practice birth control in my marriage, I'd have eight kids back at the house, not two."

"Which method?" This wasn't good at all.

"She used the birth control shot. I can't remember what the actual name is."

"And?"

"After we separated, the kids were devastated. Noah's grades dropped. He did nothing but hide in his room. Becky had nightmares almost every night. It took me six months to get them to finally sleep in their own beds. Seeing them like that pissed me off. Pissed me off enough to explode. I never felt that kind of anger. Ever." His words were harder than concrete.

Raven stroked her thigh. "I'm sorry. It still bothers you, doesn't it?"

"Yes, it does." He almost barked his reply. "They see her once a month on the weekend. And on holidays. They're leaving on Friday for Kenora. Then they'll spend the March break there. At the end of March, they'll be on a plane again for another weekend visit."

Jude ground his teeth. "No kid deserves that. None. I won't even have them for Easter. It's part of our custody arrangement. She gets them on holidays, besides one weekend a month. Over Christmas, I woke up to Emery and Darryl's dogs in my face. They drove the ice road to stay at my place. Guess they didn't want me waking up on Christmas Day alone. Dad celebrates Mass here on Christmas Eve and Christmas Day. The folks didn't fly in until Boxing Day."

He leaned in and clasped his hands together. "Before Christmas, I gave myself a present. No more kids. No more split homes. No more nothing. I wasn't gonna put another child through what my kids already suffered."

Raven bowed her head. He truly didn't want a woman to become a part of his life again. Then why should she care? This was their second official date. They both had differing dreams. Once Clayton won the election, she was buying the diner.

Jude set his hand on her knee. "I was angry at the time, but when I moved up here . . ." He blinked. "The anger faded. I started to . . . change. The kids are changing."

"Changing?"

"Yeah." He cast a solemn gaze. "They needed the change. They're used to being up here. They loved coming up here to visit their grandparents. Now they see them all the time.

"Noah misses Kyle. Bridget and Adam's son. They went to school together. Best friends, besides cousins. Noah also misses hockey. But the recreation supervisor teaches them. There are only two teams here, which means not much competition. He'll miss his golf lessons in the spring. Curling."

"Will you eventually go back? They're only seven and eight, aren't they?" She held her breath.

"It depends on how much their extracurricular interests grow. The rec supervisor is great with the kids, but he doesn't have the skills the other coaches in Thunder Bay have for teaching hockey. The same goes for golf. Curling."

"Emery attended high school here." If Raven's stomach kept dropping, her intestines would hit the truck floor.

"Yeah, he did, and there's a lot of stuff he missed out on. I taught him golf when he moved to the city for university. I taught him how to curl. When he showed up, he—"

"Was totally bush?"

Jude winced. "Well, he wasn't very fashion savvy. Hiking boots. Old t-shirts. Jeans he should've donated to charity. Bush accent."

"He dresses like that now. It sounds like he's happy with himself." There was nothing wrong with looking bush. The fashion industry had gone crazy for the plaid, grungy style in the nineties that was the norm up here.

"That's Emery. He's content hunting, fishing, trapping, camping. He loves the outdoors. I guess he made the best decision for himself. Marrying Darryl. Moving back to the rez. The only time he dresses up is for church."

"You said your kids love it up here." Why was Raven trying to point out the benefits of reserve life anyway?

"They do. They're adjusting fast. They're turning eight and nine this year. High school is still a few years away."

"The vasectomy thing. You plan on it only being the three of you?"

Jude wet his lips. "I . . . I did."

His hesitation produced hope in Raven's melancholy heart. Then she sat back, picking at her pants. *It's our third date. I shouldn't care. I never used to care.*

"I . . . Excuse me." She pulled on her mukluks and parka. Without saying anything further, she left the truck. The snow never made a sound as she quietly walked away from the daytime running headlights of the truck.

She withdrew her vape from her pocket and inhaled. Gloom and doom knotted her shoulders.

The truck door slammed shut. Jude's boots squashing against the snow carried to where she stood.

"Hey . . ." His voice had lost its direct tone.

"Um, we should get going. Your mom probably wants to call it a night." Raven needed to call it a night. What was she doing out here anyway?

Jude's arm draped her waist, and she stiffened.

"I mentioned the kids'll be away this weekend."

She nodded and sucked on the vape again.

"I'd . . . hey." Using his thumb, he gently prodded her chin upward. "I'd, uh, I'd like us to spend the weekend in the city."

The gloom and doom vanished. Shock shimmied down Raven's spine as she faced him. Hope filled his eyes, even pleading. Her feelings did mean something to him. He truly liked her. He wanted more from her than — what?

"Uh . . ." She'd never gone away with someone, unless the drive to Brandon for a drug deal Sully had been negotiating counted. And there'd been nothing exciting about that.

"How much does it cost?" Yes, the reserves up north had their own air service to make purchasing a flight easier for band members, and to haul fuel, freight, and other big items, but Raven made minimum wage.

"Don't worry about it. There'll be a ticket waiting for you. See if you can get Friday afternoon and all day Saturday off." Jude's eyes glittered.

"I'll check with Cookie. Where are we gonna stay?" A squeal invaded her throat.

"A hotel, like everyone else who comes down from the rez to spend the weekend in the city." Jude grinned.

If the family asked, she'd say she was picking up supplies for the campaign. "I'll do my best with Cookie."

"Thank you." Jude leaned in. His lips brushed hers.

Raven's heart bordered on bursting.

The diner door swung open. Clayton banged his big boots on the welcome mat. He hefted up to the counter.

The joy filling Raven's chest vanished. She'd been ready to dance across the floor after Cookie gave her the okay to take Friday afternoon and Saturday off.

"What've you got for me to look at?" Clayton turned over his coffee mug.

"What do you mean?" She filled his cup.

"For the campaign. I need to review and approve your strategy."

"Nominations were only on Monday night. It's Wednesday morning." How fast was Raven supposed to work with a busy schedule?

"We can start this weekend." Clayton fixed his coffee.

"This weekend?" Not a chance. "I already made plans."

"Plans? What plans?" Clayton frowned. He set aside his spoon, staring at her. "All you do is work, hit your recovery meetings, and go to school."

"I'm going to the city."

"The city? We need to get started on the campaign." Clayton banged his finger on the counter.

"I already bought my ticket. It's too late." Big deal, she'd lied. She wasn't passing up an opportunity to spend a weekend alone with Jude, in a real bed instead of the back of a truck like some prostitute.

Clayton's narrowed eyes narrowed even further. "What's going on?"

"What do you mean?" Was he questioning how she'd stood up for herself instead of kowtowing to him? She was thirty-one. And very grateful for his help when nobody else had helped her, but this didn't give him the right to butt into her life.

"You've been acting a little off. The other night when I mentioned the Matawapits, you didn't slam them like you always do." Clayton hunkered over his coffee, still studying her.

She couldn't care less about the church after meeting Jude.

A ball formed in Raven's stomach. This wasn't good. Her damned coochie was responsible for tossing aside the staunch convictions she'd clung to after coming home.

Jude sat back in his office chair. He held a cup of coffee in one hand and a pen in the other while Darryl continued to divulge his platform for the campaign.

"Basil's participation is a must. I consulted him last night. We both did." Darryl motioned at Emery who sat in the other chair. "He has to be a big part of the campaign. I want him to open every speech I give with a prayer."

"So that's what you're concentrating on? Culture?" Jude had spent too much time in Western society. He had to remind himself First Nations communities operated differently. Yes, they thought about economic bases, infrastructure, health care, recreation, jobs, and everything else that drove townships and cities, but their culture and spirituality were most important to them.

"Willie did a great job. He had a good team to help him, but the division's still present. The children need options. They need more than recreation, schooling, and a chance to express themselves creatively. They need to remember who they are."

Another of Darryl's strategies—the youth.

"Who takes our place after we leave here? The children. We've got a great base. *Anishinaabemowin* is taught in school. Elders provide oral stories. But we must bring the youth back to where we belong. Out there." Darryl pointed to the bush. "I went out there when I was thirteen. Basil prepared me. How many other kids do this? How many know how to dress a moose? How many know how to trap? What about the girls? I know Raven tried to help them through the Traditionalists Society before the Kabatays upped and left."

Something fluttered in Jude's stomach. Her name always made him tingle now. "Kids want to be kids. They're into hip-hop, fashion, video games—"

"That can be incorporated into what we teach them. Why can't they rap about the old stories and teachings? Why can't they play music that's an expression of us as a people? What about developing a traditional game in the computer lab? There's nothing stopping the girls from mixing the fashion of their heritage with what's *in* for kids today." Darryl reached for his coffee on the desk.

Jude's brother-in-law was every inch the traditionalist— jet-black hair knotted into two braids, bone choker necklace, deer hide vest with his clan decorated into a multi-colored beaded pattern on the left breast. Mukluks.

"What about the reserve?" Jude had better remind Darryl about other important issues. "More are going on dialysis—"

"That comes from what we eat. If we go back to tradition, this wouldn't be happening. Yeah, some of its strong in the bloodline. I have diabetes. And I manage it through proper eating. Exercise. Putting the kids outdoors where they belong will bring them pride in their roots."

Jude glanced at Emery. "How do you feel?"

Emery cleared his throat. "When one's settled inside" — he pointed at his chest — "they're then nourished emotionally, mentally, and physically. I'm with Darryl on this. Spirituality is important. This is an Ojibway community. Participation of the adults is crucial because they influence the children. I see it all the time. When adults don't set a proper example, the kids suffer."

Ouch. That had hit too close to home. Jude nibbled on the top of his pen. "Okay. Let me try to draft something over the weekend. We'll concentrate our efforts on returning to our roots. Let me try to figure out how to market it."

"The vehicle is there." Darryl pointed outside. "I finished the self-governance project eight months ago. If the Crown says this is sovereign land, then we should be sovereign. But we can't until our own people begin practicing their own ways."

Not this argument again. Jude removed the pen from his mouth. "What about those who are in twelve-step programs? Or those practicing another faith, such as Catholicism?"

Darryl grinned slyly. "Your brother's Catholic. I have the utmost respect for the faith he practices."

"I see." Jude uncrossed his legs and sat forward.

"The practice of other faiths is important. As one council member said, we must provide support or the resources to nourish all spirituality for members of Ottertail Lake," Darryl added.

"This means you'll continue to support the parish financially?"

"If we have the means." Darryl pursed his lips. "We're currently operating in a deficit 'cause we don't have a set of funds allocated for covering the church's hydro bill. I'm going to meet with the band manager later this week to see what's available in one of the budgets."

Emery again cleared his throat. "It's a legitimate concern.

Operating to budget is imperative. We don't want to see mismanaged funds during the audit."

"I wouldn't call it mismanagement. More along the lines of proper allocation. I'm an administrator myself. I'm always juggling budgets." The funds for the school were Jude's biggest concern, since dollars came from the feds and not the province, which meant the bare necessities. "The schools are operating in the red. Dad did his best, but he didn't have a money tree erected out back."

Darryl chuckled. "Education's a big concern. And what I'll address. We must work with other First Nations communities, though. One band isn't going to fare well in Ottawa. As a collective, we can make changes."

"Okay, that's what we can use for another speech." Jude typed the concerns under the education column he'd devised for the campaign spreadsheet.

"How many speeches am I giving?" Darryl leaned forward and peered at the laptop screen.

"There'll be one for the elementary-aged kids. Another for the high schoolers. And the last for those enrolled in adult education and distant ed. programs. I know you wanted to tackle non-voters, too."

"Excellent."

"I'll be in the city this weekend, so I'll gather whatever I can for the speeches. Promo material."

"This is starting to sound like a federal election." Darryl snickered. "Am I gonna have to slag my opponents?"

Jude couldn't stop the smile. "No. It goes against the Seven Grandfathers teachings. What about the adults? Are we going to break them down into demographics?"

"I think we'll have to. Let's start with age groups. Older youth from eighteen to twenty-nine. Thirty to fifty. Fifty-one to sixty-four. And sixty-five plus. Each'll have different concerns to address. The same goes for employed and unemployed. Men and women. Mothers. Single parents. Families. Carla will have that list."

"Carla's the band secretary, right?"

"Yep."

"What about you?" Jude looked up at Emery.

"I don't have a platform. I don't even know why Sadie nominated me. I never gave politics a second thought." Emery angled his leg and set his foot on his knee.

Not everyone campaigned during elections on reserves. Some simply threw their name in the hat and let the people decide. "I think you should try to find one."

"I'll try, but I didn't intend on running. I would've declined the nomination if Darryl hadn't told me I'd be insulting Sadie and Basil."

"Do what you do best — consult God about what your platform is."

Emery's mouth fell open.

"I'm not being sarcastic." Jude stifled his laugh, or he'd upset his brother. "I'm serious. You pray every day for direction and guidance. Pray about this. Talk to Dad. Or Father Bennie. Darryl consulted Basil. I'm sure he also prayed about it."

Darryl nodded.

"I'll get the demographics from Carla. Meanwhile, you two spend the weekend going over more of your platforms." Jude finished typing on the laptop. "We'll do coffee once I get back."

"Back?" Emery's slim brow arched.

Heat saturated Jude's face. "Yes, err, I said I'm going into the city this weekend . . . to . . . ah . . . visit Bridget and Adam."

Emery cast Jude a knowing look.

Chapter Sixteen: Me and You

Raven cuddled up beside Jude in the taxi. True, they were only in Thunder Bay, but with the elation consuming her while they held hands, she swore Jude had taken her to New York City for a romantic weekend getaway.

The cab driver turned into the hotel parking lot that was on the main drag of Arthur Street. They'd flown in just after six.

Raven checked her phone, since it had reset itself to Eastern Standard Time. "What are we gonna do first?"

"How about dinner in the hotel dining room? We can go out shopping tomorrow." Jude smiled at her. "And do the major shopping on Sunday. I need to stock up on perishables."

"Okay. Sounds good."

Their cab pulled up under the brick canopy at the front of the hotel. While Jude dug through his wallet, the driver vacated the vehicle. Raven also stepped from the taxi. She clutched her purse and laptop case. Well, not *her* laptop. Clayton had loaned her his older model to use for the campaign. She needed to get on the ball and buy one of her own.

Jude paid the driver and clasped the handle of his rolling suitcase. He slung her duffel bag strap over his shoulder.

Raven's face heated. Her luggage was hardly designer style. Not even a cheap suitcase. She could imagine Jude's traveling baggage was first class.

They really were from two different worlds, although both were *Anishinaabe* and had lived in cities. If Jude had resided in Winnipeg, he wouldn't have lived in Lord Selkirk Park.

"Let's go." Jude motioned at the double doors.

They headed inside to a wooden plank-style floor in patterns of browns, and a high dome-shaped-style ceiling made of cedar. The brick exterior carried inside to the walls. There were comfortable sofas and chairs to sit on. Even an eating bar-style table was available.

Jude strode up to the check-in desk. Raven sat on one of the chairs. People wandered back and forth, some emerging from the coffee shop. Others purchased coffee at an in-house *Coffee Coffee* where an *Anishinaabe-kwe* stood behind the counter. This brought comfort to Raven. At least the hotel hired Indigenous people.

"Ready?" Jude stood beside her. His fingers gripped the handle of the wheeled suitcase he'd attached his laptop case to. He leaned down and retrieved her duffel bag. "We're on the ground floor. I got us a spit-level room."

"Split level?"

"Yeah. I got us one so you can vape. C'mon."

His thoughtfulness almost melted Raven's insides.

They walked to their ground-floor room. The rest of the hotel was designed the same as the lobby. Giddiness continued to tickle Raven's stomach. Even the carpet leading to the rooms was a plush shade of brown.

Jude stopped in front of room one-twenty-six and swiped the key card.

"After you." He held open the door.

Raven peeked inside. A queen-size bed. Her chest expanded with joy. Split-level was right. since the living area was sunken and had sliding doors leading outside to a courtyard. Relaxing tones of beige and off-white wrapped Raven in coziness. Not high class or anything, but rich in comfort. Welcoming.

"Nice. Very nice." She stepped down the two stairs to the living area.

"It's a great hotel. I've attended meetings here, but I've never been in the rooms."

"Meetings with the Catholic School Board?" Raven set her laptop case and purse on the glass coffee table.

"Yeah." Jude placed their luggage on the luggage rack. His phone dinged. "I hope the kids aren't already sending me messages. Whenever they text, it's complaining. They have to get used to being at their mom's on weekends."

He checked his phone, and his eyes rounded. "It's my sister. She's, geez, she's waiting at the airport for me."

"Bridget?" Raven scooted up the two steps.

"Mom told her I was coming to the city for the weekend. Bridget must've assumed I was coming to visit her."

Raven clicked her nails together. "What're you gonna tell her?"

"That I came into the city to get groceries." Jude tapped away on the phone's screen.

Hopefully Bridget bought the lie. Raven sat on the edge of the bed.

Jude swiped at his hair. "There's no way I'm gonna get out of this. She wants me to come over for dinner. I told her I'm busy tonight. Curling and going for beers with friends. She's insisting I come over tomorrow night."

He sank on the bed beside Raven. "You musta figured out by now my family's very close."

"I understand." So much for a nice private getaway. She'd sit alone in the hotel room while he went for dinner.

Jude patted her thigh. He wet his lips. "Emery knows."

"Yeah, he does." Curiosity pricked the back of Raven's neck. What was he hinting at?

"You feel up to dinner with Adam and Bridget?"

He was inviting her? Seriously? But . . ."She doesn't like me."

"Doesn't like you?" Jude frowned. "I don't think you two

have formally met. At least not that I know of."

"We met. During Healing the Spirit." Something bristly surfaced on Raven's skin.

"When your family was protesting outside?"

Raven had no reason to feel smaller than a mouse. She was a Kabatay and proud of her family. Sure, Mom was a total bitter bitch, but she was Raven's mother. "I recognized Adam. When he came outside for a smoke during the break, I approached him at the cemetery to talk."

"Adam introduced the two of you?"

"Uh, not exactly. Adam and I talked alone. Bridget and I met after Adam went inside. I was still at the fence finishing my cigarette. We . . . talked."

Jude snickered. "I would've wisely disappeared inside if you two were lacing up the boxing gloves."

"What makes you think we fought?" Raven held her nose high. "We were polite."

"I know my sister. And I'm getting to know you. Neither of you are the type to back down. Bridget's a big believer in Healing the Spirit. She booked her holidays to volunteer at the workshop. And your family was there to protest. Even Harry and Lloyd from *Dumb and Dumber* coulda figured out you two were beating on each other with your eyes."

"Okay. I might have been a little . . . defensive."

"Defensive?" Jude stood. He kept grinning. "You got in a few sideways barbs. Huh?"

"I believed in the protest." Raven also stood. "Reconciling with religious institutions is wrong."

Jude's smile faded. "Maybe we should talk about something else?"

Raven folded her arms. "You're right. Let's unpack."

"Gotcha." He winked.

Raven opened her duffel bag. She removed the small packet where she kept her smudge bowl, cedar, and tobacco.

Morning prayer to Creator was important and a big part of her recovery. She'd also brought her daily meditation books, and her recovery book, since she'd miss that night's meeting. But some reading before bed might help her feel as if she'd attended one.

"Hey, do you need to hit a meeting? I brought work with me in case you have to." He pointed at his laptop.

"I'll be fine." Her heart pretty much exploded into a bazillion little hearts. Such respect he showed for her recovery. She motioned at the books.

"Y'know, I admire your spirituality." Jude's palms held her arms tenderly. Even his gaze was tender. "It's a beautiful thing."

"I do, too." That came out wrong. "I mean, I like how you pray, too. I've never dated a guy who believes in a higher power. Are you . . . will you go to church on Sunday?" For some reason she started shivering.

Something strange flashed in Jude's eyes, like he was uncomfortable or hiding a secret. "Uh . . . no. I'm taking Sunday off. It's our weekend."

"Okay." Honoring one's deity was important, but he'd passed on church for her. Flattery warmed her belly.

His thumb traced her cheekbone. "Let's have a bath. I think we're both needing one after working all day and then flying here.

"And you haven't vaped since we stood outside the airport. How about I run the water and you get in your nicotine fix?" He winked again. "We'll finish unpacking first."

"Okay. Deal."

"Help yourself to the mini-bar. There should be pop in there if you're thirsty."

"Thanks." Raven opened the door to the mini-bar and selected an orange juice. Vaping always tasted better with something to sip on. And Jude was very understanding, knowing she was addicted to nicotine.

There was also liquor available. She hadn't thought about Jude drinking. Alcohol was confiscated upon entry into Ottertail Lake from the plane or taken from vehicles using the ice road upon entering the reserve.

What if Jude drank this weekend? Maybe she was worrying for nothing.

Jude finished filling the bath, having unpacked his clothing and other essentials about five minutes earlier. His heart wouldn't stop hammering at finally seeing all of Raven instead of what he could glimpse in the back of his truck.

Drawers opened and closed. Footsteps pattered across the carpet.

Raven entered the bathroom sans clothing.

A thick film of saliva filled Jude's mouth. Talk about bold. He'd never expected her to come in naked, but there she stood. Beautiful high breasts. Slim hips. A landing strip of dark pubic hair. Flat stomach. Long legs.

"You look . . ." He gasped. She didn't even cover herself with her waist-length hair.

"And why're you still dressed?" Raven sashayed to the tub and placed a foot inside. "C'mon, before it gets cold." Her tone was as sassy as her hip-wiggling gait.

Jude removed his sweater. Raven's full-on stare devoured his bare chest. As he removed his jeans, her gaze dropped. There was nothing like having a woman's appreciating stare while a man shed his clothes.

He left the rest of his outfit pooling around his bare feet.

Raven's eyes altered to a smoky expression. She curled her finger in a *come on over* manner ala Jane Russell.

Jude sauntered to the tub. His cock bounced against his lower abs. She kept staring at his dick, smiling.

"Lemme see." She held out her hand.

"See?" The truck mustn't have given her a clear view the last time she'd wanted a peek, and she could peek again all she wanted.

He stepped into the tub. The hot water engulfed his calves.

Raven leaned in and lightly gripped his erection. Her warm skin melted around his boner, and a hiss snuck out from between his teeth. She eased her fingers from the tip to the base. Each stroke sucked the breath from his lungs. She held his stare, her lips forming into an O. Knowing she got off on playing with his dick left his breathing ragged.

"I waited all week for this," she whispered. Her tongue snaked from her mouth and traced her lips as if she was licking his cock. "Join me."

Jude eased onto his knees. When Raven's hand left his cock, disappointment flickered in his stomach. But they had all night to get between the sheets.

She splashed water over her full tits. Beads of moisture dribbled along her skin and trickled over her heaving breasts. "Wash me, Jude."

The sultry way she'd said his name, as if her pouty mouth had pecked his flesh, fired his nerves. From the tray, he grabbed the bar of soap he'd unwrapped earlier.

Raven moved to her knees. The water swished. Jude worked the bar into a lather. He massaged the suds along her slippery toned arm. She closed her eyes. Without the false lashes, her natural ones were as long and black as the ones she liked to wear.

"Why bother?" He massaged her other arm. Each swipe of the soap, her lean muscles flexed beneath his palm. Even her nipples remained erect. Big and beautiful with dark brown areolae. He'd never get tired of looking at her.

The way she hummed and wet her mouth was a delight to his stirring cock. Was her pussy creamy like it'd been on

Tuesday night, full of her musky scent? Even her breathing had intensified.

He traced her prominent collarbones. His fingers lingered for a second. Then he traced her wet skin. Her chest swelled. Jude grinned. He cupped her breasts. Not too big or too small. Generous enough to fill more than his palms. He ran his thumbs along her nipples.

Raven moaned. Her lids flickered. "That feels good."

"No idea why you wear them." Jude lightly pinched her nipples.

She hissed. "Wear what?"

"Your false eyelashes. Your own are gorgeous."

"I like how they make me look." She smiled.

"You're looking damn good right now without them." Boy, did she ever. Her tits needed some sucking. Too bad he'd lathered them in soap.

"Any woman is the bomb when she's naked." Raven giggled.

"I mean it." Jude leaned in and melted his lips over hers. The tip of his cock searched out her pussy, but all he got was her sexy thighs.

She again licked her mouth. "You gonna wash my cunt?"

Cunt?

"What is it?" Raven pecked his cheek. "You seem a little shocked."

"I never heard a woman call her pussy a cunt."

"Mmm . . . I'm not a fan of the pussy word. I prefer cunt."

"Then cunt it is." Who was Jude to argue? He dug the word, too. "And a washing it is."

He'd never gotten to wash pussy. Charlene had been too modest to let him slip soap between her cunt lips.

He lathered up more soap. Raven's arms encircled his neck. She lightly kissed his mouth. Her wet breasts squashed against his chest. He palmed the buzzed hairs she'd groomed into a landing strip and rubbed. The heat from her cunt warmed his hand. She ground her hips and arched her back, thrusting her pelvis in his direction.

He slid his hand between her pussy lips and spread his fingers, parting her slippery folds of flesh. When he wiggled his index finger, she slowly rolled her head about in a circle, gasping.

"Yes." Her groan was hot on his ear. "More."

His cock throbbed as he stroked her clit. Her groans grew deeper and her breaths heavy pants. She widened her thighs and wiggled along his finger.

Getting her off was creating an unbearable ache. She was fucking his finger, her pussy sliding and slipping on the tip.

His balls hurt. His dick wouldn't stop jerking. He swore she was caressing the tender spot at the head.

Her hips bucked, and she cried out, draping herself in his arms.

Chapter Seventeen: Tonight

Washing Raven's beautiful body, from her tits to her feet, left a deep ache in Jude's groin that bordered on bursting. And he'd refused to let her wash him, or he would have shot his wad into her hand.

He lavished her mouth with another kiss. Her legs wrapped his waist. Her arms encircled his neck as he guided them from the bathroom to the bed. She might be a tall woman at around five-nine, but she was light.

"Jude," she whispered. "Oh, Jude. You feel so good."

He felt good? She had no idea what her long legs, beautiful tits, and the warmth of her cunt felt like, slathering his body. And she sure knew how to groom someone. Not only had she shaved him, she'd massaged his scalp with such luxury she'd swaddled him in a cloud.

Her lips kept showering his face with tender kisses. Sure, she'd come, but her lithe body told Jude she wanted more. He eased Raven onto the bed. Hair spread out, eyes a sleepy slumber, thighs splayed, and nipples straining for his touch, she was more than ready for him.

"C'mere." She wiggled her finger, gaze sultry. "Fuck me, Jude."

Oh, he'd more than fuck her. He buried his palms into the bedspread and lay half over Raven. Her arms snaked about his neck. Their lips met. He tasted her wet tongue that played and rolled along with his. The mint toothpaste she'd used earlier to brush her teeth flavored his mouth.

Her hips came up, crotch rubbing his cock. His lips sought

160

her neck, and he suckled at Raven's throat.

"Jude . . . I said to fuck me." The words she said came out half angry and half begging.

"So bossy." He snickered and wiggled the tip of his prick at the entrance of her pussy. Her hips again came up. He plunged into snug flesh, slick and wet that swathed his erection in slippery heat. His cock pulsated. His nerves crackled from the teasing strokes her cunt lavished on his boner.

"Damn, you feel good." He pumped, working his erection back and forth.

Her nails skittered across his back.

"Harder." She panted.

He hadn't held back as it was, so he thrust quick and deep. Her pussy was as cunning as Raven, coyly taunting him with her alluring sexuality. She used her thighs to grip his hips, clasping him around her.

Shivers bumped down his spine. His prick bordered on bursting. He thrust faster and deeper as the exhilarating pleasure wrapped his skin. His release came fast, snuck up on him like fingers massaging his backside. The pleasure thumping at his groin rocketed through him, and the tautness invading his muscles slithered from his limbs.

He buried his cum inside her.

Raven nestled her head in the pit of Jude's arm. In a bed. Finally. She traced her toe along the front of his calf. His nipples stood proudly. He must be as sated as she felt. She couldn't resist and pecked the tiny bumps of his areola. His smell was marked with the scent of her pussy and the soap she'd used to wash him earlier.

Although her body cried for nicotine, she refused to leave the sheets. Too warm. Too cozy. His skin was as comforting as the cotton sheets they lay in.

She still giggled to herself that they were away for a weekend together.

"What?" Jude's voice was sleepy.

"Nothing." She scratched lightly at his flat stomach. "Tired?"

"Mmm . . . a little. What time is it?"

Raven turned her head to the clock on the nightstand. "Quarter to nine. But we're an hour ahead. Long day?"

"It's always a long day when I have to get the kids ready for their weekend away." Jude covered his mouth and yawned. "I said we'd go for dinner . . ."

"We can always order in if you're tired." It'd be nice to lounge around the room, eating and talking.

"Room service sounds excellent. They got great food here. I'm famished and could go for a steak and baked potato."

"I'll order. Let me vape first." Raven slithered out from beneath the sheets. She padded to the dresser to retrieve her leggings and a t-shirt.

A wolf whistle came from the bed.

"Like what you see?" She bent over and opened the drawer, making sure to wiggle her ass.

"Do I ever." In the mirror, Jude propped up on his elbow, grinning.

Raven grabbed the clothing and turned. "I guess I know what we're doing after we eat."

"I'm all for it." His finger made designs on top of the comforter. "Let's get dessert, too."

"Sure." Raven donned the leggings and t-shirt. "Have a quick nap. I'll wake you when the food arrives."

"Thanks, sexy." He laid his head on the pillow.

"How do you like your steak?"

"Medium rare."

Yikes. She was all about well done. "Okay."

Raven slipped on her parka and mukluks and left the room

through the sliding door. Although the courtyard possessed benches, small bare trees, and the skeleton frames of flower bushes, there wasn't much comfort with light coming from everywhere. At times the reserve had its benefits being engulfed in darkness, so she could stare up at the twinkling stars. Some nights she even got to enjoy the dancing green lights.

Once she'd satisfied her nicotine craving and called the dining room to place their order, Raven curled up on the chair in the sunken living area. Jude lay on his stomach, arms hugging the pillow.

What do you see in me?

Something resembling a bleak gray cloud formed in her chest. Maybe that was why she'd taken an instant dislike to Bridget the first time they'd crossed paths. Ms. Career. Ms. Education. Ms. Tall, Slim, and Beautiful. If Raven stacked herself up against Jude's sister, she'd come out the loser. Not because of her looks. She could give the stunning Bridget a run for her money. It was the fact Raven lacked in the other departments of sophistication, finesse, and style.

A part of her had even been a smidgen jealous when she'd found out Adam was dating the Matawapits' beautiful daughter. Raven had assumed his choice fell in the men who categorized women as the kind a guy fucks and the kind a guy marries. But she'd been wrong. Adam had wanted away from the derogatory lifestyle and people who went with gangbanging.

She'd done the same thing by choosing Jude. Wanting a life far from her previous one.

Raven clacked her nails against her drawn-up knees. At least Adam might welcome her in his house.

Someone knocked on the door. "Room service."

Jude rolled over. He swiped at his eyes.

"Our food's here." Raven padded up the steps and to the door. "Stay covered."

"Charge it to the room, and the tip."

"Okay."

Raven opened the door.

The attendant smiled. "Hello. Your dinner."

"You can leave it here. I'll take care of it. I need the order charged to the room."

The boy held out a bill for Raven to sign. She made sure to add the tip.

Once he left, she wheeled the cart in front of the dresser. "Lots of food."

"I'll say. Looks like we got salad. Bread. Our main entrée. Dessert. A drink for you. I'll get a beer from the mini-bar."

He'd smell like alcohol afterward. Raven's stomach churned. She had to accept his social drinking. A few in the program didn't mind their partners imbibing, but some couldn't, insisting they were too new in their sobriety and didn't want to be around temptation.

"Everything okay?" Jude yanked on his sweatpants.

"Um, what?"

"You lose any more of your beautiful color, you'll turn paler than these sheets." He ambled up to her. The trail of hair below his naval disappeared beneath the waistband of his pants.

"I'm fine." Raven did her best to keep the strain from her voice.

"Oh geez." Jude used the heel of his palm to thump his temple. "You don't drink. You're in recovery. I'll have an orange juice instead."

"No. It's okay. It is." She couldn't tell someone if they could or couldn't drink. It went against the program.

"It's cool. It's not like I need a beer." Jude chuckled.

"Okay." Since she couldn't wheel the cart to the living area, Raven picked up the covered plates and carried them to the table.

Jude reached into the mini-bar and uncapped an orange juice. He swaggered to the small dining table.

Raven uncovered the food and sat. Her stomach growled at the scent of well-done steak. She'd managed some toast at work that morning on her break, which hadn't satisfied her hunger.

Her plate held the steak, a stuffed baked potato, and a side of greens.

She wasn't much of a vegetable eater, but maybe she should try. Growing up poor meant passing on fresh produce and vegetables because they'd cost too much. Food had come from a box or a can since those lasted longer. Or from trapping and hunting. Or the lake when they'd fish to replenish the freezer.

"Looks good." He laid out the napkin on his lap.

"It sure does." Raven cut into her steak.

"You're not eating your salad first?" Jude poured dressing over his.

"I'll pick at it. I'll confess I didn't grow up eating the five food groups."

"A lot don't on the rez." Jude shoveled a helping of tomatoes and lettuce into his mouth. "It costs a lot of money to ship fresh goods up our way. I'm glad Mom keeps a garden. She does a lot of canning in the fall."

"We never had a garden, but we did a lot of berry picking." The meat was tender and heavenly.

"Wild rice, too?"

"You betcha. I could live off the stuff."

"Me, too. I never attended the annual ricing. I'm looking forward to it this fall. The kids have no clue how wild rice is harvested and processed."

A cold lump gathered in Raven's belly. Each extended family worked together to gather the rice. She peeked at Jude who joyfully ate his food. He'd go with his family and she'd go with hers.

"Bridget won't say anything, will she?"

"No." Jude shook his head. "She'll understand why we're . . . being quiet for now."

"For now?" Raven shivered.

"My family isn't going to disown me because I'm seeing you."

"Will they approve?"

Jude sighed and wiped his mouth. "I don't know." He pressed his lips together. "I can't see it. Even Dad, as much as he'd first disapproved of Darryl, wasn't a total jerk about it. I'll admit he wasn't happy. They did have a few . . . words for each other. But they eventually made their peace."

"My family will hate me." Raven pushed at her green beans.

"Kinda thought so." Jude kept eating.

"I mean really hate me. You don't mind us keeping quiet?"

Jude set aside his fork. He glanced up. "I guess we've been treading around this, haven't we?"

Raven nodded.

"There's not much we can do about it now. Elections are coming up. You're your brother's campaign manager."

"It's important to me."

"You want to see your brother get in. Highly understandable."

"And you want your brother-in-law to win."

"Let's stay away from this convo." Jude's shoulders caved downward. "We have the weekend, and I really wanna enjoy it."

"I do, too." Jude was right. They flew out Sunday afternoon. They could do whatever they wanted without having to worry about someone finding out, except for Bridget.

Raven sucked in a breath. She wasn't looking forward to sitting down for dinner tomorrow night.

Jude rolled over. Raven's light breaths dusted his chest. She slept on her side, knees slightly bent, and hands tucked beneath the pillow. He brushed at her hair she'd swept up and over her head. Probably a habit to keep it from tangling.

Waking up beside a woman, not just any woman but Raven, comforted Jude as much as the thick blankets they slept under. With her smooth skin, long lashes, protruding lower lip, and relaxed face, she appeared younger than thirty-one. Heck, she didn't look her age when awake. Twenty-five tops. Bridget was the same way. Maybe it had to do with their skin tone. He'd also been told too many times he didn't look like a man pushing forty.

Raven smacked her lips together. The lashes Jude admired fluttered open. When her eyes focused on his face, her mouth formed into a wide smile. Seemed she enjoyed waking to him as much as he adored waking to her.

"Good morning." They'd fallen asleep cuddling, but during the night they must've sought some sleeping space.

"Morning." Raven slipped her hands from beneath the pillow. She stretched out on her back and extended her arms and legs. "How'd you sleep?"

"Like a baby." The truth. Sleeping hadn't been the greatest ever since his marriage had fallen apart, not after drifting off from the age of twenty-two with his wife beside him every night.

"Me, too." Raven rested on her side, gazing at him. "I always get a good night's sleep. This time it's different. I never slept so good."

"It must be the body heat." Jude snuggled up to Raven's lithe form. Her warmth flooded his flesh. He kept his lips a breath from her forehead. "Coffee?"

"Hmm, sounds awesome."

"Then I'll order up a pot."

"Does smudging bother you?"

"Nope. You go ahead and do your meditations." Her commitment to prayer touched him like a feather sweeping his chest. Too bad he didn't pray anymore. Not going there. He'd rebuilt a new life where the Lord had failed.

He pecked her lips. "I'll get the coffee ordered."

While Raven dressed, Jude called room service. Once their cups of joe arrived, they both settled into their morning routine. She offered tobacco to her creator and then lit the cedar in the bowl and fanned herself off using the eagle feather. Jude settled in with the daily paper he read on his tablet.

Raven let the cedar burn out. She sipped her coffee and picked up the meditation books she'd brought.

Jude's phone dinged. He checked the message list, since he'd called the kids before he and Raven had settled in after dinner last night to watch a pay-per-view movie.

Emery.

This was strange, but Jude called up the message.

Darryl and I had a long talk last night. People do things when they're angry, and what he did isn't different from what any other single guy does when he moves to the city. I had no right judging him for his indiscretion with a . . . person of the night. Thanks for the advice. I hope in time you'll allow me to reciprocate and provide an ear for you.

Jude set the phone aside and stood to have a shower. He'd answer Emery later.

CHAPTER EIGHTEEN: COMMUNICATION BREAKDOWN

With Jude having gone to shower, Raven poured another coffee to finish the last of her meditations. Her cell phone beeped. Hopefully the texter wasn't Clayton. She reached over, fumbling for the phone while still reading the daily reflection.

Her breathing stopped cold at the message.

Darryl and I had a long talk last night. People do things when they're angry, and what he did isn't different from what any other single guy does when he moves to the city. I had no right judging him for his indiscretion with a . . . person of the night. Thanks for the advice. I hope in time you'll allow me to reciprocate and provide an ear for you.

Her mouth fell open, and her pulse points stopped fluttering for a moment. Oh shit. Oh hell. She'd grabbed Jude's phone by mistake. Her own phone remained on the table, a close replica of his expensive model, but hers was cheaper and a deep purple to his shiny black.

She flicked away the phone while pressing herself tight against the back of the chair.

If Clayton found out, he'd tell the whole reserve. He'd even probably tell everyone if they voted for Darryl, he'd use band funds to cruise the north end of Winnipeg looking for suction.

The shower stopped.

Raven jumped from the chair. She scampered for her vape.

Jude emerged from the bathroom, only a towel wrapping his hips. "I guess I'd better dress, hey?" He chuckled, motioning at the open curtains.

"I can close them." Raven twirled on her heel and yanked on the drapes.

"You didn't have to." No disappointment lurked in Jude's voice that she hadn't taken the time to appreciate his gorgeous body. "I'm gonna finish up in here. Then the bathroom's all yours. Did you have a place in mind for breakfast?"

"Anywhere's good." The anxiety running up Raven's backside demanded a shot of nicotine. "I'm going to get in a vape first."

"Gotcha." Jude wandered back into the bathroom.

Raven jerked on her mukluks and parka. She dashed outside, her poor mug handle and e-cigarette almost protesting at her strangling grip.

Jude sat in the chair by the dresser. This vantage point offered him a view of Raven in the bathroom. There was something sexy about a woman dressing. The brushes they used to swipe at their eyelids, cheekbones, and face. The way they shaped their mouths to apply lipstick or mascara. And something new — Raven gluing on false eyelashes, which had been rather interesting.

She took her time, too, letting everything *set* properly, she'd explained. Foundation must set. Concealer must set. Loose powder must set. During these setting times, she'd done something else, such as putting on her eye makeup, or curling her lashes. Interesting. He couldn't recall Charlene's process being this intense.

As alluring as Raven looked glammed up for an evening, waking to her bare face this morning, a bit puffy from sleep, she'd been just as stunning, maybe more so.

It'd been a great day. Not counting the kids, since Jude always loved his children's company, but he couldn't remember when he last had this kind of fun.

They'd eaten breakfast in the hotel coffee shop. Then they'd gone out shopping. Raven had fallen in love with a beautiful calf-length leather coat with a faux-fur-trimmed collar. When she'd set the garment back on the rack, saying even on sale she couldn't afford it, Jude had whipped out his credit card, much to Raven's protesting, and he'd bought the coat. At sixty percent off, the sale was a steal. She deserved something nice to wear, as all women did.

Afterwards, they'd returned to the hotel and spent the rest of the afternoon in bed. Exhausted, they'd napped before waking to dress for the evening.

Raven emerged from the bathroom. She'd left her hair loose. Skinny jeans clung to her slim thighs. Spiked-heeled ankle boots decorated her slim feet. Beneath her transparent teal blouse was a black camisole. The coloring lit her brownish-red skin.

"I must say, you really know how to do yourself up." Jude stood. The outfit was sexy, in a bad-girl sexy way, his new favorite kind of sexy after meeting this woman.

"I can't believe you sat there and watched." Raven snuggled up to him. "A first for me."

"Oh? Your other boyfriends didn't bother watching?"

"Them? Those—" Raven stammered.

Jude gulped. He'd said *boyfriend*. Not only had his spine frozen, Raven's tilted, narrowed eyes had popped to ovals. Red flecked her face, and she sheepishly smiled.

"Um . . ." She wet her burgundy-painted lips.

"Should we . . . ah . . . go?" Whatever Jude was trying to swallow wouldn't go down.

"Sure. We should." Raven motioned at her new coat.

He grabbed the leather jacket slung over the chair. "Here.

Lemme help you."

"Thanks." She slipped her arms into the sleeves. "You didn't have to buy this."

"I wanted to." Jude stepped back. Classy. She could pass for a mysterious spy meant to seduce the enemy. Call her Mata Hari. "I hope you didn't mind."

"Mind?" Raven grinned. "How could I mind? It's . . ." She ran her nails along the front of the coat. "It's beautiful."

"Then it was the right thing to do." He stole a quick kiss. "You ready?"

"As ready as I'll ever be."

"We should go. I asked the front desk to get us a cab for quarter after seven."

"You're okay with taking a taxi then?"

"Yep." Jude understood. Adam was cooking dinner, so Bridget would've picked them up, and Raven needed time to prepare herself to meet his sister.

As they left the room, he sent up a silent prayer the two women wouldn't get into a hot debate over dinner. He'd already texted Bridget and given her fair warning—he was bringing Raven Kabatay who'd accompanied him to the city, and yes, Emery knew about her, and no, he wouldn't discuss anything further on his weekend getaway.

The cab pulled over a good two feet from the snowbank.

Raven glanced around at the quiet neighborhood in Fort William. Rows of bungalows. A typical middle-class place. Snow covered what appeared to be flowerbeds in front of the house. She got out to a light wind.

The porch door opened. Adam's muscular, tall form almost smothered the front steps. He wore his ever-present cowboy hat. "Hey," he called out in a voice deep enough to shake the snow off the roof.

"Hey, yourself." Seeing a welcome blast from the past whom the Matawapit family now embraced, Raven flung aside her earlier anxiety. Although Adam and Bridget made trips to the reserve, usually on weekends, Raven hadn't seen him at any of the recovery meetings because none happened on Saturday nights.

His big smile lit a candle of hope in Raven's chest. If he could build a wonderful new life for himself, so could she. He'd been a worse mess than her. In and out of jail, two stints in prison, and a hardcore lush with a penchant for cocaine.

Whenever she'd seen Adam in their old stomping grounds, he'd been giving some poor guy a beatdown. But his flashing black eyes, mellow grin, and massive hands half in and half out of his jean pockets reminded her of a laid-back pile of pillows.

"How you been?" She ascended the steps.

Adam held open the porch door. "Doing good. Getting in my vape."

"This is where you vape?" Raven glanced around at the wicker table with a glass top and four matching chairs. "This is nice."

"Yup. Comfy. Good place for you to have a smoke."

"I quit."

"Did you? How you doing?"

"I have my moments." And chatty. The Adam of the past hadn't done anything but grunt and nod. "What about you?"

"We'll see how I do. Only been a couple of months."

Raven chuckled. "You don't seem too positive about it."

"I'm an old dog, and you know what they say 'bout that. A man can only change so much." He puffed on the vape.

Jude strode up the walkway. "Good to see you. What's on the menu?"

"Slow-cooked baby back ribs. My own recipe. You're gonna pop a button for sure." Adam's booming laugh threatened to crumble the porch.

"I shoulda worn my sweatpants?" Jude bared his perfect white teeth.

"Bridget's inside. Kyle's bunking at a friend's tonight. C'mon in."

"A new friend? He's not still missing Noah, is he?" Jude headed inside.

Raven entered to the scent of barbecue and a dash of honey simmering somewhere in the kitchen. Designer furniture complemented the rich light color of the walls. Not a big room, but a proper size for the family to enjoy a night of TV.

"Oh, yeah. What about Noah? Those two are always on that webcam thing or whatever it's called." Adam shut the door.

"He still misses his BFF." Jude removed his coat. "Let me get yours, Raven."

"Sure." Raven's chest lightened as Jude helped her remove the new coat.

"I'll take those. Toss 'em in the closet," Adam said.

Jude handed over the coats. "C'mon." He motioned at Raven.

He led her into the kitchen, where Bridget stood setting a basket of bread on the table in the eating area in front of sliding doors that Raven assumed led to a deck.

Bridget smiled, but her dark eyes failed to sparkle. Her long hair was braided. Like Raven, Bridget was casually dressed, but in maternity wear accentuating her slim hips and long legs. A thick sweater swathed her baby bump. Although Bridget's coloring matched Jude's, her features weren't as bold. She'd inherited her mother's willowy height, delicate features, and sleek bone structure.

"You two already met, but I'll reintroduce you. Raven, my sister Bridget. Bridget, this is my . . . Raven." Jude's face reddened.

Heat saturated Raven's cheekbones.

The forced smile Bridget had pasted on faded. "Your Raven?" She folded her arms. The stare she sent Jude could have frozen the tundra.

"My guest for this weekend." Jude narrowed his brows at his sister.

"Hello." Raven forced out the greeting. She wasn't giving an inch if the haughty Bridget wouldn't.

Bridget patted a cushioned chair. "You might as well sit. I was going to get zee wine." She twitched her nose affectionally at Jude.

Was this bitch kidding? Everyone on the reserve knew Raven didn't drink, and Adam sure didn't either. Bridget sure couldn't at about five months pregnant.

Jude snickered. "Zee wine."

"Family joke. It's alcohol-free. A sparkling cider." Bridget's words were cold. She strode to the slate-colored fridge that matched the gas range, range hood, microwave, and dishwasher. The kitchen resembled a cozy cabin with off-white cupboards and matching counters. There was even a buffet and hutch against the wall separating the living room from the kitchen.

Raven stiffly moved to the table.

Jude pulled out her chair. His gentle gesture stroked her heart. Yes, heart. His sister was being an unwelcoming bitch, and he was making sure to keep Raven comfortable.

Adam lumbered into the kitchen. "Everything should be done. Got the ribs simmering. Grilled potatoes and asparagus warming. Salad chilling."

"What kind of salad?" Jude sat adjacent to Raven, much to her relief.

Wait, she didn't need anyone to fight her fights. If the conversation got a bit heated, she'd take care of herself.

"Lemon quinoa with pistachios and sun-dried tomatoes."

Adam plodded to the oven. "Roasted the asparagus with Dijon Vinaigrette dressing. You're gonna love it."

Raven's stomach sang in approval. The scents in the kitchen washed away the annoyance sitting beneath her skin. Adam didn't mind her here. Jude wanted her here. That was good enough for her. Screw Bridget.

While they ate, Jude slipped into host mode, something he'd done on too many occasions during his own dinner parties or special gatherings held by the school board. He kept everyone's glasses filled, never stopped raving about the food, fired too many questions at Adam about his job managing the kitchen at Benny's. Anything to make sure Bridget didn't stir the pot and say something to offend Raven.

Adam followed suit, answering all the questions in his low voice, unaware he was in the game.

"That was really good." Raven wiped her mouth, having eaten the last bite of the strawberry cheesecake.

"Want some coffee?" Adam shoved back his chair and stood.

At times, it was hard for Jude to believe his brother-in-law was on parole and had spent most of his life gangbanging.

"Sounds good." Jude gazed at Raven. "Want some?"

"Sure."

Jude kept his eye on Adam moving about the kitchen while trying to sneak glances at Bridget, who'd added perfunctorily tidbits to the dinner conversation, which was unlike his talkative sister.

Adam set two coffee carafes on the table. He glanced at Bridget, sort of sighed, and then looked at Jude. "Wanna join me outside for a vape?"

Suspicion crawled along Jude's spine. "Sure."

"We can have our coffees on the porch." Adam filled the

three cups and then used the other carafe to fill Bridget's mug.

Jude stole a peek at Raven. Her shoulders remained relaxed, although she was staring at her coffee mug. He shot Bridget a warning stink-eye, grabbed his mug, and followed Adam outside to the porch.

"What's going on? I know my sister. She made you ask me to join you outside, didn't she?"

Adam snickered. "Y'know what she's like. She's the boss." He sat in the wicker chair.

Too true. Big deal Adam stood around six-five and was a wall of solid muscle. No man told Bridget what to do. Jude sat. He hugged his jacket around himself. "What's up?"

"She wanted me to give you the lowdown on Raven, nothing more." Adam shrugged. "Problem is, the Raven I knew was a hardcore addict. She's in recovery. The program changes people. Changed me, didn't it?"

Very true. Jude's brother-in-law had gone from Adam two-point-zero to Adam three-point-five. "And who's the Raven you knew?"

"I don't gotta draw you a picture. If Raven's working her program, she was probably honest with you. It's what I tried to tell Bridget."

"She was very honest." Jude sipped his coffee. The chill nipped at his exposed skin, so he kept his hands wrapped around the mug. "She told me she used guys for drugs."

"Yep."

"She told me she left school at sixteen because she was tired of the rez."

"That I don't know." Adam again shrugged. "Nobody on the streets talk about their pasts, if you get my drift. Sully was a good buddy of mine. I saw Raven around lots."

"You can tell my sister, after we leave, that Raven was open about her past." Jude should return inside to put out the fire Bridget was determined to start.

Raven had listened to Bridget speak about her job, and in turn she talked about waitressing at *Kiss the Cook* and working on her high school diploma. The conversation had lasted under ten minutes. Silence permeated the kitchen, mixing with the scent of the leftover food.

Bridget poured them another refill.

"The men are probably getting cold." Raven fixed her coffee.

"I doubt it. Adam sits out there quite a bit."

Enough of dancing around the subject. Bridget didn't strike Raven as diplomatic like Emery was. Try a firing squad.

"You sent them outside for a reason. Want to tell me why?" Raven kept her tone even. Though Jude's family loathed Raven's family, she wouldn't apologize about the protest or going after the church.

"Do you want to tell me why?" Bridget's voice was as even as Raven's.

"Why what?"

"Why Jude?"

Raven shrugged. "We enjoy each other's company."

"I see." The clicking of Bridget's nails cut into the deafening silence that almost hurt Raven's ears.

"He's turning thirty-nine this year. I think he's old enough to make his own decisions."

Bridget drew in her cheeks. "Yes, he sure is."

A lump of ice was warmer than the air swirling about the dining table. "Then I guess we have nothing else to say." Raven set down the cup. "Thanks for dinner." She stood.

She'd get Jude from the porch. Their weekend was short, and she refused to waste any more time at a place where she wasn't welcome.

She strode through the living room and opened the front

door. "You ready?"

Storm clouds formed in Jude's eyes. "What's going on?"

"Nothing." Raven's shoulders moved up and down. "I'm ready to leave. I don't have anything else to say to your sister."

"What'd she say?" Jude stood.

"Nothing."

"Nothing?"

"Nothing." Raven pointed at the door. "Can you get my coat?"

"Yes." Jude stomped inside and slammed the door shut.

Adam puffed on his vape. "Might as well join me. I think they'll be awhile. Got your vape?"

"It's in my purse."

"I'll go get it." Adam rose and headed inside.

Raven wouldn't apologize if she'd started a family feud. She'd done nothing but ask to leave.

Chapter Nineteen: Treat Me Fine, Treat Me Good

Jude stormed into the kitchen to Bridget innocently wearing a halo over her head, sipping decaf coffee.

"Raven wants to leave. Why?"

"If you're asking if we had words, we didn't." Bridget stood. She stacked the plates one on top of the other. "We talked about work. She asked me why I sent you and Adam outside. I asked why she was seeing you. She told me you two enjoy each other's company. And reminded me you're turning thirty-nine this year."

"Yes, thirty-nine, which means mind your own business."

Bridget gripped the plates and flounced to the island. "I see. It's okay for you to butt your nose into my business. Emery's business. Everyone's business with your *know-it-all-listen-up-good* speeches, but it's not okay if it's done to you. Gimme a break."

"Is that what this is about? Because I didn't involve you in my divorce?" Jude tossed the cutlery onto the tray and huffed up behind Bridget at the island.

"Get real." She threw on the tap. Water blasted from the faucet. "This is about what she did to me." Bridget thrust her finger at her chest. "She was rude. So freakin' rude. Her family protested outside a workshop we were hosting to help people in great need of healing. They called me a half-breed and other insulting names."

They did what? Jude sputtered. "She didn't tell me that."

"No? I guess she wouldn't, since it's evident what she's after. Your money." Bridget tossed the dishes into the sink. She snatched the brush and scrubbed at a plate.

"My money?" Never had anyone insulted Jude this way. He ought to point out Bridget had bought the fancy four-by-four truck parked in the garage and how she'd sold her plush condo to buy the bungalow. He could hit below the belt, too.

"I see. No other woman can like me except for my cheating ex-wife. Raven only sees dollar signs when she looks my way. Only my family thinks I'm worth being around, hey?"

Bridget set aside the brush. Her brows drooped. "I'm sorry. I wasn't trying to insult you. I can think of a dozen women who'd give anything if you'd take them on a date."

"Then why not believe Raven's one of those women?" Jude canceled the hotness in his tone. His little sister was concerned, especially if Raven had insulted Bridget. "Okay, she wasn't nice the first time you met. Maybe you two can talk about it tonight before we leave?"

A big loud throat clearing and the front door slamming carried into the kitchen. "Yeah," Adam, who never raised his voice, said in a pitch higher than his usual low timbre, "so this is the living room. Then we got three bedrooms and a bathroom down this way."

It was obvious the two had gotten cold outside, it being the end of February.

"Let's have more coffee and sit down like adults." Jude flashed his *work-with-me* grin.

Bridget's lips formed into a smile, and the sparkle returned to her eyes. She switched off the tap. "Okay. For you. It's pretty obvious you're smitten. And I know you don't fall for any—Never mind." She held up her hand. "I won't go there, or I'll be insulting your ex-wife next."

"Enough insulting other women. Let's have some coffee. Or should I say decaf for the baby mama." Jude patted

Bridget's belly and then steered her to the table.

"Speaking of other women, I know of a lovely professor at the university who was very disappointed about your move. She was giving you time to . . . heal."

"I'm not gonna ask who she is." Jude snickered. He pulled out a chair.

"I'll go get them." Bridget left the kitchen.

About five minutes later, everyone reappeared. Much to Jude's relief, hostility didn't flash in Raven's eyes. Adam looked resigned to putting up with more talking. Bridget scooted to the fridge.

"I have more sparkling cider. What's your poison?"

Geez, Bridget must've used her most welcoming and cheerful voice to get Raven to consider staying. There was hope.

"Coffee." Raven sat. "It's a recovery thing. We all drink coffee."

"Yep. Bridget threatened to buy a share in *Reggie's Donuts,* I drink so much of the stuff." Adam also sat.

Everyone chuckled. Now this was how Jude had wanted the dinner to play out.

"Sparkling cider for me." Jude shoved his wine glass forward.

"I told Raven we got off on the wrong foot." Bridget filled Jude's glass. "I said we should reboot the laptop and try again."

"I can understand. Our first meeting . . . I wasn't the most welcoming person." Raven fixed her coffee. She wet her lips. "Jude and I made a promise to stay away from . . . politics while we're together. I think we should do that here as well."

"We faced the same problem with Darryl." Bridget sat. "He and Emery worked out their differences."

Raven gripped her mug. "I don't think it's something I can speak about yet."

"Maybe it'll help if we simply enjoy our after-dinner drinks and one another's company? Getting to know one another is the best way to see someone else's point of view." Jude cringed. "Oh man, I sound like Emery."

"Well, we share the same DNA." Bridget snickered.

Raven also snickered.

Sure, the elephant in the room remained, but Emery's logic made sense. Taking the time to know the person behind the enemy line out of battle uniform was the best step to ending a battle.

Raven snuggled into her new coat while inhaling the tobacco-flavored e-liquid. They'd finished playing the last round of cards. Adam would drive them back to the hotel. The truck was pulled out and waiting on the street, engine running to warm up the interior.

First she'd let down her guard for Jude, and now Bridget. If Raven had spent the evening with Emery and Darryl, they would have produced the same result. Content. Pleased.

But the Matawapits were supposed to be the enemy. Raven hung her head. They weren't. Simply people who loved, laughed, cried, and hurt like anyone else on the Great Mother. Hadn't she seen for herself the people behind the bottle, needle, and pipe in the recovery meetings?

"They say it's hard to kill your enemy once you look him in the eye as a flesh-and-blood man." Adam puffed on his vape. "If we sat the 'Nish gangs down like we did tonight, we wouldn't have been beating and killing each other out on the streets for almost two decades."

Raven's stomach tightened. The delicious meal she'd eaten three hours ago sat kind of funny in her tummy. "They bought into what the government wanted. They're Catholics."

"So?" Adam shrugged. "Just 'cause Bridget goes to church doesn't mean I have to give up my beliefs."

"Does Kyle go to church?" Who was Raven kidding? Of course the boy did.

"Yep." Adam puffed on the vape. "He also smudges with me every morning. Take him to powwows. He's learning his language in school."

"Bridget doesn't mind?"

"Hell no. She sits on the Indigenous Women's Alliance board. Y'know she's involved in native issues."

"Jude isn't. He's a hardcore . . ." The awful *apple* word almost fell out of Raven's mouth. "Catholic."

"Our program's about acceptance. He is who he is. You got a sponsor?"

Raven shook her head. "She moved here. Dialysis. We text now and then when I'm stuck."

"When'd she move?"

"About eight months ago. I really miss her. She's the only woman who likes me."

"You'd better get another one. It's not good to go too long without a sponsor."

Raven should, but there wasn't anyone available. The other two women who had long-term sobriety were busy sponsoring the new girls. "It's tight up there, y'know? We have a small membership. The three older women who do come to meetings are in and out. I have more sobriety time than them."

"Text your old sponsor. There's that webcam thing. Doesn't that one social media thing have a way to connect face to face? Kyle uses it with Noah."

"She's sixty-eight and can barely work her cell phone." Raven's chin hit her chest.

"Then we'll talk. I know it's not as good as having a woman to talk to, but I'm here."

"Yeah, we can do that." She flipped her head back up. "Who would've thought we'd spend a Saturday night playing cards and drinking coffee? And the weird thing is, I'd choose tonight over any other night when I'd been wasted in the bar."

Adam's booming laugh echoed through the porch. "Me, too." His laughter faded, and his hard features grew serious. Funny how he'd never lost the coldness in his eyes or the rock-solid cement to his jawline. He was still every inch the ex-con from the streets.

"You're your own person. You gotta do what's best for you—even if you think the people you care about might be wrong."

Raven swallowed. But they were her family. All she had. What if it came down to choosing her brother, sisters, and mother, even the beloved dream of her own diner over Jude? And what did Jude have to offer? They were merely dating.

Bridget handed Jude his coat.

"Thanks. Thanks for understanding." He slipped on the thigh-length black leather commuter coat.

She leaned against the doorway. Concern filled her dark eyes.

"I know. I know." Jude focused his attention on the northern style Indigenous painting hanging on the living room wall. "It'll hurt Mom and Dad. You don't think I thought about this? Raven's family put them through hell."

"What do you two got going exactly?" Bridget searched his face.

Good question. "I don't know," he whispered. He buttoned the coat. "They probably had their vape by now and are waiting in the truck for me."

He turned and opened the door.

"Jude . . ."

"Yeah?" He stared straight ahead.

"Please be careful," Bridget whispered. "After what Charlene did, I don't wanna see you get hurt again."

"I won't get hurt." Or was he fooling himself?

"I know she's more than your . . . weekend guest. I saw it . . . the way you two looked at each other while we played cards." Worry dusted Bridget's words.

Jude sucked in his breath. "I gotta go. G'night. I'll phone you next week."

"Please, do. We need time to talk."

What was there to talk about? Jude didn't have answers for the questions rolling around in his sister's head.

They held hands while walking down the hall to their room. Never had anything felt so right to Raven. Jude's touch. The warmth of his hand. It was as if they belonged together.

Jude stopped in front of their room door.

Raven's heart squeezed slightly shut. They had tonight. Come tomorrow, after shopping, they'd be back on their way to Ottertail Lake. Back to hiding.

"Did you have a good time tonight?" Jude held open the door.

Raven scooted inside. If only they could stay here. "Yeah. A really nice time."

"Even your laugh is sexy." Jude slid his arms around her waist. He nuzzled the back of Raven's neck.

She cupped his hands, stroking his smooth fingers while he kissed the spot behind her ear.

"How about we get washed up and go to bed?" His voice was hot on her ear.

His suggestive words danced between Raven's pussy lips.

She turned and faced him. This was their last time together sharing a real bed. She snuggled against his chest.

"Thank you for the coat."

"You're welcome." He pecked the top of her head.

He worked the buttons free and slid the coat from her shoulders. His mouth came down on hers. Her heart jangled. Each button she unsnapped from his shirt allowed a speck of warmth to escape. She eased her hands inside his shirt and slid her palms over Jude's hard pecs. His chest drew up and down beneath the tips of her fingers.

She molded her crotch with his to meet his thick erection. He gasped in her mouth and continued to lick and taste her tongue. She flicked the button open to his pants and lowered the zipper. His cock edged out from his underwear. Pre-cum seeped from the slit. She fingered the delicious wetness on the head of his prick.

Knowing that he wanted her and had done everything to make sure his sister approved of her lit a warm fire in Raven's heart.

She yanked on his pants while urging him to walk with her to the bed. They stumbled along the way. The back of Raven's knees hit the edge of the mattress, and they collapsed on the comforter. His chest heaved on hers, his tongue still rolling and flicking around in her mouth, offering Raven a taste of his minty essence. They bumped and ground their hips together. She clasped his buttocks, caressing his firm ass.

Jude groaned and worked at his open shirt. Once he tossed aside the garment, he pushed up her camisole. Raven's heart held tight as he unclasped the front opening of her bra. His mouth left hers and claimed her breast. The heat of his breath feathered her nipple. He suckled and licked at the tip. Tingles juddered along Raven's spine, and she arched her back while he tasted her breast.

The breath burst from her lungs. She gasped, cupping the back of his head.

His tongue licked at her skin, leaving a trail of saliva. He pecked her stomach, and she kept running her hands through his short, coarse hair. His lips left a stream of suckling kisses to her naval. He worked at her jeans, lowering the zipper and unfastening the button. His teeth nipped at the skin just above her skimpy panty line. She lifted her hips so he could ease down her jeans.

He tugged a few times. She silently cursed the tight material.

Jude snickered. "Easy, sweetheart. We'll get them off."

"I can't get them off fast enough." She kicked off her ankle boots.

"Ooh, such a horny woman."

"Horny is an understatement." Her pants and socks were whisked away by Jude.

His palms settled on her inner thighs. The richness of his skin teased Raven's insides, and she jerked beneath his touch.

He spread her legs and settled his mouth at the mound of her landing strip. Anticipation stole her breathing. His wet tongue licked her slit, and she shivered from the silky sensations erupting beneath her skin. He'd never eaten her cunt yet, and Jude was too close. When he kissed her pussy lips, she groaned from the sweetness his lips produced inside her. Each peck he lavished on her slit draped her in hot velvet.

His light kisses were too teasing, too tickling. She spread her legs wider, burning for him to feast on her pussy. It'd been too long since she'd been eaten.

She slid her nails into his hair, pushing at the back of his head, urging him to delve between her slit. He must've sensed her need because his tongue parted her lips and lapped at the fold of skin guarding her clit. The sizzling sensations his hungry mouth coaxed from her cunt left her gasping. Her nerves crackled, dancing with delight.

She draped her legs around his neck, trapping him with her thighs. Her hips grinded, forcing her pussy deep against his tongue as she rubbed her flavor all over his mouth. He moaned, and his groan buried itself deep in her stomach. He was enjoying her response. He wanted her to lose control to his nibbles and licks.

"Jude. Jude." His name came deep from Raven's throat, deeper than her normal tone, but his daring feast was maddening. He'd awoken her nerves. Coaxed to life electrifying sensations hissing under her skin.

An ache surfaced, a frantic need to claim him with her clit. She worked her hips in a deep circle, slathering her wet mess all over the skin around his mouth. He lapped faster, fierce licks while burying his tongue between her cunt lips.

She slapped her hand over her mouth before the scream hurled from her throat. The maddening pleasure was trolling up her spine and caressing her spread thighs. The ecstatic sensations swirled from inside, and a heady burst of pleasure claimed her.

She fucked his face, gasping and moaning while the electrical bliss draped her in silk. Her breathing skipped. Tiny pulsations continued to flutter around her clit.

"Jude . . ."

He was on top of her, pants yanked half down, melting his bare chest against her breasts. His cock slid inside her cunt, and she held tight as he fucked her hard and fast, his gorgeous ass rising and falling.

CHAPTER TWENTY: COME ON OVER

R aven entered to the scent of sweetgrass filling the house. She shut the back door.

"Is that you?" Mom called out.

Stomach curling, Raven clutched her laptop case, duffel bag, and shopping bags. It was time to cough up a few lies.

"Hey." She poked her head around the wall where the bathroom was located and into the small eat-in kitchen.

Mom sat in the living room in her favorite recliner, sewing a small piece of moose hide, probably for mittens or moccasins. "Did you drink? Use?"

"Um, no."

"Don't lie to me. You never wanted to go to the city. Why now? Especially during a busy time. Your brother was nominated on Monday, and you take off."

"I went to get away . . . from this." Raven stomped to her bedroom that was off the living room.

"Look at me." Mom heaved her skinny body from the recliner.

Raven glared. "What?"

Hand on her stomach, Mom shuffled over, peering. "Okay. You're fine. It's only been a couple of years. And a lotta them never make it on the first try. Addicts are liars."

A fire erupted in Raven's chest. "Happy?"

Mom nodded. She turned back to the recliner. "You're late. Why?"

"I can't control the flight." Raven headed into her room and shut the door.

There wasn't a chance she'd be able to get the hell out of here. Yes, single parents and families came first for housing, but didn't a person trying to get their lives back in order count, too?

The back door opened and slammed shut.

"She get home yet?" Clayton asked.

Raven rubbed her arms. Jude was probably settling in to a wonderful night with his kids after a weekend away — while she was stuck in the house of horror.

A knock on the door.

"Yes?"

"It's me. Come have some tea."

"Be right there." Raven tossed her duffel bag on the bed. She scooped up her phone and headed into the kitchen.

Clayton yanked out a chair at the table.

Mom set the kettle on the stove.

"Did you buy anything then?" The studying stare in Clayton's beady eyes was as scrutinizing as a coyote probing a rabbit.

"Buy what?"

"You said you were going to the city to buy stuff for the campaign." Annoyance crept into Clayton's words.

Mom dashed from the stove and got in Raven's face, peering at her eyes.

"I wasn't using." Suffocation tightened around Raven, and she pushed away. "I wanted some time alone. Okay?"

"Why?" Hands on hips, Mom leaned in again, eyeballs almost popping from their sockets from her microscopic stare.

"Because I'm thirty-one and I need space. Can't I get away for some *me* time?"

"Me time?" Mom huffed and clenched her fists. "You spent how many years in Winnipeg enjoying your *me time* while your brother and sisters did what they're supposed to do. Looking after this reserve and keeping our culture alive. It's always about you. You. You. You. When are you gonna start thinking about others instead of what you want?"

"What?" Raven couldn't believe this woman. "I help lots of people. You just don't see it."

"And who do you help? It's your brother who helps. He helps everyone as a band councilor."

"You all get paid when you help." The words burst from Raven's mouth.

"Paid?" Mom wrapped the table. "That is the old way. You received something if you gave your time. Elders received blankets and food for their advice. Medicine men were brought gifts as payment."

"And the most revered of the band were those who gave away what they had. The more they gave, the more they were honored for their generosity. The chief was the poorest in the community because he cared for those in need. Everyone went to him for help if they had nowhere to go." Hot anger pounded in Raven's throat.

"And daughters listened to their mothers." Clayton's tone was the same one when he used to admonish Raven as a child. "Show some respect."

"I'm trying to . . ." For cripe sake, they never wanted to hear what she had to say. All they gave a shit about was telling her what to do, and what not to do. "But you're making this hard for me. All everyone does is belittle me."

"You brought this on yourself when you shamed us by becoming the cliché drunken loose Indian." Mom scowled.

Pain closed in around Raven's heart. The knife cut deep into her belly. She turned and fled to the bedroom to grab her parka and mukluks.

Raven had spent the last hour out in the cold, walking the roads and puffing on the vape. She'd made the ten-minute walk to downtown. Three houses away was Jude's place. Not even the lovely scent of burning wood coming from the chimneys of the many houses could produce a glimmer in her gray chest.

She typed in the message on her phone.

What's up?

Working. Finally got the kids in bed. What about you?

She furiously typed back . . .

I had a fight with my family.

I'm sorry to hear that. What happened?

Same bullshit.

Her phone rang. She checked the caller. It was Jude. He did care. She was more than a weekend guest. Hands shaking, she pressed the button. Jude's face appeared on the screen.

"What's going on?" Concern filled his gaze and voice.

"Like I said, the same bullshit that's been going on since I was born."

"Are you outside?" He looked to be trying to peer behind her.

"Yes."

Jude frowned. "Why don't you come over? I don't want you standing out in the cold."

"I'm used to the cold." At least the icy air had chilled Raven's hot anger.

"Yeah, everyone is, but you walked from Old Main. How long have you been outside?"

"About an hour."

Jude kept frowning. "C'mon over. I'll turn off the outside light so nobody sees you. The kids are asleep. I'll make some tea."

"I can't come over. Downtown's busier than the Trans Canada."

"It's also nine o'clock. Come over. Now." He disappeared from the screen.

Raven shoved the cell phone into her pocket and inched down the road. She glanced around. Everyone was still at bingo. She had time to sneak over without anyone seeing. Nobody was peering out their windows, either.

Bursting into a sprint, she darted up Jude's driveway. Thank goodness there were no streetlights like in the towns and cities. She shimmied up the steps just as Jude opened the back door. He put his finger over his lips.

How were they supposed to talk? Most of the reserve houses were built the same. Open kitchen and living room facing the front of the house and the bedrooms at the back.

"C'mon in."

Raven entered to much-needed warmth and the lovely scent of a fire burning in the woodstove. She stood beside the bathroom door.

"We can talk in there." Jude pointed.

"The bathroom?" Raven mouthed. It was the farthest room from the children's bedrooms, since the main bedroom door opened into the kitchen. This was too much like her using days. Everything had occurred in a place meant for showering and other personal stuff.

She didn't dare stamp her mukluks. While Jude disappeared around the corner, Raven eased into the tidy room no different than the one she used at home.

Jude reentered and closed the door behind him. They were squished. Bathrooms weren't that big in band-owned homes. Only enough to hold the tub, a toilet, and a vanity wide enough to fit the sink.

He held out the mug and leaned against the towels folded

over the rack. Raven squashed against the vanity. She wouldn't sit on the toilet, although it'd give her more room.

"What's up?" He sipped his tea.

This was stupid. She'd made a big deal out of nothing. "I feel like I overreacted now."

"What's going on?" He raised his hand and stroked her chin.

This man could do anything to melt her into a pile of goo. Even a simple reassuring brushing of his finger uncoiled the knots that had frozen her shoulders after the latest family feud.

"The same bullshit." Why couldn't she come out and say it? The recovery program had taught her to speak about her feelings. A person was only as sick as their secrets, she'd heard too many times.

"Out with it." Jude's order was a silken whisper sliding along Raven's ear.

His comforting gaze caressed her cheekbones, coaxing her to trust him. "I just want their respect. I know I screwed up bad —"

"Who's respect?" Jude asked in a soothing tone.

"Mom's. Clayton's. My sisters'." Raven shrugged.

"And why's their respect important?"

"They've never given me any." The walls were bare. Nothing hung yet. Not even *the sprinkle if you tinkle* sign.

"Look at me." His order was a gentle prodding.

Raven returned her gaze to his dark eyes full of compassion. "I feel stupid talking about this. Like some whiny kid."

"There's nothing wrong with what you're feeling. Who doesn't want their family's respect?"

"I've always been the fuck-up," she whispered. "Bringing home bad grades. Barely passing before I dropped out of school. Getting into trouble. Maybe I came along too late? Maybe after raising four kids on her own, another baby was too much for Mom? I dunno."

"Emery was a bonus baby. That didn't stop Mom from raising him properly."

Raven bristled. "Your mom wasn't a single mother."

"No, she wasn't, and she stayed home, but a mother's a mother. Get it?"

True. Just because a woman worked full-time didn't give her an excuse to be short-tempered with a child. Raven hadn't asked to be born. Maybe Mom should take some responsibility.

"Is that why you started using drugs?"

"I was sick of . . . sick of being at home. Sick of Mom always bitching me out. Nothing I did pleased her. Ever. It's like she hated me from the moment she conceived me. She probably spit on me after she gave birth to me." A scowl burned in Raven's chest.

Jude's eyes widened. "Hey, I wouldn't go that far—"

"I'm not kidding. Really, I'm not. And I wanted out. Y'know? I wanted to be like any other girl I saw on TV. Winnipeg was fun—for a time. Lots of guys. Lots of partying. The first five years there I had a blast. Then I started hanging around the Winnipeg Warriors . . ."

"Is that when you got into the heavy stuff?"

Holding his stare wasn't easy. Raven's brain screamed to lower her gaze to the floor, but she kept her chin lifted. "Yeah, they introduced me to every drug you can think of. When I met heroin, I couldn't believe the feeling it gave me." She bit down on her lip. "I know I screwed up. I know I spent too much time feeling sorry for myself. I've been in the program for two and a half years. I've heard it all from the older members.

"I'm making myself the center of the universe again. Poor Raven. Her family doesn't believe in her. Her family treats her like a fuck-up. Center of self leads to relapses. And lately that's what I've been doing. Worrying about how my family treats me. Trying to suck respect from a stone."

"You said a stone. So you don't think it's possible to gain their respect?" Concern continued to fill Jude's gaze.

"The program teaches us to use action instead of words. We're supposed to show them we've changed, because by the time we get sober, the family is sick of us. Sick of our disease. Whatever comes out of our mouths they don't believe because they've heard our lies in the past."

"What do you think should be your priority? What would the program tell you to do?"

"It'd tell me to go to meetings, keep working my steps, leave everything in the hands of my higher power, and help other addicts."

"Then maybe that's what you should do. You can't change how people think. You can't force them to respect you. All you can do is keep doing what you're doing. And what you're doing is a good thing. You're working toward your high school diploma. You're working full-time at *Kiss the Cook*. You're helping other addicts. You're opening the recovery meetings twice a week. Maybe that's what you're meant to do."

Everything Jude said was right.

"I think you're a winner." Jude set the cup on the vanity. He placed Raven's cup beside his. She was drawn into his arms, swaddled in warmth cozier than a big blanket in front of the woodstove.

His lips brushed her forehead.

"Thanks," she murmured. The thick weight on her chest lightened. Talking had helped. Marty from the program was famous for saying *share your problem and you got half a problem*. "Ever since I met you, you're helping me see different things. You're such a great listener."

"No, *thank you*. I guess I wasn't the greatest listener during my marriage. Maybe you're helping me learn how to really hear someone." He nuzzled her hair.

"Something your ex-wife said?"

"Yep."

"You always listen to me. You're a wonderful listener." He was. Nobody had taken the time to hear her out until Jude. The people in the twelve-step program didn't count, because that was one of their purposes for attending meetings.

She was supposed to start campaigning for Clayton, but did he even deserve to be chief? Before Jude, she wouldn't have questioned her brother leading the community. But if Clayton didn't become chief, she didn't get a diner.

Jude stood at the living room window. He couldn't see Raven's slim silhouette on the road anymore. Not that he hadn't seen her when she'd left his back door and vanished into the night moments ago. But she was out there, somewhere, starting home.

The bedroom door squeaked. "Dad?"

For a second, Jude's breath vanished. He always shut the kids' doors until he went to bed so the TV wouldn't bother them. When he turned in for the night, he opened their doors to allow them to experience the full heat from the woodstove.

He whipped about on his heel. "You're supposed to be asleep."

"I'm not feeling good." Rebekah's voice sounded whiny, like it did whenever she was ill.

"Did you not feel good when you saw Mom?" Jude strode over and pressed the back of his hand against her forehead. She was warm.

"No. I was fine." Rebekah cuddled up to him. Her small head rested against his stomach. "Who was here?"

The blood drained from Jude's veins. "Wh-what?"

"The lady in the bathroom. I went there. You two were talking."

"Oh . . . uh . . ." Jude gulped for air. "Yes, that was a student. She was having homework problems. I didn't want to wake you two, so I asked her if we could speak in the bathroom."

"She sounded sad. Did she feel better when she left?" Rebekah's big blue eyes peered at him—her mother's almond-shaped, striking eyes set off dramatically by reddish-brown Ojibway coloring. She was even petite like Charlene.

"Yes. She felt better. I'll see her Tuesday night at class."

"You're not gonna work late again?" Rebekah's girlish voice was begging. "I missed you."

Jude patted the back of Rebekah's head. Guilt pricked the back of his neck. Yes, he'd thought about the kids while in Thunder Bay, but he'd enjoyed himself immensely. And while he'd been having a great time, his baby girl's heart had cracked from loneliness.

"You were with Mom. Didn't that make you happy?"

Rebekah shrugged. She kept her face buried in Jude's stomach.

"C'mon. You can tell me anything." Jude kept rubbing the back of her head.

"It's not the same."

"What's not the same?"

"Mom. Mr. Baker. I don't think she's happy. She looks sad sometimes. Maybe you can come next time? She was always happy with you." Rebekah peered up at him.

Huh? He'd made his ex-wife so miserable she'd had an affair, actively pursued a man who'd been trying to date Bridget at the time. "Remember what I told you about grown-ups? That we can be sad like you get sad. We can be confused like you can be confused. Mom's going through a lot of changes right now. When you visit her, it makes her happy, because she loves you two."

He brushed at Rebekah's long, glossy black hair. "Mr. Baker's going to be Mom's new husband soon. She's probably a tiny bit scared, like you were scared when I told you we were going to move where Grandma and Grandpa live."

"Is that how it will always be, Dad? Me, you, Noah, Grandma, Grandpa, Uncle Emery, and Uncle Darryl?"

Jude swallowed. What did he want? He clutched Rebekah tightly.

Chapter Twenty-one: When You Gonna Tell the Truth?

The bell above the door tinkled.

Raven glanced up from wiping down the counter, having served two men earlier who'd left ten minutes ago. Clayton swaggered into the diner. Her blood turned to ice. Had he come back to finish spanking her like a ten-year-old?

He plopped on a stool at the counter and turned over the coffee mug in front of him. "Mom was really upset. You gotta start showing her more respect."

Raven snatched the coffee pot from the burner. She filled Clayton's mug. "She was sleeping when I got home."

"Yeah. You hurt her feelings." Clayton pinched a couple of creamers from the small bowl. "She tries, y'know." He dumped the cream into his coffee. "It's not easy raising five kids alone. Even when Dad was alive, all he did was drink up the welfare check."

"Great. I'm supposed to pay because of what happened to her?" Raven set the pot back on the burner.

"No. But start seeing things from her point of view. She told me you do nothing but cause problems."

"What exactly do I do? I cook, clean, and do the laundry."

Laundry wasn't easy, either. They didn't own a drier. Dryers were rare up at a reserve where hydro cost two kidneys and a liver. Even in the winter, everything had to be hung outside to dry. Then brought inside to further dry. Then ironed to remove the stiffness and wrinkles. Clayton knew how enormous the chore was.

"It's your attitude. It's under your skin. And it's crawling out. I see it. Mom sees it. What's going on? It was always there, but not like now. It started over a month ago."

A month ago, she'd met Jude. "I don't know what you're talking about. Look, we need to meet about the campaign."

"Yeah, the campaign. Are you in this or not?" Clayton's narrowed eyes turned to slits. "Or am I gonna have to ask Fawn?"

Everyone's Mrs. Perfect. "I can do this." Raven wasn't giving up the diner. If she had to force people to vote for this loser, she would. With the diner, at least she could possibly sleep here, have something away from the family.

She almost slapped her hand over her mouth. Oh my God, she'd thought of Clayton as a loser. He wasn't a loser. He'd saved her from drugs.

"Okay. Get over to my place tonight. For supper." Clayton shoved away the mug. "I'll see you then."

He turned and swaggered out the door.

Raven reached inside her apron to pay for his coffee.

Emery's text message flashed at the back of her mind—a sure thing to win Clayton the election if she told him about what she'd read.

She wrung her hands, glancing back and forth at the customers. Fuck! She snatched the mug and darted for the kitchen.

When Jude entered the diner, he had to swerve around a few people. This place was a gold mine. At seventy-two, which was the new sixty-two, Cookie was a spry man, so the rumors of his retirement must be false.

Although Jude had come to meet with his brother and brother-in-law, he couldn't resist searching out Raven. She dashed from table to table, setting down plates of food. When she whipped on her heel, her gaze rested on him briefly. A half-smile cracked her lips, and he sent a clandestine grin her way. He then wound through the crowd to where Emery and Darryl sat at a back table.

"Glad you could meet us." Darryl wiped his mouth and set the napkin on his empty plate.

Emery continued to work through the last of his pancakes.

Funny how their eating even matched their personalities. Darryl always tackled his food with gusto, while Emery grazed through one side dish at a time. He'd probably already picked his way through his bacon and eggs.

"Where're your shadows?" Jude turned over a coffee mug.

"Outside, running around somewhere." Emery glanced out the window. "They came down with me in the truck. Darryl took the snowmobile to work."

"You have the schedule?" Darryl glanced at his empty coffee cup. "Be right back." He rose and headed off.

Emery slid another cut piece of pancake into his mouth.

Jude reached into his briefcase and set the spreadsheet on the table. "I thought we should start at the senior center first."

"Bridget texted me."

"Yeah? I can imagine what she said. Pissed because you knew first? Did you tell her you found out by accident?"

"Yes. And she broke my eardrum for not telling her." Emery waved his fork in resignation.

Jude could imagine Bridget's shrieking and hollering. "Now I know how you and Darryl felt."

"It's not fun having your personal life in the spotlight, hey?" About six bites of pancakes were left on Emery's plate. He squirted a dollop of syrup over them.

"Those have gotta be pretty soggy."

"They're fine. Are you getting anything?" Using his fork, Emery pierced another bite.

Darryl returned, carrying the coffee pot. "I think we should consider buying the diner from Cookie," he said under his breath. "If the rumor is true about him retiring." He filled everyone's mugs.

"What?" Jude had enough to juggle without owning a diner. "Where would we get the money? No bank'll loan us a nickel, no matter if we have five-star credit ratings."

Darryl patted Jude's shoulder and leaned in. "I'm talking about the new band council. I think it's something we should promote. Think about what we could do with the profits. We could use the money to fund activities for the youth instead of always relying on government funding."

A rather shrewd and smart idea. Jude glanced at Emery who nodded while chewing on his food.

"Do you want me to use it as part of the campaign?" To make a note to himself, Jude whipped out his cell phone.

"We'd have to speak to Cookie first." Emery wiped his mouth and pushed away his pancakes, leaving three bites left. "Maybe we could arrange a meeting?"

"Let me talk to him. He's manning the grill." Darryl stood.

"Who'd we get to cook?" Jude fixed his coffee. "If Cookie's retiring, he won't hang around to keep flipping burgers."

"Perhaps we could look at expanding to catering events, too?" This came from Emery.

"It'd draw in more business." Darryl swiveled on his heel. "Let me find out if he's free tonight."

Raven used the delivery door at the diner to bring in the supplies shipped to the airport. She grabbed the dolly they kept on hand.

Five minutes ago, when she'd pulled up, Emery and Darryl's truck had been parked out front, which was strange, because the diner closed at ten. Mildred, who worked from two-thirty until closing should have locked up by now.

Something was going on. Raven made sure to keep quiet, not an easy feat while hauling in chicken strips, chicken nuggets, onion rings, and French fries.

She set the stock by one of the deep freezers and then inched toward the delivery window where Cookie set readied food orders.

Although the lights were dimmed, voices came from the main area.

"There's much more we can do, besides what we already proposed. We can support other spiritual endeavors for band members." The soft-spoken voice belonged to Emery. "Like the church. Outreach facilities for the people in—"

"I hear ya. I hear ya." Cookie response was jovial, as usual. "Ya know, I think it's a great idea. But the thing is—and you can't say anything—I already promised to sell to someone else. If this person can come up with the money, it's their diner."

Raven's breath heaved. Stifling her gasp, she slapped her hand over her mouth. From the moment Willie had passed away, her gut instinct had been right. Darryl was hot on the campaign trail, ready to put the entire reserve under his treasonous fist.

"When does this person have to come up with the money?"

If Raven didn't manage to breathe, she'd pass out, but drawing in air was impossible because the deep, authoritative tone asking about the buying deadline was Jude. To think she'd kept her trap shut tonight at Clayton's while going over their campaign strategy.

Knees ready to give out from under her, Raven lurched to the main island where she usually chopped vegetables. She set her hand on the island to steady her balance, but her foot caught something in the dark, which she kicked, and a clatter thundered through the kitchen, loud enough to wake every house in the Downtown area.

"Oh geez, geez, geez," Cookie cried out. "That's probably Raven. She was bringing supplies from the airport after meeting with her brother at his house tonight."

Raven put out one mukluk to race for the back door, but footsteps scampered into the kitchen. The light flew on. She swiveled, gaping at Jude, Emery, and Darryl staring in shock, and Cookie hovering behind them.

Hot coals settled in her stomach. "You want the diner," she spat out and folded her arms, "then you're gonna have to get through me. Cookie said if I came up with the money, it's mine. Only mine."

Jude's mouth fell open. Eyes bulging, Emery gaped at Darryl.

Darryl held Raven's stare. "You're the buyer?" he asked, his voice slow and easy.

Raven thrust her finger. "Damn right. And I see you're going behind my back—"

"We had no idea Cookie planned on selling to you until a few moments ago," Darryl said in the same slow and easy tone.

"Right. Yeah, right." Raven spun on her heel. "And to think I kept my mouth shut tonight because of . . ."

She faced Darryl, again thrusting her finger. "What happened to you, huh? You wanna buy this place to keep funding *his* church?" She pointed at Emery. "All so the band doesn't keep going into deficit? You're supposed to put the *Anishinaabeg* first, not what almost destroyed us."

Scrubbing at his face, Darryl sighed. "Raven, if you'd give me a chance to explain, finally listen to me instead of what your family keeps insisting I'm doing, you'll know—"

"Know what? That you like cruising around for male prostitutes?" Raven stumbled backward. She'd never meant to blurt out what she'd said. The words had simply vaulted from her mouth.

Emery's face turned up red, and his jaw slackened enough to hit the floor. Cookie sputtered. As for Darryl, he drew in his cheeks, eyes narrowed.

"Let me . . . let me handle this." Jude raised his hands, stepping between Darryl and Raven. He gazed at her. Not harshly. Simply somber. "Can we talk?"

There was nothing to speak about. They weren't on the same wavelength, much less the same frequency. She shook her head and stormed for the door before she said more regretful words.

Just as she dashed from the diner's back entrance and reached her brother's truck—the man who'd saved her, the man she'd eaten dinner with tonight, the man she was to help after all he'd done for her—Jude's hot breath invaded Raven's ear.

She clutched the driver's side door handle. The ice-cold metal on her fingers sparked hot flames on her flesh. Wincing, she withdrew her hand and fired her burning fingers straight into the mitten.

"Raven . . ." Jude's palms held her shoulders. "Look at me. Please."

She huddled closer to the vehicle.

"Please . . ."

There was nothing to say. She dug into her pocket and withdrew Clayton's truck key. When she attempted to wrench the door open, Jude swathed her in his strong embrace. She stumbled backward, hitting his chest.

"What do you want?" Her words hissed.

"I want you to talk to me. Please?" His usual low timbre was an octave higher.

To be held in his arms, his voice full of pleading . . . Raven's heart told her head to piss off. She huddled against his chest. Fool. She should run. But with her dream sitting at her feet, the ache in her chest demanded comfort, even if the comforter was the enemy — the one person who always kissed away the bad cuts life inflicted on her.

She nodded.

"I'm freezing." His body trembled, something she hadn't noticed until now. "If I get my coat, will you wait for me?"

Rave again nodded.

"Promise? Promise you won't leave?"

"I . . ." She huffed out the word. "I promise."

They rode in silence. Jude wasn't sure about being inside Clayton's truck, but he'd walked over to the diner for the meeting. Mom had already texted him, asking what was going on. He'd said he had to speak to someone and then he'd be home.

Raven stared straight ahead. She stopped at the church, threw the gear into park, and pointed. "That's what's going to cost me my dream, huh?"

"No, it isn't." Jude turned to face her.

"I heard Emery say — "

"You didn't hear everything. Yes, the church is part of the plan, but not all of it. A biggie is the tight funding for recovery."

"Recovery?" Raven's head jerked. "What do you mean?"

"Darryl mentioned a lot of addicts are coming out of recovery programs but don't have any place to stay to keep working on their recovery. He said a lot return to their same homes, places where people are still practicing . . . err, let's say they're not sober. It makes it hard — "

"That's true. A lot have a hard time sticking to the program when they return."

"I guess John Morrison, the guy in charge of recovery, tried for a sober living home at one point. Four beds. A kitchen.

Living room."

"It's where we hold our meetings. Down in the basement."

"We wanted to use profits from the diner to reopen the up-stairs. The sober house."

When Raven's eyes lit, the knots of tension released from Jude's shoulders.

"I love the idea." She tapped her nails against her lip. "I really do. A lot fail because they don't have the proper sup-ports when they leave treatment."

"That's all we were trying to do—figure out ways to gen-erate money that members of the reserve can benefit from." Jude set his hand on the console between them. "We weren't trying to take away anyone's dream. I wish you would've told me."

"It's . . . something very personal." Raven wet her lips. She stared at the church's silhouette in the headlights. "I'm sure there are personal . . . matters . . . you keep to yourself."

Jude swallowed. He gripped his knee. "Perhaps . . . there are."

"See?" She turned her head, gaze searching his. "Now that you know one of my secrets, what's yours?"

"You ever hear of Job?"

"Job who?"

"From the Bible."

"I never read it. Who is he?"

"A man . . ." His tongue seemed to grow thicker and larger. "A man who was completely faithful to God. Then one day the Devil challenged God. He said anyone can worship the Lord when they're forever blessed by Him. He dared God to take everything away from Job and see if he'd still praise the Lord. In a nutshell, terrible things happened to Job after he spent his life honoring God."

"Your divorce? Leaving your job? Having to live up here?" Raven's questions were slow and precise.

"I-I . . ." Jude's ears burned. Finally seeing through new eyes, he came across as a spoiled child, mad because he didn't get his way, and spiting himself in the process. "I take the kids to church but don't . . . I'm there but not there . . . like I used to be."

"So you're going through the motions."

Jude nodded.

"Maybe . . . maybe we've both been behaving . . . um, a bit selfishly." Raven fingered the keychain dangling from the ignition. "I acted like a little kid when I heard you guys talking. I had no right saying what I did to Darryl. I didn't even mean to. The words jumped from my mouth."

"It's okay. You had a dream. A big dream. And we almost took it from you."

"In the program, I'm supposed to accept what I can't change. And change what I can." Her lower lip quivered. "I can't change where I live, but I can change how I react. I guess I haven't been fully practicing my program."

"Hey, you told me they're giving you a pretty rough time. It's only natural to respond the way you did."

"What about you? Are you finally going to listen in church?"

Her question punched Jude's gut. As a hardcore traditionalist, Raven was concerned about his faith. She wasn't telling him he deserved his misery for following an outdated religion that had no place in today's world, or as Ojibway, he should honor his culture.

"Raven . . ." He inched his hand across the console. This woman truly cared about him.

Her gaze seemed to stroke his face.

Jude's heart banged against his chest. The three words sat on the tip of his tongue. What he felt had happened on its own accord. He'd gone into this simply wanting to date and instead found a wonderful gift. A wonderful treasure during his darkest time given to him by God.

"Raven . . ."

Her long lashes fluttered. "Yes?"

Chapter Twenty-two: If You Want My Love

The look in Jude's eyes, the way his irises sparkled brighter than a full moon glowing luminously in the night sky, the way his lips relaxed, Raven's hand snaked out on its own accord and gripped his fingers.

Yes, she wanted him to keep honoring his god. Yes, she wanted him to be the man she'd assumed was loyal to his religion. Yes, she loved him. Loved him for simply being sweet, kind, caring Jude.

"I . . . I . . . I don't want to scare you off . . ." His other hand cupped her chin.

"Scare me? Why would you scare me?" But his supple statement did. Shivers and tremors shook her bones.

"No, not in that kind of way. I . . . uh . . . I don't want to scare you off."

"Scare me off?"

He massaged her fingers. His gentle touch dispelled the shivers. So did his tender gaze. He brushed his lips along her knuckles, pecking each one.

Her limbs began to melt. She was ready to dissolve into a puddle all over the truck seat. What she'd longed for but had kept telling herself she didn't want or need seeped into his potent stare, was in his gentle caresses, and dangling on his gorgeous mouth.

"I . . . I love you."

A lump formed in Raven's throat. "I love you, too. I love

212

you so much. I . . . I never thought I'd love . . . someone." She strained to move over the console. Dammit, there was always something coming between them.

Jude's lips met hers. Silky. Sweet. The kiss he rained on her was as velvet as the comfort he'd swathed her in. Each suckle, each peck moving along her mouth, each pucker of his lips was gentler than an autumn breeze Raven experienced down at the lake with the water lapping against the rocks.

The breaths from Jude's nostrils coated her lips in sugary warmth. She fingered his cheekbone.

His lashes fluttered.

They were nose to nose. Raven couldn't resist and rubbed the tip. Jude's mouth formed into a wide grin, eyes twinkling.

"I never imagined I'd feel this way about anyone." Her words seemed to stay between their lips that almost brushed. "I wasn't looking, didn't think I needed—"

"Same here," Jude whispered. His palms still grazed her cheeks. His forehead touched hers.

"What about . . . what about your kids?"

"There's a lot we must consider." He traced her cheekbone. "We can talk more tomorrow night. After class. I have to get back to the house. Mom agreed to watch the kids so I could see Cookie."

"Cookie . . ." Raven sighed. She still had to tell Jude about the deal she'd made. "Tomorrow night then."

Jude wasn't surprised when Emery and Darryl showed up at his office at eight in the morning. After last night's disclosure by Raven, both were probably in a panic, wondering what she'd said.

"Hey. Have a seat." Jude motioned at the two chairs in front of his desk.

Darryl's hair was braided off his face to the crown and the

back left loose. The severe style he'd chosen matched the intense expression on his round face.

Emery wilted into the chair. Dark circles sat beneath his green eyes.

"We talked, but not about . . . your adventure in Winnipeg." Jude had had time to think about his feelings and think about if word got out how it might impact the campaign.

"You're meeting her tonight?" Darryl's puzzled expression said he'd had no clue Jude was seeing Raven. Naturally, Emery hadn't disclosed anything to Darryl, because little brother's confidence was that of a priest in a confessional.

Emery cleared his throat. "Maybe you should tell him."

Jude tossed his pen on the desk. "I've been . . . seeing Raven since the first week I moved here."

"Wh-what?" Darryl's eyes bulged at Jude and then he whipped his shocked gaze to Emery. "You knew about this and didn't tell me?"

Squirming in the chair, Emery patted his thick waves of hair. "Uh . . . I . . . I can't say anything to you that's told to me in confidence. You know this. I don't ask about in-camera band council meetings."

Darryl's face reddened. "Is this how she found out?"

"I don't know how she found out. I'll ask her tonight." Jude did his best to keep the exasperation tightening around his shoulders from his voice.

"Tonight." Darryl's words were a nip from a dog. "Tonight." He drummed his fingers on the armrest of the chair.

"Easy . . ." Emery set his hand over Darryl's. "Remember what we talked about last night? Responsibility for our own choices, are own actions, our own behaviors?"

Nodding, the tension around Darryl's mouth vanished. "Yeah." He sank in the chair. "I guess I got nobody to blame but myself. I guess I never thought about a political career when I was . . . being an idiot."

He thrust out his hands, scampering forward in the chair. "I was twenty-four. Everyone does dumb shit when they're young."

"Look, lemme figure out a way to put a spin on this." Jude adjusted his laptop in front of him. "Give me time to think, and I'll present you with something that I'll write up if word gets out."

"If word gets out . . ." Darryl grumbled. "She's a Kabatay. She's Clayton's campaign manager. It'll get out."

"We don't know that yet." Like a stone wall, Jude's defenses rose, ready to protect the woman he loved who faced horrible challenges from her family — horrible enough to chase Raven out into the winter nights instead of seeking warmth and comfort from a place supposedly called home.

Emery again patted his thick waves. "What happened to honesty is the best policy, and leaving everything in your creator's hands?"

Jude nibbled on his pen cap. "You two discussed this already?"

Emery nodded.

"Then what's it gonna be?" Jude readjusted his attention on a scowling Darryl.

"Gimme time to think." Darryl stood. "I gotta get to work. I'll text you later."

After opening the diner, Raven had danced her way through the kitchen, danced while performing her chores, and still danced as she set out fresh creamers and packets of sugar on each table.

Jude loved her. He wanted more than sex from her. More than dates. More than weekends in Thunder Bay. He wanted her to be a part of his life.

The bell tinkled. Raven turned to see Clayton rushing

inside. He crooked his finger, barreling straight for the counter.

She switched off the speaker, silencing Rapsody's *Power*. As she approached the back counter to pour him a coffee, her feet dragged.

"What's up?" Raven turned over his mug with a wrist limper than noon's spaghetti noodle special.

He again curled his finger, indicating for Raven to lean in closer.

She did while filling his mug.

"Did you see or hear anything last night when you delivered the food?"

A horrible ball of shock filled Raven's throat. "Uh . . ."

"Did you see anything?"

"Oh . . . uh . . . see what?"

Clayton's nose pinched. "You didn't see or hear anything?"

"Well . . . I know Cookie was there. He was talking to s-someone in the eating area, but I didn't stick around. I wanted to unload the stuff and take a drive . . . think about our strategy."

"You should've stuck around." Clayton banged his fist on the counter. "You woulda heard more than I did."

"H-heard wh-what?" Raven held her breath.

"Get this." Clayton remained almost nose to nose. "Bryan tipped me off. He texted me last night. He saw Emery and Darryl pulling up at the diner. Then he saw Jude walking over. I borrowed Tanya's car and went to check it out."

Dread coasted along Raven's spine.

"I waited around the corner." Clayton pointed to the side window. "Get this. Darryl was scouting hookers in the 'Peg. He cheated on Emery with one." His grin spread into a devious wide smile.

Raven swallowed the sputter. Her tongue searched for an even tone. "Are you sure?"

"More than sure. Heard it with my own ears. They were heading for their truck. He said, and I quote, *What're we gonna do? If word gets out about the hooker, I'm finished. I never shoulda went near the 'Peg.*"

"I . . . I . . ." She must respond . . . like the old Raven. "I see . . ." She grabbed the batch of napkins.

"This is what I got in mind." Clayton remained hunched over. He used his finger to draw on the counter. "We hold a debate. Invite everyone. During the debate, that's when I confront Darryl about his . . . hehe, indiscretion in Winnipeg. If his own husband can't trust Darryl to remain loyal in their marriage, why should the rez trust him with money, with the well-being of the community, with everything?"

At least Clayton didn't know the whole truth, but having their dirty laundry aired to everyone would embarrass Emery and Darryl, and even cost Darryl's chance at chief.

"Set it up for the end of March. And keep this under your hat." Clayton tapped his finger on the counter. "I don't want anything leaking until the debate."

At least Raven had time — time to think, time to talk to Jude, time to . . . oh hell, she might kiss her dream goodbye.

Raven closed her binder and textbook. The other students rose and filed out of the classroom. Jude continued to type on his laptop, having already dismissed everyone.

When the last person left, Raven rose and strolled over to Jude. She trailed her fingers along the desk's smooth finish. A new feeling. She'd never loved a man. Not like this.

"I'm almost finished." He kept typing away.

"What are you working on?" She sidled around his chair, standing behind him.

This time Jude didn't slam his laptop lid closed. Her chest glowed. She leaned in and nibbled at his neck. A barely perceptible scent of the cologne he'd sprayed on this morning lingered on his skin.

"A strategy for the campaign. How'd your lesson go?" He clicked *save* and closed the window, the file vanishing into the laptop's hard drive.

"Great." Raven sat on the desk. Where should she start?

"Hey, once we talk, it'll seem better." He patted her knee.

A feather seemed to stroke her belly. "What makes you think I'm . . . distracted?"

"A lot went down last night." He smiled lightly. "C'mon. I already have the truck warming up. We'll go to the camp."

Once Raven donned her jacket, she followed Jude outside, making sure to glance around so nobody saw them. Within ten minutes, they were parked at their hiding spot.

"Who's watching the kids?" Raven removed the vape from her purse.

"Emery." Jude uncapped the thermos.

"Black tea?"

"Yep." He filled them each a cup.

They got out of the truck and stood in the headlights.

Raven removed her vape. She puffed, taking in the tobacco flavor that eased away some of the tension.

"I think we should . . ." Jude spanked his gloved hands together. "I think we should talk about what we promised not to talk about."

A numbness seemed to invade Raven's mouth. She nodded. But what answers could she give? She wasn't sure what to do or think, or what to disclose. Clayton trusted her.

"Can I ask how you found out about Darryl?" Jude's voice lacked authority. Nor was a hint of demanding present.

The recovery program told Raven to answer honestly. Rigorous honesty, if it didn't hurt another, was mandatory. "I . . . I . . . when we . . . our trip to the city."

Jude pursed his lips. "May I ask *how* during our trip?"

"I need you to believe me," Raven blurted out. "It was an accident. No way was I going through your phone."

His eyes widened, and his cheeks drew in.

"My phone buzzed. I picked up. I thought it was mine. We-we have the same phones. Yours is black. Mine's purple. I was meditating. Reading. Praying. I read the text. I knew it wasn't mine." The words raced fast and high from her mouth, matching the galloping speed of her pulse points.

The tightness of Jude's cheeks relaxed. He nodded.

"You gotta believe—"

"I do."

"Wh-what? You do?" Raven croaked out. Nobody believed her, not after years of lying.

"Yes. I do. I trust you wouldn't intentionally go through my phone."

"Thank you." A rush of relief swept through her. She leaned into Jude, head on his shoulder. "Thank you. Thank you so much. You're the first . . . the first . . . besides people in the program . . ."

"The first to what?" He stroked her back.

"To believe me. My family always thinks I'm lying," Raven murmured. "I guess I deserve it after what I—"

"What you did is in the past."

"I know. But after what your ex-wife did, I thought you'd have—"

"You're not Charlene. Why should you pay for what she did to me?"

She lifted her head from his shoulder. "Really?"

He nodded, dimples exposed.

She wrapped her arms around his waist. "I . . . I . . . can I have time to think, first? I need to talk to my . . . sponsor." Well, there was Adam who'd said they could video chat.

"Sure." He pecked her cheek. "May I interest you in the back of my truck?" His tone was teasing.

"Sure." For the first time, she'd experience sex while she loved someone. And she couldn't wait to find out if it was different.

Jude opened the door. He flipped the seats up while Raven shrugged off her parka.

"After you . . ." He gestured at her.

Giggling, Raven climbed inside. She tossed her parka in the front seat.

He climbed in after her. "Boy, someone is excited. Should I be flattered?"

"I, um, never had sex with someone I loved. Uh, not that I ever loved a guy." Raven licked her lips.

"It's the best. The best sex you'll ever experience." His grin and devilish twinkle said he spoke the truth.

"Oh wow . . ." Her voice resembled the croak of a frog.

Jude kept grinning and melted his lips over hers. What he lavished on her wasn't steamy or sensual, but sweet and filled with affection.

Raven trembled. Affection was a foreign emotion. And it left her warm, the same feeling of being draped in satin. He was satin—his skin she ran her fingers along, having sneaked her hands up his sweater, his hard nipples she caressed, the exploration of his mouth on her lips that was as tender as a whisper in her ear.

He eased off his sweater and tossed the garment in the front seat. Left was his thermal shirt to keep the cold away. Once he removed it, he worked on the buttons to her cardigan. Each unfastening, slow and gallant, left Raven shivering. No rush. No hurry to get undressed.

She panted because the waiting was drawing the air from her lungs. After the longest moment of her life while continuing to accept his delicate kisses, experience the heat of his breath on her skin, and his small moans, her sweater was open. He slid his hand up her camisole. His palm edged from her stomach and trailed her ribcage.

She couldn't get over his leisurely exploration. He was

loving her with his flesh, touching every part of her, and not just the good bits. Elation consumed her. He wanted to know the tiny dips and curves of her body. His fingers brushed back and forth, tenderly skimming her tummy. Then he drew a circle around her naval. She shivered from the goosebumps pushing to the surface beneath her skin.

He didn't slip his tongue between her lips, either, but kept showering her with kisses as slow and affectionate as his finger skimming around her belly button.

Heat built in Raven's crotch. The dampness in her panties prickled and itched. Want and need consumed her, like getting out of her clothes to let some air relieve the fever in her pants. Again, she tried to capture Jude's tongue with hers, but he didn't open his mouth. Instead, his lips left a tender path of kisses to her throat where he suckled. He didn't draw the skin between his teeth but offered simple pecks full of steam and light breaths that whispered along her neck.

Her heart seemed to rattle upward. Her insides bubbled. Her lungs were swelling, almost seeming to fill with too much air.

"Jude . . ." She gasped and dug her nails into his bare back. She wiggled her hips, searching out his crotch. Anything to dampen the eruption coiling upward and threatening to burst.

"Easy." His gentle command was moist on her neck. His palm moved from her belly button and flicked at the opening of her leggings. His fingers toyed with the elastic band of the waist.

"Mmm . . . I love how you made it easy for me tonight, sweetheart." His words were part teasing and part raspy.

He never slipped inside. His finger kept toying with the elastic band, slithering back and forth until she squirmed, her body an angry fire of impatience. She wiggled. She wormed. But he didn't take the hint. His breaths continued to steam her neck, and his finger kept roving along her waist.

Gosh, she had to find a way to get him moving. But when Raven inched her hand from his chest to the trail of hair leading into his jeans, he moved on top of her. His hard cock melted against her sopping wet pussy where her clit throbbed, begging for his finger to stroke her off.

"Easy," he whispered. "Don't you want me to love you?"

Love her? Raven squealed. Her words came out ragged. "I . . . I need you. I need you bad. Please . . ."

He brushed at her damp hairline and pecked her forehead. "You don't think I feel the same way?" His warm palm cupped her cheek.

"Please . . ." Goodness, she was begging, because her body was begging. Her tits begging. Her clit begging. Her cunt begging.

"Sure. I want you as bad as you want me."

He shifted to lower his jeans. Raven fought to peel off the leggings. She kicked them from her ankles just as Jude laid back over her. His bare skin saturated her already hot flesh with too much warmth. His nipples met hers that stood hard and proud. His cock nestled on her landing strip of pubic hair.

She locked her legs around him. "Inside me. Fuck me."

"Uh-uh. Bad girl. What do you say?" His voice was as toying as his magical fingers.

"Make . . . make . . ." Oh my God, she'd never asked this of a man. "Make . . . make love to me."

"Gladly."

His swollen cock feathered the opening of her cunt. She twisted to draw him inside. When the tip breached her pussy, her shaking body seemed to breathe a sigh of relief. She gathered her legs around his hips.

So much pressure. Her fluttering clit was being teased with his lazy pumps that brought his stomach to her bare skin. She had no time for air with his tongue finally deep in her mouth, delivering slow licks along hers, a lingering exploration.

Her skin seemed to gather tight around her taut muscles the more the sweet pumps of Jude's cock and delicate licks he lavished on her tongue rolled Raven into sheer bliss. This wasn't fucking. This wasn't sex. He was cherishing her. Loving her, as he'd promised.

She groaned and cupped his buttocks that flexed and unflexed each time he glided sweetly into her wet mess of a cunt.

"Jude. Jude." Her voice didn't sound like her own. Groaning. Moaning. Panting.

The pressure was building. The fire he'd lit inside her with his delightful touches, gentle licks, sighing thrusts had curled her into a ball ready to burst. Her damp skin and slippery pussy were a tangle of musk that permeated the truck.

She cried out, burying herself against his shoulder as the heady sensations washed over her. The words flew from her mouth in gasps and sighs, "I love you. I love you so much."

Chapter Twenty-three: Secrets

Raven sat on her bed. She'd already texted Adam to expect to hear from her. He'd texted back about having no clue how to video chat, but Bridget would set up everything. With Mom at bingo, now was the time.

After making a few clicks of the mouse, Raven called up Adam. His strong square face appeared on the laptop screen.

"'Sup?" He held a coffee.

"Are you alone?"

"Yep. In the kitchen. Bridget's in the bedroom. Kyle's sleeping."

Where to start? Raven clacked her nails on the laptop.

"Spit it out. You know the saying—share your problem, you got half a problem."

"I know. I know. Um, I never had a male sponsor." She giggled.

Adam gave a booming laugh. "Old-timers don't like it. They say it should always be men sponsoring men and women sponsoring women, but anything to help." He sipped his coffee again. "Start at the beginning. We both know there's always a beginning. The underlying issue."

"You're right. You must be sponsoring quite a few guys. You know your program. You've been sober longer than me."

"Years of sobriety don't matter. The day I graduate from this program, I'll graduate on top of a bar stool."

His humbleness was as comforting as cotton. "I know." She drew out her vape.

"Lucky you."

"'Cause I get to vape?"

"Yep. Quit stalling. Out with it."

"Boy, you're a hard-ass. Are you this way with your other sponsees?"

"One sponsee. Now two. You. Out with it."

He'd be one of those sponsors, hey? Raven curled her fingers into a fist. Embarrassing. Humiliating. But she managed to choke out what she'd told Jude already. About her family treating her like a liar, a baby, an irresponsible thief not to be trusted, about Mom's shit behavior from birth, how Clayton had saved Raven from drugs, how she needed the diner to prove to herself, her family, and the community that she wasn't a nobody. That she, too, could succeed instead of bringing shame to the Kabatay name. How being Clayton's campaign manager and seeing him to a win would finally earn her some respect. How she was tired of the women on the reserve shunning her and calling her *slut* behind her back.

Adam relaxed in his chair, folding his arms. "Y'know what I'm gonna say, right?"

"What?" Raven sucked on the vape, although her dry throat needed a glass of water after her huffing-puffing-blow-the-house-down fifteen-minute rant.

"You can't force people to respect you. Can't buy their trust either. Or make them like you. Or change their mind about you."

"I know. I know." Raven picked at her pillow. "I knew you'd say that."

"I'm only telling you what the program says."

"Yeah, yeah. Actions speak louder than words." Something Raven was sick of hearing. If she heard it one more time, she'd tear the hair from her scalp.

"So if you can't change your home life, what does the program say?"

"I have to practice patience and tolerance with Mom," she

muttered. "That my disease affected her for years, and since she's not in the program, she'll be full of resentments against me, 'cause she thought I abandoned her."

"What about step three?"

Raven sighed. "I'm s'posed to leave this in Creator's hands. If I don't, I'll drive myself crazy in the process. Trusting Creator means it'll work out how it's supposed to work out."

"Y'see, you know your program."

"It doesn't make it easier. Now here's the biggie and why I wanted to talk." She hugged herself.

"Fire away."

She admitted to him what she'd learned during her romantic getaway to the city.

Adam snickered. "Ain't no biggie. Lots of men use hookers."

"I'm not finished." She told Adam about the meeting between Cookie, Emery, Darryl, and Jude. Her part in it. Then laid out the clincher—Clayton's plan.

Fingering his mouth, Adam glanced away from the monitor. He glanced back. "You already know your answer."

Raven's chest seemed to plop to the mattress. "Yeah. Uh-huh. There goes everything I worked for."

"Answer this. How would you feel owning that place, knowing how you got it?"

She rubbed her bare arms. Cold. Clammy. "Then what am I supposed to do? Tell Clayton not to do it?"

"He's always talking about how he lives the *Anishinaabe* way. Always claiming to walk the red road. I guess it's time he walked it instead of talked it, hey?"

"I'll . . . I'll speak to him."

"Remember to pray to Creator before you talk to him. Lemme know how it goes."

"I already know how it'll go." Frustration burned in Raven's throat. "But I'll talk to him. Thanks." *For nothing.*

"No prob. Call me any time."

This time only Darryl appeared in Jude's office.

"Well? Did you talk to her?" Darryl set his hands on his hips.

Jude pushed away his laptop and motioned at the chair. What he had to say would set off ten firecrackers in his hot-headed brother-in-law. "Help yourself to a coffee." He pointed to the carafe on the side table.

"Just one cup. I gotta get to work." Once Darryl poured and fixed his coffee, he plopped in the chair facing the desk that had seen better days. It sure wasn't the plush oak Jude had used at his former job.

Jude stuck the pen cap in his mouth and nibbled. "Where's Emery?"

"He has a couple of assignments due." Darryl sipped his coffee. The face he made said he'd drunk from a pot that had been left on the burner for ten hours. "I think he hates talking about this."

Jude might as well deliver the bad news. "We didn't talk. She said she needed time to speak to her sponsor in the recovery program." At Darryl's frown, Jude made sure to add in a firm tone, "Which is a wise idea. This is why they have sponsors. Their sponsors make sure they make the right decisions. In the same way you consult Basil first."

"Yeah, I hear you." Thoughtfulness replaced Darryl's frown. He massaged his temples. "I wish there was a way I could undo all this."

"Because of the election?"

"Honestly, I couldn't give a shit," Darryl muttered. "What matters is Em. I really hurt him."

"He'll get over it. Trust me."

"It's not about getting over it." Darryl slumped in the chair.

"I know he will. I know he's forgiven me. I just don't like disappointing him."

"Get used to it." Jude sipped his coffee.

Darryl scowled and sat up. "Get used to it?"

"Yep. Marriage's full of ups and downs. There'll be a lot more times you're gonna disappoint him. You're human. It's what we do. What makes a marriage stronger is when you get through the tough times together."

"I see . . ." Darryl's mouth moved into a straight line of aggravation. "Then I guess I'll be the guilty culprit forever, always disappointing my partner. Em isn't capable of disappointing anyone."

"He's human. He'll come up with something." Jude winked. "Hey, lookit the rift he caused between you two. He disappointed you when he chose religion the first time, didn't he?"

"Well, that's different." Darryl shrugged. "He wasn't out to intentionally hurt anyone."

"Neither were you," Jude replied. "You were a single man, enjoying a bachelor party."

"True. So when do you think you'll hear from Raven?"

"I'm not sure. But I can guarantee she won't say anything to anyone. She's not like that."

The look on Darryl's face said he had misgivings.

With everyone gone to bingo, now was the perfect time for Raven to speak to Clayton. She stood at the sink, washing the cutlery Tanya had left behind before racing out the door. As for Tyrell, he was working his shift at the diner.

Light snow fell in front of the window, big fat flakes lazily making their way to the ground.

Clayton sat at the kitchen table, drinking his tea.

Raven set the plates in the sink. At least eating at her

brother's was full of laughter and joking, instead of Mom's tight face at home. But in a few minutes, Clayton wouldn't be laughing.

"Did you have an objective for the debate?" *Besides outing someone.*

"Yep. Our roots. What else."

So the debate would turn into mud-slinging. "Exposing Darryl will be considered wrong by many." She washed another plate but studied Clayton's reflection in the window.

The sneer on Clayton's face formed into a scowl. He glared at her backside. "What's that supposed to mean? What he did is wrong. The people got a right to know if he can cheat on his husband, lie to his face, he'll do the same to them."

"But you don't have all the facts. What if you—?"

"I didn't hear anything wrong. I told you what I heard. I made a note in my phone because I'm going to quote him word for word at the debate. Now get it set up." Clayton shoved away his tea.

The cup spilled over, and tea seeped across the table. Raven whipped on her heel, gripping the dishrag. "I spend all day cleaning up after people. I don't need to start cleaning up here."

"Chill out." Clayton righted the cup. "Pass me that." He held out his hand.

Raven dumped the dishrag into his palm.

"I wanna start with community development first. That'll lead us into his . . . cheating." Clayton mopped up the tea.

"I see. You want to bring it up when you're debating something." Raven plopped in the chair.

"Yep. I'm gonna ask him if he'll show the same loyalty to band members that he did to his husband." Clayton glanced up, mouth a half smirk. "Nobody's gonna call me unfair. It's a legitimate question, isn't it?"

Her brother's spirit animal should be coyote, because he was as cunning as one. "It's the way you're going about doing it. You're setting him up. The whole point of the debate is to set him up. Respect is the biggest—"

"Don't you talk to me about the Grandfathers." He angled his chin in her direction.

"Will you please listen to me?" If she didn't sway him, she'd be forced to break his confidence by telling Jude about Clayton's strategy. But she was her brother's campaign manager. Dumb old Adam made everything sound simple when it wasn't.

"Go ahead. I'm listening."

Raven set her hands on the table. "You can win without . . . uh . . . using the information."

"You think I'm going to lose?" His brows pinched.

"No. I wouldn't be your campaign manager if I didn't think you were right for the job." Damn those second thoughts, because she did now have doubts. "I simply want us to do this fairly. Leave it in Creator's hands, as you taught me."

"I am leaving it in Creator's hands, but I'm not about to let that lying cheat con band members into voting for him." Clayton banged his finger on the table.

"You didn't hear the whole story. You heard Darryl talking about something they spoke about inside the diner."

"Then he can explain himself at the debate." Clayton stood and shoved the chair into the table. "Discussion over. Set up the debate." He strode across the floor to the living room and plopped on the couch.

Raven again sat at her desk, pretending to write while the other students filed from the room. Thursday night. She couldn't wait for the week to end, which was pointless, because she'd go home to Mom anyway.

The perennial pen tip sat in Jude's mouth. Throughout class, he always remained professional, but whenever the students left, he'd steal coy glances Raven's way. Normally, she enjoyed this, but not tonight when her heart seemed to sit thick in her throat.

She closed her textbook and binder. Jude also packed away his laptop and files. Maybe she'd luck out and he'd tell her he didn't have a babysitter.

"Do you have to go straight home?"

"Emery's watching the kids. He knows we're going to talk." Jude zipped his laptop case closed.

"How're they doing?"

"Fine." Jude slid on his coat.

Raven also slipped on her coat. She followed him from the classroom and out to his truck since she'd walked over.

They got in. Raven stared at her mittens.

"You're normally a chatterbox," Jude murmured. "Everything okay?"

"Yeah . . . sure." What was she going to say when they pulled up at Geoff's Camp?

Even worse, the drive was too short. Moments later, Jude shifted the gear into park.

Raven's jittering nerves needed a vape. She opened the truck door and got out. The sky was clear, stars twinkling, but the familiar cold produced by a cloudless night didn't result in freezing air waiting to smother her skin.

She withdrew the e-cigarette from her pocket. Jude's boots crunched against the snow.

"You gonna talk to me?" Concern filled his voice. "Something's really off."

Raven stared up at the silver dots the stars resembled. "Tell Darryl I won't say anything."

"Okay. But I think there's more going on than you're telling me. What happened to the woman who likes telling people, and me, what's on her mind?" His words were cozy against Raven's ear. His hands rested on her waist.

She inhaled his crisp scent.

"Talk to me, please." A hint of pleading crept into Jude's natural authoritative tone.

How could she tell him? What were they doing, anyway? The odds were stacked against them.

His hands slipped from her waist. He walked around her and stopped. They stared at one another. His finger grazed her chin. "Can you please tell me what's going on?"

"I'm . . . I'm a Kabatay. My family will hate me if . . ." Something awful was burning in Raven's throat.

"C'mon, we're getting ahead of ourselves."

"How long are we gonna keep this a secret? Forever? My brother will never understand." She shook her head. The burning was almost a fire. Eyes pinching, hurting.

"There are always solutions."

"Solutions?" Her voice cracked. "There're no solutions." When she tried to lower her head, his finger beneath her chin refused to let Raven hide in the comfort of her thick coat collar. She was forced to keep facing him.

"Let's start with what I *can't* tell you." Fuck, they had no choice to . . ."We're gonna be fuck buddies forever." And that wasn't enough for her anymore, not after experiencing his love.

"Fuck buddies?" His mouth dropped open. "You are not a fuck buddy. I love you. Don't you understand?" His searching stare was sharper than a fillet knife.

"Yeah . . . love." She jittered. "A love we can't tell anyone about. Even your brother and sister can't tell anyone. Darryl doesn't have a clue about me—"

"He does. Emery and I . . ." Jude's gaze begged for understanding. "We had no choice but to tell him."

Raven's chest pinched. "See? More people are finding out. Someone's gonna let it slip. They're gonna say something to the wrong person. If my family finds out—"

"Nobody'll find out. The only people who know are

Bridget, Adam, Emery, and Darryl. That's it."

"It's hopeless. I can't share anything with you. Because what I share . . . it betrays the people who trust me, and I've broken their trust enough." The burning sensation in her throat was a ball of fire, almost choking her. Hot tears spilled and rolled down her cheeks.

"What're you talking about?" He cupped her face, wiping away her tears. "What can't you share with me? It's okay. In time, when you feel you can share, you will. I don't need to know everything right away."

"You don't . . ." The lump was awful to try to talk through. A big ball lodged at the back of her throat. Even her chest hurt. "You don't understand. Things I can't tell you, you might not . . . like."

"What do you mean?"

"I can't . . . say. Don't you see? There're parts of my life I can't share. All because of our families." Raven didn't want to wrench herself free from his grasp full of the love he'd declared to her the other night. But standing here, she ached to flee and lick her wounds alone.

She buried herself in his chest and let the sobs finally leave her aching throat, aching chest, aching heart. "There'll never be a right time," she whispered into his coat. "And . . . and . . . and . . . what I can't tell you, you'll hate me for."

"Hate you?" His fingers grasped her chin, urging Raven to gaze into his shocked black eyes. "Why would I hate you?"

"We . . . We . . . We can't see each other anymore."

Chapter Twenty-four: She Keeps on Cryin'

Jude's lungs seemed to squeeze shut for a moment. What Raven said made no sense. She kept edging around the real problem by talking gibberish. And he wasn't letting her go until she told him the truth.

"What do you mean? Talk to me. We're not leaving until you talk to me." Although her pain sliced at his heart, he wasn't about to let his emotions rule him. They had to get to the bottom of what was making her upset enough to try to end things between them, when it was apparent with the number of tears running down her face, she loved him and wanted to be with him.

"You—you don't understand." Sniffles and sobs soaked her words.

"Why don't you think I'll understand?"

"Because . . . your family isn't mine. I . . . I have nothing."

"You have me." The frustration left his voice and dropped to a delicate echo. He slid his hand along her silky hair.

"But . . . but for how long?" Through her tears, she searched his face. "You have kids to think about. You'll be moving back when they start high school. You'll—"

"Whoa. Hold up. Time out." He laid the palm of his left hand over the tips of his fingers on his right hand.

Raven hugged herself.

"You're getting way ahead of yourself. Doesn't your program teach you one day at a time?"

She nodded through a sniffle. With mascara running down her cheeks, makeup washed away from her tears, lipstick smeared, she was a little girl in need of a friend. So much younger-looking than her thirty-one years.

"Then let's take it one day at a time. Okay?" His thumb lightly brushed at her tears. "It sounds like you've been keeping a lot inside. C'mon, where's the girl who'd tell me anything?"

"I . . . I don't know where she went." Raven shivered.

"You cold?"

Her head bobbed in agreement.

"C'mon, let's sit in the truck. We can talk some more in there. I have some tea."

"I . . . I need to vape."

"You can vape in the truck. We'll keep the window down a crack. It's only vapor."

"Okay."

With his palm against Raven's back, she shuffled to the truck. Her mukluks left a line resembling ski trails in the snow. He opened the back door, and they got in.

He fixed their teas and handed Raven hers. With a trembling hand, she took the cup.

He put his arm around her shoulder and held out a tissue he'd retrieved from the front console where he kept them on hand for the kids. "How you feeling?"

She took the tissue and wiped her eyes. "A bit better."

"Y'know, it'll feel better if you tell me what's going on. I won't say anything. I won't offer advice."

"That's the problem." Her voice was huskier than usual from her crying. Gritty. Sandpaper. "I can't tell you."

"I see . . ." Something was up with the Kabatays, and it no doubt concerned the election. Clayton had probably trapped Raven in the crossfire.

"This has to do with Darryl, doesn't it?"

Raven's head dipped.

"You read my text by accident. Did Clayton find out somehow?"

She wrung her hands. "Please . . . please don't ask me questions I can't answer."

Great. Clayton was pulling out the tricks from his trickster bag, just like a true coyote. That was what Darryl would say, who'd taught Jude about the Ojibway trickster.

"Can you answer this?"

She nodded.

"Are we still together?"

Raven nestled against him. "I . . . I wanna be with you, but I don't know how it'll work. Your ex-wife kept secrets from you, and now I am. I don't want to, but I have no choice."

"But you're being honest. There's something you can't tell me because you promised your brother you'd keep it to yourself. Right?"

"Yes." She dabbed at her eyes again.

"Then it's enough for me. You want to tell me. And you can't. Right?"

"Yes."

He pecked her temple. "I'm fine with it. I'm not going to ask you to break the confidence your brother has in you."

"But . . . but . . ."

"This isn't the first time my family's dealt with his . . . stratagems."

"Stratagems?"

"It's a nice way of saying your brother's plan to outwit the terrible Matawapit family."

Raven half giggled.

"Hey, I got you laughing. Was that a giggle?" He couldn't help the coyness in his tone, because coyness galloped up his spine.

She laid her hand across his stomach. "Just hold me."

He would. And this had better not be the last time he'd get to hold Raven.

Jude was about to leave the church after going through the motions of Mass again when Dad called out to him, "Do you have a minute?"

He swiveled. Dad still had to retire his dalmatic, surplice, and alb. "Sure."

"Come." Dad beckoned. He ascended the three stairs leading to the sacristy.

"Catch a ride with your uncle. I'll bring Grandpa to the house," Jude told his kids. His stomach rumbled for Mom's home-cooked brunch.

"Okay." Rebekah and Noah scampered from the church.

Jude passed through the two other doorways as he walked the half-circle of the sacristy. He stopped at the sink and wardrobe area where Dad liked to disrobe.

Dad had already removed his dalmatic and was untying his cincture.

"What's up?" Jude retrieved the dalmatic laying over the old chair. He hung the long, wide-sleeved tunic in the wardrobe. His chest constricted slightly. At one time he'd almost worn this garment.

"I thought you could tell me. As of late, you're very preoccupied." Dad handed Jude the alb, surplice, and stole.

"Lots going on at work . . . and this campaign." Which left Jude racking his brain about Clayton's latest plan.

"I do have an ear. Maybe we could retire downstairs and sit. We'll have coffee before we go to the house." Hope filled Dad's eyes.

A regretful knot seemed to tighten around Jude's rib cage. He'd always confided in Dad. This damned divorce was to blame. "Sure. Coffee sounds good."

He slipped his arm around his father's shoulder and

steered them from the sacristy. "I've been so busy, too busy. I can't believe it's already March and the break is around the corner."

"The kids are going to Kenora?"

"Yeah. I already have it set up." Jude followed Dad down the main aisle of the church. "Booked their flights. Texted Charlene about it."

"They'll be much missed at Easter."

They sure would be. In the past, he and Charlene had always flown to the reserve to participate in Holy Week at Mom and Dad's. During their separation last year, the kids had accompanied him to the reserve. He'd have to save their Easter treats for Easter Monday.

Dad patted Jude's back. "A lot of adjustments, hmm?"

"Too many adjustments." Jude headed down the stairs the older people used since it had the lift chair. He glanced to the seating area where he'd talked to Raven on their first unofficial date.

"You sit. I'll make the coffee."

Jude plopped in the chair Raven had previously occupied. He fiddled with some of the prayer books left on the round table, books he'd ignored as of late. Maybe the Lord was attempting to show him that without the Big Guy, Jude could do nothing, since life kept growing more difficult.

Five minutes later, Dad returned, carrying the coffees. He sat in the chair Jude had used with Raven. "How's school going?"

"We text every day about the school, Dad." Jude set his elbow on the armrest and crossed his legs while holding the mug of freshly brewed *Coffee Coffee* he still donated to the church.

Maybe this chat was meant to happen. He continued to support the church, even financially.

"Yes, we do." Dad cleared his throat, which meant he had

something of grave concern to address.

Jude sipped his coffee and waited. Unlike Emery and Bridget who complained about Dad's interference, Jude didn't mind and always considered his father's words. Maybe because Dad never did this supposed *talk-down* Emery and Bridget insisted Dad was famous for.

"How are you doing?" Dad asked again.

Jude rubbed his brow. "Better than I thought I'd be. Honestly."

"And how are you and the Lord?"

Jude glanced to the lift chair. "I decided to try to repair the shambles I made of Our relationship."

"You have?"

"You knew?" So much for fooling everyone.

"It's easy to see in one's eyes when there's distance." Dad wet his lips. "Remember, the Lord gave us free will. The divorce wasn't Him punishing you or testing you. Charlene made her choice."

"I'm learning." Jude crossed and un-crossed his legs. "I have a great teacher."

"Learning?"

"Yeah, learning. She's . . . very understanding." The words left his mouth of their own accord.

Dad peered. "I thought as much."

"That I'm seeing someone?"

"Yes."

"I know it goes against Catechism, but at the time . . . I wasn't much for practicing Catholicism. I'm still not quite practicing what I was baptized to do."

"I never wanted to see you go through a divorce, but they do happen."

"Neither did I." The relaxing brew of *Coffee Coffee* warmed Jude's chest. He gazed at Dad's sympathy-filled reflection. "But now that it's happened, I can't say I'm unhappy about it.

The kids . . . no, I didn't want them to experience it. They're better off, though, being in a home where two people . . . love each other."

"It's gotten serious . . . already?"

"Uh . . . yeah . . . I guess so. She hasn't met the kids. We've been keeping it very quiet."

"May I ask when this started?"

Emery and Bridget were right. Dad never demanded answers from Jude. Thankfully, he'd always given Jude a wide berth. "First week here."

"Ah . . . I see. Is she Catholic?"

Jude swallowed. "No. She's . . . traditional."

"She's from here?" Dad squinted. "Your trip into the city wasn't to see *someone*?"

"It was to be alone with her. She's only been at the house once, and that was an emergency. Like I said, we've been keeping it quiet."

"I'm assuming Bridget knows. You can't go to the city without your sister demanding you visit her." At least Dad's eyes twinkled.

"Oh yeah. Bridget knows. She texted me as soon as my plane touched down. At first, she disapproved, but she came around."

Dad's jaw slackened. "Disapproved? May I ask who she is?"

Oh boy, here went nothing. "We're keeping it quiet because . . . because we're both campaign managers."

"Campaign—campaign . . . you mean . . ." Dad sputtered. "Raven Kabatay?"

"Yes. Raven."

Sitting forward, Dad set his hand over his chest, blinking. He shook his head, as if trying to clear his mind. "At times . . . at times I wonder if my children—"

"Don't go on a guilt trip. Please." Jude set aside the coffee and scooted forward. Their knees almost touched. "Many people who worshiped God faced tough trials. And they grew from them."

"Yes, uh, yes." Dad cleared his throat. "And you've grown?" Moisture seemed to gather in his eyes, but not tears, something else Jude couldn't put his finger on.

"Maybe she's showing me how a man should behave. I made a lot of mistakes in my marriage. A lot. I tried . . ." Jude searched his mind for answers, something he'd never wanted to admit. "Maybe I tried too hard to be like you. Maybe I went into the marriage thinking I had to have one like yours."

He stood. He grasped the coffee cup. There was a lovely painting of Mary the Blessed Virgin on the wall. A beautiful blue background and Mary draped in sky blue and white robes with a crown of stars above her head. Her hands out, index fingers pointed. Compassion in her eyes. As a child, he'd been taught to pray for her intercession.

"Maybe part of me wanted to be you."

The slightest gasp, maybe a puff, came from Dad.

"Charlene's right to seek the annulment. Perhaps I married her for the wrong reasons. Maybe I didn't love Char for Char. Maybe I wanted her to share in this dream I had." Jude stuffed his hand in his pocket, fisting his fingers. "This dream of being like you and Mom.

"I contemplated the diaconate for the wrong reasons. I believed I was supposed to carry on your work after you left this earth. I assumed I was supposed to do so as a deacon. But during the orientation session . . . it wasn't for me. I can't embrace the teachings like you can. It was all for the best. Lookit the scandal I would've caused the diocese. Divorced deacon."

"Maybe I can't embrace all the teachings, either." Dad's words were quiet, even contemplative.

Jude whipped on his heel to Dad still holding his hand over his chest. "Wh-what?"

"Would I have wanted you to stay with a wife who isn't fully committed to her vows?" Dad's body seemed to cave into the chair. "No. I want a woman who loves my eldest son for who he is. Faults and all. Nobody's perfect."

"There were changes I had to make, too. And I didn't." Jude leaned against the wall, his head inches from the painting of Mary. He tightened his grip on the cup.

"I admire your objectivity in considering your contribution, but don't take any more than fifty percent. Remember, Charlene must reflect on her share, too. There were children involved, and she didn't consider Noah or Becky." Dad's hand remained on his chest, which was a bit strange. Or maybe the shock hadn't worn off yet.

"Maybe Char is. I haven't asked. I only keep her informed, nothing more."

"About the kids?"

"Yeah." Jude sidled from the wall and sat.

"About Raven . . ." Dad cleared his throat again.

"I know already what you're gonna say. Don't think we talked about it. And she has nothing but respect for my religion. She was concerned my brain's taken a leave of absence."

"She was?" For the second time, Dad sputtered.

"Yep. Surprised me, too." Jude sipped his coffee. "She was concerned enough to almost call it quits last night. Don't think she doesn't worry about how this'll affect everyone."

"I guess this is a side of her I never got to meet. The most I know of her was from her youth. As for now, she wasn't keen on me when I taught the adult education classes after the principal up and resigned." Dad continued to stare off somewhere.

"We're trying to say away from political discussions."

"Sooner or later you two will have to have that discussion. Especially if you wish to continue your, uh, relationship."

"Yeah . . . that." They did have to sit down and address the ten purple elephants in the room. "I'd rather wait until after the election."

"You might not have a choice. We know what Clayton's like. I agree, he has strong leadership abilities. When it comes to his own, he'll fight to the death. I admire his valor in that respect, but he also has issues of his own to address."

"They're close. Very close." Jude squeezed the paper cup. "I guess I'm worried." *Worried she'll choose me over him.*

Raven finished drying the last of the dishes.

Clayton yanked out a chair and sat beside Tanya, who went through her wallet, conducting her counting ritual of money she'd use for purchasing bingo cards and pull-tabs. Lucky Tyrell was again cooking at the diner for his evening shift. Maybe Raven should reschedule her days off and start working on Sunday.

She set the last dried bowl in the cupboard.

"You listen to your brother from now on. You're his campaign manager. Help him. Don't dissuade him." Mom shut her bedroom door, having finished dressing for bingo. Her hair was tied off her angular face.

Raven gripped the tea towel. "What are you talking about?"

"Clayton said you tried to talk him out of having the debate." Mom headed for the entryway at the back door.

"I . . . I . . ." Raven whipped about and glared at her brother who stared right back. "You told her?"

"I told her I wanted to hold the debate and you weren't on board." Clayton shrugged.

"What kind of campaign manager are you?" Mom's voice carried from the entryway. She reappeared, parka over the crook of her arm.

The house, small as it was, seemed to shrink around Raven.

She barreled to her bedroom and snatched her purse and cell phone. When she reentered the living room, Clayton, Tanya, and Mom stared at her.

Raven huffed past them.

"Where are you going?" Mom called out.

Why had Clayton involved Mom? At least she didn't know the whole truth or the reason why he wanted the debate. Raven threw on her parka and stormed outside.

She'd never win. Ever. And to think she'd almost called it off with Jude on Thursday night. Why? The family wasn't worth losing the first bit of happiness she'd found after finally sobering up.

She withdrew the cell phone from her jacket pocket and texted Jude.

Chapter Twenty-five: Are You with Me?

While reviewing his paperwork, Jude sat at the dining room table. His cell phone dinged. He grabbed his tea and phone at the same time, checking the message.

It's me. I'm ready to tell you the truth.

He held his breath and quickly typed back . . .

Where are you?

The diner having coffee.

I can't leave right now. The kids still need to bathe. They're watching a movie and having a snack. Can it wait until Tuesday night after class?

No. I'm sick and tired of . . . keeping this to myself.

Jude stood. He typed back . . .

Give me one second.

"Hey. I'm gonna take a private call."
The kids glanced from the TV screen, nodding.
He opened and closed the door to his bedroom. The lack of a walk-in closet, master bathroom, dressing area, and sitting

area didn't bother him anymore. The room served its purpose of a place to lay his head and store his clothes—well, more like squash his clothes, because the closet wasn't big enough to accommodate his full wardrobe, leaving him to store his spring, summer, and fall outfits in the spare bedroom at Mom's.

Calling up the video chat, he sat on the edge of the mattress. Raven's stunning face appeared on the screen. Her skin was lush and brown, so she hadn't been crying. False eye lashes perfectly applied. Makeup not smudged or smeared.

"Hey . . . you okay?"

"I thought it over. I need to speak to Darryl."

"Darryl?"

"Yeah. I need to offer him tobacco. I need to—"

"Whoa. Hold up. Time out. Can you at least tell me first?"

"Please. I need to talk to Darryl. I need to do a sweat."

"A sweat?"

Raven couldn't keep her eyes still in their sockets. They bounced around, darting at whatever she was taking in at the diner. "I don't know what'll happen to me or you, or us—"

"Hang on. Not so fast. What do you mean *us*?"

"Because . . . I must, I must make a decision. I can't do this anymore." Her lower lip quivered.

"Let me call Emery. He can watch the kids. I'll come get you. I'll take you to Darryl's." Panic thumped at Jude's backside.

"Okay. I'm sorry, Jude." Her husky voice was full of regret. "I don't mean to interrupt you. Or make you have to call in a babysitter. Or—"

"Enough. I'll see you in a bit."

A half hour later, Raven rode shotgun in Jude's truck, him having explained the delay because Emery had to dress and drive from Long River first.

"He'll make sure the kids bathe and get them off to bed." Jude's hand rested on the steering wheel. "Are you ready to talk to me?"

Raven might as well blurt it out, but a niggling of guilt crawled up her spine. "Clayton was at the diner the night you met with Cookie."

"He was?" Jude's head whipped in her direction then back to the road. "Where?"

"Outside." She fingered the beads on her mittens. "My nephew tipped him off. Clayton used Tanya's car. He was waiting outside. He overheard Darryl talking. He only caught part of it. He thinks Darryl cheated on Emery. With a hooker. When Darryl was last in the 'Peg."

"Wh-what?"

"Clayton . . . Clayton . . ." Raven gripped the mittens. "Clayton wants me to set up a debate. He wants to confront Darryl. At the debate. Expose Darryl's secret."

"Wh-what?"

She held the mittens to her face, rubbing the rabbit fur against her chin. "I tried, really tried to talk him out of it. He won't budge. Tonight . . . he . . . I guess he told Mom about our talk. He told Mom I wasn't for the debate. Clayton refuses to understand. Neither will she."

A gasp Raven had never heard before hurled from Jude's mouth. "Your mother knows?"

Raven kept rubbing the rabbit fur against her chin. "Only that I didn't want the debate to happen."

"This is what you couldn't tell me?"

"Uh . . . yes. I . . . I'm betraying my family." She looked to the passenger window and into the blackness of the night.

"Hey, it's gonna be okay." His fingers brushed at her hands still clutching the mittens.

"Yeah right." She wet her lips. Her heart trembled. "My

family isn't yours. They're — "

"They're your family. Family's family." Jude steered the truck down the road to Darryl and Emery's log home.

"They're not your family. Not even close." She might have called the Matawapits a bunch of traitorous do-gooders in the past, but they were behaving a hell of a lot better than her family.

Jude pulled up in front of the small log home.

Three dogs bounded around outside, playing in the snow.

"They got their own zoo going on. Two cats, too." Jude shifted the gear into park.

"It's great someone's taking in the strays. I asked Mom about a dog. She said no." Raven opened the door and got out.

The dogs raced to her, yipping. She plopped to her haunches, letting the black-and-white one with the illusion of a mask around its face, a mixed golden lab, and the small black one sniff and lick her.

Caring for animals was part of tradition, respecting their four-legged teachers, but Mom called the stray pet problem a pain in the ass.

"What are their names?"

"That's Bandit." Jude pointed at the black-and-white one aptly named. "She's the first one they got. The golden one is Lucky because he should've died but lived. And the little one is Keemooch."

"The sly one?" Raven giggled and petted the small dog shaped like a wiener.

"Yep. Darryl named him. He always figures out a way to steal food, socks, you name it. And instigates trouble. And sneakily gets his way."

Raven snuggled against Keemooch who wagged his tail and drooped his ears, giving her the *I'm-so-adorable* stare. "You're a manipulator. Always up to something. You are *keemooch.*"

"C'mon. They'll play outside until Emery gets home." Jude started up the shoveled walkway.

Standing, Raven patted the dogs one more time. They sprang off down the road like typical rez mutts. Free. Aimlessly going wherever they wished until they got cold or hungry and wanted to come home.

Darryl opened the back door. He'd yet to tie or braid his damp hair. Sweatpants and a t-shirt draped his stocky body. "C'mon in. I made some tea and scones."

"Thank you." Raven meant it, since she hadn't eaten yet, and her growling belly demanded a feeding.

She removed her mukluks and hung her coat on the hook. A fluffy gray cat curled around her leg.

"That's Smokey. The last time I saw Pumpkin, he was sleeping on the bed in the spare room." Darryl shut the door. "C'mon in."

Raven didn't have to enter far. She pulled out a kitchen chair and sat. The scent of fried scones filled the small log home. Jude joined her at the table while Darryl readied the tea and snack.

Compared to Mom's place in dire need of renovations since the house still had the original bland cabinets, linoleum flooring, and cheap doors because their home was one of the package deals the band had bought, Darryl had worked fiercely on his crib, from the new hardwood flooring and woodstove to the refinished cupboards and brand-new white fridge, stove, and microwave.

Besides the scent of scones, cedar hanging over the doorways added a nice pop of fragrance. A man nailed to a cross hung on the center wall in the living room. A log-style coffee table and matching side tables added a nice touch of comfort to the cozy home.

"Where does Emery do his homework?"

"In there." Darryl pointed to a bedroom, which Raven guessed to be the spare one. "I bought him a desk so he can close the door and work in peace."

Jude fixed a scone. "We didn't interrupt anything, did we?"

Darryl's face reddened. "No? Why?"

"Emery's hair was also wet when he showed up. And he was also wearing sweatpants and a t-shirt." A grin crept onto Jude's face.

Raven couldn't help the giggle. Funny, coming here had put a brightness in her chest, wiping away the storm of gloom from earlier.

"Nope. Didn't interrupt anything. We were watching a movie." Darryl's round face remained red. He drummed his fingers on the table. "Tea?" He poured from the pot, filling the three mugs.

Jude held out the honey.

"Thanks." Raven added the honey to her mug and stirred. Again, guilt surfaced.

She'd been starving moments ago, but the buttered scone made her stomach slightly cramp. To not eat offered food was rude, though. She picked up the treat and bit into the fried bread.

"I know we interrupted." Jude winked. He bit into his snack, dimples bared. "Anyway," he continued on through a mouthful of food. "Raven needs to talk to you."

"Okay." Darryl directed his small-eyed gaze on Jude and then Raven.

Under his curious peering, Raven squirmed. "I . . ." She set the scone on the plate. "I . . ." She dug inside her purse and withdrew the tobacco pouch. "Here." She placed the pinch of tobacco in front of him.

Darryl's brows drew together. "Thank you. What do you need?"

"A sweat. In your backyard." Where the skeleton for his lodge was erected.

"Consider it done. When would you like to?"

"As soon as possible."

"We can do that. I'll get Emery to take something out of the freezer for our meal afterward. You know I've been teaching Tyrell to become a firekeeper. We'll ask him to participate. We'll go to Basil and ask him to conduct one for us."

"Okay." Tyrell's being close to Emery and Darryl was a big thorn in Clayton's and Tanya's sides. But if Raven's foster nephew could find the courage to stand up for what he desired, so could she.

"I'll let you know when Basil decides is the best time." Darryl sipped his tea. "Is there anything else you need of me?"

Raven palmed the mug. The heat warmed her moist hands. She was at her lowest, and the supposed enemy was helping her.

The truth sat on her tongue, urging her to blurt out Clayton's plan. "No . . . just — just the sweat."

"Gotcha. I'll call Basil." Darryl grabbed the cordless off the counter.

Jude shut the back door. Emery sat on the sofa, having sent the kids off to sleep already. If Raven was going to undertake a spiritual journey for answers, Jude would do the same. After the sweat, knowing she'd make her decision about them, about her beloved diner, about her dreams, her hopes, all could be wiped out if she chose him, and he needed a moment to talk to his brother, something God desired.

He removed his parka and boots.

"Want some?" Emery held up the bowl of chips and dip.

"Pass." Jude meandered into the living room and plopped in the recliner. "Not in a million years did I believe a Kabatay was capable of making me discern my own spiritual path."

Emery dipped the chip and bit into it. "What do you mean?"

"Raven and Darryl are doing a sweat together. She said she needs spiritual guidance. There's a lot happening."

"That's promising. The best place to seek answers is from the one you worship." Emery bulldozed the remainder of the chip through the dip and lathered up a huge portion.

"You double-dipped." Jude rubbed his jaw.

"I always do."

Half snickering, since his aching chest couldn't produce a true laugh, Jude sat forward. "I wanted to ask you to accompany me, but Darryl wants you to cook the dinner for the sweat."

Emery's brows hiked upward. "Accompany you where?"

"The church."

"You need prayer?"

Jude's chest constricted. Asking for help wasn't easy. He wasn't Dad. He'd never be Dad. He was Jude Norman Matawapit. Not Norman Earl Matawapit. The word *yes* left the back of his throat.

"I have kids to think about. An annulment coming up. I'm divorced and disobeying Catechism. It's easy to be Catholic when everything's going great. But when it's not . . ." Jude's chest seemed to fold into his rib cage. "I always knew it wasn't black and white. I never had to face the shades of gray."

"One size doesn't fit all. I'm honored you wanted me to accompany you." Emery's words were drawn-out and softer than his usual pitch.

"Once I find out when the sweat is, I'll text Mom to watch the kids. I gotta admit, her spirituality is something I really admire."

"Mom?"

"No. Raven's." Jude clasped his hands together. The

252

crunch, crunch of chips filled the living room. "Don't you ever stop eating?"

"Darryl says the same thing." Emery reached for another chip.

"And you're supposed to eat the whole chip. Not bites at a time."

"I savor each bite." Emery shrugged and smiled, his green eyes flashing.

"Wait until middle age hits you. You won't be eating like that for long." Jude reached over and grabbed a chip, a rare treat for him, or he'd blow up into next year.

"I mean it." Emery's voice returned to his usual *put-anyone-into-a-trance* tone. "I'm honored you wanted to ask me."

"It wasn't my intention to leave you out." The chip's salty flavor didn't cheer up Jude's taste buds. He sat back in the chair. "I guess . . . I guess part of me tried too hard to be like Dad. But I'm not. Dad didn't end up divorced. Dad didn't run away from the diaconate—"

"You didn't run away. You discerned, and the Lord—"

"Discerned? I never made it past the orientation session." Jude snorted.

"That's because God already had a plan for you."

"I'd sure love to know what His plan is."

"He'll reveal it when He's ready."

"Yeah, that's what's freaking me out. What if I lose . . ." *What if I lose everything again? My home was my sanctuary. My marriage was my sanctuary. My family was my sanctuary. Now what I have with Raven . . . it is becoming my sanctuary.*

"Hey." Emery reached over and patted Jude's hand, coating his skin with grease from the chips. "I don't know what's going on. I won't ask. But I can assure you the Lord is present, and He's here for you."

"Yeah, like last time." Jude couldn't help the bitterness creeping into his mouth. "Mom and Dad shoulda named me Job instead of Jude."

"We all face tough trials in our lives. I don't know why you believed you'd be exempt."

Fire filled Jude's chest, and he snatched away his hand. "What's that supposed to mean?"

"We grow spiritually through the most painful moments in our lives, when our faiths are tested. Can you tell me you truly suffered? Ever?"

A glare raged behind Jude's eyes. No, he hadn't suffered. No, he hadn't been reduced to his knees, begging the Lord for help. He'd been . . . blessed. A wonderful life in school. Girlfriends. Good grades. Sports. A solid education. A wife. Two healthy children. A great career. People seeking him for help or guidance. Loved by just about everyone.

"Maybe . . . maybe I grew too much of an ego." He swiped at his hair.

"Not an ego. There's nothing wrong with confidence. I'd simply say you've never experienced true humility."

"Humility." The scowl constricting Jude's muscles pinched his lips into a grimace.

"You do know humility is about being humble. The ability to seek help. The ability to extend your hand and beg for help. Maybe this is what the Lord wants."

"Y'see, He took everything from me just like Job."

"No, He didn't take everything from you. You still have your health. You still have your children — full care of them, too. You still have a job. A home. A family who cares about you. Respect. Money. A truck. A solid education. You have much more than Raven does."

Jude flopped back in the chair. Emery was right. This was about Raven. She had a lot to lose. And this meant he had to respect her decision, whichever one she made.

Chapter Twenty-six: Are You Really Gonna Walk Out?

In the morning, Raven had helped Darryl ready the sweat lodge by placing tarps over it to keep away the light. With the fire pit already constructed from previous sweats, they'd laid the cedar boughs from the pit to the lodge for the spiritual path. There was plenty of wood stacked for Tyrell, who now manned the fire, pitchfork at his side. The Grandfathers were steeping in the deep heat, had sat in the pit for a long time.

No food had touched Raven's mouth yet. Only water. The sun wouldn't set until after six. Her stomach grumbled, so she sipped more water held in a container.

Emery moved about the kitchen. The scents of bannock baking in the oven, a roast cooking in the Crock-Pot, and potatoes bubbling on the stove from the ingredients Raven had purchased at the *Northern Lights Store* the other day filled the home. Buying the food was important, to thank Emery and Darryl, even though the high prices had put a dent in her wallet. Because Darryl had set up the sweat, he'd given gifts and offerings to Basil.

"Do you need help?" Raven had put on her light cotton robe in the spare bedroom. Having always sweated with her female relations, this evening would be her first among men. She'd already informed Darryl she'd be sans clothes, needing to completely expose herself to the spirits. May they help her.

"I got it under control." Emery continued to move about the small kitchen. "You worry about the sweat."

"Have you done one?"

"Actually, yes." Emery turned from the stove where he stirred the potatoes. His gaze was as gentle as Raven's cotton robe.

"Really? I thought you were a . . ." It wouldn't be appropriate to say *hard-core Catholic*. "Dedicated to the church."

"I am. But I enjoy joining Darryl for his sweats."

"Really?"

"Uh-huh." Sincerity filled Emery's gaze. "They're very spiritually cleansing."

"The church isn't enough for you?"

"It's more than enough." An easy smile cracked Emery's rose lips. "I attend confession on a weekly basis, but as I said—"

"What's confession?"

"Where one receives absolution for the mistakes they've made, or what they failed to do. Where they wrongfully thought or said in words."

"So it's also a spiritual cleansing," Raven said more to herself. This was interesting.

"Yes." Emery opened the lid to the roaster. He sniffed at the meat in the pot. "There's a confessional where you meet with the priest."

"Is it dark?"

"Yes. Complete blackness."

"The sweat lodge is the same way."

"Err, the sweat lodge is extremely hot." Emery chuckled.

"Do you think Darryl will become a Catholic?"

"No. He practices his beliefs and I practice mine."

Raven folded her arms. Maybe she stood a chance with Jude. She didn't wish to see him walk away from his spirituality he received from the church. Well, he was meeting with his dad during the sweat lodge ceremony.

Darryl ascended the stairs of the deck, motioning at her.

It was time.

Raven opened the door to the chill of March, clutching the canister of water. Darryl held out his hand, and she grasped it. He helped her down the rest of the stairs so she wouldn't slip.

The cold touched through the deer hide of her moccasins and chilled her feet. Her exposed and even wrapped skin received a good nip from the ice in the air.

Darryl let go of her hand. Raven gingerly walked on the cedar boughs. Once she reached the lodge, she moved in the direction of the sacred circle until she came upon the entrance that faced east.

Before opening the flap, she shifted to her haunches and offered a short prayer. When she entered the lodge, she moved in the same path she'd walked—west to east, not stopping until she found her place on the right side where women sat if joining men for the ceremony.

She removed the bathrobe and tucked it beneath her. As expected from women while inside the lodge, she sat with her legs to the side.

Darryl entered next. He sat cross-legged opposite Raven and also disrobed.

Basil made his appearance. He heaved his old body next to Darryl.

The first round would consist of prayers from Basil.

Tyrell moved back the flap. He placed the pot of medicines next to the pit. Just as quickly, he vanished. A few moments later he reappeared with the first Grandfather, which he set in the pit.

Darryl sprinkled a dash of medicine from his pouch onto the rock the size of a human head. Each time Tyrell brought in a Grandfather, Darryl kept sprinkling medicine on the spirits.

The small lodge, chilly at first, warmed Raven's icy skin.

When the seventh Grandfather was laid in the pit, Tyrell left, closing the flap.

Heat curled around Raven's limbs from the glowing Grandfathers.

Basil launched into his prayer. Darryl tapped his hand drum in sync with the words coming from the old man's mouth, honoring Mother Earth, Creator, and the five directions.

Raven bowed her head. She needed direction from the three, and the east, west, north, south, and sky that represented respect, humility, truth, sharing, caring, kindness, and strength.

The hiss of the medicine splashing the rocks whispered through the lodge. Raven kept her head bowed, although no words came from Darryl, which meant he was holding the eagle feather and praying quietly. After a few moments, shuffling sounded. Darryl was feeling his way to offer Raven the eagle feather.

She stuck out her hand, and her palm met the beaded, leather stem. Holding the eagle feather to her chest, Raven prayed to the Grandfathers, Grandmothers, and Creator, giving thanks for the sweat lodge ceremony, the air in her lungs, the heat climbing around her skin, the chance to return to womb and become reborn inside the skin of the lodge, and her sobriety. During her prayer, Basil kept splashing water on the rocks.

For about a half hour Basil prayed. He then stopped.

"*Nindinawemaganidog,*" they said at once.

Basil opened the flap and signaled for more spirits.

Tyrell appeared. The heat snuck into the cold air outside. One at a time, he loaded the pit with seven more Grandfathers. Darryl sprinkled the medicine on them.

Second round. The hiss of the water and the steam moistened Raven's skin and hairline. Once the entrance closed, she'd be encased in a bursting volcano meant to purge the negative emotions from her body through the sweat of her flesh, bringing her to new life as an infant came out pure from its mother's womb.

They'd pray for their natural brothers and sisters. The four-legged, winged, finned, and two-legged. Raven kept her head bowed. Basil sang quietly while Darryl beat his hand drum.

After about fifteen minutes, there was silence, meaning Darryl held the eagle feather and was praying silently again. Once finished, he crawled along the earthen floor and handed Raven the eagle feather. She said her prayer and passed the eagle feather back to Basil while more medicine was splashed on the Grandfathers.

When the third round started, Tyrell having brought in seven more Grandfathers, the sweat seemed to rain from Raven's pores. She made sure to drink the water since her scalp was soaked in sweat.

This round was meant for her sisters, her brother, and mother — those suffering greatly from the effects of the Indian Residential Schools. Raven must remember their pain, why they behaved the way they did, and most important, that Creator's work be done, not hers.

Creator's wishes. Creator's desires. Creator's wants.

Raven was one simple spirit in the circle. *Center of self. Center of self.* This was what treatment had taught her to draw away from. Western society preached that one put themselves inside the circle, the wrong place for *Anishinaabeg* to be, because everyone came from the Great Mother, so they were linked around the circle, not inside it. She couldn't let life revolve around her, she must revolve around life, and life was happening to her family as she prayed.

Her family loved her. Her family wasn't perfect, since nobody was perfect. She had faults. They had faults. She must pray for what they suffered inside. What Clayton suffered.

What Fawn suffered. What Wren suffered. What Lark suffered. What Mom suffered.

They went through their prayers, and the flap was again opened. Raven readjusted her legs to the other side of her. It wasn't easy sitting this way when she longed to cross her legs as the men did. Each time Tyrell set a new Grandfather into the pit, the heat climbed in the lodge. Too small. Raven was used to sweating with about twelve to fifteen of her female relations in a much bigger lodge.

The heat seemed to find her lungs, her heart, her liver, even her kidneys, while swathing her flesh in its tormenting blanket of hot moisture. The Grandfathers sizzled from the water Basil splashed on them.

He sang his song, and again Darryl beat his hand drum.

This last and final round was for Raven's own self. Black dots appeared in front of the glowing Grandfathers. Her head lightened. She could leave if the heat became too much, but she'd stay. This prayer must be done.

The singing, praying, and drumming were never-ending. Basil's old voice was moist and rich, not the grit of a man in his eighties.

Raven clutched the water canteen against her chest. She curled up slightly, anything to try to cool down and escape being plopped inside a blasting oven full of bubbling water.

Wait, she was fighting the heat, fighting the spirits, fighting what must leave her body. She set aside the canteen, shakily raised her chin, placed her hands on the ground, and sat straight and tall.

Suffering was part of the ceremony. She must suffer for Creator to grant her answers that she sought.

The drumming and singing stopped. Only the hiss of the Grandfathers permeated the lodge. Darryl was praying.

Raven bowed her head. Creator had extended His hand for her to walk the red road. She'd taken it. Creator had sent

Clayton to help her, and she'd gladly accepted the help.

Creator had brought Jude Matawapit into her life — a Catholic man of mixed-blood heritage, but oh so *Anishinaabe* in his physical features, and much so in his spiritual beliefs because he unknowingly lived by the Seven Grandfathers teachings since he'd been honest with her, showed her respect, took a leap of courage to welcome her into his life, even though she was his enemy, which made him a brave man. And his kindness, his willingness to understand, while knowing she'd make her decision today. He was at the church, searching for his truth. He possessed the qualities that made an *Anishinaabe* man a great warrior.

She had the diner to think about. Did she desire to serve and host those in the community for the right reasons? Or was she being greedy, wanting the money for herself? In the past, their ancestors honored generosity. The more one gave away, the more this person was respected and revered.

The diner was something she'd pursued for the wrong reasons. She'd wanted the gold mine for respect, not because she loved cooking and waiting on people. Then if the diner was meant for someone else . . . No, she trusted Creator.

As for Clayton, she'd desired to become his campaign manager for the wrong reasons. Her own selfishness had goaded her to say *yes*, because she'd been too busy thinking about what she could get from his generous offering. By agreeing to his offer for the wrong reasons, she'd put herself in this quagmire, and the reason for her sweat.

Then there was Mom. Raven had a right to ask for respect. For two and a half years, she'd walked the right road. The tension between them came from Mom, who was responsible for addressing the resentment and anger simmering inside her. Raven shouldn't and wouldn't accept Mom's pain and ire any longer.

There was shuffling. Raven reached for the eagle feather

handed over by Darryl. Creator was asking for faith. And Raven knew what she must do now. All the answers were inside her heart. They'd been there all along, but she'd been too afraid, too worried, too frightened to acknowledge them. This evening, Creator was in charge.

CHAPTER TWENTY-SEVEN: SECRET IN- FORMATION

Jude squeezed the rosary in his fist. He flopped back in the pew. They were in the first row, front and center of the unlit sanctuary. Only the emergency lights gave off a hint of red. To keep costs down, the thermostat was lowered to around sixteen degrees, and he shivered.

"A coffee?" Dad asked.

"Yeah. I could use a warming up."

"Let's go to the rectory."

It was across the road. Father Bennie had flown out on Friday to conduct Mass for a couple of other reserves this weekend. Dad would lead a communion service at the church tomorrow.

Jude rose. His heels dragged the carpet as he followed Dad down the main aisle. There wasn't much to shut off because they'd entered using the main door and only needed to switch off the light inside the narthex.

With the church locked, Jude stepped out into the cold of March. One more week of school. On Friday, the kids would leave for Kenora. He started down the steps. No answers had come during his praying. The Lord was asking him to share with another person, finally let go of what burned inside him.

They descended the steps and walked across the plowed lot and then the road to the rectory — a quaint two-bedroom home with a porch, white-trimmed shutters, and light-gray siding. The only sound was the crunching of their boots on the snow.

Whenever Father Bennie had to fly out to another reserve in the diocese, Dad cared for the rectory by keeping the wood stove burning, imperative so the pipes didn't freeze.

Each had a key. Jude withdrew his from the big set on his neck strap. He unlocked the door to a small table lamp in the foyer giving off a delicate glow.

"Father Bennie really enjoys the coffee you supply." Dad ambled to the kitchen.

"Everyone should have access to *Coffee Coffee*, no matter where they are," Jude couldn't help saying. He headed into the kitchen. Dad had already turned on the light.

"This won't take long. I made sure to run water through each day." Dad strolled to the coffee machine Jude had purchased for the rectory around five years ago—the expensive kind that hosted hot water in a tank to perk a cup of joe in under two minutes.

Jude pulled out one of the two chairs at the small table. His mind wouldn't shut down. What if Raven—?

"Out with it."

Dad's firm tone hit Jude's spine, and he jumped.

"We're here to talk. You're too much like me." Dad added coffee to the filter. "Everything stays in here." He tapped his head. "It drives your mother crazy."

"It . . . it drove Char crazy." Jude clasped the salt and pepper shakers.

"I know. Don't think I didn't catch her sly barbs whenever we'd visit." Dad poured in the water.

"Yeah, she liked to get a few shots in." Such as in her roll-of-the-eyes little-girl voice, *Jude, listen? Jude only listens so he can tell you what to do*. Those barbs had always pinched his balls. *Oh yes, date night. Your one-night-a-week obligatory time when you try and listen to what I have to say over dinner*.

Funny, Raven wouldn't have taken a passive-aggressive approach. She would have told Jude, *shut up and listen, and I don't wanna hear one word from you.*

"What's producing such a smile?" Dad asked.

Jude didn't know he smiled, but the glow in his chest said he was. "Thinking about Raven."

Dad set the two coffees on the table. He sat, clearing his throat.

"I understand Raven means a lot to you." Dad sat straight in the chair. He wore a thoughtful expression while staring at the white cupboards Emery had repainted last summer for Father Bennie.

"She does."

"This sweat lodge ceremony Darryl's hosting, does this have to do with your . . . ah . . . relationship?"

Jude tightened his grip on the coffee mug. "It hasn't been easy for her. She thinks her family'll disapprove."

Dad kept stealing peeks at the cupboards. His brows gathered in the middle. "I'm sorry."

"Sorry? It's not your fault her family's . . . the way they are." Jude lifted the mug and sipped. The coffee draining down his throat warmed the goosebumps peppering his arms and back.

"Maybe it is. Arlene has a lot of reasons for her anger."

"You mean Mrs. Kabatay?"

Dad's nod was as precise and methodical as him.

"Having a hate-on for the church isn't a reason for her to despise our family." This wasn't like Dad to excuse a person's asshat behavior. Jude angled his leg and rested his foot on his knee. "I know what they'll do if Clayton gets in. They'll kick me out of the school, they'll—"

"I simply feel bad that you and Raven are suffering the consequences because of . . ." Dad rose. He meandered to the sink and set his palms on the counter. His face reflected in the window. Frowning.

"Understand, if I could do it again, knowing how the future would play out, I'd still marry your mother. She means everything to me." Dad's words came out deliberate, and lingering on them was a tinge of regret.

"Uh . . . what're you talking about?" Jude set his foot on the floor and straightened.

"Arlene's a year younger than me. We went to the same school."

A sponge seemed to soak up the saliva in Jude's mouth and throat. "Wh-what?"

"The nuns did their best to keep the boys and girls apart, but kids always find a way." A limp smile tugged at Dad's lips.

"You and Raven's moth-mother . . ." Jude sputtered. No. Not this. Anything but this.

"It isn't what you're thinking." Dad's reflection studied Jude. "We fell in love a long time ago. A very long time ago. But it wasn't meant to be."

"Oh . . ." Geez, for a second Jude had thought . . . never mind that. "Y'mean you dated Raven's mother?" Okay, this was weird. Sure, he'd wanted to follow in Dad's footsteps as a kid, but not that close.

Dad meandered back to the table and flopped in the chair. "I told you already, the schools separated kids by ages. We went in holding the hands of our brothers and sisters, and if they weren't in your age group, that was the last time you saw them.

"It was a lonely place. She was lonely. I was lonely." Grief pooled around Dad's dark irises. "We became . . . friends."

"How — if they separated you?"

"You find a way. It isn't easy. You manage to sneak off and see each other . . ." Dad shrugged. "It was one of the reasons why I got into so much trouble."

"They caught you two?" An egg or something bombarded Jude's throat.

"Yep." Dad fiddled with the mug handle, staring into the

coffee. "The nuns were especially hard on Arlene. Times were different. Women weren't supposed to . . . we were kids. All we wanted to do was kiss and talk. The nuns believed Arlene was shaming herself."

"Geez."

"And word gets out. She was accused of being a . . . well, there're names they gave certain girls in those days." Dad picked up his mug, looked at the coffee as if it was dirt, and set the mug back on the table.

"When I turned sixteen, I went to the high school in town. I didn't fit. We were starting grade nine, and the other kids were two years younger than us. I mostly hung around to wait for Arlene. She joined me a year later. We didn't last long there. We left and hitchhiked to Thunder Bay. We joined a group of other kids we knew who'd attended residential school."

Dad had previously mentioned dropping out in grade ten and hitchhiking to Thunder Bay, but he'd failed to disclose Arlene Kabatay had accompanied him.

As a parent, Jude understood his children perceived him as nothing more than a father. Not a man who had needs and wants. Still, sitting here with his own father, knowing Dad was a man who also had needs and wants, Jude did his best not to squirm.

"We tried. But I found . . . booze. And she was lonely for home. She begged me to go back. I don't blame her. The school gave us skills to work low-paying jobs. We lived in a slum-house with others who'd come from the school. It wasn't a pretty life."

Dad's residential school experience always left Jude's stomach tight from the suffering his father had endured.

"Annie Keejik was there, too."

"Really?" Jude leaned in closer. Dad hadn't mentioned this.

"Annie liked to drink as much as I did. I wasn't a faithful boyfriend. I wasn't any kind of a man."

"Dad, you were seventeen." Jude raised his finger. "Eighteen. Nobody's a man at that age—"

"It's still no excuse for how I treated . . . Arlene."

"You mean you and Annie . . ." This was surreal. "Old Annie? Darryl's aunt? Darryl's dead aunt?"

"She wasn't always old. Annie, in her days, was a pretty girl. Not as stunning as Arlene, mind you. And booze can make a man do a lot of awful things." Dad glanced back at the coffee mug. He hunched over in the chair. "Arlene lasted two years. She went back home. Angry. Hurt. Then she married Ernest. And you know the rest. Children came along. Ernest had also attended the school. So he was also drinking. Poor Arlene . . ."

Dad shook his head back and forth slowly. "She couldn't escape it. Everywhere she looked, the nightmare of the school was around her."

"Does Mom know about Arlene? Annie?"

"No." Dad's answer was as hushed as his shoulders rounded in regret. "There's no need for me to tell her. It's in the past."

"You said even after what you did to Arlene, you'd still choose Mom." This was worse than making a wish like Noah had—unable to handle his father loving anyone other than Mom.

"I love your mother very much." At least Dad's dull eyes had brightened when mentioning Mom. "She's everything to me."

Jude brushed at his bangs, although they didn't reach near his eyes. He'd loved Charlene the same way once.

"I know Arlene'll never forgive me." Dad pushed out a breath. "If she learns about you and Raven . . ."

Jude's legs fell open, and he sank against the back of the

chair. "I don't wanna come between Raven and her mom."

"Sometimes it's out of our hands. This is Raven's decision to make. And she doesn't feel right about what her brother's doing."

"No, she doesn't." Jude's words came out supple. "I . . . I wasn't looking for anything when I came up here. I just—"

"Wanted to start over? Get away from everything?"

"Yeah."

"God grants us free will, but He also has a plan for our life. Have faith." Dad reached over and patted Jude's hand. "There's something else we should discuss."

"What's that?"

"How you feel. You told me you sincerely started praying again."

"Oh . . . that." Jude picked up his mug and sipped. *Coffee Coffee* sure wasn't living up to its name of *a roast so rich you'll float away*. More like fall into a dumpster. "Maybe I don't need to talk about—"

"Jude, please . . ." It was rare when Dad used this tone, concern, even pleading. Worry rimmed his pitch-black eyes. "Don't shut me out. We both tend to shut out others. And it's hurtful to them."

Jude again picked apart the cupboards Emery had repainted. Little brother had done a great job. New hardware, too. A fine nickel finish. Maybe he'd ask Emery to refurbish the cabinets at the principal's house.

"I apologized to Emery." The words were quiet, so unlike Jude's usual forceful tone. "I told him I sort of wished he could join us."

"Really?" Dad arched his black brow.

"Yeah." Jude traced the rim of his mug. "I recognize he's great at spiritual guidance. I guess part of me . . . Aw, shit, I wanted to be like you. Not needing anyone. Not relying on anyone to fix my . . . problems." What a kick to the ego. "I was . . . I was wrong."

"I see too much of me in you." Dad thumbed the coffee mug. "I'm an old dog. It's hard to change. But you're young. There's still time. I hate to say this, but we're not easy men to live with. We . . . must be in charge. We want everyone to listen to us. We rarely seek or take advice."

Jude leaned forward and palmed the coffee mug. "Charlene said that to me. We were fighting. She told me she was sick of . . . she called me bossy."

"That, too."

"Then if we're so awful—"

"Everyone has their good traits and traits they need to work on." Dad raised his finger. His tone became one of authority. "It seems you and Raven are finding common ground, are you not?"

"We are." Jude kept palming the cup. "She's easy to talk to. I enjoy her company. She stands up for herself. I don't wanna compare her to Charlene. It's not fair to either of them. But Raven's the kind of woman who won't let me get away with . . . err, I guess being bossy."

He rested his chin in his palm. The tightness in his chest uncoiled. "She's a great person. I'd say we're pretty good together."

"What about the church?" Dad peered.

"She respects it. She's the one who told me to get my act together. I gotta admit, I was pretty pissed at God."

"What you experienced is only natural," Dad said gently. "And I'm glad to hear she respects your beliefs."

"It surprised me, too."

"How're you feeling about our Lord now?"

Jude stood. He sauntered to the counter and lifted the pot off the burner. "I asked to pray today 'cause prayer's been . . . well, it's been absent. At church, there's no connection."

He refilled his mug. "I'm not feeling it." He finished fixing his coffee and swiveled. "Refill?"

"Please." Dad held out his mug.

While Jude poured, Dad kept speaking. "Every Catholic faces this problem. Losing their connection with God or the Church. Even both. It's a true test of faith. Don't think I didn't feel removed from our Savior and His Church during times in my life."

Jude almost dropped the pot on the burner. Dad? A deacon? Lost his faith? "Really?" He scooted back to the chair and sat.

"What happened with Emery is a fine example." Dad sat back. Melancholy filled his weary stare. "I believed our Lord had truly called Emery to the priesthood. My own ego was involved and to blame." He exhaled deeply. "I'll admit I disliked Darryl very much at the time. I believed he was at fault. That he . . . he made Emery gay.

"When Emery withdrew from seminary, I was very angry at our Lord." Dad lips moved into a straight line. There was no sound in the rectory. Only Dad staring beyond Jude's shoulder. "But I learned I had to change. This is what God wanted. And it wasn't easy. I had to take a lot of baby steps. The first was to acknowledge my tendency to . . . control.

"Bridget and Adam . . . that was another tough one." Dad lifted the mug and sipped. "Now, I understand the Lord wanted my faith to grow. The night you called and told me your marriage was finished, I swore to myself I'd handle your problem differently. I made a mess with Emery and Bridget, but I won't with you.

"If Raven makes you happy, then I'm happy." The small smile on Dad's lips, the gentle look in his eyes was enough to engulf Jude in an embrace he'd experienced as a child from his father.

"Thank you." Relief swooped through Jude's chest.

Dad reached over the table and clasped Jude's hand. "As I

said, have faith. The Lord brought you this far, he'll be there for the whole journey."

"I sure hope so. Raven's probably making her decision right now. About . . . us."

Having used Darryl and Emery's shower earlier, Raven sat at the kitchen table sans makeup, which was a little strange. Oh well, she couldn't be made up all the time, and this was how she finished a sweat with her female relations. As for the meal, Emery should enter one of those reality TV shows for cooking. The roast, mashed potatoes, green beans, and bannock sat pleasantly pleased in Raven's stomach.

She shoved the last of the pie between her lips. The rich sweet blueberries and whipped cream slid along her happy taste buds.

Darryl poured another round of black tea.

Basil burped and patted his stomach. "Good."

"Very good." Raven finished off the last of the pie. "Thanks." Her mug was full, so she added a dash of honey.

Too bad Tyrell couldn't have stayed, but right after the sweat, Emery had driven the boy to the diner for his evening shift.

"I need a little nap to digest." Basil rose and shuffled to the recliner. He engaged the handle to set back the chair.

"You need anything else?" Darryl stood at the sink rinsing off the dishes.

"No. Sleep. Tired and full."

"Don't die on me over there." A snicker came from Darryl.

Basil also chuckled. "I won't die. Not yet. It'll happen when my work's done."

"Are . . . is . . . Jude eating at your parents'?" Raven stirred her tea.

"Probably. Mom's watching the kids. He'll go over there

after he leaves the church," Emery said.

Basil's quiet snores carried from the small living room.

"I . . ." The words seemed to stick to Raven's throat. She squeezed her hands together. "I . . . I made a decision."

"Oh?" Emery shoveled a helping of pie between his lips.

"Could . . . could I speak to you privately." She gazed at Darryl.

"Sure." Darryl set the last of the rinsed plates into the soapy water. "We can take a drive, if you want."

"It's okay. I got homework to finish. I'll take this to the spare room." Emery stood. He picked up his plate and disappeared into the room behind him and shut the door.

Darryl sat at the spot he'd used while they'd eaten dinner. "You're ready?"

Raven nodded. She ran her big toe along her calf covered in black leggings. "You three are so . . . generous. So nice."

"It's the way of our people. We give away what we have."

"Yeah, we do. It's what the twelve-step program follows, too." She'd simply spit it out. "I tried to reason with Clayton, but he wouldn't listen."

"Reason about what?"

The words sat in Raven's gut, seeming to press against her esophagus, fighting to stay inside while she worked for what she had to say outward. "Clayton knows." Heat infiltered her veins.

"Knows?" Darryl's small eyes rounded. "Knows what exactly?"

Again, Raven forced the words from her gut, forced out the horrible assumptions Clayton had revealed to her that she told Darryl. The pain and humiliation on his face cut at her stomach.

"I'm sorry," she whispered. "I couldn't tell him the truth. He'd know then that I always knew."

"He's going around saying I ch-cheated on Emery with a

h-h-hooker?" Darryl gasped out in heavy breaths.

The words rushed from Raven's mouth to reassure Darryl. "He's not saying anything to anyone. It's part of his strategy at the debate."

"What debate?"

"He wants to hold a debate at the end of March. And at the debate he's going to . . . accuse you of what he assumes to be true."

"Son of a bitch." Darryl's thin lips clamped together. "That son of a bitch." He shoved away his tea and stood. Hands on hips, he faced the kitchen window. "I shouldn't be surprised. Man, he really is coyote."

Raven melted into the chair. She locked her fingers together into a ball so tight, her joints pinched. As a traditional man, Clayton was failing to follow the teachings. A man she'd looked up to, admired, and respected. "I'm sorry . . ."

"There's nothing to apologize for," Darryl ground out through clenched teeth. "This is your brother's doing. Not yours."

"I know, but . . ." She squirmed. "When Clayton finds out, Mom'll boot me out. They'll all hate me."

"You don't know that. I'll talk to him. I'll text him right now and arrange a meeting." Darryl swiped his phone off the table.

Chapter Twenty-eight: I Know, You Know

Jude rested on Mom's sofa, feet up on the coffee table. Rebekah cuddled next to him. He'd forgotten how many times he'd seen this cartoon. But after this evening's tough talk, his daughter's cuddles had turned his clammy skin to a fluffy marshmallow of warmth.

"We gotta go soon, kiddo." He patted her delicate back. "Still got baths. Prayers before bed."

"It's only seven." Rebekah's little-girl voice that matched her mother's was a full-on pout mirroring her disappointed blue eyes.

"You got the rest of the week to come over." Mom folded her arms, staring down at them.

"But then we gotta go to Kenora." Rebekah buried her face into Jude's chest. "Do we have to go, Dad?"

"Yep. Your mom's expecting you. She misses you when you're not there."

"But we don't know anyone." Rebekah's words were muffled, and her breaths penetrated Jude's sweater, toasting his skin beneath.

"You will. It takes time to make new friends. Mom said she'll bring you to the recreation center for snow week. You'll meet other kids there."

"But I have friends here." Her voice remained a pout.

"It doesn't hurt to—" Jude's cell phone buzzed. He scooped it from the end table and checked the message.

Darryl. His brother-in-law had learned the truth. This meant Raven had chosen . . . had chosen to . . .

Jude scrambled to sit up.

"Dad . . . what're you doing?" Rebekah had come along for the ride, half on his lap and half holding his back.

Holy shit, Raven had chosen him. She wanted them to . . .

"Woohoo!" He spun Rebekah around, who still clung to his back.

"Dad, you're goofy." She giggled. "What's so funny?"

Jude adjusted Rebekah so she faced him. Her little legs wrapped his waist, and tiny arms locked around his neck. "Something that makes your dad happy. I'll let you know as soon as I can." He pecked her cute upturned nose, which she'd inherited from Charlene.

"Dad? Dad? What's going on?" Noah raced into the living room.

If only Jude could share his happiness, but the kids first needed a sit-down once they returned from Kenora to learn he had a new friend in his life, a very special friend. After their shock wore off, he'd then invite Raven over for dinner to meet them.

Jude pulled up at Darryl's place, having left Emery with the kids ten minutes ago, who'd get them bathed, prayers said, and off to bed.

Although Raven had chosen Jude, she'd be grieving, because her family would never understand, so he simply walked the shoveled path instead of dancing up the stairs.

Raven sat at the kitchen table, hands tucked between her thighs and head bowed.

Darryl also sat at the table, nursing a cup of tea.

"Hey . . ." Jude removed his parka and boots. He strolled up to Raven and stopped at the back of her chair. "How're you?" He kissed her head that smelled of shampoo.

"I'm okay." Raven managed a half smile. "Darryl and I talked. I'm gonna tell Clayton. Tell him and Mom. Darryl and Emery are gonna let me stay here when I get the boot."

"You don't know if they'll ask you to leave." Jude must reassure her to have faith. He pulled out a chair. "They might understand."

"Nope. You don't know them like I do. Especially Mom. She's always had it out for me." For such a husky voice, Raven's words were soft.

"Are you sure you wanna do this, then?" He cupped her shoulder.

"Yep. More than sure."

"Okay. I'm here for you." He reached for the teapot on the table.

"Everyone's at bingo. And Clayton will be at the band office like he always is tomorrow. Thought I'd tell them late tomorrow afternoon once Clayton's done for the day." Raven scratched her bare arm.

Jude poured a refill for a somber Darryl. "How're you doing?"

"Not good. Em wasn't impressed when he overheard us." Darryl's scowl was darker than looming low gray clouds ready to unleash a blizzard. "I can't believe Clayton thinks I was boning a hooker when I went to the 'Peg for biz after the Christmas break."

A snicker tried to crawl up Jude's throat, but he refused to laugh. This was not a laughing matter, no matter how absurd Clayton's conclusion was.

"What the hell kind of a man does he think I am?" Darryl swiped at his spoon. "I'm a married man." He added honey to his fresh cup of tea. "Fuck, he upset Em again. He's pissed. We keep trying to put this behind us and someone keeps bringing up hookers."

Raven ran her nails along the back of her thumbs. "My

family sucks ass."

Jude couldn't admit why Mrs. Kabatay had spent her life poisoning the minds of her children starting from childhood. Dad trusted him to keep his trap shut. "Nobody's family's perfect."

"No, they're not. But none are like mine." Raven stared into her tea.

"You said you wanted to tell them first?" Darryl was still strangling his tea mug, from the way his knuckles whitened.

"Yeah." Raven nodded. "I didn't mean to cause any trouble for you and Emery."

"You didn't. Your brother made his decision, which doesn't involve you." Darryl lifted his tea and sipped.

"I should get home." Raven pushed away her mug. "And start packing. It'll probably be my last night there."

A shot of guilt seemed to fill Jude's veins. "Look, there has to be a solution to—"

"Sexy, there's not a damned thing you can do." Raven patted Jude's hand. "It is what it is." She shrugged, but her shoulders remained sunken.

"Err . . . sexy? Jude?" Darryl covered his mouth, snickering.

"I see something got your mind off of your troubles," Jude couldn't help saying, smirking.

Darryl dropped his hand, mouth open.

"C'mon, I'll take you home." Jude pushed back his chair and stood. With a wink, he added to Darryl, "And you, enjoy another night in bed—alone." He grabbed his parka off the back of the chair and strolled to the doorway, chuckling.

"Not funny." Darryl's sharp tone was a deep scowl.

The next morning, Jude sat at his office desk. Darryl faced him, leg angled and mukluk resting on his knee.

"Did you . . . ah . . . have a good sleep?" Jude bit his tongue so he wouldn't laugh.

"Save it. It's eight o'clock." Darryl checked his cell phone. "I'm due at work in a half hour. Let's get this over with. What're we gonna do? She's talking to Clayton today. Should I hold a conference?"

Darryl wasn't the only one wondering if Clayton would keep his mouth shut. Jude had stayed up until midnight last night, trying to figure out a plan.

"We should address this right away." He tapped his pen against the desktop. "I guarantee Clayton'll open his mouth once he learns we're on to him. We don't have the luxury of holding a special meeting. We'll have to address this in the form of a letter. If we all pitch in, we can have everything delivered before he can say anything."

"Letter?" Darryl squinted. "What letter?"

"You're going to write a letter, disclosing your . . . ah . . . indiscretion." Shit, this was hard not to laugh. But it did border on sort of funny.

"Keep your lips straight. If I even see a hint of a smile . . ." Darryl set his feet on the floor and sat forward, finger directed at Jude.

This was beyond bad news if Darryl had his finger out, because traditionalists considered the gesture highly rude.

"I'm sorry. I am. But you gotta admit it's funny in a morbid way." Jude swallowed the snicker trying to edge out of his mouth.

Darryl sat back in the chair. "The letter . . ."

"Yes, the letter." Jude cleared his throat and made sure to don his most serious look. "Write one about your . . . indiscretion. Say you're sorry. You were young. It never happened again. You want the community to know in case they received the wrong information. Then reaffirm your commitment to them if you become chief. That's it. Something simple. We can make enough copies for each household. We'll deliver them tonight."

Darryl's face reddened. "I can't believe I gotta do this." He set his elbow on the chair, his fingers grazing his temple. "I really can't believe this. By the time this election's done, I probably won't be married."

"Don't worry about it. All we're trying to do is address this before Clayton starts rumors. Nobody'll care. It's not like you're one of those TV evangelists caught in a hotel room cheating on your wife."

Maybe Jude should've tried a different approach, because fire blazed in Darryl's fierce stare.

"Do you even care how this is gonna humiliate Em?"

"Emery's a big boy. He'll get over it." Jude stood to refill his coffee.

"Yeah? Tell that to my dick, 'cause I slept alone last night."

"Again?" Jude swiveled at the counter where he kept the carafe and condiments.

"I told you already—we think we're over it, and then it comes back and bites us."

"He's gotta learn we all have pasts." Jude poured a fresh cup. "You don't see me upset about Raven's past."

"You don't get it. You and Raven don't have a history. Em and I do. This is about everyone knowing our personal biz. He's a private guy."

"I think it's more about the fact you did something he doesn't approve of, and his pride doesn't like how his marriage isn't perfect now. Whose marriage is? Spouses always do something to unintentionally embarrass the other. He's gotta learn to work past it. You didn't do anything wrong, other than not telling him you got a blow job by a hooker when you were twenty-four. Nuff said."

"Thanks a lot. Now I know why your brother's the counselor and not you." Darryl's answer was sour enough to curdle the cream Jude added to his coffee.

Jude turned. Darryl had made a good point. Wasn't this why Charlene had cheated? She'd called Jude an insensitive ass who believed upon handing out his advice, everyone should file back into place and get over their problem.

"Hey . . ." He meandered back to his desk and sat. "Easy. I understand it's been rough. Char and I hit a few rough patches of our own."

Darryl glanced back and forth, face whitening. "Wh-what's that s'posed to mean?"

Great. Jude was digging a bigger hole. How did Emery handle people? What would Emery say? For starters, Emery called upon the Lord to speak for him. Everything Emery did, he relied on God.

"Y'know, this isn't gonna be solved overnight. It takes time to get past hurt. And if you give Emery time, he'll understand."

When the snarl softened around Darryl's mouth and his eyes no longer flashed, Jude took this as his cue that he could keep talking. "You're a great guy. I'm glad my brother married you, and I'm proud to call you my brother-in-law. I know you'll never do Emery wrong. Give him another week or two, and he'll see what I see."

"I guess you're right." Darryl sank in the chair. He resumed his previous relaxed pose of leg angled and mukluk resting on his knee. "I'm worrying about myself too much and not considering Em's feelings."

Funny, if Jude had taken this approach in his marriage and had shown Charlene the same consideration and sympathy he gave Raven, his ex-wife might not have cheated on him. But that was then, and this was now. The Lord was helping him rebuild and become more sensitive.

Raven had spent her day off quietly packing in her room. At

four o'clock in the afternoon, and having already texted Clayton, she braced herself for getting tossed from the family and booted from the house.

She cracked open the door, which gave her a direct line into the kitchen and living room, since hers was the middle bedroom. Mom stood at the counter, chopping something for supper.

Taking a deep breath, Raven forced herself to walk out to the kitchen. "Clayton's coming over. I'll make some tea."

"Clayton?" Mom checked the clock above the oven. "It's only four."

"I asked him to come over." Raven filled the kettle for probably the last time. She set it on the element to boil. Her suitcases, well, more like the only duffel bag she owned and a couple of garbage bags, and two boxes she'd picked up at the diner, sat at her bedroom door, waiting for the inevitable boot.

The back door opened and closed. A few seconds later, Clayton poked his head around the corner of the bathroom. "I came as soon as you texted. What's up?" He strode to the table and pulled out a chair.

"I put some tea on. I need to speak to you and Mom."

"About what?" Mom slapped the spatula onto the counter. "I'm in the middle of cooking."

Raven set the mugs on the table. "It's important."

"Important?" Mom clucked her tongue. "My ass. You're always making a big deal out of nothing. Grow up."

The cruel reply reaffirmed Raven had made the right decision. She'd never win. Mom hated her.

Raven placed the honey on the table. The kettle whistled.

"Everything has to revolve around you," Mom said under her breath. She switched off the element and oven. "Fine. Make me late for bingo."

"If you want, I can talk to Clayton. We'll go to his place."

Raven wrenched the kettle off the stove. She filled the teapot.

"Too late." Mom yanked out a chair. "Where's my tea?"

"It's steeping." Raven set the pot on the oven mitt in the center of the table.

Mom drummed her fingers. "Well, go on. No use waiting."

No, there wasn't any point in waiting. Too bad Raven couldn't ease them into the news for Clayton's sake, who'd done nothing wrong but have Mom for a mother. "I can't be your campaign manager if you're going to use the debate to accuse Darryl falsely."

Mom's mouth fell open. Clayton didn't bat an eye.

"What're you talking about?" Mom's voice that Raven had inherited rose to a screech. "Your brother's—"

Clayton raised his hand. "I got this." His gaze traveled from Mom to Raven. "I had a very good hunch you already knew the truth. I was waiting to see if you'd fess up."

A shiver claimed Raven's spine. "What're you talking about?"

"You were there. I saw my truck." He kept staring at her. His gaze didn't convey hurt or anger. But betrayal lurked.

The magnitude of what Raven had done hit her like a flash flood, and she was pulled beneath the water, trying to kick and claw her way to the surface. The blood seemed to drain from her veins, leaving her wrapped in ice.

"Your brother. You betrayed your own brother?" Mom banged her fist on the table. "What'd you do? You tell me." She tossed aside her chair and shoved her face into Raven's. "Answer me, dammit."

Raven kept her face an inch from Mom's. "No. This is between me and Clayton. To hell with you."

"Hey, watch the language." Clayton's tone was sharp.

When Mom raised her hand, a fire erupted in Raven's gut.

"You hit me, I'll hit back," Raven warned her through clenched teeth. Her thumping heart bordered on accelerating through her chest.

Mom's deep breaths coming from her flared nostrils were heavy enough to hit Raven's face like a raging bull bearing down on a matador.

"That's enough. She knows about Darryl cheating on his ol' man." Clayton's voice butted into the stand-off between Raven and Mom.

Mom lifted her hand from the edge of Raven's chair and gaped at Clayton. "Cheating on Emery? When?"

"Get off it." Raven was going to clear this up, pronto. "Nobody was cheating. It happened when Darryl lived in Winnipeg. Lived. As in past tense."

The sparkle in Clayton's eyes died. "How do you know?"

"I read the text. That's how. I read the text Emery sent Jude." Raven pushed back the chair and stood. Her heart continued to bang against her rib cage.

"And how'd you read the text?" Clayton also threw back his chair and stood. He planted his hands on the table, stare boring straight into Raven's. If his look was any sharper, he would've sliced off her eyes.

"I was in Thunder Bay. A hotel room. With Jude. He was in the bathroom. I was in the chair. The text came in. I picked his phone up by mistake."

Chapter Twenty-nine: Hit Him with Another Egg

"I always knew you were a slut and would screw anything." Mom raised her hand.

The crack across Raven's cheek was a stinging smack of sharp red heat.

"Him?" Clayton thrust his finger in the direction of downtown. "You went to Thunder Bay with him? That goddamned Matawapit is Darryl's campaign manager. What else have you told him?"

"I only told him what you assumed." Raven wouldn't give anyone the benefit of rubbing her stinging face. "And I told him about the debate."

"I can't believe you. I really can't. I trusted you." Betrayal flashed in Clayton's eyes.

Raven's heart curled for a moment. "And I trusted you. I trusted you to—"

"Get out." Mom pointed at the bedroom door. "Get your stuff and get out. After all we've done for you, after what your brother did for you, this is how you repay us?"

"Why?" Confusion and pain lingered in Clayton's question.

Raven had expected her brother's wrath. His disbelief and pain were knives carving into her chest. "Don't you see what we're doing is wrong?" She inched forward.

Clayton stepped back, shaking his head.

"Wrong?" Mom smacked the teacups on the kitchen table,

285

and they crashed to the floor. Broken shards flew everywhere. "This has nothing to do with us. You wanted Norman's son. His dumb dick and money. That's all you care about. Let me tell you something about the Matawapits. I know them better than you. Oh, do I ever know them better than you."

"Yeah, and I've gotten to know them, too," Raven fired back. She had to scoot around the broken china to save her socked feet from cuts.

"You don't know them." Mom slammed her palm on the table. "You don't know anything about them. Jude's just like his father. And his father is a womanizing bastard."

Deacon Matawapit? A callous user? "You're lying."

"No. I'm. Not." Mom kicked aside some of the shards with her moccasin and shoved her face into Raven's.

"And how do you know he is one?"

"I went to the residential school with him. And I was in Thunder Bay when he moved there after he was let out of the school. I watched him carry on like a drunken Romeo." Mom's face shone up bright red, eyes a thunderstorm of flashing lightning.

Mom would never let go of her anger or resentment. Raven couldn't live in this poisonous environment any longer.

"Both of you are wrong. You can't do this to Darryl."

"Bitch. You bitch. Whore." Mom raised her palm and struck Raven again. "Get out of my house. Get out. Now. You're no longer welcome here if you're going to side with *that* family."

Raven rubbed her raw cheek. "I'm not siding with anyone. I'm telling you what I learned in the twelve-step program. And I'm sorry you think I'm betraying you. But starting rumors to hurt another isn't fair. What's Darryl done to you, other than marrying someone from the Matawapit family?"

"What he's done to us?" Clayton sputtered. "He joined them. He joined them when he knows damned well what that place they worship did to our people."

"Y'know, I used to feel the same way, but I can admit I was wrong." Creator had to be helping Raven, because her voice remained calm, although her insides quaked.

"Wrong. You only agree with them because you're thinking with your twat again." Mom threw up her hands. "You'll never change. Get out. Get out of here."

Mom stormed to her bedroom, and the door slammed shut.

Clayton bolted around the kitchen table and banged on the door. "Lookit what you did," he hissed. Then he banged again. "Mom. Mom. Let me in. She's leaving."

Raven hopped around the broken china and fled to her own room.

The texts never stopped coming in. From Wren. Fawn. Lark. Aunties. All accusing Raven of turning her back on the family to screw Jude Matawapit.

She sat curled up on the double bed in the spare bedroom at Darryl and Emery's place. The little dog, Keemooch, snuggled against her knees. She petted the dog's silky fur. The gray cat, Smokey, lolled on her duffel bag. Pumpkin, the aptly named tabby, had vanished under the bed as soon as she'd arrived, Emery explaining the big tomcat loathed strangers.

A knock came at the door. "Hungry?" Emery asked, Darryl having been absent, along with the snowmobile, when Emery had retrieved Raven from Mom's.

Raven's stomach growled. She should eat, even though her gut twisted from the argument and being disowned by her own family. "Sure."

Lying on the quilt was her cell phone she'd switched off. She should turn it back on in case she'd missed a call from Jude, or maybe he'd texted. Someone must have told him what had happened.

She opened the bedroom door to Emery standing at the

kitchen counter dishing up supper.

"Did you . . . did you tell Jude?"

"No."

"No? I . . . I assumed you would." Raven pulled out a chair.

"It's not my place. What happened is your personal business." Emery set the platter of hamburgers on the table.

"Looks good. I like homemade burgers." Raven reached for a bun. "Where's Darryl?"

"Delivering letters with everyone else." Emery sat across from her.

"Letters?"

"Yes." Emery glumly stared at the food.

"I shouldn't be here. It's a small house—"

"We don't mind." Emery cut open a bun. "I made a salad. Do you like salad?"

"Salad's fine." She wouldn't admit to not having a palate for vegetables, because Emery offering up these precious gems had cost a lot of money.

"It's chilling in the fridge." Emery stood.

While he retrieved the salad, Raven fixed her own burger. They ate in silence for the longest time. Only the satellite radio played. The other two dogs had most likely accompanied Darryl. Keemooch was on Emery's side of the table, because his light panting came from below.

Raven squirmed. Anyone else would press her to talk or say something. "The salad's good. I feel guilty for eating it. This stuff's so expensive."

"We open our wallets for fresh produce." Emery returned the salad to the fridge. "We have a garden, but this time of the year means eating what we canned in the fall. And fresh is nice from time to time. Darryl's health comes first. If it means doing without other treats, it's worth it."

If Raven had diabetes, the day would never come that Mom would purchase special food to keep her disease in check. "Thanks. I appreciate it."

Keemooch kept panting under the table. Didn't Emery believe in small talk? Or did he want her to speak? After what she'd endured late this afternoon, he probably assumed she needed quiet time. "What's the letter about?"

Emery wiped his mouth. "Darryl's addressing the . . . he wants to address what your brother's going to tell everyone." A bright shade of pink climbed up his neck to his forehead.

"I'm sorry." How could she have previously thought of him as Mr. Perfect who shit golden nuggets, or as a man who never suffered and had six silver spoons shoved up his ass? "This is all my fault. If I wouldn't have read your text —"

"It's okay. Really." Emery reached across the table and laid his palm over the back of Raven's hand.

After how cruel she'd previously been in her thoughts about him, after the way her family had treated him, the peapod on her plate was taller than her. "I'd be . . . I'd be so proud to . . ."

Raven's spine froze. She'd almost said, *I'd be proud to call you my brother-in-law.* Marriage? She'd only known Jude since the beginning of February. Yet, somehow, besides Jude, the Matawapit family had wormed their way into her heart.

"I . . . I owe you an apology." She kept her hand under Emery's warm palm.

"An apology?" Emery peered.

"Yeah." Raven wet her lips. "The way I treated you, your family . . . before I got to know Jude."

"It's okay." He squeezed her fingers. "What matters is we're not on opposite sides anymore. Right?"

Raven nodded, not surprised Emery refused her apology. "Who has the kids?"

"They're with Jude. He's driving while they run from house to house delivering the letters."

"He's been busy? I wasn't sure if he knew what

happened."

Emery removed his palm from Raven's hand. "He doesn't know. When you texted, Darryl was getting ready to head out. He took the snowmobile instead. Like I said, it's not my place to tell him."

The sound of the snowmobile's *vroom vroom* invaded the kitchen. Keemooch shot out from under the table and bolted for the back door, barking.

Emery stood and opened the fridge. He withdrew the salad and dished up Darryl a plate of food.

The back door opened. Keemooch ran out just as a red-faced, eyes-flashing Darryl stormed inside, holding a piece of paper he thrust in Emery's face.

"Read this," he said through clenched teeth. "I can't believe him. I really can't believe him."

While Emery read the piece of paper, Darryl huffed back and forth across the small kitchen. When Emery's jawline tightened, Raven pressed her back into the chair. Clayton. She should've known he'd act fast if he knew Darryl was on to him.

"This is . . ." Emery sputtered, which seemed so unlike him to react with a face seen in comedic movies. "This is . . ."

"Can I see?" Raven asked. This had to be really bad.

Emery dropped the letter on the table. He placed his fingers at his temples, chin on his chest.

Raven scooped up the letter.

Boozhoo, *my fellow members of Ottertail Lake,*

It is I, Clayton Kabatay, a proud Anishinaabe *currently running for chief of your community. As a candidate, I'm dedicated to preserving the culture and integrity of a place we call home. However, I regret to inform you that my opponent, Darryl Keejik, does not.*

In his own words, Mr. Keejik admitted to soliciting the sexual services of male prostitutes while in Winnipeg. Ask him yourself and see if he can deny this, because I heard his admission with my own ears.

Is this who you want to run your community? A man who lies and deceives his own spouse? Think hard, my fellow people, because charity starts at home, does it not? And if a man lies and is unfaithful to the person he claims to love above all others, would he not do the same to those he's leading? Lie to the people? Be unfaithful to the people?

Greed is what's in his heart. This more than proves Mr. Keejik lives to serve his own agenda — which goes against the teachings of our ancestors, and something our people abhor.

Furthermore, this incident — and who knows how many others occurred — happened while Mr. Keejik was on business for Ottertail Lake. What kind of man uses time allocated for his people to seek his own immoral pleasure? Think about how he fought to fund a place responsible for the cultural genocide of our people. What else is Mr. Keejik planning if he becomes chief?

I know Mr. Keejik will respond in protest to my accusations, and I ask him to please do. But keep in mind if he can lie to his own spouse, he'll lie to you.

As for me, I'm only passing on information I heard Mr. Keejik say outside of Kiss the Cook. *Ask him if he can deny his words.*

Meegwetch,
Clayton Kabatay

Just like Emery had done, Raven dropped the letter.

Chapter Thirty: Lean on Me

Raven rode in the back of the truck for the emergency meeting at the Matawapits' house. She continued to squeeze Keemooch's fur. Bandit and Lucky barked and yipped, both fidgeting so much they'd squashed Raven against the passenger door.

"That son of a bitch." Darryl hadn't stopped swearing. He'd cursed when they'd left the house. Had cussed during the drive. And continued to utter profanities as they pulled up to the small abode with the blue siding and white trim on Sucker Road.

At the sight of Jude's dark-blue truck, Raven engulfed Keemooch in a bear hug.

Darryl threw the gearshift into park. "Let's fucking go." He tossed open the door and slammed it shut.

Emery inched from the vehicle. The dogs squirmed, and both jumped the console to get out. Raven cracked open her door. Keemooch squealed and leaped off her lap. The black dog bolted after his bigger counterparts.

Raven stayed behind Emery, both dragging their feet along the shoveled walkway while Darryl trounced ahead, already stomping up the four stairs leading to the porch. He threw open the door and disappeared inside.

"I wish I never would've seen the text—"

"The past is the past. There's nothing you can do about it. Let's stay in the present." Emery's suggestion was smooth and comforting. "C'mon." He motioned at the door.

"You go ahead first."

"No. Guests first." He opened the door and gestured.

Raven edged inside to a hallway spanning the width of the house. To her right was an archway, welcoming her to the living room, where Noah sat in front of the coffee table, working on something. Rebekah colored beside him.

Emery took their coats. He hung them on the jacket tree. Raven removed her mukluks and placed them beside Darryl's.

"Who're . . ." Noah, Jude's mini-me, covered his mouth. "I mean, may I ask who you are? I'm Noah."

Emery must've sent his nephew a cautionary look, since Noah had turned into the child of manners. As for Rebekah, she also possessed Jude's coloring, except for her bright-blue eyes and willowy limbs. Her black hair was French-braided, the tail tumbling down her delicate back. She offered a small smile.

"This is Raven Kabatay—"

"Oh wow, a Kabatay?" Noah's mouth fell open.

"Hey . . ." A warning lingered in Emery's gentle tone. "What did we say about treating everyone with respect?"

"But Uncle Darryl called Clayton a—" Noah closed his trap again, since Emery must have shot another look.

"Your uncle shouldn't speak about anyone that way. I'll talk to him." Emery took Raven's arm and led her through the living room to the dining room.

The cozy home was straight out of an old-fashioned movie with its older pieces of traditional furniture and decor. There was even a china cabinet. Jude sat at the foot of the cherrywood table and the deacon at the head. Darryl occupied one of the chairs on the right.

Raven glanced to her left, where Mrs. Matawapit busied herself preparing drinks in the kitchen, a sweet room as dainty as the rest of the home. The only masculine piece of furniture was the brown recliner in the living room, no doubt where the deacon liked to relax.

"Have a seat." Emery pulled out a chair adjacent from the deacon. At least he'd wisely chosen to seat Raven far from Jude.

"Thanks." Raven stared at the elegant lace place setting in front of her, but Jude's gaze seemed to burn into her skin. She peered to the left. He sat straight in the chair, hands clasped together and pressed against his mouth, elbows on the table.

Emery drew out the chair beside Raven, serving as a barrier between her and Jude.

Mrs. Matawapit entered, carrying a tray of goodies and a teapot. She set everything down and sat across from Raven and adjacent to the deacon.

"I'm glad you could join us. We never formally met. Please call me Maria," Mrs. Matawapit said in a stiff, graceful voice.

"It's good to meet you, too," Raven squeaked out.

From Mrs. Matawapit's pinched expression, she probably knew Raven was seeing her son. "Would you like some tea?"

"Thanks. I would."

"I'll pour." Emery reached for the teapot.

The deacon held the letter from Clayton. Darryl must've given it to him earlier. He frowned. "There isn't much we can do. We delivered your letter to everyone. It's up to the community to decide who they'll believe."

"Not much we can do?" Darryl's small black eyes flashed sharper than the glare of light reflecting off a knife blade. "I'm gonna phone—"

"The kids are here. Enough swearing. They already heard you calling Clayton ten different kinds of names." Exasperation filled Emery's words.

Darryl sank in the chair, firing his knife-piercing glare at the table.

"I think the debate should proceed." Without Raven having to look his way, she knew the deep baritone belonged to

Jude.

"The debate?" Confusion flecked Mrs. Matawapit's gaze.

"Clayton planned on calling me out at a debate in April," Darryl muttered. He shoved his spoon around in his cup.

"We should consider an open forum, though. And it'll happen sooner, because we're going to call him out." Jude's hard stare traveled around the table, intense enough for Raven to squirm and duck her head. "Next week's March break. We'll have time to prepare an agenda and for me to get Darryl up to snuff on everything. We'll host the forum the following Monday."

"And what am I s'posed to say that I haven't already said in my letter?" Darryl snorted.

"You'll reiterate what you said in the letter and then allow the people to ask questions." Jude pinned his hard stare on Darryl.

"What?" Darryl wrinkled his nose. "I already let people into my personal life the last time the Kabatays pulled this kind of stunt. I had to speak on behalf of the Traditionalists Society when they wanted to cut the church's hydro bill. Enough, man. Enough. I'm not dragging Em through anymore bullshit."

"So, what are you saying exactly?" Jude leaned in, still staring at Darryl.

"I'm done." Darryl threw out his hands. "When I signed on to run as chief, it was to help the people, help our community, not have everyone asking me what I do when I'm away on a business trip."

Face reddening, Jude's look formed into a disgusted glower. "For crying out loud —"

"It's okay." The soft reply came from Emery.

Darryl gasped. "Okay?"

"There's nothing to hide. And if you're going to be in a public position, I must accept people will try get a glimpse into our personal life. I'm used to everyone poking their noses in my space. I did so as a seminarian." Emery reached for a napkin and crumbled the paper in his fist.

"I know what being chief means to you. This is the start of your political career. It's why you worked hard for your master's. I fully support what you want. It's what spouses do." Emery released the napkin.

Raven gripped her teacup. "I'm sorry."

The stares from the Matawapits seemed to pinch into her flesh without Raven having to glance up.

"There's nothing to be sorry about." Jude's voice was his firm authoritative tone. "Look at me." This time his command was pure silk.

Raven raised her head to meet Jude's comforting eyes, as soothing as being draped in his arms.

"It's not your fault," he continued in his silken tone. "Your brother had choices. So did your sisters. The rest of your family. You had a choice, too, and you chose to honor the Seven Grandfathers."

"I know." Raven squared her shoulders. If Kokum was alive, she'd tell Raven, in her thick *Anishinaabe* accent, to be proud of who she was, not hide in her chair.

"Raven's decision cost her more than her family." Jude banged his finger on the table. "It cost her a dream."

Everyone's eyes shifted back and forth in their sockets. Then their curious peers settled on Raven.

"She was set to buy the diner. Cookie offered it to her. She wanted a chance to make more than minimum wage. This is her sacrifice for us. For Creator." Jude shoved away his tea. "I don't wanna hear any more about withdrawing your nomination." He thrust his finger at Darryl.

"Oh, my Lord. Your family abandoned you?" Mrs. Matawapit gasped. "But housing's so tight." She gaped at the deacon. "She'll stay here. We have a spare bedroom."

Raven almost fell out of her chair. "Oh . . . uh . . . it's okay. I'm staying at Emery and Darryl's."

"Heavens." Mrs. Matawapit placed her hand on her chest. "It's a two-bedroom like ours and crowded with dogs and cats. Please, I insist you stay here."

"Well . . . I don't know . . ." What could Raven say? It went against tradition to rudely turn down such a generous offer. "Thank you. I accept."

The deacon looked at his teacup. His pinched expression softened. His mouth, the same one Jude had inherited, spread into a kind smile. "It'll be a pleasure to have you here."

Jude slid his hands into his pants pockets. His intense eyes settled on the deacon. "We'll . . . uh . . . talk later. I gotta get the kids home. It's late."

"We should go, too." Darryl stood.

"I need to retrieve my stuff." Raven also stood.

The room was small. A double bed. A wood dresser and mirror. A nightstand. Raven had already hung her belongings in a wardrobe and had stored away her beauty essentials in the bathroom. Mrs. Matawapit had explained Jude's and the kids' fall, spring, and summer clothes were stuffed in the closet.

She'd shown Raven around the house. There hadn't been much to see, but it'd been nice to steal glimpses at the rest of the feminine furniture. As for the deck's wicker furnishings, everything sat in the shed for the winter months, but there'd been a table and a couple of old chairs where Raven could vape. Mrs. Matawapit had explained this was where the deacon enjoyed a cigarette.

Raven's cell phone dinged. She scooped it off the homemade quilt and relaxed on the bed. The texter was Jude.

How're you? I wish we could have talked, but I had the kids.

She typed back . . .

I'm fine. It's a little strange being here. I'll admit I feel out of place. But I'll get used to it.

Raven would. Her female ancestors had endured worse at the hands of the residential schools and government. Still, she needed time to digest the loss of her family.

Her phone rang. She accepted the video chat. Jude's handsome face appeared on the screen. This lightened the loneliness sitting at the bottom of her chest.

"Hey," he said, his strong voice quiet for once.

"Hey, yourself." His deep-set eyes warmed her skin and produced a light glow in her belly.

"I don't like this." He frowned.

"Don't like what?"

"Not being there when you really need me." He lowered his gaze and glanced away.

"I'm a big girl." But Raven did wish he was here to see her through such a dark time. "I can handle it."

"I wanted to let you know I'm here for you. Okay?" Jude's gaze returned to the phone screen, mouth firm. "I'll see you tomorrow night at class."

"Okay."

"If you need a ride anywhere, let me know. I'll make sure you always have one." His voice took on his serious tone.

"It's okay. Your dad's driving me to work tomorrow. He's also driving me to class."

"Dad . . ." Jude glanced away. Was Raven's imagination running wild, or did a look of guilt creep momentarily into his eyes? "Sure. Sounds good. Let him know you won't need a ride after class."

The Matawapits were pretty religious. Would they frown upon Raven sneaking off to see Jude? At least Mrs. Matawapit no longer stiffened her shoulders. Once she'd heard what

Raven had lost, Jude's mother seemed to change her attitude.

"Well?" Jude winked. "Am I seeing you after class?"

"Yep. I can hardly wait."

Jude set the thermos in the back seat of the truck. This was getting old — sneaking off to Geoff's Camp for the sake of the kids.

"If I could talk to them this week, I would, but they're pretty stressed. They don't want to go to Kenora." He tilted the cup and sipped the black tea he'd made earlier.

"I understand." Raven placed her hand over Jude's resting on the console between them.

"But you deserve . . ." She'd sacrificed too much. "You deserve more."

"They're kids. I understand. Really, I do." Her gaze lingered on his. "They've only been here since February. I'm fine meeting them when you think it's the best time."

"I know." Jude set the cup between his thighs. He squeezed Raven's fingers with his other hand.

"I don't need you to fix this. Isn't that what you do?" Raven's sensual mouth formed into a coy smile. "You're trying to fix this."

"You're right." Again, Jude squeezed her fingers. "I am."

"All I need is your support. Nothing more."

Her reassuring words eased away the knots in Jude's shoulders. He couldn't help but ask, "Need anything else?"

Raven giggled. "I think we'd better wait. Your mom's probably staring at the clock."

"My mother . . ." Jude snickered. "Dad and I had a great chat at the church . . ." Too great of a chat. He loathed hiding the truth about Dad and Mrs. Kabatay's love affair from Raven.

He lifted her hand and pressed his lips against her satiny

skin. The glitter in Raven's eyes said she wanted him as much as he wanted her. "Perhaps I can interest you in staying at my place while the kids are away. They leave Friday afternoon."

"I thought you'd never ask." She planted a supple kiss on his mouth. Her tender skin warmed his lips. "Looking forward to it, sexy."

"For all that happened, you're certainly in a good mood." He ran his hand along her hair. The lovely scent of her soap was a rich taste of an autumn night.

"I'm always in a good mood when I'm with you." Her husky voice scratched at his skin in a kittenish way.

"If I lean in any closer, I'll dump my tea." Jude kept his mouth a breath away from hers.

"We gotta get you a bigger truck." She again pecked his lips. The velvety pucker was an invitation to keep kissing.

"An RV?" He couldn't help the amusement in his voice. "Then we can disappear here without having to strain over a console?"

"Yeah." Her husky voice was an octave lower, grazing at the lobe of Jude's ear.

"If I get one, the kids'll wanna come along. Kids love shiny new things." He leaned in to brush her lips again. His cell phone dinged. Grunting, he reached inside the console. "Gimme one sec."

"Sure." Raven released their entwined fingers. She picked up her cup of tea.

Jude checked the caller who asked for a video chat. A shot of anger filled his chest. What the heck did Charlene want?

What's up? I'm in the middle of something.

I need to talk to you when you're free.

I'll call you later tonight.

I tried the landline. Emery answered.

I'm busy. We'll talk later.

Jude stuck the phone back into the console.
"Who was that?" Raven asked.
After everything she'd been through, Jude wasn't going to upset her again. "Emery."

Chapter Thirty-one: Tell It to the Telephone

Jude picked up the landline and flopped in the recliner with a cup of black tea. They were in the same time zone, and it was ten o'clock. He punched in the number for Charlene and Stephen's place.

The phone only rang once. Charlene's little-girl voice came through the line. "Hi."

His number must have come up on her call display. "Hey. What can I do for you?"

"Is it okay if I call your cell and we video chat?"

"I guess we can."

"Great."

Just as he hung up, his cell phone rang. He switched off the cordless and picked up the cell. Charlene's face appeared on the screen. Her wavy blonde hair was tied back in a ponytail, just like she'd used to do in the late evenings. She also used to scrub off her makeup upon getting home and only reapply it if she was going out to a meeting after dinner. Her rosy pale face was minus the light application of blush, foundation, and whatever else women liked to slap on. A hint of fine lines gathered around her piercing blue eyes, and a smidgen of dark circles, too.

"You okay?" He'd seen this stare many times. Quiet resignation. But he wasn't around to make her feel this way anymore.

"I'm fine. A little tired." She wet her pink lips with the

cupid's bow that he used to trace.

"What'd you need to talk about?"

"You look great." Her mouth curved upward, but her eyes failed to sparkle.

"Thanks." He reached for his tea. She probably had some concerns about the kids.

Her eyes darted back and forth. Ten bucks she was squeezing and un-squeezing her fingers. Even tensing her legs. Whenever she'd sat with the laptop on her thighs, the computer had always moved with her coiling muscles.

"What is it?" Thanks to Raven, he didn't use his direct tone. He'd learned how insensitive he'd been, but no more.

Charlene's delicate mouth formed into an O. "I . . . uh . . . oh . . ."

Jude had to stifle his chuckle. Yeah, she sure wasn't used to this approach from him.

"I . . . uh . . . Stephen's out of town. He . . . he had a meeting to attend for the school board." She lifted a glass of wine to her lips.

No wonder they'd divorced. Charlene hated talking about her feelings. And, like a true ass, he'd taken a direct approach with her, which had only worsened their situation. He almost had to bite his tongue to refrain from telling her to spit it out.

"Are you making friends?" He set the tea on his lap. It'd been the first time he'd ever inquired sincerely about her personal interests or life since their separation.

"Yes. Quite a few. It's . . . I'll admit . . . I miss . . . I miss Thunder Bay." Her titter was forced, the strain coming from between her teeth. "Do you . . . um . . . miss Thunder Bay?"

Good question. And no, he didn't. Strange. At first, he'd had misgivings about his sudden up and move, but he'd dove headfirst into the community, like he did regarding everything about his life. "No. Can't say I do."

"I . . . I didn't think so." She sipped more wine, the glass trembling in her elegant hand.

As much as Jude didn't wish to be an insensitive ass, it was after ten and time to turn in. He cleared his throat. "You're calling about the kids?" He was pretty sure Emery had mentioned the children had video chatted with their mom earlier this evening.

"I hope whoever bought our house likes it." Charlene set her long nail against her lip.

"Char," he delicately began, "it's after ten. Did you need to talk about something?"

Her gaze kept hovering about. Jude tapped his teacup, waiting.

Finally, after a very long few moments, she said, "I'm wondering about the annulment."

"What about the annulment? I thought you would've started the process by now." She had asked Emery to serve as a witness.

"I have the paperwork and everything." She drained the last of the wine. Her gaze continued to roam about. "I wasn't sure how comfortable you were. At first . . . I . . . I thought it was for the best, but . . ."

She glanced away.

"I have no problem with it." Maybe she assumed he did. "Whatever you wanna do is fine. I'll sign off on it, no problem. Just don't bash me too much," he added to lighten the mood, so humor slid into his voice.

Funny, he'd been furious over her affair, but now, water under the bridge. They were doing not too shabby co-parenting the kids from two different places.

"That's it . . . should we . . . should we go through with it?" She wouldn't look into the phone and kept staring somewhere else.

Come again? He wanted the annulment. They were Catholics. In the eyes of the Church and God, they were still married. "Yes. You're building a new life. You plan on remarrying. While we're seeing other people, in your case, living with someone, it puts a strain on our participation at Mass."

Her eyes widened. "Uh . . . wh-what? You're seeing someone?"

Great, Jude had spoken hypothetically. "If I do consider introducing the children to someone, I'll be sure to let you know. As of right now, it's me and the kids." Which was true. But once Charlene got wind of Raven living at Mom and Dad's, who knew how Jude's ex might react. Was this why Charlene was having a change of heart about the annulment?

"Oh . . . okay." Her voice relaxed.

Annoyance twitched at the back of Jude's neck. What was her problem anyway? She'd cheated. He'd filed for a legal separation to initiate their divorce. She'd run off to Kenora. He'd signed the divorce papers. The realtor had sold their once beautiful sanctuary. Case closed.

He'd better get his rising temper under control. She was the mother of his children. And a great mother. Charlene might be in Kenora, but she kept in close contact, video chatting with them every night if she wasn't busy. He'd hear the kids laughing and talking to their mom while he made dinner.

"Remember, I accepted your relationship. I do hope you'll accept mine." This time he used his normal tone.

Her face reddened. "There's someone, isn't there?"

"Like I said, if I choose for the kids to meet someone, I'll let you know. They're your kids, too. What affects them affects you."

Charlene's gaze darted around again. "I feel . . . never mind." She sighed. "You're right. They're *our* kids. Nobody else's."

"I want us to do this the best way we can."

"Do-do wh-what?"

"Parent." He shifted in the chair. "They deserve to have us

get along and make the best decisions for them by putting aside our differences. I don't want us to fight. They've been through enough."

"They miss us as ... well, together." Her lower lip twitched.

"They're kids. Of course they do. But they're starting to accept their new normal. They still have a hard time with going to Kenora, but give them a few more visits. They'll eventually look forward to going."

"I don't want to interfere ... you know. They're schooling. I'd like to see them a bit more. One weekend a month and holidays are tough. I worry ..." She pressed her lips together.

"You're their mother. I'll be sure if I introduce a new woman to them, they understand—"

"There's someone. Just say it." The words huffed from her mouth.

"For now, there's nobody."

"Jude ..." Her reddening face meant she was growing frustrated and ready to snap. And then stalk off, as she'd done a million times in the past.

"Char ... please. Okay? Let me handle this." Trying to consider his ex-wife's feelings and not set her off was like being dragged down the dirt road by Emery's four-wheeler.

"Just be honest with me."

He kneaded his thigh. "This stays between you and me. If the kids find out from you, there'll be—"

"I won't say anything." She gasped. "Do you really think I'd tell them something that might hurt them?"

"Then yes, there's someone. She's staying at Mom and Dad's."

"What?" The background in the phone's screen moved. Charlene was sitting up. Maybe standing. And probably tightening her fist. "Why's your ... girl-girlfriend staying at Maria and Norman's?"

"Because they asked her to."

"Asked?" Charlene's eyes popped.

"There's a lot going on. A lot. It'll take all night for me to explain. I'll send you an email in the morning."

Charlene nodded, but her mouth remained grim.

"I'll talk to you after you had time to read the email."

"Fine." Her tone was snappish.

"Goodnight." Jude switched off the cell.

First Clayton and his bullshit, and now Charlene having second thoughts about the annulment and getting all pissy because he'd moved on without her. What the hell was going to happen next?

Just like on Tuesday, Wednesday morning wasn't any different. Everyone at the diner was still talking about Clayton's and Darryl's letters.

Raven balanced three plates she took to where three regulars sat by the window, copies of the letters on the table. She braced herself for the same questions.

"Hey, this part of you and your brother's strategy?" Hank held up the paper.

Again, Raven explained she wasn't campaigning for Clayton anymore. She set the three plates down.

"Then who's campaigning for him?" Roger asked. "Can't believe how shit hit the fan while I was away." His old eyes crinkled mischievously.

"I don't know. You'll have to ask Clayton." Raven turned to fetch the coffee pot from the counter to begin pouring refills. She couldn't believe her brother wasn't around to address the numerous questions asked by the community.

At least Darryl was doing his part. He'd stated in his letter his office door at the band office was open to anyone who needed to talk. And from what Raven had heard, the band office was busier than the diner.

"Hehehe, there he is," someone said.

Raven swiveled with the just-fetched coffee pot. Through one of the main windows, she saw Clayton had pulled up in the parking lot. She gripped the handle. Great. Everyone would soon hear about the family feud.

For once the main area of the diner went quiet. The only noise carried from the kitchen. Everyone stared at the glass door while Raven forced her legs to move. She proceeded to refill empty mugs.

When Clayton strutted inside, flanked by Fawn and her youngest son, the diner became so quiet, Raven's eardrums hurt. Cookie stood at the swinging doors, hands buried in a dishtowel.

"I stand by what I wrote." Like a too-confident cowboy from a spaghetti western, Clayton ambled up to the counter. "If you have any questions, I'm right here to answer them."

He sat on the stool, Fawn on his left and Louie on his uncle's right.

"I got a question." This came from Max at the back table. "Raven said she's not your campaign manager anymore. And the deacon dropped her off for work, again. What's going on?"

Oh great, now everyone would hear about what a horrible person Raven was, because Fawn and Louie wouldn't even look her way.

"Those questions'll be answered at a special forum."

Raven spun on her heel. The customers had been so intent on Clayton, they hadn't heard the bell above the door tinkle or witnessed Jude strolling in and answering the question.

"Special forum? What forum?" This came from Moses.

"What? Forum?" Clayton stood.

"A special forum Darryl is challenging you to the Monday after March break." Jude held out the paper.

Clayton snatched it. As he read, his frown formed into a smirk. "I see. He needs time to come up with a proper excuse for cheating on his ol' man, hey?"

"What about the hooker?" Barney stared at them.

"Everything'll be addressed at the forum. I already stopped by the band office and told Darryl not to answer any more questions. Please respect the forum we're hosting and save your questions till then. The agenda's being delivered this evening by the high school students."

"Then we'll find out why Clayton fired Raven as his campaign manager?" Charlie asked.

"I didn't fire anyone." Clayton sputtered. "Raven resigned."

Everyone looked at Raven. She turned and headed into the kitchen. Her involvement in the election was finished. She wouldn't answer any questions. Darryl could on her behalf.

She washed her hands at the sink to tackle the next round of orders, since Cookie was still standing out in the main area. One of the swinging doors squeaked.

"Go ahead and take a break," Raven said. "I got these."

"It's me."

Raven pivoted. She reached for the tea towel to dry her hands.

"How you holding up?" Concern filled Jude's voice.

"Okay . . ." Her insides mirrored a car careening all over the road, trying to find traction to right itself.

"Don't give me that. It's an answer I'd expect from . . ." The concern in Jude's eyes faded, and he glanced to the upright freezer.

"Your ex-wife?"

Jude nodded, shrugging.

"I'll give you the gory details when we have time alone." Raven picked up an order. "I should get back to work. Your mom said you're stopping by for dinner."

"Yeah. The kids wanna spend time with their grandparents before they leave." Jude smiled. "I'll see you tonight."

Raven shivered. She'd be officially eating a meal with his kids and parents. But this didn't mean it was an official serious dinner. It was for the kids, and she merely happened to be living there. "Okay. See you tonight."

Mrs. Matawapit insisted Raven relax in the living room instead of helping in the kitchen. After spending from seven to two-thirty at the diner, Jude's mom said a woman had a right to relax. Raven was doing just that after completing her school assignments earlier. She'd also had a shower to freshen up for Jude and the kids.

Before getting kicked out of Mom's house, Raven had tanned the deer hide for the moccasins she was crafting. Already, she'd cut the vamp and bottom. She was working on the sole, top, heel, and welt. Hopefully Rebekah and Noah would like the gifts.

"Woodlands style?" the deacon asked, peeking over the top of his newspaper. He sat in the recliner.

"Yes. We're woodlands people." Raven had expected to be uncomfortable here, but the Matawapits were excellent hosts. Instead of true sinew, she used artificial to sew the material.

"You do beautiful work." The deacon flicked his gaze to the moccasins on Raven's feet—the ones she liked lounging in.

"Thanks. My kokums taught me."

"It's a lost art. I heard you used to teach the young girls . . ." The deacon's face reddened.

She knew he was referring to the protest two summers ago, when Clayton had insisted the family leave the Traditionalists Society.

"I plan on returning." Raven made another stitch with the leather needle. "I want the girls to learn what my kokums wisely taught me. I asked Emery and Darryl to get me another hide the next time they're out hunting."

"From scratch? You'll teach them how to tan and dress one?"

"Yep. It's the best material to use. Fresh. Not the store-bought stuff. I do sincerely believe in using as much from the deer as possible. And a brain-softened smoked hide is the best kind. But I buy the sinew. It's easier. I should make my own. I just don't have the time."

"Understandable. You're very talented. Do you sell your items on the powwow trail?"

"No. My schedule's too crazy. I was considering starting a website. I planned on it . . ." She made another stitch. "Clayton loaned me his spare laptop. I'm without one now."

"We have one here you're more than welcome to use." The deacon nodded at the laptop resting on the side table.

Maybe all wasn't lost? Raven's heart was in crafting. Yes, she loved the restaurant, and she'd viewed the diner as her only hope to become financially independent, but if she could sell her crafts full-time and make enough money, she'd be in heaven.

She made ribbon skirts. Ribbon shirts. Mittens. Mukluks. Vests. Purses. Dream catchers. Key chains. Crafting had always been a hobby and a way to de-stress.

Jude's truck pulled up in the driveway.

Raven kept working. If she greeted Jude at the door, since she was supposed to be merely a guest, the kids might become suspicious.

The door burst open, and the kids stampeded inside. They shucked off their boots, mittens, toques, and coats.

"Whoa. Whoa. Hold up. Hang your stuff."

A smile tugged at Raven's mouth, since Jude had used his authoritative tone.

"Well . . . hello . . ." Mrs. Matawapit's voice carried into the living room. She probably stood in the main hall off the kitchen.

The kids dashed by the archway, most likely hurrying to their kokum.

Jude sauntered into the living room, grinning. He sat on the sofa beside Raven. "How'd your day go?"

"Pretty good." Raven kept stitching. "How about you?"

"It's pretty excellent now." He kept grinning. "What're you making?"

"Don't say anything. It's a secret. Moccasins for Rebekah and Noah. I hope to have them done when they get back from Kenora."

"That's when I plan on talking to them," Jude murmured. "Maybe you can bring the gifts over on that Friday? I think it's the best time to sit down together and have dinner with the kids."

Raven's heart fluttered. She was so close to life finally going her way. But there was the forum to address, the Monday after March break.

CHAPTER THIRTY-TWO: WE CAN MAKE IT

Mom yanked a wooden spoon from the cutlery drawer and used her hip to slam it shut. Then she attacked the jug of orange juice. With the amount of force the big wooden spoon generated through the liquid, a hurricane should erupt any second. Jude had expected a cocked brow from Dad when he'd told them Raven was staying at his place until the kids returned, not for Mom to be pissed.

"Can you keep it down? She's in the spare room. She'll hear you."

"The kids have been through enough." Mom kept attacking the jug like a tsunami ready to unleash its torment on a tiny island. "What if someone tells them what's going on before you can?"

"I'm telling them Sunday night when I get them from the airport." Why should Jude explain himself anyway?

Mom set aside the wooden spoon. She looked up, wiping her hands on a tea towel. "This couldn't wait until after your annulment?"

"No." Was she serious? "The annulment could take a year or two. The marriage tribunal has more red tape than the government."

"We're trying to teach the kids the obligations of Catholicism. And what you're doing—"

" . . . happens to a lot of other Catholics." Jude set his hand on the counter.

"Yes, it does, but . . ." She waved her hand in a dismissing manner. "Never mind. Your father and I already talked. He's right."

"Right?"

"He admitted he made a lot of mistakes with Emery and Bridget. He said he wasn't going to do the same with you." Mom capped the orange juice. "Understand, I like Raven. She's been most helpful here, even when I ask her to relax because she has a full schedule. Work. School. Recovery meetings. This is my problem. Not yours."

"And your problem is . . . '

She touched Jude's cheek. "You're not the only one upset about your divorce and what Charlene did." The corners of Mom's green eyes Emery had inherited wilted. "I wanted you to be happy—"

"Who says I'm not?" Mom's palm on his cheek warmed Jude's heart.

"You're truly happy? You had it all . . ."

"And who says I can't have it all here? I have my job. It doesn't pay six figures, but what I earn is tax free, so I'm making a more than generous salary. I have a home. It's not a fraction close to what Char and I had, but it's free and a roof over my head. I can build one if I want to. The best part? I have full custody of the kids." And he had Raven.

"Mom, I'm happy. Really, I am."

"Okay." She leaned in and pecked his cheek. "If you're happy, then I'm happy."

That was all that Jude needed to hear. He just had to pass his children's test.

At his own home, Jude picked up the dinner dishes and set them on the kitchen counter. Raven also stood, retrieving the leftovers they'd cooked. Pork chops. Baked potatoes. Brussel sprouts. Nothing fancy, but it'd been a lot of fun preparing dinner. Now they'd clean up, since there wasn't a dishwasher.

"They left without much fuss?" Raven asked for the third time.

"They're fine. They gotta get used to it." Jude filled the sink. He added a helping of dish soap. "I'm sure Charl will keep them busy. Stephen's back from his meeting, so they'll probably go to the movies."

"Oh? What meeting?"

"School board." Jude switched off the taps. He turned to meet Raven standing behind him. He wrapped her in his arms and drew her against his chest. "I'm glad you're staying here. It's been a rough week."

"It has." Raven rested her head on his shoulder. "The gossip hasn't stopped."

"I'm glad we finally have some alone time. It's been busy but great having dinner with you every night. I lucked out, hey? Y'know, the kids wanting to eat at their grandparents' all week."

"It was awesome. It gave me a chance to know them. What do you think they'll say when you tell them the truth?" She lifted her head.

"They'll be fine." He toyed with her braid. "Becky can hardly wait to finish her dream catcher."

Pride had filled his heart when Rebekah had begged to make something after watching Raven work on the moccasins this week, so Raven had put aside her project and had shown not only Rebekah, but an eager Noah how to make dream catchers. The kids weren't done yet. They'd wanted to take their crafts with them to Kenora, but Jude had urged them to keep the material at home in case they needed Raven's help.

Raven had brought over her crafts. The moccasins she was working on rested in a bag beside the woodstove, along with her assignments from class.

"You're a dictator." She pecked his nose. "Giving out

homework on Thursday before the March break."

"Hey, the break's the best time to tackle assignments. What'd you think I'm doing? Playing catch-up. What else?" Her slim body pressed against his was an invitation to whisk to the bedroom. But there was the DVD he'd purchased.

"I think you'll like the movie I bought us."

"Oh? Which one?"

"*Indian Horse.*"

"*Indian Horse*?" She grinned. "I never woulda expected you to watch something about the residential school. I saw it this summer. When we were in the city. Did you read the book? It's excellent."

"No, but I plan on to. Dad read it. He told me I'd really like it. I figured we'd watch that instead of *Some Like It Hot.*"

"Sounds kinky. A porn?" She giggled. "I do a mean imitation of a porn star." She bumped her hips back and forth.

He swatted her luscious butt. "Not a porn. It's a classic. Marilyn Monroe. You must've heard of her, at least."

"Duh, who hasn't?" She giggled again. "Miss Iconic Blonde. I've never watched any old movies." She rubbed his nose. "Let's watch it."

"You're on."

And they did. Jude was as content as a trusted blanket wrapped around him to ward off the cold while they watched one of his favorite movies. Around eleven, while Raven washed up, Jude readied the queen-size bed he'd bought since his king couldn't fit in the small bedroom. Plus, he'd wanted something new instead of what he'd previously shared with Charlene.

The thick duvet kept him warm during the chilly winter nights. He used flannel sheets because when he woke at six, he had to reload the woodstove, the fire having died down to ashes in the middle of the night. Very chilly. But he was used to waking to a cold floor and cold house. As long as the place was toasty before the kids woke, he was fine.

"Well, what do you think?" Raven's husky voice scratched along Jude's shoulders.

He turned. His cock thickened. The black teddy he'd bought her during their trip to Thunder Bay was cut high to elongate her already long legs. She did a little twirl to show off the sheer material riding high up her backside to give him a nice view of her sexy ass.

"I'd say I made a great purchase." He shoved aside the pillows he'd fluffed and strolled about the bed.

"I'd say you did, too." Her slim arms draped his shoulders.

He leaned in and slid his mouth along hers. They stood there for a few moments, simply kissing. It'd been ages since he'd last held Raven. But his hand couldn't resist trailing up and down her bare back and exposed ass. Her flesh was warm and silky, urging him to explore.

He kept kissing her while cupping her bare buttocks. His cock was rock-hard. She grinded her crotch on his. He wasn't the only horny one needing some action. Her tongue searched every inch of his mouth while he kept feeling up her nice ass. He traced her spine, and she shivered.

His cock sought out her warmth, and he caressed the hot, damp area that was an invitation to fuck. Her heat coated his prick with a fever. He kneaded her ass, pinching at Raven's backside while she wiggled her hips.

He tugged at one of the flimsy straps to the teddy. She moaned into his mouth. Her breaths came fast, a groan of delight while continuing to bathe his tongue with slow licks. Her excitement was his excitement. He began peeling off the sheer material pasted to her sleek body.

Her mouth moved to his neck where she suckled. The wet trail she left on his throat was a tease to his cock. He lowered the teddy around her thighs, and she stepped from the sexy lingerie.

She edged her hands into his sweatpants and lowered them. His cock burst from its confinement. He traced her contracting abs and cupped her cunt. She moaned into his ear and licked at his lobe. Her sassy groans were enough to make him come. This woman was too sexy for her own good. He eased his finger between her slit and was greeted by ripe, wet heat. Her hips thrust, and he spread her pussy juice along the folds of flesh.

"Oh, Jude." Her husky voice was an octave lower. "Fuck me. Fuck me—"

The hood of her clit had eased away. Her pussy lips were thick and wet, her cunt more than ready for him. She panted and groaned, calling out his name as he kept fingering her clit. Her hips rocked, gyrating in rhythm with his teasing strokes.

She humped his finger hard and fast, her groans filling the bedroom, calling out his name between heavy panting.

He expected her to wait a moment and savor what his finger had done to her, but Raven whipped about and slithered onto the bed. Her hands and knees braced the mattress. She raised her ass to him.

"Fuck me. Fuck me now," she said hoarsely.

Cock throbbing, Jude scurried onto the bed. He settled behind Raven and grabbed her hips. He didn't even get to ease his cock into her. She slid down his length and rocked back and forth along his prick.

He was close to bursting. Damn, she was horny. He fucked her hard. He didn't let up until the head of his cock burst from his excitement.

Raven kept her arm looped through Jude's. The outdoor chill attempted to nip at any part of her body not covered. Still, this was winter, and any evening hovering around minus twenty was a good evening. The fresh scent of snow and the outdoors was the perfect way to wind down after a wonderful day since she'd started her Saturday by waking in Jude's arms, before showering and heading for work.

Now they were making their way down the road, which earned them plenty of looks from the passing vehicles. But Jude would tell the kids once they returned from Kenora. There was no point in hiding their relationship anymore. After all, he'd stopped by on the lunch hour at the diner to tease her at the counter while enjoying his soup and sandwich, and tongues had wagged. Since he lived downtown, people had most likely spied Raven leaving his place that morning.

An evening stroll after a delicious dinner she'd brought home from the diner was the perfect way to work off bannock burgers smothered in cheese and bacon, French fries bathed in gravy, and key-lime pie for dessert. They'd gone all the way to the Grassy junction, a flat walk with a bit of a curve to the road. They were on their way back.

"Full?" She squeezed his fingers through her mittens.

"Very. But it was worth it. I can't eat that stuff all the time. I'm too much like Dad. I'd blow up to the size of a beach ball." He chuckled.

"That's okay. I'll eat enough for the both of us." She couldn't help teasing him.

"Yeah, you would. Bridget, she's slim like Mom and Emery, but she has to watch what she eats, too. She curses Dad's genes."

"Really? I thought she was one of those naturally slim girls. She's got the ballerina build."

"She's gotta—" Jude's cell phone rang. "Hang on. It might be the kids. Hello." He stopped, brows crinkling. "Walking." He frowned, listening. "Look, I'm a good half hour away from the house. Can this wait?" His lips remained tight. "I'll call you back . . . okay . . . bye."

"You okay?"

"The ex. C'mon, we'd better get our butts in gear. She says it's important." Doubt lingered in his tone.

After hanging up his coat and grabbing a cup of tea Raven had made, Jude shut the door to his room. The covers on the bed were pulled down and the pillows plumped, waiting for him and Raven to retire.

He sat on the edge of the bed and pressed Charlene's contact button. She came up on the screen, looking the same as the last time they'd talked — tired, even defeated.

"What is it?" He sipped his tea. Raven was probably loading *Indian Horse* into the DVD player. They'd decided to watch the late *Anishinaabe* author Richard Wagamese's book that had been made into a movie.

As usual, Charlene's gaze roamed around. Regret filled his chest. He should've been more patient with her over the years, instead of wanting an answer right away. In some ways his ex-wife was a lot like Mom, a woman who held everything inside.

He'd wait to let her speak. Raven and *Indian Horse* weren't going anywhere, and his new girlfriend understood his responsibilities to his family.

"I . . . I got some news today from the reserve." Charlene's voice was tinier than her natural little-girl pitch.

"My rez? This rez?"

Charlene nodded. She licked her lips. "Is she there?"

A wall of defense quickly built around Jude. "What're you talking about?"

"Your new . . . new girlfriend." She wouldn't look at the camera.

The pain in Charlene's blue eyes ruffled the former agony she'd handed to him after unearthing her affair. He fought to stamp down the fire rising in his gut and not spit out *you got a lot of nerve. A helluva lot of nerve after what you did. I got every damned right to see who I wanna see. You threw in the towel on us. Not me.*

Sending up a silent prayer that unwound the tension in his muscles, he managed to say in a controlled voice, "I told you we'd talk about it when I think it's best. Being the mother of my children doesn't include you in my personal affairs unless it impacts our kids. And right now, it isn't."

"I knew you'd be this way. You never listen." Her jawline stiffened. She was going to withdraw into herself. There'd be hisses under her breath while she trounced around her home, a book maybe banged, perhaps some snapping at the children, and then she'd retire to bed, refusing to speak to anyone.

Jude wasn't going to placate Charlene. He had a right to stand up for himself. "I listened and I answered."

"Fine. Whatever." She didn't snap. She didn't fade off into sadness. Her words were quiet resignation. "Goodnight." She disappeared from the screen.

He rose off the bed, tossing the cell phone on the duvet. At least he'd spoken low enough so Raven might not have overheard. When he opened the door, Raven stood at the kitchen counter pouring some fresh drinks. The microwave hummed, popcorn cooking.

She glanced over her shoulder. "Everything okay?"

Her concern washed away the damage of Charlene's phone call. He was starting a new life. There'd be no more paying penance for the old one. Yes, he could've been a better husband — more attentive, more sympathetic, a better listener, but he couldn't take one hundred percent of the blame for his failed marriage. Charlene had to take fifty, and he had easily owned up to his fifty percent.

The woman at the counter with the long black hair, the sexy seductive eyes, the sensual body, and take-charge-take-no-shit attitude was who he wanted to introduce to his children. He wanted Raven to become a part of his life.

"Y'know something? I'm fine. Seriously." He ambled up to her and wrapped his arms around Raven's slim waist and pecked her cheek. He nuzzled her ear. "Ready for the movie?"

"Ready." She giggled and bestowed a light kiss on his mouth.

"Then let's put it on and enjoy ourselves. We got two more hurdles."

"Two?"

"Yep, two. The forum. And telling my kids. I wanna forget for now and enjoy your company. You're the best company I've had who's older than twelve."

They both burst out laughing.

CHAPTER THIRTY-THREE: TRIAL BY FIRE

Jude finished off the last of the green and yellow beans. Noah continued to shove his veggies around on his plate. Rebekah, like the good girl she was, munched on hers.

"You gotta finish. No dessert if you don't." Jude pushed back his chair.

"They taste like wax." Noah made a face.

"And how do you know what wax tastes like?" They really had to get a dishwasher, instead of having to scrape the plates and wash them. Jude switched on the taps.

Noah's face reddened. "I didn't do it. It was Lucas. He ate the candles."

"The votive candles at the church?" Jude's jaw almost hit the floor. In his altar serving days, he'd snuck into the wine, but eating candles sure hadn't entered his mind. "Seriously?"

What a way to start a Sunday evening. He was in for a manic Monday tomorrow, because he'd wanted to speak to the kids about Raven, not lecture about eating candles, for crying out loud. Screw it. He'd bought a strawberry shortcake from the diner, and of course he'd purchased the kids' favorite cartoon to pop into the DVD player afterwards.

"Can we watch the Z Men now?" Noah whined.

"Not yet. We need to talk." Jude finished filling up the sink. "Let me cut the cake."

"Yeet!" Noah drummed on the table.

Oh yeah, *yeet* was the new *it* word at school, meaning a very strong *yes*. "And you get an extra-big slice."

"Why?" Noah crinkled his brows.

Double oh yeah, because his son had reached the age of suspicion. Too bad. "I have something important to tell you." Jude cut three slices.

"Lay it on me." Noah winked.

This kid was too smart for his own good. *Too much like me.* "Here." Jude set the three plates on the table and sat.

Noah dug into his right away. He ate so fast, a dollop of whipped cream sat on his nose. Rebekah gingerly picked away as her mother would.

"What da word? What da word?" Noah asked in between shoveling bite after bite into his mouth.

"Can you speak in English? No slang."

"Ookay." Noah grinned.

Jude reached over and ruffled his son's coarse black hair that was as poker straight as his own. "I have something important to say."

"What's important?" Rebekah smiled like a true angel.

"Something chief." Noah giggled at his sister.

"Rez slang now?" Jude should know better than to ask.

"Yep. Important is totally chief."

"Remember when Mom first moved out? I explained she had a new friend?"

Noah's black eyes clouded. "Yeah. Mr. Baker."

"He's always nice to us." Rebekah ate some more of her cake.

"I'm glad he's nice. He should be nice. He's Mom's friend."

"You mean he's gonna be our stepdad soon." Noah glared at his plate.

"Why the face? Mr. Baker likes you both."

"Yeah, I know. He's . . . okay." Noah's shoulders sagged. "He takes us places. He does stuff with us." His dark eyes lost their luster. "But he's not you."

"No, he's not. He'll never be me. But he can be your friend." Jude used his faintest tone. He reached over and squeezed Noah's fingers.

"Are you . . . do you . . . do you have a friend?" Noah's lower lip trembled.

Jude kept squeezing Noah's fingers and nodded.

"She — she's gonna live here?"

Jude shook his head. "No. She won't be like Mr. Baker and Mom. She's my friend. I told you about how adults need friends. Your mom needed an adult friend, and that's why she's with Mr. Baker."

"He — he told us to call him Stephen." A tear rolled down Noah's cheek.

This was getting serious if Charlene's fiancé wanted to be on a first-name basis. But it had to happen. He'd one day be Noah and Rebekah's stepfather. "Calling him Stephen's okay. I told you. If an adult gives permission, you can call them by their first name."

"And your friend? What're we gonna call her?" Noah's hand dampened in Jude's palm.

"You'll call her Miss Kabatay."

Relief flooded Noah's gaze. "Okay. Miss Kabatay."

"I asked her to join us for dinner on Friday night."

"Miss Kabatay," Rebekah exclaimed. "The Miss Kabatay who lives with Grandma and Grandpa?"

"*That* Miss Kabatay?" Noah's mouth fell open.

"Yes, *that* Miss Kabatay."

"But . . . but Grandma said Miss Kabatay was living there 'cause she has no place to live."

"Yes. Uncle Darryl and Uncle Emery offered Miss Kabatay their spare room, but Grandma and Grandpa insisted Miss Kabatay stay there," Jude reassured them.

"And you're only friends." Suspicion lurked in Noah's eyes. "She won't live with us like Mr. Baker lives with Mom?"

"No. We're friends."

When Noah stared at his plate of crumbs and then eyed the

strawberry shortcake on the counter, Jude let out a breath of relief. One hurdle jumped. The kids needed time to get to know Raven. He wasn't going to spring her on them like Charlene had done with Stephen. The kids were still fighting to accept that their Mom loved someone who wasn't Dad.

"More?" Noah pointed at the cake, brows waggling.

Jude snickered. "Sure. Let's go watch *Z Men*."

Since Monday was Raven's day off, she helped Mrs. Matawapit with the laundry. They worked quietly in the back area of the house at seven-thirty in the morning. There was no Mass today for the deacon and his wife to race off to.

"Are you going to the forum tonight?" Mrs. Matawapit asked. She stood at the washing machine, sorting darks from lights.

Good question. "I'm not sure. I haven't made up my mind." Raven scooped up the load from the wash to hang on the line outside. "Are you and the deacon?"

"I'm watching the kids. Norman's going."

Raven hefted the laundry basket to take the clothes outside on the main deck.

The sliding door opening and closing carried to the back area.

"Good cigarette?" Raven called out, having already been outside to get her nicotine fix from her vape.

"Always a delight." The deacon's chuckle followed him. He stood in the hallway, holding a mug of coffee. "How about you? Did you get outside yet?"

"Yeah. While you were in the shower." Raven opened the back door and stepped out into the cold. The scraped coating of snow clinging to the wooden deck seeped through her moccasins and iced her feet. She shivered.

"Will you be joining me this evening at the forum?" The

deacon had followed her outside. He leaned against the doorway.

"I haven't made up my mind." Mom would be there, and Raven's sisters. She'd be snubbed. Maybe she'd worsen the event for Darryl, too.

"Understandable." Sympathy reflected in the deacon's voice.

Raven had sorted the pants on top first. She secured her brown leggings with the clothes pins on the line.

"I'm sorry. I truly am," the deacon said.

"There's nothing to be sorry about." Raven pushed on the wheel and sent the leggings out a foot. She reached for another pair of pants. "I expected Mom to act the way she did."

The deacon frowned, but quickly used his hand to cover his hard-set lips. "You'll always have a place here."

The sincerity in his black eyes warmed Raven's heart. Never in a million years—if someone had told her at the beginning of February that she'd not only fall in love with the family enemy, but turn to them in her time of need and live under the roof of a man she'd once detested, she wouldn't have believed them.

Raven rode shotgun in the deacon's truck to the multi-use center where the forum was taking place. They'd dropped off Mrs. Matawapit at Jude's house. Jude's truck cruised along up ahead of them.

She glanced at the deacon and then back to Jude's truck.

The deacon followed Jude onto Lynx Road. Already, the parking lot was full. They stopped behind Jude's truck. Raven didn't realize Emery and Darryl were behind them, and they also parked.

Just as Emery cracked open the door, the dogs stampeded over him and leaped from the vehicle.

"Keemooch." Raven squatted and petted the little black

dog. "You take them everywhere, hey?"

"Yes." Emery tapped his gloved fingers against his thighs. He peeked at the building.

Darryl trounced off without a hello. He stared straight ahead.

While Emery, the deacon, and Jude talked, Raven trailed behind. Her family's vehicles were also parked. The food she'd eaten during supper a half an hour ago seemed to try to crawl from her intestines. When they entered the big hall, Roy stood at a table where others from the church sat, waving them over.

Raven stopped for a moment. Last month she'd accompanied her family here. Now she sat with the enemy. Although she'd never embrace the Catholic religion, she could at least accept it, especially for Jude's sake.

Darryl and Jude headed for the platform where Clayton already sat, flanked by Fawn and Mom. Lark, Wren, and the others sat at a nearby table.

"Coffee?" The deacon motioned at the long table set up against the wall.

"Sure."

"I'll fetch the java. You go on ahead. Jenny saved a seat for you."

Raven turned to the Catholic table. Jenny waved, pointing at the chair.

Staring straight ahead, not daring to even look in her family's direction, Raven squared her shoulders, lifted her chin, and gave a go at her confident sashay as she headed for Jenny.

At least nobody from the family had called Raven names during her journey across the community center. She removed the leather coat she'd proudly chosen to wear tonight—the very coat Jude had bought her.

"Oh my, gorgeous." Jenny smiled. "Wherever did you get this?"

"Jude bought it for me when we took a trip into T. Bay." Raven set the coat over the chair.

Surprise reflected in Jenny's eyes. But her smile remained. "That's Jude for you. He's as generous as they come."

Pride lit a warm candle in Raven's chest. "Yes, he is." How wonderful not to have to hide the fact Jude was her boyfriend.

Chief Willie's son, Lonn, stepped up to the microphone. Raven approved of the MC. Lonn stood on neutral ground as Willie had while alive, practicing both ways.

"*Boozhoo.* Welcome, welcome." Lonn grinned. Around forty-five, he was the splitting image of his departed dad. Long black braids, cowboy hat, jeans, cowboy boots, and sharp features.

"It's great to see many out for tonight's forum. Before we get started, I asked Basil to say the opening prayer. My dad taught me prayer is the best way to begin anything of importance, and this is a very important event. My wish is we all remember we're *Anishinaabe*, and to conduct ourselves as our ancestors did. Let's make them proud we are continuing to honor tradition. Okay?" He nodded at Basil.

Relief seeped across Raven's stiff lower back. Lonn's reminder was important. Copies of the two letters were on the table. She grasped both.

Everyone stood as Basil launched into the opening prayer.

After about ten minutes, Basil shuffled back to his seat. The debate would commence.

Lonn came forward. "Remember, this is a forum. As the MC, I'll chair this on behalf of the two candidates. I'll first let Darryl Keejik begin, because he is the man defending himself. I placed both letters on the tables. If you haven't read a copy yet, which I highly doubt, seeing how the moccasin telegraph is quite reliable around here . . ."

Everyone chuckled.

" . . . I suggest you read both before asking any questions."

Lonn swiveled. "You have the floor."

Darryl murmured something to Jude who sat beside him. Jude had his laptop open and papers in front of him. He motioned at the microphone.

Clearing his throat, Darryl moved the microphone closer. He sipped from the glass of water. "Good evening. I'm glad to see many out tonight. I'm sure you have questions, and I'm here to answer them. I'll start by giving you some background. I won't take up too much time speaking about the past, but the past's important."

Raven snuck a peek at Emery, who sat, head bowed. He seemed to be fiddling with something beneath the table that she couldn't see.

"I'm looking at all the faces here, and I'd say it's almost the same who were here during a special meeting held two summers ago. It involved the church." Darryl's gaze roamed around the many tables. "At that meeting, I shared my story. This is pointed out in my letter on the tables."

There were murmurs and nods from the people.

"As I said in my letter, I was an angry, young, single man in my twenties living in Winnipeg when the—I'll call it *the incident* in respect to the diverse group present. Yes, this happened when I was twenty-four during a bachelor party.

"A friend was marrying, and we took him out for his last hurrah as a single man. No, we did not encourage him to engage in any kind of activities with the escort we propositioned. We were, and I still am, men who believed in faithfulness to our partners. It was the single men who participated in *the incident*."

Darryl wet his lips, his gaze still addressing the many people present. "Am I proud of what I did? No." His voice flattened. "I'm not proud at all. If I could go back and erase what I did, I would, but I can't. Why? Because although the young man was of age and selling certain . . . services, I don't know what put him in that position — selling illegal services . . . to others.

"There are many people out there forced into this line of . . . service. Some have no choice and need the money. Some have an addiction they need to feed. But I'm not here to judge why people do what they do. I'm here to address me and me only.

"Have I ever cheated on any of my partners over the years? A flat-out no." The intensity of Darryl's dark eyes more than said he spoke the truth. "Have I ever cheated on my husband? Never. As I said two years ago in this same facility, my husband is the only person I ever wanted for a partner — a person I wanted to always and will always spend my life with."

He cleared his throat and sipped more water. His hand holding the glass never shook. "If you have any questions, now is the time to ask."

Albert, an older man, stood.

Lonn walked across the floor. "One at a time. Whoever has the microphone is the only person allowed to speak."

Raven glanced at Clayton's hard stare directed at Darryl. Her brother was moving into annihilation mode. And Albert was a friend of the family. If Clayton had dared to plant spectators in the crowd whose sole purpose was to embarrass Darryl, she wasn't sure what she'd do. But one thing — she'd lose the last smidge of respect she had for her brother.

"You did something illegal," Albert said in his thick bush accent while Lonn held the microphone. "What if you do it again?"

Jude faced Darryl, his left hand resting on the laptop.

Darryl clasped his fingers together. "Yes, I did something illegal. Soliciting the services of another selling his . . . favors . . . is a crime in our country. And no, I won't ever do something illegal again."

Marlice, another friend of the family, raised her hand. Lonn hurried over. He held the microphone to her mouth.

"I can't vote for a person who does something like that." Marlice wagged her finger. "What you did is wrong."

"I agree." Darryl's amplified voice carried through the hall. "What I did was very wrong. I'm sorry you lost your confidence in me. I hope you will reconsider at the voting booth come voting day."

"Never." Marlice flicked her hand in a dismissive manner and sat.

"May I speak." Clayton's cheeks were drawn in. He stared at Darryl.

"Go ahead." Lonn motioned at the microphone in front of Clayton.

"How a man conducts his personal life says a lot about how he'll conduct his professional life," Clayton began, hunched over the microphone, still firing his hard stare at Darryl.

"Yes, it does. I completely agree." Darryl sat tall in his chair, having adjusted the microphone so he wouldn't have to hunch over. "I fully agree how a man conducts his personal life says a lot about him."

When Darryl broke his stare and let his gaze wander to where Raven sat, the air drained from her lungs.

"Yes, it says a lot about a man." Darryl kept staring at her.

The color depleted from Clayton's face. His naturally narrow, dark eyes settled on Raven for the first time since she'd been booted from Mom's house.

"If a man can't protect his very own . . . what does that say about him?" Darryl asked, voice calm.

"It says a lot. A man . . ." Clayton kept staring at Raven.

His lingering look seemed to pierce her insides. The saliva dried in her mouth. He was her big brother. He'd always done right by her, had done his best, but Mom had taken a good man and poisoned his mind since he was but a baby. Clayton didn't have the twelve-step program to help him through his dilemma, but he did have the Seven Grandfathers. She could only pray that he'd turn to Creator and finally be the man Creator wished him to be.

"I have no more questions for you, Darryl." Clayton's words were a low rumbling of quiet resignation. "The people will decide who they wish to lead them."

CHAPTER THIRTY-FOUR: ROAD TO PARADISE

R aven clutched the gift bags against her chest. She was on her way to Jude's, being chauffeured by Mrs. Matawapit who'd insisted on taking her.

"If Norman and I accept you, the children will follow suit. It's how we taught our grandchildren to behave. Don't worry." Mrs. Matawapit patted Raven's hand.

"I hope they like their gifts." Raven fingered the moccasins.

"They'll love them. They love their dream catchers, don't they?" Mrs. Matawapit stared straight ahead, smiling.

"It was fun . . . a lot of fun."

It had been. This week, the kids had come over to eat every night because they loved being at their grandparents'. On Tuesday night, they'd curiously peered at her, since Jude had told them on Sunday evening their dad was seeing Miss Kabatay, the special lady who lived at Grandpa and Grandma's.

The children had fun working on the dream catchers. Rebekah had even sat on Raven's lap. Noah had been slightly leery for the first couple of dinners, which was normal. The poor boy had been through a lot of changes. But by Thursday night, he'd turned into a mischievous imp who loved surprising and teasing people.

This reaffirmed to Raven they'd move at the kids' pace. The last thing she wanted to do was make Noah and Rebekah uncomfortable or even upset them. Just as they needed time to get to know her, she needed time to get to know the two most important people in Jude's life.

Mrs. Matawapit guided the truck into Jude's driveway. She shifted the gear into park. "Here you go."

Raven gulped. This was it. Her first official dinner with Jude and the kids. But she'd made sure to slide on her big girl panties before leaving the house. She didn't need the deacon or his wife to hold her hand as they'd done all week.

"You'll do fine. Simply be yourself. I very much like the Raven I see at our house. So does my son. And so do his children." Mrs. Matawapit again patted Raven's hand.

The heartfelt words fired a shot of courage into Raven's veins. "Thanks for the vote of confidence and the lift."

"Just call when you need a ride," Mrs. Matawapit said in a voice as delicate as her willowy build.

"I will." Raven cracked open the door. "I'd better go. Can't be late. Jude's making prime rib."

"Oh? He is? The kids love prime rib."

"Yeah. And expensive." To get such a succulent slab of meat up this way must have cost Jude a pretty penny.

"Don't worry about the expense."

The back door opened. Noah stuck his head out. "Dad wants to know if you're okay."

"I'd better go." This was promising. The family was eager to see her. Raven slipped from the truck and shut the door. She hurried up the steps. "Sorry. I was talking to your kokum."

"My kokum?" Noah squinted.

"Yes. I used to always call my grandma Kokum. All *Anishinaabe* grandchildren use this name."

"Really? So Grandma is Kokum instead of Grandma?" Noah moved aside to let Raven inside the house.

"You can call your grandmother whatever you wish." Raven removed her boots. The scent of prime rib turning in the rotisserie wafted under her nose.

"C'mon." Noah used his finger to beckon and took the three short strides into the kitchen. "Dad, Miss Kabatay's here."

This Miss Kabatay business was nonsense. She'd talk to Jude and ask if he'd relent and let the children call her Raven. Maybe not. Jude knew his kids best, and he'd tell her when they were comfortable enough using her first name. Then again, children had addressed Jude as Mr. Matawapit since he'd become a teacher. Maybe she'd always be Miss Kabatay.

"Hi, Miss Kabatay." Rebekah closed her bedroom door. She twirled, showing off a ruffled teal dress. "I only wear this for church or special places, but Dad said I can wear it tonight."

"It's gorgeous. I'm so glad you did." Thankfully, Raven had slipped on wide-legged black pants that cinched tightly at her waist and a sheer blouse with a camisole underneath.

"Let me take your coat. Geez, it's really nice. I wonder where you got that." Jude winked. He'd also dressed for the occasion in his metrosexual dress pants, a deep-blue shirt that hugged his strong upper build, and hair slicked back.

"Someone was kind enough to gift it to me." Raven giggled and shrugged off the long, black leather jacket.

"Santa?" Noah exclaimed.

"Yes. Santa." Raven grinned at Jude.

Noah, also done up as if he was ready for church, leaned in, whispering, "I don't believe in Santa, but Becky does. I'm too old for that stuff."

"He's real, Noah. He is." Rebekah set her hands on her hips.

"I agree. Santa's very real." Kids. They were too adorable. "I make him cookies and set out a glass of milk at the woodstove before I go to sleep."

"Do you really?" Noah's eyes widened. He glanced at Jude

and then back to Raven, brows knitted and a finger on his lip.

Maybe someone was reconsidering their stance on Santa.

"See. I was right. He's real. C'mon," Rebekah urged in her little girl voice. "I set up your spot, Miss Kabatay."

Raven took Rebekah's hand and was led to the table, which was only a step away.

"Here." Rebekah pointed at the seat at the end of the table.

"I get the foot? I'm honored." Raven sat.

"Yes. Mom and Grandma always sit there. But you can sit there tonight." Rebekah pulled out a chair.

"I just have to finish carving." Jude ambled to the cluttered counter full of a platter of meat and every other small appliance known to man. The table was weighed down with salad, baked potatoes wrapped in tin foil, some kind of strange cakes, and something else Raven wasn't sure about.

"We really need a bigger house." Jude reached for the knife.

"Dad says he's going to build us one," Noah announced proudly. He took the chair opposite of Rebekah. "This one is really small."

"I'm sure your last house was beautiful."

Glumness flickered in Noah's black eyes for a moment. "It was. I had a really cool room. It was big. But I like living with Grandma and Grandpa, and Uncle Emery and Uncle Darryl. I miss Auntie Bridget and Kyle, and my new uncle. They were always doing stuff with us when we lived in Thunder Bay."

"I bet they miss you, too." There wasn't a better time for Raven to present her gifts to coax the children from homesickness. "Look what I have." She held up the two gift bags.

"For me?" Noah exclaimed.

"Me?" Rebekah pointed at her chest. Goodness, she was as sweet as maple syrup.

Speaking of maple syrup. "It's almost time to tap the maple trees."

"Tap the what?" Noah squinted.

"I—I learned what maple trees are in class." Rebekah raised her hand as if she was in school.

"Yes, they're special. My family still taps them for syrup."

"Can we go?" Noah asked, eyes glimmering.

"I think we might be able to. You must have tapped maple syrup with your kokum."

"No." Noah shook his head. "But we pick blueberries. And Uncle Darryl picks wild rice."

Just as traplines were inherited, so were stands of maple trees and stands of rice.

"Then we'll go with Uncle Darryl. It's fun bending the plants and knocking them into the canoe." Raven refrained from mentioning the spiders and other creepy crawlers that snuck into the canoe during the process.

Jude set the platter of meat on the table. "It sounds like your schedule's growing, hmm?" He peered at his kids.

"We're going to pick wild rice." Rebekah's sweet upturned nose made her grin on the impish side.

A person picked blueberries but *knocked* wild rice. Raven wouldn't correct Rebekah until they were in a canoe and she showed her how harvesting from the sacred plant was done.

"I think your uncle won't mind. You're old enough to sit in the canoe for a whole afternoon." Jude pulled out the chair and sat.

"Yeah, I'm going, too." Noah drummed on the table. He rapped the salad bowl as if bashing a pretend symbol.

"Maybe you can wear these while we're harvesting the rice." They'd have to accompany Darryl, since Raven had been ousted from her family and would be unable to join them at their stand.

"Wear what?" Rebekah tilted her head, placing her finger on her cheek.

"These." Raven held up the gift bags.

"Cool. Presents!" Noah reached over to snatch his.

"Hey. Hey. What do you say and do?"

"Aww, Dad." Noah hung his head.

"What's the rule?"

"We wait to be given the gift and then say thank you." Noah looked to be trying not to roll his eyes.

"I think you waited long enough." Raven handed the gift bags over to the kids.

Both eagerly dug into the packages, and their faces glowed when they unearthed the moccasins.

"Yeet. Now I'll—"

"What did I say about proper language?" Jude folded his arms.

"I have to speak properly at the dinner table." Poor Noah's tone matched the rolling eyes he again tried to stop.

Raven bit her lower lip to suppress her giggle. The kids weren't any different than her rambunctious and mischievous nieces and nephews.

Of course dinner was held up so the children could try on their new gifts. Then they had to walk about the house in their moccasins. Ten minutes later, everyone sat at the table. Both kids bowed their heads.

Jude clasped his fingers together and also bowed his head. Raven decided to join in, although she never participated at the Matawapits house, choosing to say her own prayer to Creator instead.

"Bless us, O Lord, and these Thy gifts, which we are about to receive from Thy bounty, through Christ our Lord. Amen." Jude's voice was loud and clear, Noah's the same but a pitch higher, and Rebekah's sweet and quiet.

Raven's heart warmed. She truly did belong here, and wanted to belong here, surrounded by three Catholics.

Having played a board game Rebekah had picked since find-ing candy-filled adventures was her favorite, and with the kids now off to sleep, it was time to clean up. Jude draped the tea towel over his shoulder.

Raven stood in front of the sink, scrubbing a plate, helping him tidy the kitchen. But they wouldn't turn in for the night together. She'd text Mom or Dad afterward and go home to his parents' house.

That was okay. They were letting nature take its course. He wrapped his arms around her waist. Her reflection in the win-dow over the sink gazed at him, beautiful lips moving into a deep smile.

"Did you have a good time?" He pecked her cheek.

"A really great time." She giggled. "Wanna know some-thing?"

"Sure." He nuzzled her ear.

"I was a bit nervous. I mean, I've had nieces and nephews, like, forever. Um, I wasn't sure how I'd do with kids."

"You did great." He blew into her ear.

"That tickles." She squirmed in his embrace, her sexy ass rubbing against his crotch.

"Keep it up and we'll be in big trouble," he murmured.

"It's not my intention to cause trouble." Her voice was as impish as her answer.

"Admit it, you love causing trouble." He nibbled on her lobe with the gold studded earing.

"Mmm . . . I love making major trouble, depending on who my partner in crime is." She bumped her hips back and forth ala Marilyn Monroe, fluttering her perfectly applied fake lashes at him in the window.

His cock thickened. "Y'know, we might have to make a special trip on Tuesday night to our old stomping grounds."

"Should we invest in an RV then?" She rinsed off the plate and set it in the rack.

"We might have to . . ." And Jude meant each word. Having Raven staying over one weekend a month was too tough on his dick. "Or never get out of bed for the two nights we're alone out of the month."

"Now that's gonna be difficult." Raven swiveled. They were crotch to crotch. She plucked the tea towel from his shoulder and dried her wet hands.

Jude couldn't resist stealing a kiss. Her arms snaked around his shoulders in the perfect slinky way she had of coiling around a man. The lips he explored were as sassy and bold as Raven, nibbling away at his mouth, a pucker and then slow and lingering.

He broke the kiss, or they would get into trouble.

Using the tip of her nose, she rubbed his.

"Northern kiss?"

"Northern kiss." Her voice was scratchy, a delicate, dreamy echo capable of loosening his muscles.

"The most we can do right now is cuddle on the couch and watch some TV." He kept rubbing the tip of her nose with his.

"Remember, I have to call by at least ten."

"I understand." And he did. There were no complaints on his part, because this woman was offering him a true sanctuary again, gifting him with something he'd once lost and thought he'd never recapture.

"I love you." His lips were a breath of air from hers.

"I love you, too, Jude. I love you so much." Her love was in the softness of her words, in the glow of her eyes, the lushness of her face, and the warmth of her breath.

"Same here, sweetheart. Same here. With all of my heart." His mouth claimed hers, and he lavished a kiss on her silken lips.

Other Books in The Matawapit Family Series

Blessed
Redeemed
Renewed

You may also enjoy the following from eXtasy Books Inc:

Redeemed
Maggie Blackbird

Excerpt

Lying was what Adam did best. He'd learned how to lie as a punk-ass kid. Believing the lie for the complete truth was key in confusing the cops, the Crown attorney, the judge—anyone trained to search his face, voice, or body language for signs of dishonesty. Only booze had tripped him up, nailed him good enough to send him down below because of his love for the bottle.

He wouldn't lie today. He hadn't lied during his parole hearing, either. Lying wasn't a part of his new life. Neither was whiskey.

From now on, fatherhood was what he'd do best.

Other parents sat in the waiting room at Children and Family Services. One paced the floor wearing yesterday's stubble. Another shifted in her seat, bleary-eyed, either from a hangover or crying. The tall guy with holes in his clothes crossed and uncrossed his legs. The girl, not much older than twenty, rocked back and forth, slurping coffee, while her legs twitched. A tweaker, probably.

The smell was the same in all government buildings. A lingering of something old and outdated, and the walls either a bland beige, faded white, or dull light gray. Off-white was the color of choice at Children and Family Services.

"Mr. Guimond?" The receptionist rose from behind the rounded counter against the wall. "Your caseworker's ready to see you. Second floor. The fourth office on your right." She used a pen to point in the direction of the elevator.

Adam stood. His feet remained rooted to the floor, and he forced his legs to make the ten-yard trek to the elevator. Once he was enclosed inside the stuffy chute no bigger than the drunk tank he'd been tossed in after coming off a bender, he fumbled for the second-floor button.

There was no turning back. He was going up.

He could face a judge sentencing him, cops tossing him on the hood of a cruiser to handcuff him, scouting his range for the first time while being sized up by the toughest of toughs, or a beat-out from the Winnipeg Warriors to drop his colors. He could face anything but a caseworker who'd decide if and when he'd see his boy.

He checked his reflection in the mirror, smoothing his hair that kinked this way and waved that way. Damned wind was to blame after his walk to and from the bus stop. Since t-shirts, jeans, and running shoes wouldn't impress the caseworker, he'd borrowed a too-snug dress shirt and dress pants off a guy at the halfway house. The buttoned cuffs were silver bracelets locked around his wrists, and the starched collar a noose.

The doors opened. His breathing mirrored the rattle and hops when he'd been chased by the cops. The same for the hot pressure pounding at the back of his neck.

There were offices in both directions. Some doors were open, a couple of them closed. Voices carried out from the offices, workers either on the phone or meeting with a loser like himself.

He gave his left a try first and trudged down the hallway.

The fourth door on the right was closed.

Show time. He'd done this lots — getting his shit together before his execution. He fisted and un-fisted his fingers while huffing and puffing three quick breaths of air.

He rapped his knuckles against the fake wood.

"One moment, Mr. Guimond," a woman said in a stern voice.

Adam's heartbeat slowed, and the ball of tension behind his neck vanished. A few more seconds. He leaned on the wall and folded his arms. At least he'd gotten the right door. He'd also made sure not to smoke outside. First impressions counted, whether at a parole hearing, before a judge, anything. Smelling like an old cigarette butt was the wrong impression, but the blood threading through his veins could use a dart right now.

"You may enter." The woman's supposed invitation came out as an order. She must have worked at the iron house or had a husband as a CO.

He opened the door to a hawk — a birdlike biddy in her sixties with gray hair pulled off her narrow face and twisted into a bun. Beady cold eyes looked him up and down with the scrutiny of a judge on the bench. Her nose, the shape of a beak, she held high in the air. She pointed her skinny finger at the chair positioned in front of the desk, square in the middle.

"You may sit." She lowered her hard gaze to a neat stack of papers and started writing.

Adam sat. The chair was positioned too close to the desk. Even when he opened his legs, his knees hit the cheap laminate. Maybe this was part of the caseworker's strategy to make clients uncomfortable.

"I'm Mrs. Dale. Your son's caseworker." She kept writing on the pad, her scrawny knuckles a bright red from how hard she gripped the pen.

There wasn't a smidgen of dust on the filing cabinet, desk, or bookshelf. One lone picture faced her. Pens kept in order of color sat in a tray. Even the essentials for an office were set square on the desk. There were no other files present but one manila folder which also sat square beside the paper she wrote on. The off-white vertical blinds were adjusted to keep the sunlight off her but allow the two blooming plants on a shelf to take in a tan.

With all this silence, she must want him to speak first. He swallowed a helping of saliva to keep his voice strong and calm. "I'm Adam Guimond. Kyle's father."

"I already know who you are and why you are here, Mr. Guimond." The Hawk kept writing. "I have been responsible for your file since your incarceration."

Double great. This old biddy had it out for him. Adam kept his arms unfolded. He stared at her rolled bun. He wouldn't look anywhere else or shift in his chair.

After five more minutes, and Adam refusing to twitch, the Hawk raised her head. She laid aside the pen vertical to the pad of paper, which she rested her skinny fingers on. "Why are you requesting approval to see your son?"

Adam hadn't expected this question. He continued to stare at her narrowed eyes tucked behind matching glasses. Again, he made sure to keep his voice even. "He's my son."

"I know he's your son, a son you lost to care, because you not only abused alcohol, but also committed a serious crime while under the influence. Tell me, why are you requesting approval to see your son?"

She'd made a damned good point. He'd cut the old biddy some slack. The twelve steps of his recovery program, the Seven Grandfathers teachings of the Ojibway, and the anger management course he'd followed while in the iron house had prepared him for this moment.

"Saved up enough money working on day parole. Gonna use the coin to rent a small apartment. Got a plan."

"What plan would that be?"

With her shitload of questions, her unchanging cold stare that was a block of ice, The Hawk was in the wrong line of work. Adam should recommend she become a detective instead of a caseworker.

"Good place for my kid."

"Mr. Guimond, you are going to have to be specific and find your tongue to elaborate. We are discussing the welfare of your child." Her voice remained the same stern tone.

She was good. Really good. Better than the too-many cops who'd hauled Adam into an interrogation room for questioning.

"You got the info on me. Came up with a plan in the pen." He squeezed his toes, a great way to destress when under scrutinizing eyes and effectively hide the flicker of anxiety twitching along his spine.

"A plan?"

"Yeah. Got my grade twelve. Went to twelve-step meetings. Was part of the aboriginal healing program. Took my anger management class and passed. It was my plan. To change. Become a true dad to my son."

"This is why you relocated from Winnipeg to Thunder Bay — again?"

"My boy lives here. I wanna live here."

"Why else do you wish to reside here? As I said, you had better be more specific and talk." She tightened her jaw and lifted her brow.

Adam kept the smile itching to stretch his lips tucked deep inside him. She'd broke first. Confidence swelled in his chest. Maybe, just maybe, he stood a chance at getting his son back. "After my last rubbie bit, I dropped my colors—"

"This is not the federal corrections institution, Mr. Guimond. Proper English. Not street code." Her voice rose an octave.

He'd broken her again. So he set his hands on his thighs and leaned in a smidgen. Crowding her space was imperative to force her to lean back. He kept his stare rigid and spoke in the same low monologue. "During my second last incarceration, the mother of my kid told me she was pregnant. I wanted a better life for my son. Stopped drinking and left the gang. Went to rehab. My back was against the wall. No protection anymore. Other gangs wanted a piece of me still. Moved here to start a better life. Didn't wanna get in any more trouble."

The Hawk failed to recoil into her chair. She remained a statue in her seat. "But you did when you first lived here with your son . . ."

"I shouldn't have moved back to . . ." Nope, he'd better not say the 'Peg. " . . . Winnipeg after things fell apart here. That was a big mistake."

"Then why did you move back to Winnipeg, again, if you knew trouble awaited?" The Hawk's tone shifted to her natural sternness.

Adam kept returning her stare. "It was a mistake. Told you already. Things fell apart here."

"You mean your ex-fiancée, who's been responsible for your son for almost four years now, ended your engagement and you couldn't handle the rejection." The Hawk's mask of plaster cracked into a half-smile of part sneer and part triumph.

So this was her game, huh? She did want Adam to fail. Authority. They were all the same. Good thing he'd come in here with the right kind of attitude and game plan. "My ex-fiancée had every right to do what she did. I started drinking again. She gave me the boot."

"What about your drinking now?" Mrs. Dale redonned her mask of plaster.

"Kept sober while doing my time. Attended twelve-step meetings at the jail in Winnipeg while I was on day parole. A guy from the outside came in and chaired them. I'm still sober. First thing I did when I got into town was check where all the meetings are. Attending one tonight."

"And when your parole term is finished?"

"I don't plan on going back to drinking. I'm done with that."

Mrs. Dale clucked her tongue and crooked her narrowed

brow in a we'll-wait-and-see manner.

She didn't have to wait and see. He'd tell her right now. "My old boss lined me up a job here. Chain restaurant. He called his buddy here at the Thunder Bay chain."

"When do you start?"

"He's gonna call me. Once I find out, I'll let you know what my hours are."

Mrs. Dale sat back in her chair.

Confident, much? She could take her confidence and shove it. She'd lose. Nothing was stopping Adam from getting his boy back.

"I see men and women like you every single day in my office, Mr. Guimond. I also visit the homes of people like you to remove your children whom you are not providing adequate care for. Do you know how many times people such as yourself regain custody of your children, and then lose them again?"

"I thought the purpose here was to care for the kids until we . . ." He couldn't say get our shit together. " . . . until we've taken care of biz, made our lives better?"

"I will recommend to my supervisor one hour per week, supervised visits in the family room." Mrs. Dale sat up in her chair and began writing again.

One hour? One measly hour to see his boy after he hadn't seen Kyle in almost four years? "Why?" The word flew from Adam's mouth.

He squeezed his toes. Careless. Fucking careless. Dammit, she'd broken him. Now she knew his weakness. How to get under his skin. He'd failed.

"Mr. Guimond . . ." The Hawk's half-sneer returned. Even her cold eyes glimmered. "I am considering the welfare of your child. Not your welfare. Your son has not seen you in almost four years. He recently celebrated his seventh birthday. This means he was extremely young when you were institutionalized. He has only known the care of his foster mother. Don't you think reacquainting yourselves should be the priority so he can make the emotional adjustments he will require to have you back in his life? Or do you not care? Is this about what you want, instead of what your child needs?"

Adam's gut burned. She was right. This meeting wasn't about who played a better game of chess. Kyle's feelings came first. "Whatever you recommend," he managed to grunt out.

If he had one measly hour to give to his boy, he'd make their time the best hour possible.

I'm coming, kiddo. Daddy's here. He's made a lot of mistakes. A lot of bad mistakes that you're paying for, when you shouldn't be. I won't let you down this time. That's a promise.

He ran the tip of his tongue along the roof of his mouth. But from the day he'd kicked and clawed his way from the womb, whenever he challenged authority, he'd lost.

Bridget slammed the door shut and stormed to the building. She smacked the button on her key set to lock the truck. Nobody had to tell her what this meeting was about. Nobody had to tell her Adam had raced back to Thunder Bay once the son of a bitch had finished his day parole. Nobody had to tell her he'd overlooked informing anyone about his intentions. Adam only thought about Adam.

She stomped into Children and Family Services and huffed to the front desk. "I have an appointment to see Mrs. Dale. She's my caseworker."

"One moment." The receptionist picked up the phone. "Ms. Matawapit's here . . . Okay . . . Thank you . . . I'll send her right up."

The receptionist set down the phone. "Go on up. She's waiting."

"Thank you." Bridget stamped to the elevator and got in. She used her knuckle to punch the button for the second floor.

Adam was going to try to gain full custody of Kyle, after she'd looked after the boy for almost four years, after she'd refused to allow Adam to take Kyle to Winnipeg, after agreeing not to call Children and Family Services on him when the bastard had fallen off the wagon. After all she'd done for the loser.

The elevator doors opened. Bridget trounced to Mrs. Dale's office and rapped on the door.

"Enter, Ms. Matawapit."

Bridget opened the door and flounced to the chair in front of the desk.

"I am grateful you could come on your lunch hour." Mrs. Dale shuffled some papers. "What I have to say merits a face-to-face meeting. How is Kyle? Did he enjoy his birthday party?"

The angry, raw heat faded. Mrs. Dale was a straight-to-the-point woman who never engaged in small talk. And like any proud mother, Bridget loved talking about her child. "I held his party at Sleeping Giant Park. The kids had a lot of fun. They swam and hiked. I even arranged to have his favorite hero show up—Laser from the Z Men."

"Wonderful." Mrs. Dale tapped her pen against the desk. "I met with Kyle's father yesterday for a full assessment. Mr. Guimond has relocated here. My supervisor and I agreed to one hour, once a week supervised visits for Kyle and his father."

The blood flowing through Bridget's veins slowed. "I see . . . Does . . . does this mean, uh, does this mean—" She dug her nails into the arm of the chair.

"Understand, Kyle hasn't seen his father in almost four years." Mrs. Dale's normal sharper-than-her-pointed-nose voice warmed to a reassuring tone. Even her hard gaze softened, liquifying her cold gray eyes to melted clay.

"This doesn't mean he'll gain full custody. He may never gain full custody. Transitions, especially those of Adam Guimond's case, take a long time. A very long time." The melted clay of Mrs. Dale's eyes re-hardened to their natural concrete. Her thin upper lip twitched.

All Bridget had to do was stay silent and let Mrs. Dale

sabotage Adam's chances at regaining custody of Kyle. Was this what the woman was insinuating?

But Bridget was Catholic. Her parents, the church, and God expected her to handle the most important facet of her life with faith—a faith as shaky as her trembling knees and clacking teeth after what she'd endured at Adam's recklessness.

ABOUT THE AUTHOR

An Ojibway from Northwestern Ontario, Maggie resides in the country with her husband and their fur babies, two beautiful Alaskan Malamutes. When she's not writing, she can be found pulling weeds in the flower beds, mowing the huge lawn, walking the Mals deep in the bush, teeing up a ball at the golf course, fishing in the boat for walleye, or sitting on the deck at her sister's house, making more wonderful memories with the people she loves most.

https://maggieblackbird.com/
https://www.facebook.com/maggieblackbirdauthor/
https://twitter.com/BlackbirdMaggie/

www.ingramcontent.com/pod-product-compliance
Lightning Source LLC
Chambersburg PA
CBHW062010170626
46813CB00001B/103